MARIAH

BLOOD of the NEW MOON

B. A. Mealer

Copyright

Dedication

To all those people who work where they must to earn a living. Until you've walked that mile in their shoes, any judgement you make might be wrong

This is for those men and women who risk their lives to keep us safe. I took a lot of literary license in the jobs, but you are appreciated for your hard work.

And last but not least, all those people out there who have lost a friend or family to violence. No matter what you do, it is hard to move past that loss, even if justice is served.

Acknowledgements

Thank you to Mark Stone of https://100covers.com for making the cover. Great job.

Also, I'd like to thank Jamie Brydone-Jack for her hard work in editing this book. I know I didn't see most of the errors she found. It's because of wonderful people like her authors have professional works published.

Quotation

They say a person needs just three things to be truly happy in this world: someone to love, something to do, and something to hope for. *---Tom Bodett*

Table of Contents

Prologue

Saturday, June 21, 1986

THE SMOKE RISING FROM the candles on the stone alter drifted over the worship area to gather by the walls. The gentle breeze set the leaves on the tree above him to dancing, sending the smoke in his direction. The young boy liked the way the waxy scent of the smoke tickled his nose. Flames dancing on their wicks before the statue of Xolotl made moving shadows across the alter.

This was the night of darkness. Time to appease the jaguar who would eat the moon, leaving the blood behind. All done in hopes of pleasing Xolotl, their very demanding god.

The young boy remained seated at the base of the wall with only his head moving. His wide-eyed gaze darted over the scene before him. The chants and the drums called for him to join the dancers. He forced himself to remain where he was, seated by the rough stone wall still warm from the sun.

His grandmother said he was too young to dance. She wanted him to see and understand how they appeased the jaguar. Today, like those before, he was to stay where he was until the ceremony was completed. Soon, very soon, he would be worshipping with them, dancing and helping with the ritual handed down over thousands of years.

His dark-eyed wonder followed the dancers. They twirled, dipped and raised their cups to the dark sky, offering the blood the cups would soon hold to the darkened moon. The four groups, each containing four worshipers, followed the ancient ritual that only they knew. They separated and came together again in an ever-changing pattern passed down from one generation to the next. Mesmerized with the dancers' feet that kept rhythm with the drums and flutes, his lips were parted, enjoying the ancient ritual like he had for the past two years.

A light spilling from a doorway drew his gaze to the small building on the right side of the gates. Two men helped a blindfolded woman dressed in a gauzy beribboned robe along the path the dancers made for them. There was a man leading them, ringing a bell in-time with each step, and one behind the woman swinging a censor that added the sweet odor of burning sweet grass to the smoke of the candles.

The procession was slow. The woman didn't seem to be able to get her legs to work. She stumbled, her toes catching in the dirt, the robe parting to show she wore nothing underneath.

The drums changed to a slow measured rhythm matching that of his beating heart. The feet of the men slid forward with each heavy beat, helping the woman walk to the stone slab before the raised alter. The boy held his breath, following the compact group with the woman with an intent gaze.

The sizzle of tension rose along his lower back when the chant segued into the repetition of one phrase that matched the beat of the drums. The worshippers sang the words from the ancient language. He didn't understand the words yet, but he was working on it by studying the ancient writings in secret. His fingers tapped out the beat, wetting his lips for what was coming next.

The sounds of the worshipers' song filled him, sending his spirit soaring. He swung his head back to examine the man in the decorated mask and dark robe leading the ceremony. The priest's musical voice wove among those of the worshippers, reciting the prayer directed to the statue of Xolotl on the raised altar, his back to the worshippers.

After the woman was placed on her back on the long flat stone, the priest turned around to face the stone. The worshippers were gathered in a semicircle facing him, holding the small stone cups in their hands. They continued the chant they had begun when the men appeared with the woman.

The knuckles of the young boy's hands were white as he gripped them in his lap. His gaze flitted over the scene, attempting to remember all the details. He leaned forward slightly, lips parted in anticipation.

Two of the men held the women in place. The priest pressed his left hand to the chest of the woman on the sacrificial stone. A dull glint from the candlelight, revealed the gently curved blade of the ancient dark green volcanic glass knife. The white of the bone handle was visible in the dim light. The boy sucked in a large breath and held it, his eyes on the priest while waiting in eagerness.

A heavy cloth decorated with colorful woven designs was placed over the woman's face. The drums became louder and faster as the priest continued his prayer, sending the powerful words to Xolotl, the god who demanded they do this. The hand with the knife rose as his deep voice competed with the drum and chanters. Swiftly, the raised hand descended. The curved blade entered the woman just below the breastbone. Her scream was muffled with the cloth held tightly over her face by one of the men who had walked her to the slab.

A quick movement of the priest's hand drove the curve of the blade into the woman's heart. Blood began to pump out of her around the knife and onto the stone. The worshippers caught the blood in the cups they held as it ran from the corners of the stone. His grandmother was responsible for the priest's cup. When all the cups were filled, the priest removed the knife. He hooked the tip under the muscle, sliding the blade toward the woman's feet. Her intestines slithered onto the alter as the slit widened. The worshippers drank the warm blood they had collected, inviting the spirit of the sacrificed to enter them and make them stronger.

The metallic scent of the fresh blood drifted to the boy. He licked his lips again. He wanted to be there in the group drinking the blood. Not sitting by the wall.

What came next was his favorite part of the ceremony. The priest dipped his hands into the opening he had made in the woman, covering his hands in her blood until they were dripping. He turned to the altar where a thin loosely woven white cloth lay before the statue of Xolotl and the four candles. He placed his hands on it with his thumbs touching, leaving wet bloody handprints on the cloth.

The priest washed his hands in the basin of water at the side of the altar. Two of the men who had escorted the woman to the stone took the corners of the cloth. They held the bloodied square over the grouping of four candles. The cloth began to smoke, then burn. The men placed it on a metal tray, letting the flames burn the dry parts of the cloth, leaving the two bloody handprints connected at the thumbs undamaged.

The worshippers began to dance again as the priest chanted. When the dance finished, the priest placed the bloody handprints onto the open abdomen of the woman. The dancers began a new chant. The priest's sonorous voice was easily heard with the prayer he sang while he washed the stone knife. When the knife was clean, he placed it below the statue between the candles, the worn bone handle decorated with designs only the priest understood facing to the priest's right.

The green glass-like blade glistened in the wavering candlelight.

The drums stopped. Silence lay heavy until a breeze set the leaves on the trees to rustling. The ritual was over.

The four men and the priest lifted the woman onto a pole stretcher covered in a colorful cloth. They wrapped the cloth about her, folding it over before tucking it so it wouldn't open. The four men lifted the stretcher from the ground and returned to the building at the entrance in measured footsteps, reciting words only the initiated understood. The priest followed them, saying the words with them.

Instinctively, the boy felt the words were a blessing for the sacrifice. They were encouraging the jaguar to allow the moon to return. His gaze followed the procession until it was out of sight.

When his attention returned to the worshippers, he waited patiently for his grandmother and parents to finish their devotions. They cleaned the stone where the woman had been, singing a song in the old language. A quick glance around the enclosure showed it was bare other than the sacrificial stone and the altar with the statues. What grass there was in the compound was short and brown. The bare spots coincided with where the earth had been packed by generations of worshippers.

His grandmother was the first to finish. She placed the picture of the next sacrificial offering before the statue for all to see, leaving the candles to burn. When she approached him, he stood to greet her, a smile on his face. His eyes shone in the candlelight with unshed tears at the beauty of the ceremony. She returned his smile, then patted him on the cheek.

"Someday, my boy, you will be the priest, keeping our traditions alive," she said before his parents joined them.

They left the sacrificial grounds to walk back to their small adobe house on the outskirts of the little town. He couldn't stop smiling. His grandmother had given him hope of achieving his goal to become the high priest for the Nahua. This year he would honor San La Muerte on Dios de Los Muertos with a sacrifice. There was no time like the present to prepare for the future.

Chapter One

MARIAH WAS TIRED. BONE tired. Unable to move tired. Her eight hours of bringing drinks and food to the men in the club had been profitable, but at a cost. The constant propositions resulted in a smiling refusal, but the men coming into the Golden Cat Gentlemen's Club didn't want to hear a no from her. Shuttling drinks and empties back and forth for the night while staving off wandering hands and multiple proposals for things she would never do was taking a physical and mental toll.

At twenty-six, Mariah Lansing had learned a lot about the seamier side of El Paso. When she moved here, she hadn't planned on working in a strip club, but it was the only place that was willing to hire her with enough pay to support herself at the age of eighteen with no skills. She had to live. Minimum wage for a twenty-four-hour week wasn't going to cut it. Even now she had to watch what she spent if she wanted to be able to pay her bills while saving enough to complete her education.

Sitting on the hard, narrow bench in the locker room, Mariah sighed. After removing the heels all waitresses were required to wear, she rubbed her aching feet. She could hardly wait to get into comfortable clothes and shoes.

This was the first time she had been able to get off her feet. Her break had been taken while standing up in the kitchen leaning against the wall. Eating was accomplished by shoving food into her mouth with her fingers when no clean utensil could be found. All the seats at the small table assigned to the girls for their lunch break were taken and none of the girls were about to move for her. On top of that, the outfit she wore was tight and uncomfortable with all the stays and spandex.

"Hey kid, you all right?" Zelda asked, reaching into her locker to get a robe to cover her nakedness after completing her turn on stage. Zelda was one of the few who talked to her at the club.

"Yeah. My feet hurt. And that creep is back again. He still hasn't gotten the message that I'm not going anywhere with him."

Zelda plopped onto the bench beside her. The scent of sweat and sex swept over Mariah. "Honey, you be careful. He's not one you want to upset."

Mariah grimaced. "I know. Rachel told me about him." She let out a tired sigh. "Speaking of Rachel, have you heard from her? I've called her several times, but her phone only goes to a message saying the phone is out of service."

Zelda shrugged, readjusting her robe so it was fully closed. "Not today. She called me a couple of days ago. Said she had a meeting with her counselor on the twelfth."

Twisting so she could see Zelda, Mariah's worried eyes went to her face. Zelda immediately looked away and began to rummage in her locker.

"I'm concerned about her. I haven't heard from her since Wednesday. She didn't call in tonight and is being given a no-show. The same with last night. That's not like her." Mariah returned her gaze to the heels she was holding.

Zelda bent over to remove her shoes. Her voice muffled when she spoke. "She could be using again. I know she's been under a lot of stress with breaking up with her boyfriend, moving, and whatever else she is doing on the side."

Mariah paused to consider Zelda's take on what was happening with Rachel. She leaned over and rested her elbows on her knees, the heels dangling from the fingers of her right hand. "I don't believe so. She wanted to break up with the creep. He was using. She was so proud of being clean, so I don't believe she would use again. Also, she's excited about moving and is making plans for her future.

"I've got this gut feeling something's wrong. She's never a no-show, and she always answers her phone. On those rare occasions when she hasn't answered, it went to voicemail. She always returned my call. Usually within the hour. It's like her phone has been off since she called me Wednesday morning."

Mariah sat for a few more minutes while Zelda prepared for her next show. She couldn't shake the feeling that something was very wrong. Why would Rachel be using again with all the plans she had made? The scenario Zelda gave didn't fit.

The breakup with the boyfriend was old news. In fact, she had been glad to get rid of him and was looking for a job away from the club. Her not showing up for work was out of character. Rachel always showed up for work, even if she was sick.

Pushing her concerns aside, Mariah changed into running clothes and shoes. She wasn't ready to go home to her apartment. A quick run should help her sleep for a couple of hours.

Her tenuous sleep schedule was in shambles with worry over Rachel. Insomnia was the normal for her, but she had developed a schedule for sleeping and resting so she didn't burn out. Seventy-two hours was longer than she liked to go without actual sleep.

With keys in her hand, Mariah left the club. Danny, a bouncer and her friend, met her outside the door. He had a big smile on his face while he walked with her to her truck. She was only able to give him a partial smile this evening before unlocking the truck door.

"Thanks, Danny."

He leaned over from his six-foot-four height to kiss her cheek. "Anything for you kid. You do need to find a better place to work."

Mariah stepped onto the running board of her truck then pivoted back to one of the few people she considered a friend. He leaned on the door watching her.

She let out a frustrated sigh. "I'm working on it. I have six more credits to graduate. Hopefully, I can find a decent job away from here after that."

"Great." He stared at the bed of her truck, the smile slipping from his face. "You don't belong here." He returned his gaze to her and cupped her cheek with a gentle hand. "Kid, get out of here as soon as you can. This place is getting worse by the day." The dark eyes studied her for a second. "Look, there's a club over on the east side. It's got a classier clientele. You should go and apply there. It would be a lot safer than here. And the tips would be better. You could work there until you get the job you really want."

She understood what he was saying. Over the last year, the men who frequented the Golden Cat Gentlemen's Club had gotten rougher and slimier. Along with the change in clientele, the tips had decreased for the waitresses. Maybe changing clubs might be worth a shot even if it was for less than a year.

"Which one?"

"The Platinum Slipper. It opened about six months ago."

Unsure of why he was wanting her to work there, she took a wild guess. "I take it you got a job there?"

Danny chuckled, ducking his head. "Yeah. My last night here is Saturday." His face was serious when he returned his gaze to her. "I know Sam and Greg will watch out for you, but I'd like to see you in a better place than here. You'd fit in at the Slipper because you're classy. It's a higher end club and would make it safer and more pleasant until you get that dream job."

With pursed lips, she thought about what he said while staring at her shoes. Maybe she should apply for a job there. Glancing back at the blinking neon sign, she knew there was nothing holding her here if Rachel were fired. Over the past week the bouncers had to remove disorderly men from the club almost nightly. Also, several of the clientele were carrying guns, not bothering to hide them. Danny was right. Time to find another job, even if it was only for a few more months.

"Okay. I'll check it out after I get out of my class tomorrow. The worst that could happen is them not hiring me. Right?"

"Right, but I don't believe that'll be the case." Danny was beaming when she raised her misty gray eyes to his face.

"Why?" she asked, brows raised.

Danny moved a stone with the toe of his shoe and shoved his hands into his pockets. "I've already put in a good word for you. I happen to know the manager. He would love to have you there."

He peeked over at her. She didn't miss the uncertainty in the way his brown eyes were watching her. He was afraid she would be upset with him. Mariah reached out and pulled him over to kiss his cheek.

"Thanks Danny. I appreciate the help. I'll go tomorrow and apply. If he offers me better than here, I'm there."

With a big grin, Danny said, "He'll offer you a good raise. Trust me on that."

After she slid behind the wheel of her truck, Danny closed the door. She rolled down the window. "I'll let you know if I take the job. Thanks again."

"My pleasure. You be careful now."

He patted the door when the engine turned over before taking a step back from the truck. With a wave, she pulled out, heading to Sunland Park and the path beside the river where she normally ran.

Next to Rachel, Danny was her best friend. He was like a big brother who looked out for her. The regular customers knew to leave her alone. On more than one occasion he had thrown a customer out who continued to hassle her when she turned down their offers of money for dates and sex. Some men couldn't seem to understand she was a waitress, not a prostitute.

Traffic was light at this hour of the morning. She pulled into her normal spot under the light in the parking lot before shutting off the engine. Prior to exiting the truck, she hid her purse and grabbed a bottle of water. A short run for her was usually eight miles. This morning a stiff breeze made the 70 degrees feel cool. She pulled on a lightweight dark windbreaker over her thin light-colored shirt.

Mariah slammed the door of the old beat-up truck, tucking the keys into her pocket before jogging on the path going to her right from the parking lot. With the lead on a better job, she felt more relaxed. Danny was right. She needed to find a better place to work until she could qualify for a respectable job with decent pay. Four more months until she graduated. Another three to wait to find out if she got into law school. She did have a plan.

It would be great if she could find a job using her criminal justice degree. One which would pay more than minimum wage. If she was accepted into law school, she needed enough to pay for her living expenses for the next four years. By living thriftily, she had saved enough to pay for her tuition and books at any of the in-state law schools. She would have to move again, but that wasn't a problem. All she needed was a part-time job while in school. There were times when her insomnia came in handy.

The light from the parking lot disappeared. Mariah ran in the dark along the path she knew well. Her gaze darted around the ethereal landscape of faint light and dark shadows. The sound of her feet hitting the pavement was loud in the quiet along the bank of the dry riverbed. The temperature was comfortable for running. This was part of the reason she preferred coming here after work during the summers...the quiet and slight breeze.

The path ended in the rutted dirt of the never-ending construction along the river. The scent of stagnant water came to her on the breeze when she slowed to go from the paved walkway to the packed dirt. A gentle incline indicated she was moving away from the riverbed.

Not breaking her stride, she followed the dirt track, having run this path since moving into her apartment eight years ago. The shadowy outlines of various plants bordering the path could be seen more clearly now that a little light filtered down from the street above. But that would only last for a short distance. Mariah peered intently into the dark, picking out what she could see of the road without slowing, the night wrapping around her. The night hid all but a few steps before her. The dirt track turned back toward the river. She ran in the general direction of the Country Club Road bridge, four and a half miles from the Sunland bridge.

She was close to the Country Club Road bridge when a cough and a thump startled her. She stopped and listened, unable to tell which direction the sounds had come from in the darkness. She moved into a large shadowy bush to her left, hoping it would hide her. Another thump and a grunt reached her, slightly fainter than the previous sounds. Crouching so she would look like part of the bush or a rock, she scanned the area, unable to see anything moving.

Unintelligible words came to her from the direction of the bridge. Mariah remained where she was, holding her breath as someone grunted again and another thump sounded. A person walked into view from the shadow of the bridge located twenty to twenty-five yards up the path.

Another man joined him. They stood as if waiting for something. A third person joined them from the shadows. She couldn't see any details, just enough of the forms to tell they were men.

"Did you see anyone?" a man with a Spanish accent asked.

"No. Let's go. If we can't see them, they can't see us," a rough and raspy voice responded.

The three men hurried away in the direction of the river. An engine started then moved away from her. She remained hidden, shivering as much from fear as the cool temperature on her sweaty skin.

No way they were doing anything law-abiding at this hour using what sounded like a large ATV. They could have picked any area along the river and been safer than here at the bridge. Then again, many of those areas didn't have the easy access to places where they could disappear. There were subdivisions and warehouses on both sides of the river and bridge.

She waited until the sounds of the engine couldn't be heard before moving from the bush. The fear of what the men were doing meant cutting her run short. There was no way she was going under the bridge to see what they had been doing. After a quick glance at the dark shadow of the bridge, Mariah started back to her truck. The goal was to get away from this area as quickly as possible. Instead of her normal fast jog, she ran back.

When near the parking area, she slowed. The light was out above her truck, leaving it in the dark. Going to a walk, she went on high alert. Other than the dark shadows of the bushes and trees, nothing else could be seen. At her truck, she quickly got in and locked the doors. In all her years of coming here, the light had never been out.

A movement under the bridge caught her attention. An indistinct form of a person moving in the heavy shadow of the bridge set her hands to trembling. He was coming toward her. She started the engine and threw the truck into reverse, almost hitting a dark colored car she hadn't seen parked in the shadow of the bridge. Shifting into first gear, Mariah popped the clutch and raced into the darkness. A sliding turn to the right put her on the steep rutted ramp to the road before she turned on her lights. She pushed on the gas when car lights from the parking area turned to follow her.

With no traffic on the cross street, Mariah made a left turn. Shifting rather than braking, she made several sharp turns until merging into the early morning traffic on the main thoroughfare. After passing another pickup that looked like hers, she pulled into the right-hand lane, keeping an eye on the rearview mirror. When she merged onto the interstate, no one was behind her.

Mariah drove for another ten minutes before pulling off I-10 to get gas. When no one paid any attention to her at the gas station, she headed to what she called home. Luckily her truck looked like hundreds of others. Unless they had her license plate number, finding her would be like looking for another earth in the Milky Way.

Her phone said just before eight AM when she pulled into her parking space at the apartment building. The complex was quiet with nothing out of place. She entered her apartment, automatically throwing the deadbolt before dropping her keys into the bowl on the small stand beside the door. The bowl made the ringing sound she associated with being in her haven.

The incident at the river confused her. What were these people doing out there at that time of the morning? What had they done? The thumps could have been almost anything, but....

Mariah didn't want to contemplate what they had done. This was the first time she had run into anyone at that hour of the morning who wasn't also running. That meant the likelihood of them doing something illegal was high. She shivered, but it wasn't from being cold.

Her favorite place to run was along the river. The quiet and the water the Rio Grande held at various times of the year was the big draw for her. Maybe she needed to change her routine...then again, there wasn't anywhere else other than the streets she could use at that time of the morning. The mountain path was closed until sunup.

Mariah pulled out her cellphone and attempted to call Rachel. A message saying, *"The phone you are trying to reach is not in service at this time,"* played instantly. The sense of something wrong washed over her again. What could have happened to her? They were supposed to clean out her apartment today. The plan had been for Rachel to move in and share expenses so they could save more money for the next six months.

They had agreed for Rachel to keep the apartment when Mariah moved to Dallas for law school. Unless something changed, she planned to come back to El Paso. When she returned, she wanted a decent place to live and someone pleasant to share it with.

For what she was paying for the apartment, she couldn't get much better. The apartment consisted of two bedrooms, two baths, a decent-sized kitchen, washer and dryer, small dining area, a comfortable living room with a fireplace. She had a small enclosed patio so she could sit outside when the weather was nice. It was close to a mall and grocery store. The interstate that would take you from one end of El Paso to the other wasn't far away.

Mariah pushed the incident at the bridge and Rachel into the background. The scare from her run nixed getting any sleep. Instead, she decided to return to work on her senior thesis. Because she was still doing research, she had papers and printouts spread out over the coffee table and couch.

After booting up her laptop, she got busy looking for verifiable information on the drug trade, smuggling and the cartels in the area. She was also looking through the criminal trials connected with the drug trade which had made the newspapers. If she needed the transcripts from the trials, she could get them at the courthouse, but for now, she only needed a ton of background information to figure out what facts she needed or didn't need. Unlike most of those in her class, she had gotten her thesis approved before the end of last semester so she would have the summer to work on it.

Mariah was so engrossed in what she was reading about the Sinaloa Cartel, Cartel de Golfo, Juárez Cartel and the feuds over territory, she didn't notice the knock on the door. When it was repeated louder, the sound pulled her from her reading. A frown formed on her face. She wasn't expecting any visitors. Automatically she closed her laptop and pushed up from the couch to peer through the peephole.

Three men were standing outside her door. One was older, dressed in a dirt brown sports coat which didn't cover his belly, a white shirt with straining buttons and dress pants. There was a thin man with graying hair in a Mexican police uniform. The third one was a young man in jeans and t-shirt, covered with a plaid flannel shirt hanging open and the sleeves rolled up to just below his elbows. He was someone from her past. It had been eight years since she last saw him. At least she thought it was him.

Mariah opened the door as far as the security chain allowed before the rotund man could knock again. "May I help you?" she asked, her eyes gravitating to the young man who stared at her. She thought she was wrong when the young man didn't show any signs of recognition.

"Are you Mariah Lansing?" the big man asked, his voice gruff, disdain showing on his face. He had a paper with her picture on it, so he knew who she was.

"Yes." Fear zipped through her. No one was smiling. Their faces were grim, with eyes that seemed to be accusing her of something.

"We need to talk to you. May we come in?" the older man asked. It was more of a command than asking permission.

"Who are you?" Mariah shot back, not sure if they were law enforcement as she assumed.

Badges and IDs were produced. The older man was a Daniel Jamison, Detective. The man in uniform was Juan Lopez of the Mexican police. When she turned to the young man, he produced his ID with obvious reluctance. Dale Warner, DEA. She examined his face. This time his eyes didn't hold what they had the last time she had seen him. A little sliver of her heart broke off and fell. Some dreams were never meant to be.

Mariah stepped back, closing the door enough to release the chain before opening it to let the three men into her sanctuary. They gathered inside the door, scanning her apartment and the mess on the couch and coffee table. She led them to the table in the dining area, not willing to move her papers and taking a chance on mixing them up.

"Would you like something to drink?" she offered, going to the refrigerator to get a bottle of water.

"No, but thank you," Jamison answered for the men, the politeness gruff and given with a grudging condescension.

After opening her water, she took a long drink before joining the three men at the table, letting the silence grow. Inside she was trembling, her heart racing, but on the outside, she remained composed and calm. The police needed to tell her what they wanted. The way they were watching her made her believe this wasn't going to be a pleasant interview for her.

Jamison began the questioning. "When was the last time you saw Rachel Hartley?" He was scowling, as if questioning her was distasteful. The crossed arms above his belly showed he was prepared to classify everything she said as a lie.

"Tuesday morning. We spent a couple of hours here after we got off from work."

"You didn't see her on Wednesday, the twelfth?"

"No."

Holding to what she had learning from Wes, her cousin, she wasn't going to give them anything more than what was asked until she knew what they wanted.

"Did you talk to her after you last saw her?"

"We talked on the phone Wednesday morning."

Jamison was grinding his teeth. The big hands were fisted, and his knuckles were white at her short answers. Too bad. Until he explained his questions, she wasn't giving him anything but what he asked.

"What was your relationship with Rachel?" It was the first open ended question he had asked.

Mariah glanced at the other two men who were remaining silent. Neither one offered her any help. She took a drink then set the bottle on the table. Her fingers picked at the label as she concentrated on the water.

"We're best friends and have been for the past five years since she cleaned up her act. She was supposed to contact me yesterday. Today was the day we had set for her to move in with me." Mariah stopped, waiting for the next question.

"When did she start using again?" Jamison asked.

Mariah shook her head. "She wasn't using. There's no way she would go back to drugs again. Like I said, she's been clean for five years. She's registered to go for the fall session at U of T. She has a plan and it doesn't involve using drugs."

Juan Lopez leaned forward and asked, "It there any reason she would have gone to Ciudad Juárez?" His English was heavily accented.

Mariah only knew of a couple of reasons for Rachel to be in Mexico. "She has family there and some friends she stayed in contact with over the years. Other than that, I've no idea. She didn't mention going there when I talked to her." Mariah scanned the men before asking, "What is this all about?"

Lopez didn't answer her question. Instead he asked, "Can you explain the $25,000 deposit made to her account on the twelfth?"

She stared at him while processing what he said. She shook her head, frowning. "I've no idea. It wasn't there on the eleventh when we balanced her checkbook. She had over $85,000 in her savings and $5,000 in her checking. She didn't need money."

"You sure about that?" Lopez asked.

"Very sure. We earn good money at the club. There was no reason to use or sell anything. Her last check would be somewhere around two thousand for the week before. Like I said, she didn't need money."

"So, you didn't know about the $25,000 deposited in her account on the twelfth?" Jamison's sneer showed he didn't believe her.

"No."

His next words were like slaps to her face and explained why they were here. "Were you helping her smuggle drugs?"

Anger lashed through her. She clamped her mouth shut, shoving the anger down into her roiling stomach, a cold fear sending a shiver up her spine. Her voice hid the emotions raging inside of her. "Rachel wouldn't be smuggling. She hated what it did to the people who got hooked on drugs. I've never had anything to do with drugs. I'd become a prostitute first before getting involved with drug smuggling."

"Is that what you're doing at the Golden Cat?" Jamison asked, openly leering at her.

She didn't back down from him. "Never. I have enough self-respect and don't need the money. I get enough in pay and tips to do what I want within reason." She crossed her arms and dared him to disagree with her.

"Okay. Then explain the $20,000 deposit in *your* account?"

"I don't have a $20,000 deposit. My last deposit was for $1,150 for my tips from Thursday and Friday." A crease formed between her brows. Why would they be checking her bank account? How could they justify getting a warrant without her being a suspect in Rachel's death?

"You might want to recant that statement, Ms. Lansing," Jamison said before pursing his lips. He was happy and Mariah suspected he was up to something.

Getting her laptop from the couch, she opened her bank account. She'd had no reason to check her balance since last Monday. When her account came up, she studied the screen. Someone had deposited $20,000 into her account.

It was all she could do to hit the button with her shaking hand to view the particulars of the deposit. The transaction was made during the time she was working her internship at the courthouse. Someone was playing games with her, but why? What could she say? The money was there, but she wasn't responsible for the deposit.

"You don't have a $20,000 deposit in your account, hm?" Jamison's voice was almost gleeful.

"Oh, I see $20,000 in my account, only I didn't make that deposit. In fact, it would have been physically impossible for me to have done so. I was working at the courthouse."

"Doing what?" Dale asked.

"Criminal Justice internship. I have to attend my sessions, or they won't allow me to continue the internship." She attempted to stuff the fear that was trying to take over back into its cubbyhole. What were they accusing her of doing?

"Will we be able to verify you were there?" Dale asked, his voice melding her past into the present.

With a nod, she said, "Yes, I was with Judge Newcombe. He'll be able to verify I was working for him and my hours. I'm required to clock in and out." Her eyes went back to Jamison. He was back to glaring at her.

"We will verify your alibi, but I want to know where that money came from."

She looked back at the screen and the offending deposit. "I've no idea. Absolutely none. No one else should have my account numbers." She raised her head and stared into Jamison's eyes. "How did you get access to my account?"

He handed her a folded paper. She took it and opened it. The warrant was signed by a judge she knew, giving access to her account on the supposition she was dealing drugs secondary to her relationship to one Rachel Hartley.

"How does my relationship with Rachel give you the right to probe into my private affairs?"

Dale's voice cut into her glaring contest with Jamison. "Rachel was found dead last evening. According to the coroner's preliminary report she was using heroin, cocaine and oxycodone. There's reason to believe she was smuggling drugs across the border."

It took a few seconds to comprehend what he said. Mariah blinked back tears, her head down. She didn't want to show how much his words upset her while processing the reason for their visit.

"No, she wasn't," Mariah emphatically said, not raising her head. "First of all, she wouldn't have gone near heroin or cocaine. The oxycodone and oxycontin were her drugs of choice. She didn't do needles so if the drugs were injected, she wasn't taking it by choice. As to smuggling, no way!"

Jamison glared at her. "Then explain away the packets of drugs found inside of her along with the drugs which showed on her lab work."

Mariah's head rose, the tears beginning to run down her face. He had it all wrong. Rachel wouldn't have used any of those drugs let alone smuggling them. Even when she was at her worst, she didn't stoop to selling drugs.

"I can't. I do know there's no way she would have ever voluntarily done what you're saying. I've no idea of where those deposits came from in my account or hers. What I do know is there's more going on here than you're seeing. If you won't find out who did this, I will."

Mariah was positive about her assessment of Rachel and what she would have done. The officers were basing what they believed Rachel was doing on her past, negating what she had done over the past five years. There was something fishy with this whole setup.

Dale asked, "What about her boyfriend? Maybe she was helping him?"

"Definitely not. When she found out he was using, she told him to get lost and never contact her again. She loved being clean and wanted nothing to do with that scene again."

"Are you sure about that?" Dale asked, studying her.

"Positive." She didn't waver from his direct gaze.

He leaned back in his chair with his brows drawn together, not taking his eyes from her. "Juan, I don't know. I can't get the pieces to fit."

"Señorita, do you know of any other acquaintances of Señorita Hartley?"

"There's Zelda. She and Rachel worked together for almost seven years. Then there is her counselor, Father Rivers at the Saint Vincent of Leon treatment center where she went when she wanted to get off the drugs she was taking. Other than Andrew, the ex, I don't know of any others she hung out with or talked to regularly. From what she said last week, she hasn't talked to Andrew in three months."

Jamison opened a folder and pushed a grainy photo across the table. "Who is this man?"

Mariah studied the photo. She shook her head with a shrug, pushing the photo back to him. "I've absolutely no idea. As far as I can remember, I've never seen or met him before."

"Then explain this," Jamison gloated as he placed a second photo on the table of the man and a person who appeared to be her. She noted the date and time on the photo.

"I have no idea who the man is, and that isn't me in the picture."

"Hmm. Looks like you to me," he said, picking up the photo and studying it with a gloat.

She glanced at the photo again. "Look at her eyes and then mine. Close but not close enough. She has dark eyes, and they're closer together than mine are. Also, they aren't slanted like mine. Nice makeup but it doesn't change the way they're made." Mariah tilted her head and dared him to refute what she'd said. Juan picked up the photo and studied it, then her, before passing it to Dale.

Dale scrutinized the picture and handed it back to Jamison. "It isn't her. She's right. The eyes are all wrong. So, my question is: why would someone pretend to be her and deposit money into her account?"

Jamison didn't answer Dale's question. "Ms. Lansing, Ms. Hartley had drug packets inside of her stomach, plus the cocktail of drugs in her system. The only explanation would be her acting as a mule for one of the cartels."

Mariah's gaze locked with his. "I don't care what the tests show. She wasn't using again. I don't know what happened, but there's no way she would be running drugs willingly. When she got clean, she avoided all her old contacts, even erasing them from her phone."

Flopping back in her chair, arms crossed, Mariah scowled. Something was so wrong with this picture. All the evidence pointed to Rachel running drugs, but it didn't fit with how she was living. No way would she willingly use again or agree to help any of the cartels.

"All I can say is that things aren't as they appear on the surface. I know Rachel almost as well as I know myself. Whatever happened, it had to be coerced. She wouldn't willingly take any drugs. You need to find out where she went and why, because something isn't right about this whole thing."

Detective Jamison blew out an audible breath. "Ms. Lansing, so far we can't find anyone who saw her other than at the bank on Monday evening. The picture shows her with a known enforcer for the Sinaloa. The last confirmed contact was with you."

"Did you talk to Father Rivers? She had an appointment with him at two in the afternoon on the twelfth."

"Yes. She missed her appointment." Jamison was set on his theory of Rachel running drugs. It would make his life a lot easier than doing the footwork needed to trace where she had gone before she died.

Lopez glanced at Jamison before saying, "We know who the man is in the pictures. What we need to discover is why she was with him. He's well known to us in Mexico and is part of the Sinaloa Cartel."

"The man in the picture with the woman pretending to be me was with Rachel also?"

"Si," Lopez answered.

Jamison's jowls trembled when he glared at Lopez.

"We'll check out your story about the money in your account. Don't leave town without letting me know," Jamison warned throwing his card on the table in front of her.

Lopez put a hand on her arm. He smiled when he asked, "Do you know a Wesley Lansing?"

She had no reason to lie. Connecting her to Wes would be easy enough. "Yes. He's my cousin."

Lopez turned to Dale and nodded. "Connection confirmed," he said before turning back to her. "We will look into the money in your account. Don't spend it. It will become evidence. Thank you for your time."

The three men stood, the interview over. When she looked at Dale, he was staring at her, his face grim. Mariah wondered what he was thinking. He had to know she wouldn't get involved in anything illegal. Wes would kill her if she did. Besides, she loved her cousin too much to put his job with the Border Patrol in jeopardy, regardless of their estrangement.

She walked them to the door and watched as they left. After locking the deadbolt, she rested her forehead against the door, the tears she had held back flowing freely. What was she going to do now? This would destroy her future if she couldn't prove she was being framed.

Then there was Jamison who was smearing Rachel and her both. Rachel had been murdered. Why? Who would have done this to her?

Wes might have some answers for her. If he didn't, she'd start digging them up herself. No matter what Jamison said, Rachel wasn't using, and she'd never smuggle drugs.

Mariah had no intention of setting back and letting them blame her for something she didn't even know about! This was all she needed. More stress.

Chapter Two

SUNDAY NIGHT AT THE club was normally quiet. Mariah left at four in the morning with only two hundred and fifty in tips for the night. The tips and clientele were getting worse each week.

Danny walked her to her truck. She looked and felt like a child next to him, her five-foot two-inch height coming about mid-chest, if that, on him. He was a six-foot-four muscled man with a face that created fear in most who met him. Very few people attempted to argue with him, even when drunk. She was lucky he liked her enough to make sure she was safe.

"You going to stop by the Slipper after class today?"

"Planning on it. After tonight, I need a new job."

"I guess you didn't get much. What did you do to piss off Madeline for her to stuff you out in no man's land?"

"I told her about Rachel. I guess it was my punishment for ruining her night. That, or she figured I needed a quiet shift when what I actually needed a busy one."

Danny nodded, blinking back tears. He had like Rachel and respected how she had maintained her dignity and morals while stripping. She had never resorted to sex to get money, even when she'd been using.

Mariah opened the door to her truck then pivoted back to Danny. He grinned when he lifted her and placed her on the seat as if she weighed only a couple of pounds.

"You be careful going home. I should be at the club this afternoon. I'll be looking for you."

Mariah leaned over and kissed his cheek. "Thanks Danny. I'll see you later."

He closed the door to the truck and watched as she drove away. If she got hired, it would be nice to have him at the new place. He wouldn't let anything happen to her. After rescuing her one time, she became his little imp. He said he liked having her around because she kept him entertained.

Mariah decided to skip her morning run. After yesterday, she wasn't keen about going to the river. It meant she would have a couple of hours to rest. She wasn't sleepy, only tired. There was a difference. Sleepy meant she needed to actually sleep and recharge. Tired meant she was overstressed and needed to close her eyes and purposefully clear her mind so she could relax.

She pulled into her parking space, gathered her things, and let herself into her apartment. Per her normal routine, as soon as she closed the door, she dropped her keys into the bowl on the little table before doing anything else. The bowl rang as the keys hit it. After locking the door, she went to her bedroom to rest, hoping things would make more sense when she got up.

At seven, she decided to go for a run. Instead of going to the river, she ran the city blocks in her neighborhood. It worked for today, even though she didn't like running on the hot concrete. The city was beginning to wake up when she returned home, showered and prepared for her day with Judge Newcombe. This would be a short day since the judge was leaving town. He gave her some research to do for him for Wednesday, which was close to being completed.

Before she left the parking lot, she put on Enigma's *Cross of Changes,* the music suiting her mood. She hadn't gone two blocks before she noticed the dark sedan. The car had pulled out behind her when she left the apartment complex and was still following at that distance. While paying attention to the heavy traffic, she kept close tabs on the vehicle in her rearview mirror. The sedan remained one car back, making every turn she did. Not until she pulled into the courthouse parking lot did the car pass her. It contained one person. A man with dark glasses concealing his eyes turned and scrutinized her and her truck before speeding away.

Before she got out of her vehicle, Mariah scanned the area, but didn't see anyone standing around. Maybe it was her imagination—then again—maybe not. Either way, the whole incident was strange. No one had ever followed her before today.

After the judge left, it didn't take her long to finish the research he wanted done. Mariah made her way to the Platinum Slipper, using the GPS on her phone to get her there without getting lost. The place wasn't hard to find. It was easy to get to from I-10, unlike the Golden Cat, which was hidden in a maze of streets in a rundown section of town. This club was in a decent neighborhood of stores, restaurants, and movie theaters where it should be reasonably safe.

Few cars were in the parking lot, but then again, late afternoons normally weren't a busy time for gentlemen's clubs. She pulled close to the building since she wouldn't be here long. When she started for the door, Danny was watching her, a big grin on his face.

He met her halfway to the building, bending over to give her a kiss. "Glad you are here. Mr. Becker will be over the moon when he sees you. Got to say, I love the outfit."

"Really?" she asked.

The summery flowered dress with a full skirt and sandals weren't anything special. She had gotten them to wear for her summer classes, unwilling to wear the shorts and crop tops the other girls wore.

"Really. He loved the picture I have of you. Come on in. I'll show you around."

He gave her a quick tour of the club, introducing her to Miguel and Rico, two other bouncers at the club. The place was still new looking and was heads and shoulders above the Golden Cat. Taking in the large room, Mariah noted that the area next to the stage was set up with comfortable chairs and loveseats to handle the higher end clients. Each grouping had mobile tables for drinks and food along with a coffee table. The seating was arranged into conversational groups. allowing for a good view of the large stage containing three poles for the dancers.

The pit, as the girls called the area next to the stage, was roomy and would be easy to work for the waitresses. The rest of the floor was also spacious with enough room between tables to allow people to get through easily. The floor gave the impression of a comfortable nightclub instead of a sleazy strip joint.

A girl walked onto the floor to deliver a drink to a customer. Mariah noted the costume was skimpier than the ones she now wore, but it covered all the necessary areas well enough and wasn't made up of stays and spandex.

"Well, Danny, I'll say it's a few steps up from the Golden Cat for sure."

Danny chuckled, guiding her to the bar. "It's more than a few steps up. This is top of the line. You'll like it here. They treat you good, and you'll get paid a hell of a lot better. With you being a class act, I'm sure you can play 'let's make a deal' to get more. All you'll need to do is give him one of your brilliant smiles."

She grimaced. "Yeah. Right. Then he'll want me to sleep with him for the extra pay. Not happening. I'll take a decent raise and let it be."

"You do know if you were to dance, you could make a fortune in tips." Danny was looking down at her when she turned to him with a withering glare.

"Not happening. There's no way I would ever get out there on a pole and take off my clothes. I have more self-respect than that. I'll leave the dancing to the exhibitionists who enjoy it." He had tried before to get her to dance, but Danny should know by now she wasn't going to change her mind.

"With that figure of yours, I don't see why not. So few women have what you do. Also, that innocent look you have makes it so you could command your own price for dancing and whatever else you might want to do."

"Enough, Danny. It's not going to happen, and you know it. Besides, how would stripper as my occupation look on an application for a job in law enforcement or to law school? It would guarantee my never finding a decent job away from these types of places."

"So, cocktail waitress is a better recommendation?" Danny challenged with raised brows.

"It's better than stripper. They at least know how much crap I can take and still smile."

Danny laughed. Mariah knew he was aware of how much she was hassled as she smiled and tiptoed through the veritable minefield of keeping the customers happy without compromising her morals. She was one of the few who didn't date the customers or make use of the private rooms like many of the girls did when they found someone they liked.

She was different and hadn't changed from the time she started to work at the club. Her sticking to her morals was one of the reasons the bouncers looked after her. They knew she didn't participate in the sexual games like the other girls.

They were standing at the bar drinking water when a man in a three-piece gray suit walked down the hall to the left of the bar. Danny stood up, smiling at the man. The man assessed Mariah before giving Danny a raised-brow look. When he stopped, Danny introduced them. "Mr. Becker, this is Mariah, the girl I told you about. She's a whiz on the floor."

Mr. Becker slowly took her in from head to toe before coming back and studying her face. "Sure I can't get you to dance? I'd pay top dollar if you did."

She glanced at Danny before saying, "No, but thanks. I prefer keeping my clothes on while working. Stripping isn't my style."

He sighed, keeping his gaze on her, shaking his head. "Danny, you were right. She's gorgeous and will fit in here. Too bad she won't go on stage. I could see her as the main attraction."

"Yeah. I get it, but there's no way she'll dance. They tried at the Cat to get her on stage and she always refused. Instead, she's been the best girl they've had on the floor for years."

Becker's eyes came back to her. "Years? She can't be over twenty-two max!"

Mariah and Danny grinned. "I'm twenty-six," she said.

Becker's eyes widened before he said, "I'll need to see proof to believe that. If I were to see you on the street, I'd think you were a teenager. I can see why you get a lot of attention." He sighed and shook his head again. "I guess I'd better get you an application to complete before you change your mind. Once that's done, we can talk pay."

He started back down the hall, a wave of his hand indicating she was to follow him to the business area of the club. The office area was as nice as the rest of the place. He guided her to a conference room and handed her an application and pen. When he left the room, Mariah could hear him and Danny conversing in the hall before they moved away.

The standardized application was short and didn't take her long to complete. She didn't have a lot to put on it. Her only paying job had been at the Golden Cat.

While waiting for Mr. Becker to return, she examined the room. The walls were a light mauve with a darker mauve carpeting on the floor. On each wall were oil paintings, not reproductions, with live plants in the corners of the room. The table against the wall to her left had neat stacks of papers on it, one of which she knew was applications. On the right was a wet bar with glasses neatly arranged on a corner shelf.

The conference table where she was sitting was a large light-colored wood oval with twelve comfortable chairs around it. Opposite to her were two narrow windows with sheer white curtains overlaid with dark mauve drapes pulled back with cord ties. The room was pleasant, but it wasn't masculine. She'd bet a day's tips that there was a woman who had planned the décor for it to be so feminine.

Mr. Becker silently appeared at her side, Startling her. "I see you're finished," he said before picking up the application and taking the seat beside her to look it over while she waited. "I see you have some college education. What were you studying?"

"I'm currently taking courses to complete my Criminal Justice degree. I should graduate after this next semester. I'm planning to go to law school in the fall if I'm accepted at one of the schools."

He didn't react to her statement of currently going to school, his eyes on her application. "Okay. It looks good. Danny says you're excellent with customers. What sort of tips did you get on a normal night at the Golden Cat?"

Mariah shrugged, not caring if he knew what she was earning. "Somewhere between two and three hundred during the week and up to a thousand most weekends."

His eyes rounded before turning away from her and leaning on the table, folding his hands together. "Do you know what the other girls were getting in tips?"

She was honest. "Most of them got half of what I did. Sheryl and I were the ones who got the best tips."

"Did you have to pool tips, or did you get to keep what you got?"

"We got to keep what we collected. They would move our area each shift, but it didn't seem to make a big difference for Sheryl and me. We still got good tips from the back of the room. I was kept in the back a lot because the others complained when they discovered that I would get a couple of thousand from the pit on the weekends."

He sat for a few seconds before he spoke again. She couldn't tell what he was thinking from his face.

"Don't get angry with me, but do you service the customers, along with waiting on them?"

"No, I don't. I'm a cocktail waitress. Nothing more. If they want to be serviced, they need to get one of the dancers or a floor girl who does that on the side. I turn down all propositions and proposals. In the five years I've worked on the floor, I've dated only one person from the club. It only lasted two dates. When he discovered I don't sleep around, he became upset and left and never asked me out again."

Mr. Becker flicked a glance in her direction before nodding. "Yet you bring in really good money. It tells me a lot. Here's the deal. We pay you twenty an hour plus you get to keep all your tips. You will work eight-hour shifts. Your choice is whether you want full time or part time. We offer insurance and a 401(k) if you're full time, along with two weeks of vacation. We also provide you with uniforms and clean them for you. Probation is two weeks."

Mariah couldn't believe it. Twenty an hour! That was close to twice what she was getting now. Plus, the tips here should be a lot better. This meant she could work three or four days a week and still come out ahead. She didn't need the insurance or 401(k). With the decreased hours, she'd have more time to concentrate on her schoolwork. Carrying the maximum credits, she had a difficult time keeping up with her assignments while working full time even with her insomnia. It was the reason she got a head start on her thesis.

"Okay. I'll take the job but would prefer part time since I'm in school. Weekends are good. I don't have Saturday classes and Tuesday and Thursday are my light days. I'm flexible other than day shift during the week."

He smiled, turning to face her. "Great. When can you start?"

"Next week. I need to give notice at the Golden Cat. I'll do that tonight."

"What size uniform will you need?"

"An eight. From what I saw when I came in, I'll need a ten top. It would fit better and still give the effect you want."

He wrote the information at the top of her application. "You got it. I can almost see the jealousy of some of the girls now. You will show them up without faking it. I'll have Theresa call you about starting orientation. With your experience, I would guess one or two days should do it. If you have any questions, call me." He handed her his card before saying. "Welcome aboard. I believe you'll find it's a change from the

Golden Cat. Our clientele is upper class and we plan on keeping it that way."

"Thank you. I appreciate it. I'll see you next week."

She stood to leave when his hand on her arm stopped her. She turned her head to see what he wanted. "Are you sure I can't talk you into dancing once a week. You could easily pick up eight or nine thousand for the night."

She smiled. "No thanks. My self-respect means more than the money. I'll stick to waiting tables."

"If you should change your mind, let me know."

"Not going to happen, but thanks for the offer."

He shrugged and shook his head with a wry grin even though she had turned him down. "I can always hope. With that angelic face framed by your glossy dark hair and the body of a goddess, you would rake in more money than you could imagine for less than an hour of actual work."

"Sorry. Not my thing," she sweetly told him as she would one of her persistent customers.

Pursing his lips, he nodded. "I see how you get those tips. See you in a week."

"Thank you again," she said before leaving, aware he was watching her as she left.

The interview had gone better than she expected. What she was prepared for had never happened. The manager at the Cat had been trying ever since she turned twenty-one to get her to dance and sleep with him. She wasn't about to sleep with a man she wasn't married to, and no way could she hang on a pole and take off her clothes. Going to the beach wearing a two-piece bathing suit which covered her was hard enough.

As she was going out the door, Danny came up behind her. "Well how did it go?"

She put her arm around his waist when he joined her as she walked. "Great. I got the job and start in a week. I'm only going to be doing part time, so I'll have an extra day for schoolwork." She walked a few steps with him before asking, "Did you hear about Rachel?" Blinking to keep the tears at bay, she waited for him to speak.

"No. What about her?" Mariah felt him tense with the question.

"She was murdered. The cops seem to think it was drug related and that I was working with her."

Danny stopped and faced her, brows drawn down and his eyes boring into hers. "You've got to be kidding! I can understand Rachel, but you—never!"

"Well, there's this thing about a deposit of $20,000 into my account. I've no idea where it came from, but it's there. Then they had a picture of someone pretending to be me with this man they recognized as being part of the Sinaloa Cartel. I hope they get it straightened out. I was at the courthouse when the deposit was made, so they need to start looking beyond me."

They turned and began walking again, remaining silent until they reached her truck. Danny turned her to him. "Mariah, be careful. This isn't something to play around with. I don't know what's going on, but you shouldn't have been drawn into whatever Rachel may or may not have been doing."

Mariah leaned into him to hide her tears. His arms came around her. "I don't believe she was doing drugs again. She was set up, but I don't know how to prove it. How they could even think I was involved is beyond me. I've never done drugs and never will." She moved away from him before tilting her head to see his face not hiding her tears. "Maybe someone at the Golden Cat assumed I was like Rachel, but then again, I still don't think she went back to drugs. It just doesn't fit." She sniffed and swiped at the tears.

"Leave it alone. Let the authorities handle it," Danny warned.

"I am for now. Depends on what they do to make it look like I was involved in what happened to Rachel." She opened the door and slid behind the steering wheel before saying, "I do believe that it's one of the slimy characters at the Golden Cat. I wouldn't put it past them to do something to me for refusing their advances."

"Maybe," Danny said, a worried frown marring his face. "You need to stay out of it, like I said."

She studied her key before putting it in the ignition. "I'm trying to do just that, but someone seems to want me involved and I haven't a clue as to who or why."

Danny shut the door. She rolled down the window, a half-smile on her face. "I'll see you in a week."

"Take care, imp."

Mariah could see she had worried him. She probably shouldn't have told him, but she had to tell someone. He didn't believe her about Rachel either. She knew it from the way he reacted. Who could she turn to for help now? Wes? He had his job to consider. Dale? He didn't let on he knew her, so she couldn't see him being willing to help. Perhaps the only thing she could do at this point was to wait to see what happened next.

The trip home was quick. If traffic was this good when she was scheduled to work, she could make it to the Platinum Slipper in less time than she needed to get to the Golden Cat. She jumped down from her truck and pulled her backpack from behind the seat. She was unlocking her front door when Dale's soft voice startled her. "Mariah, we need to talk."

She didn't look in his direction. When she opened the door, she let him go in first. No one was around when she scanned the parking lot. The old jeep with a canvas top that she didn't recognize, had to be his. She closed and locked the door before dropping her keys in the bowl with a ringing clatter. Using the bowl was the only way she could keep from losing her keys, then spending an hour looking for where she had left them. The sound of the bowl ringing was her welcome home.

Dale was studying the papers strewn on the coffee table and couch. The mess was organized. She knew where to locate what she needed in the stacks of paper, even though they appeared to be haphazardly thrown into random piles.

Mariah didn't care what he thought before going to the kitchen to fix herself something to eat. She was hungry. Hopefully this discussion would be concluded quickly since she had a lot of things to do before work tonight.

From the kitchen, she asked, "Okay. What did you need to talk to me about?"

When she turned, he was beside her, leaving her off balance. His hands steadied her, sending sparks and frissons of electricity through her. That much hadn't changed in their years apart.

"I believe your assessment of Rachel not using again is correct. I find most of the pieces don't fit in the way Jamison is trying to force them together."

Mariah moved away from him, turning her back so he didn't see how his touch affected her. "Really? I thought you'd be trying to close the case the quickest way possible. That way you could move onto something more important than finding a dead stripper."

"I do want to close the case but not until I discover the truth about her death. Too many things don't add up. Things like the $20,000 in your account. I know you wouldn't ever do anything illegal, but Jamison doesn't."

Turning to face him, Mariah rested her hip against the counter, arms crossed as she glared at him. "What are you attempting to tell me, Dale?"

"That you're being framed. I don't know why though. I would have let things drop but he made a big mistake. If he was accusing anyone else, I would have been following up on their involvement in the supposed drug smuggling with Rachel. With you, I know there's no way you'd be connected to anyone dealing, let alone helping them." Dale hadn't looked away from her. Somewhere along the way, he had stopped being afraid of her.

"You positive about that?"

He chuckled. "Yeah, I'm sure. You're as likely to be involved in the drug trade as I am."

"Thanks for the vote of confidence," she said with a sigh, not really believing him, before returning to putting a meal together. "What now?"

"I'd like you to read this and tell me what you think." He handed her a bound book which had *'Diary'* written in calligraphy on the cover. She opened it and immediately recognized Rachel's writing.

"Where did you get this?" Fear zipped up her spine, leaving sparks in her brain.

"I managed to snag some evidence before Jamison got there. The case is out of his precinct. That makes me wonder why he is investigating the murder instead of Patterson, who normally covers that precinct."

Her gaze returned to the diary she held. Forgetting about fixing food, she sat at the table and began to read Rachel's words. A smile crossed her face as she relived some of the things she and Rachel had talked about or done together. Rachel had thought of her as a smart kid sister.

It wasn't until the last few pages that the tone of the diary changed. Her dead friend insinuated someone was stalking her. On the last entry, she wrote: "*I need to go and see Father Rivers. I'm so confused right now. Why? I'm terrified for myself and Mariah. If what Javier told me is true, I don't know what to do to stop it.*" Mariah reread the entry, brows furrowed while she attempted to make sense of it. Why would Rachel be so terrified for *her*? And who was it that had terrified her in her last days?

Dale set a plate of food before her. "You need to eat."

Mariah glanced at the clock. Over an hour had passed while reading Rachel's diary.

"Do you have any idea what she was talking about?" Mariah asked, staring at the final passage in the diary.

"No, and from your question you don't either. Like I said, the pieces don't fit. I'm hoping to find Javier Gutiérrez. So far, we haven't been able to locate him. My guess is he's feeling the heat from talking with Rachel."

Mariah shook her head. "How do you know which Javier she was talking about?"

Dale shoved a paper with Rachel's writing across the table. The person's full name and address were written on it.

"I guess you do know which one. I wonder what he told her that made her so afraid."

"My guess is he told her about some deals, a few murders and the Sinaloa. He has hated them since they put him and most of the Juárez Cartel out of business. They've been feuding with the Sinaloa for years over their businesses and territory."

Mariah nodded. "I know. The Sinaloa wants it all and has already absorbed several smaller cartels. taking control of their territory, businesses and contacts."

Dale frowned, his fork pausing midway to his mouth. "How do you know that?"

"It's part of my senior thesis. There's been an uptick in smuggling with rumors of a new drug coming across the border. No one in authority can prove it though from what I've found so far. Then again, most of my information is from six months or more ago."

"I've seen the new drug and even have a sample of it. Pretty dangerous stuff and deadly if not cut enough. A quarter ounce will become over two pounds when cut. At fifteen hundred a quarter bag, you know it's better than cocaine or heroin." He stared at her before saying, "Stay out of this. These guys aren't very nice, and I don't want you hurt."

"As if you care about what happens to me," she mumbled without thinking. She kept her eyes on her plate as she ate, mulling over what he had told her and what she had read in Rachel's diary. A tap on the shoulder had her turning to see what he wanted.

"Girl, I care a lot about what happens to you."

"Why?" she questioned, his words summoning the anger from its hiding place.

He hadn't cared when she was at the farm with him. Or when Wes had her leave. He hadn't even bothered to speak to her back then, no matter what she did to get his attention. Why would he care about her now?

"Because I do. I cared when we were on the farm, and I care about you now. I was just too stupid and scared to say it."

She put her fork down. "Scared of what?"

"You."

"Huh?" Scared of her. He had to be kidding! She was too tiny to create fear in any man.

"Yeah. You. Every time you would come around, I couldn't think let alone speak. No matter how hard I tried, I couldn't put two words together when you were there. Believe me, I wanted to, but my mouth and brain wouldn't cooperate." He played with his food, unable to look at her. "You're so beautiful. So perfect. I can barely look away from your eyes. And the smile you have reaches out and grabs me each time I see it. Wes did what he could, but no matter how much I practiced, the minute you showed up, I would freeze. No matter what I did, I could barely speak to you.

She sighed. "What changed?"

"I guess being in the DEA role made it so I could say something without my brain turning to mush."

"Does that mean Dale, the agent, is speaking to me now, or am I talking to the Dale I knew at the farm?" For her, his answer made a difference. If the agent was speaking, she could give up on the man permanently.

"It's me. I got past that first few words." His lips twitched up into a crooked grin.

"Well, it's about time. Nothing like waiting ten years for you to say something to me."

His eyes widened before he spat out, "You waited ten years for me to talk to you?" His face reddened when he realized what he had said.

She grinned and chuckled. "Sort of. I figured you weren't interested in me when you walked away as I was leaving."

He hung his head, playing with his food. "I wanted to beat Wes to a pulp for making you leave. I probably would have if I had stayed. We argued over him making you leave. He told me to stay out of it unless I was going to man up and start dating you. I left right after you did."

Mariah leaned back in her chair, watching the man who had been so scared of her he couldn't even talk to her to keep her there. None of this made sense. But then again, she didn't understand his inability to talk to her. Being only five-one and weighing all of a hundred pounds at the time, she definitely wasn't intimidating.

"So, what's next?" she asked, keeping the question vague to allow him to determine what she meant.

"I need to discover the truth about what happened to Rachel. Also, I need to keep you safe. What she wrote means you're in danger, and I'm not about to let anything happen to you."

"Why?" she again questioned.

"Because you're important to me. When I saw you standing at the door, I wanted to jump for joy. Wes wouldn't tell me where you were, and I wasn't about to get fired for trying to track you down through the computers at work. I've been given a second chance and I've no intention of letting you disappear from my life again."

She mentally cursed Wes. The least he could have done was tell him where she was and let him take it from there. Wes knew she was interested in Dale. He had even encouraged it. Bastard. He should have helped rather than hindered things between them.

Her eyes went to the clock. It was almost six. Time for her to get ready for work. "Look, I have to work tonight. Give me some way to contact you. I'll let you know if anything happens or changes. I'd call in, but I'm giving my notice tonight. I have a new job starting next week."

Dale's head came up. "Where are you going to be working?"

"The Platinum Slipper. It's a strip joint, but it's classy. I'm doing the same job as I am at the Golden Cat."

He didn't look away when asking, "Doing what?"

"I'm a waitress." A second later she realized what he was really asking. "You didn't think I'd be stripping, did you?"

His face turned the color of a fire truck. "I didn't think so, but I had to ask."

"Wes would kill me if I was dancing. Besides, I have more self-respect than that. At least give me some credit for brains."

"Oh, you have brains. That I do know. Like I said, I didn't believe you would be dancing, knowing how you dressed at home. I'm surprised you even agree to wear the skimpy outfits the waitresses wear."

"They aren't that bad. They cover me more than any bikini. I can live with it for now. I'm hoping I'll be able to find a more respectable job when I graduate until I can get into law school."

"Okay but

0.61be careful. I'll be working to prove Rachel wasn't using and she was set up. Meanwhile, you stay out of it," he again warned.

"I'm planning on it. Unless somethin happens, I'm going to let you guys handle it."

He nodded before standing. "I'd better get going and let you get to work. Let me know if you have any concerns or information."

"Will do," she said before walking him to the door.

"He pivoted and stared down at her. "Mariah, when this is all over, I want to talk about us getting together."

"It's about time," she told him with a smile.

He bent over and brushed his lips across hers before abruptly leaving. She couldn't believe it! He had finally talked to her, then kissed her.

After all this time she was still attracted to him. He had manned up and had done something right. Maybe there was hope for him after all

Chapter Three

MARIAH WENT TO WORK, hoping to have a decent night. Zelda made it not so good. She'd been off on Monday and hadn't heard about Rachel. She came to the locker room to take her break. Mariah sat on the bench staring at Rachel's locker attempting to hold back the pending tears.

"Hey, kid. You look like you lost your best friend," Zelda said.

Mariah blinked. "I did. Rachel's dead." She used the heel of her hand to scrub away the tears that didn't stay put.

Zelda dropped onto the bench with a gasp at the news. She put her arm across Mariah's shoulders. "I'm so sorry. I didn't know. When?"

"The twelfth. The police came to talk to me. They want to believe she was smuggling drugs and that I'm connected somehow." Mariah turned to Zelda only to find her studying the lockers in front of her.

Zelda removed her arm. "I was wondering when she was a no-show. Sometimes things seem to come crashing in and you start using again. I know I did. I found it easier to get cleaned up the second time. Crap happens."

"I can't believe that. She was on top of the world and was starting school."

"Whatever. She's gone, and there's nothing we can do about it. Life goes on. Sorry, but I've got to get ready for the next show. You'd better get back to work." Zelda left to get her costume. Mariah returned to staring at Rachel's locker.

She finally opened the combination lock and cleaned out the personal items, leaving the skimpy costumes for someone else to dispose of. The lock joined the other things in the bag. Most of what she had was trash, but she wasn't about to let Madeline clean it out and toss everything. Something worth saving might be hidden in the trash.

She couldn't believe how Zelda had immediately traveled down the same road as the police. With the cold way she had dismissed the news of Rachel's death, Mariah guessed that they weren't close friends after all. The rest of the night was a blur. Business was slow, and Mariah wanted to be anywhere else but the club. The end of her shift couldn't come fast enough.

Greg walked her to her truck, but he wasn't Danny. With the way her night had gone, she decided to go for a run before returning home. At four AM, there shouldn't be anyone else out running. She parked in her normal spot at Sunland park. The light that had been out, was now fixed.

She was about a third of the way back to the truck when she heard footsteps behind her. Glancing back over her shoulder, she saw two men dressed in running shorts and shoes. She wasn't worried about them. This wasn't the first time she had seen others running before daylight.

Around halfway back to the parking lot, she became concerned. The men were staying the same distance behind her, neither slowing down or speeding up to pass. Time for a sprint.

When she arrived at her truck, she jumped in and was backing out of the parking space before the men made it to the small lot. They had a dark sedan parked out of the light in the shadow of the bridge. They were getting into the car when she turned on to the ramp out of the park.

Mariah turned onto the main thoroughfare, keeping tabs on the car behind her. They followed her until she turned into the apartment complex. The incident spooked her. She couldn't be sure if they were really following her or if it was her imagination.

Mariah opened the door and entered her apartment without turning on the light. Her keys clinked into the bowl before she threw the deadbolt.

"It's about time you got home," a soft male voice with a Texas twang stated from the shadows of the living room. She whipped around, fear zinging throughout her, freezing her stomach and chest. The fear left as quickly as it came when she recognized the voice.

"What in the hell are you doing here, Wes?" Mariah asked, turning in the arms enveloping her in a hug. "How did you get in?" she questioned with a smile, looking into the eyes which mirrored hers in shape and color. Only he wasn't smiling. Her smile ran away, leaving behind a crushing pain. She pushed out of his arms and waited for him to answer her questions.

He held up a key, eyebrow quirked. "I guess you forgot you gave me this when you moved in for the just-in-case scenario."

"I did forget. It was so long ago. Nice seeing you. How long are you staying?"

To hide the hurt, her voice was almost cold. She stuffed the joy at seeing at him back into the box where it belonged. There had been no warmth in his greeting, so this wasn't a social visit.

Wes reached around her and flipped the switch, bathing the area by the door in the soft light from the lamp on the table with her key bowl. Mariah drank in the sight of him. At five-foot-ten and a young thirty-six he wasn't imposing. He was well-toned from the hard work on the farm he owned. She was aware of the strength that went with those hard muscles.

Most people took him for being laid back and not too bright. He played on that assumption, only they couldn't have been more wrong. He was extremely intelligent and as fast as lightening when necessary. The job he did with the border patrol was mostly administrative now.

Back when he was active on the front lines, he had always found time for her when she was in his care. He had gone from babysitting her to raising her when her parents moved, leaving her behind. She was eight and he was eighteen.

The three years since she last saw him, he hadn't changed much. The last time she had gone back to the farm, which had been her home, he had been cold and distant like now. What that meant was that something was seriously wrong for him to be here now.

She walked to the end of the couch and turned on the lamp to be able to see him without a lot of shadows. He still wasn't smiling. She was right. Not a social call. Figured. Like everyone else, he cast her out of his life without telling her why.

Mariah plopped onto the sofa and waited for him to talk. With her arms crossed over her middle, she totally quelled the initial happiness at seeing him. She stared at the feet she had propped on the coffee table, hiding as best she could the hurt and disappointment.

His face and demeanor showed he didn't want to be here. She watched from lowered lids when he stalked to the chair placed to the right of the couch. He gave the impression he was forcing himself to be close to her. The straight-lined mouth and eyebrows drawn together creasing his forehead showed his distaste. He leaned forward with his elbows on his knees and folded his hands together. His gaze was on his hands like he was avoiding looking in her direction.

"What's going on with you?" he asked, his voice soft but holding not one iota of warmth.

"The same old stuff. Work and school." She kept her answer short, blinking rapidly to hold back the tears. He didn't give a damn what was going on in her life and it showed.

"Heard you're taking a new job."

"Just a change of place. Same job."

"Why?" he asked, turning his head enough to see her face.

"The Golden Cat has gone to the riffraff and low-class sleaze balls. It's gotten to the point where I almost feel I should be packing when I go in there. The new place is high-class. I'll earn more and work less hours." She glared at him and let her anger show when she asked, "Why the visit? I can tell you don't want to be here."

The muscles in his jaw jumped when he clenched his teeth. She didn't think he was going to speak until he said, "Tell me about Rachel," avoiding answering her question or commenting on her accusation of his not wanting to visit her.

"Not much to tell. She's dead. Murdered to be exact. The police believe she was using and smuggling, but I'm sure she wasn't."

His eyes assessed her. "Mariah, I'm here to help you. Dale talked to me. You're in big trouble and don't even know it."

"Do you want coffee or tea?" she asked abruptly, jumping up and going to the kitchen to get away from him.

"Coffee," he said.

She turned on the coffee maker. Tears ran down her face while she stared at the light and the screen which said *Not Ready*. Should have known. He was only here because she was having problems. If it weren't for that, he wouldn't have contacted her.

If only she could figure out what she had done three years ago to make him not want her near him. The last time she went to visit him, she had planned to spend a week, but ended up leaving after two days. If he hadn't wanted her there, he should have said so when she let him know about the planned visit.

As for today, he could have called, saving himself a lot of time and trouble. Everything he wanted to know she could have told him over the phone. Then again, she probably would have hung up at the icy tone he was using.

She fixed his coffee as he liked it and returned to the living room, handing him the cup. He hadn't moved. He glanced at her and blew out a breath through his nose. "What do you know about the drug trade in this area?"

"A lot. I'm doing a paper on it for my senior seminar. Why?"

"How many cartel members do you know?"

She wondered where he was going with this line of questioning. "None that I'm aware of. I try to remain ignorant about what people do for a living. If you know too much, you become a problem. It's the 'I leave them alone and they leave me alone' type of thing. If your next question is about me possibly being involved in drugs and smuggling, don't bother. I'm a cocktail waitress and earn a decent living. I've never used drugs and would never knowingly get involved in smuggling."

Her anger had seeped through by the last sentence. What she wanted to do was to ask him to leave and not bother coming back. She didn't need his professional help. What she needed was what she had believed was her family. Her only family. A tear dropped onto her hand at his insinuation she was involved with drugs in any shape or form.

He ignored her anger and tears. "Then why the extra money in your checking account?"

"I've no idea where it came from, and it isn't mine. I have no intention of using it. The detective seemed to believe I was helping Rachel in whatever he thinks she did."

"And were you?" Wes asked, his expression not changing.

Mariah's voice was overly calm when she said, "You may leave now, Wes. This conversation is over."

He didn't move. The silence was pregnant with what she hadn't said to his implication she was doing something illegal.

"Are you dancing along with waiting tables?" Wes asked.

"Get out!" Mariah commanded, her voice rising in pitch and volume, deeming the question unworthy of an answer. She now knew what he thought of her. Consuming pain gripped her as she bit her lower lip, blinking back as many tears as she could.

"Answer me, Mariah. I need to hear from you what you're really doing." The voice was harsher than she had ever heard from him. It was also alienating in his belief that she was dancing and smuggling drugs.

"I'm nothing more than a cocktail waitress. I don't strip or dance and never will. I don't have sex with the customers. I don't date them. What I do is go to school five days a week. In my free time, I study. I don't use drugs and never will, and I won't have anything to do with them." She hadn't added how he had raised her to respect herself.

"I didn't think so, but that isn't what I've been led to believe."

She didn't bother to wipe away the tears. "All you had to do was ask. You told me to leave. I needed a job where I could support myself, so I took the highest paying job I could find with no experience or skills."

Where in the hell had he expected her to work? McDonald's? So she could live on the streets?

In the eight years since he told her to leave, she hadn't asked him for a damn thing. All she wanted was the loving cousin who had raised her to return. As it was, she had no family, leaving her to deal with everything on her own.

"Tell me about Rachel. I know she was a friend?" Wes's voice had softened. She had heard him use the technique before to get information. He could play good cop all he wanted. The pain of his kicking her out of his life over a lie left another deep wound, deeper than the cold way he had treated her before she left three years ago.

With a sigh, Mariah repeated what she told the police and Dale. She ended with, "She was supposed to move in with me. She was my best friend, and yes, she was a stripper. Her preference would have been working in a factory, office or even a store, but like me, she needed to live.

"The drugs she used dulled the pain of what she was doing. When she got clean, she started making plans to get out of the club. Next week she was supposed to start school. I don't care what they say, she never would have gone back to using drugs, let alone smuggling them for money. She had plenty of money that she had saved over the past five years. Enough for her to get her degree and to live comfortably until she found a decent job."

Wes leaned back, placing his elbows on the arms of the chair with his hands clasped together. He tapped his chin with his steepled index fingers while studying her. "Who else did she associate with that you know about?"

"She was friends with Zelda, another stripper. They were close until Rachel got clean. Zelda still uses, but they talked and hung out at times. Rachel was trying to get Zelda into counseling. Then there was Father Rivers, her counselor at the rehab center where she stayed to get sober. She saw him regularly. Then the boyfriend she dumped when she discovered he was using.

"She was moving away from Zelda because she didn't want to be tempted into using again. Zelda keeps control of what she does, but sooner or later she'll lose that control."

Wes picked up his coffee and took a sip, staring out the window beside the front door. He gnawed on his bottom lip, then he took another sip before setting the cup on the table beside him. The coldness was gone from his features. He leaned over again with slumped shoulders. He scrubbed his face with his hands.

"I'm sorry, Mariah. I should have asked you about your job." The soft voice hitched. "Dale told me I had it all wrong, but I heard from several others you were stripping. I couldn't have you around if that was true. It would have put my job in jeopardy."

A heavy sigh escaped her. "Come on Wes. Think about it. You raised me with more self-respect than to disrobe on a stage in front of a bunch of drooling men. I told you about my plans to become a lawyer. As if I could get into law school with stripper as my occupation. It's going to be hard enough with cocktail waitress on the application. I honestly thought you knew me better than that." The sharp pang in her heart made it difficult to catch her breath. How could he have believed that she would strip for a living?

"I'll admit to being young enough to be swayed by those I thought I knew and could trust. When two of the guys told me essentially the same story, I believed them. Then you came to visit, and I didn't know what to do, so I avoided being around you and was cold to hide how much it was hurting me." The fingers on his hands knotted together. He kept his head lowered so she couldn't see his face. "I can't apologize enough. I hurt both of us. I've missed you a lot. This time I screwed up big time by not checking for myself when they told me you were stripping."

"As if you would ever go to a strip joint. Next time ask me. I'll always tell you the truth. I'll never strip. It's all I can do to parade around in the skimpy outfits I have to wear. Think about it; if I won't go to the beach in a bikini, why would I take everything off for a bunch of nasty, leering, slime-balls? I thought you were smarter than that."

Disappointment filled her. The last thing she thought he would do was to believe the worst of her. The story most likely came from a couple of men who recognized her. Their story was most likely conceived after she turned down their offers of money for things she didn't do.

"You're right. I'm smarter than that but got sucked into their story. No matter what I believed, I couldn't leave you hanging out there with what is going on now."

"What *is* going on?" Mariah asked.

"Seems you are being set up, but we don't know why. Dale gave me a rundown of the interview with Jamison. You need to be careful with him. He's not what he seems to be."

"Uh, duh! If he isn't dirty, I'll eat a shoe, your choice," she said, disgust lacing her words.

Wes chuckled. "I see you caught onto him."

"It would take a really dumb person to not see what he's doing. He knew exactly when to get the warrant to check my account. That warrant came from a judge who is questionable at best. I've done my research and found many dubious things concerning the syndicates where that particular judge is concerned."

"Hmm. That explains some things. You must have run across something which sent up alarms to those who aren't exactly on the up and up. You're going to need to be extremely careful. My belief is they weren't after Rachel so much as you."

"Huh?" She wasn't sure she had heard him right.

"Tell me, has anything odd, unusual, or strange happened since Rachel's death?" He appeared to know there had been from the way he stared at her as if daring her to say no.

Mariah curled into the corner of the couch. "Yes. A couple of guys were following me as I was running today. Then a car followed me to the courthouse. Of course, there's the money in my account I didn't put there."

She hesitated before saying, "The day the police came to see me, I went for a run after my shift was over. That night .

there wasn't a moon. No one should have been around, but three men were there. Before I saw them, I heard some thumps which sounded as if someone was hitting another person. They left in what sounded like a ATV. When I got back to my truck, the streetlight was out, and someone attempted to follow me from the park."

"From here on out, run with someone you trust."

"Yeah, like I'm going to find someone to run at four or five in the morning."

"Find someone or go later when more people are in the park. These people don't play around, and I don't want to lose you."

She couldn't keep the sarcasm out of her voice when she said, "You couldn't prove that with the way you've treated me for the last few years."

Her barb hit home. He hung his head. "I know I hurt you bad. You have every right to be angry with me. From here on out, I'll not believe anyone without checking it out thoroughly. Stupidity comes in all forms, as you should know. Besides, I hadn't heard from you in months and made the incorrect assumption that you were ashamed."

"That's because you wouldn't talk to me on the phone. I'd call and you didn't return my calls, so I finally gave up. The visit was my last try to find out what I did wrong."

Wes hid his face, almost curling in on himself in the chair. When he raised his head a few moments later, he was crying. "I can't change the past, but I can make sure I don't repeat that mistake ever again."

Mariah moved to the arm of the chair to hug him. He pulled her onto his lap. "I want my little girl around as much as possible. She needed to fly and find herself. I love who she is, and I'll do my best to never hurt her again."

He cuddled her to his chest like he had when she was small. He added some information no one had mentioned. "The day you ran in the dark and heard those thumps, a runner was killed. I'm almost sure that person was supposed to have been you. Instead, an innocent runner was beaten to death."

A spike of fear went through her. "They were using an ATV, right?"

"Yes. They're after you. Don't trust anyone but me and Dale. No one. Understood?"

"Yes, sir."

"Also, be careful what you tell people. Don't talk about Rachel. Don't let them know what you think or why. They're going to attempt to set you up for a fall, so please be careful. Let me know if you need help. I'll be there for you."

Her arms went around the man she thought of as her father. "I love you Wes. Please don't push me away again. You're all I have."

"I know. No matter what I believed, I couldn't let you take a fall for something you didn't do."

"I take it you and Dale work together a lot."

"You could say that," he said with a chuckle. He turned her head until they were facing each other. "He cares for you. Stay close to him on this. He'll watch over you like I would."

A smile lit her face. "I know he cares since he's now talking to me. He finally gave me a kiss. Not that It was much, but still, he kissed me."

Wes kissed her forehead before setting her on her feet. She had no idea of what he was thinking when his eyes scanned her face with a slight frown on his lips.

"Okay, girl. You going to eat before you go to your internship?"

Mariah giggled. "Of course. An omelet with raisin bread okay?"

"Sounds perfect."

As they ate, the strain on their relationship began to recede. The hole caused by his pushing her away was closing, but she was going to have a scar. The scar might get littler and fade, but it would always be there, like the one she got when her parents took off without telling her they were leaving. She knew how hard things could be when abandoned by your family. Wes's reaction to her over the past few years could be construed as abandonment as well. A niggling doubt remained as to whether he meant what he said about wanting to keep her in his life.

When they finished eating, Wes sent her off to school, saying he would do the cleanup and lock her apartment before he left. He promised to see her in a week or so if he could get away. If not, he'd call her. She wasn't sure if they would go back to the weekly calls they had shared when she first moved out, but it didn't matter. He would be calling her again. That was enough to keep her from feeling totally alone. The question she asked herself was: But how long would it last this time?

Chapter Four

WORK TODAY WENT WELL until after lunch. Mariah had become sleepy, making it hard to read the fine print in the legal tomes. Thankfully she'd be home before two and could squeeze in some actual sleep. In the last three days, she had only slept for an hour.

She managed to make it home before crashing. The bookbag landed on the chair in the living room on her way to the bedroom. Without bothering to undress, Mariah kicked off her shoes and crawled onto the bed. Within seconds she was in a sound sleep, oblivious to the world around her.

In her dream, there was an annoying hammering. The noise wouldn't stop. Slowly, she came back to awareness. What she thought was hammering, was someone pounding on her door. Alertness returned as she padded to the door in her bare feet to find out who was disturbing the first real sleep she had gotten in over a week.

She checked the peephole. Jamison was lifting his hand to pound on the door again. A young man in uniform was standing behind him. Mariah considered letting the detective continue with his assault on her door but thought better of it.

The last thing she needed was her neighbors being disturbed, bringing attention to her problems with the police. The deadbolt clicking open had Jamison moving to give him a clear view of her when the door opened. The young officer had his hand on his gun as if he was expecting her to create a problem.

With a scowl, she asked, "What do you want now?" She blocked the doorway, wanting to go back to bed. His being here meant she wouldn't get those few precious hours of sleep she needed.

"We need to discuss a new issue," Jamison responded with a sneer. "May we come in?"

With a sigh, she opened the door and let them in, leading them to the dining room. This time she didn't offer them anything as she grabbed a bottle of water from her fridge. Her gut told her he was going to attempt to frame her again for something she hadn't done. Wes made sense when he told her she had stumbled upon something, and somehow, they believed she knew more than she did. If only she knew what she had found which made them so afraid.

"Ms. Lansing, please explain why another $20,000 has shown up in your account." This time Jamison didn't bother with pleasantries.

She went to the living room and retrieved her tablet, pulling up her account before rejoining them at the table. He was right, another $20,000 was in her account. She checked the time it was deposited and wanted to laugh. These guys needed to check her internship schedule.

"You're right. Like before, I have no idea who put it there. Again, I couldn't have deposited it since I was giving a presentation at the time. That is easily verified with Professor Lowenstein." She leaned back in her chair, her eyes challenging him to come up with something else.

"I'll check your alibi, but I want to know who you hired to make the deposit." He wasn't giving up easily this time.

"Hmm. If I hired someone to make the deposit, where did I get the money to pay them? There've been no unusual withdrawals from my accounts, and my deposits are in line with my normal tips." Her eyes again dared him to come up with some sort of proof she was doing something wrong.

Jamison leaned toward her, close enough she could smell the garlic, onion, and coffee on his breath. "I know you're involved in the smuggling like Rachel. You can play games with me, but you won't win. From what I know, you could have easily skimmed part of your tips to pay a person to make those deposits."

She kept eye contact, not backing down from him. "Again, you'll have to prove those suppositions. If you check, you'll find the tips for everyone at the club have been slowly declining over the past few months. Also, I declare how much I make in tips each night for them to add it to my pay for tax purposes. They have a nice system where they take the taxes out for me. You have nothing, but you might want to look into why someone is attempting to frame me."

She noted the momentary change in his face. If she hadn't read it wrong, she had seen fear before he covered it up with a false bravado.

"I promise I'll get the proof you're working with them. I'm positive you won't be able to provide alibis every time. Soon you'll be sitting on the inside looking out. People like you always slip up, and when you do, I'll be there," he threatened.

"Until you have enough proof to arrest me, I'd appreciate you leaving me alone. I've a busy schedule and you awakened me from some much-needed sleep. Next time, please call and make an appointment if you have any further questions."

The young officer had been studying her during the exchange with Jamison. He drew himself up and puffed out his chest, a holier-than-thou expression on his face. "We aren't required by law to give you any advance notice when we want to question you. This investigation is showing you are deeply involved with the cartels. Once we put all the details together, you'll join the rest of the scum in jail."

With a sugary sweetness, Mariah asked, "Are you finished? I need to eat and get ready for work."

Jamison glared at her. "We're finished for now. The next deposit we find, you'll be going downtown until it's proven where the money came from."

Okay. She now knew the plan. They really wanted her out of the way. If only she knew the reason why. What had she come across that had them so scared? If she knew that, she could circumvent their plans.

As soon as the two men left, she called Wes. What she needed was how to handle Jamison's threat. That was what it was, a threat to put her in jail.

Wes answered on the first ring as if he had been waiting on her call. "Mariah, what's wrong?" he questioned without a hello.

"Jamison was here again. There's another $20,000 in my account. He's trying his best to prove I'm doing something wrong. The plan is to take me in when another deposit shows up and hold me until they discover where the money came from. How do I counteract this?"

Wes didn't answer right away. She knew he was considering all her options, so she waited patiently for his advice.

"Contact Dale. He'll be able to help you where I can't without sending up alarms. There's more to this than I'm able to tell you. Go along with whatever Dale suggests. He'll keep me informed."

She frowned, positive there was a lot he wasn't telling her, but she didn't have any other options. Asking questions wouldn't get any answers. It was something she had learned over the years.

The last thing she needed was to be arrested for something she didn't do or even know about. Law schools could be extremely picky, and something like that could disqualify her from the couple of schools at the top of her list to attend. As of now, she couldn't even apply until this was finished.

"Okay. Give me his number. He neglected to give it to me.

Wes chuckled. "Somethings just don't change. You still rattle the poor boy. His number is 915-555-0139. Call him now, Mariah." It was a command, not a request.

"Okay. Thanks."

She hung up and dialed Dale's number.

"Hello," he answered, giving the impression, he didn't recognize her number.

"It's Mariah. Wes told me to call you." Hopefully Dale wouldn't be upset with her cousin. Maybe he didn't want her to have his number.

"What happened?" He was all business, somehow knowing something was wrong.

"Jamison showed up again. Seems like there's more unexplained money in my account. He nicely threatened to get me one way or another."

"I'll be there in twenty minutes. We'll develop a plan when I get there." He abruptly hung up, preventing her from telling him she needed to get to work.

The clock said six thirty. She didn't have to be to work until nine, but if she was going to call in, she needed to do it soon. That would be the first issue she'd get out of the way, even if he had another agenda.

Dale arrived in less than twenty minutes. She took her favorite seat on the couch. He took the chair Wes had used earlier.

"Okay, I know Wes wouldn't have given you my number unless there was more than you gave me on the phone."

She had been right. He hadn't wanted her to have his number. Figured. "Jamison showed up with the threat of taking me to jail with the next deposit to my account. There's a second $20,000 deposit. Again, he neglected to make sure I didn't have a solid alibi. But he had an explanation for that. He changed it to me hiring someone to deposit the money once he discovered I was giving a presentation at the time."

Dale studied her as she talked. He stayed quiet, waiting for the whole story.

"I can't go to jail right now. I'm starting a new job next week. Then there's school. I can't afford to miss too much and keep my grades up."

Dale remained silent. She sighed, wondering if he had any idea what this was doing to her.

"Look, I can't have this type of problem hanging over me. I need to apply for law school within the next two months if I want to start in the fall. There's no way I can have any outstanding criminal charges when I send in those applications. It's going to be rough enough with having to explain my job in a strip joint."

She watched him, trying not to breakdown. Dale leaned back in the chair and stretched out his legs, his gaze fixed on the wall. Meanwhile she chewed on her bottom lip, wanting to give up and go find someplace to hide where she didn't have to deal with the mess she had apparently created with her research.

"Do you have to work tonight?" Dale finally asked, bringing her out of her musings.

"I'm supposed to, but I can call in if I do so within the next ten minutes."

"Call in and take a vacation for the rest of your notice if you have any time coming to you. They have a man who's been watching you. I'd feel better if you weren't there."

"Who has someone watching me?" Mariah asked, not sure if he meant Jamison or the others he had referred to from her runs.

"The Sinaloa. I believe Jamison is being paid by them."

That was a good enough reason for her to call in. She picked up her phone and did as he requested. Madeline wasn't happy, but then again, she wasn't pissed either. From her voice, she was relieved when Mariah said she didn't want to work out her notice, making her curious as to why.

When she hung up, Dale was staring at his folded hands. "You do have an extra bedroom, correct?"

"Yes. It was cleaned since Rachel was supposed to have moved in Sunday, but then she was killed."

"Any major problem with me becoming your roommate. I don't want to be far from you now that they're stepping up the heat. If someone is watching you, they'll back off some if I'm here."

"Uh, you forgot something. Jamison knows you and is aware you're DEA. Your moving in might be a problem for you, not me, if he thinks you're protecting me."

Dale actually laughed. "He's seen me multiple times elsewhere and didn't recognize me. A simple change in my style of clothes and a pair of glasses and I might seem familiar, but he won't recognize me. The man has the memory of a gnat and the brains of an amoeba."

Staring at him, she asked, "You're kidding, right?"

"Nope."

"How did he ever make detective?"

Dale shook his head and made a face. "My guess is money crossed the palms of a few higherups. They're gone now, but he isn't. The current captain is doing his best to get rid of him. I know you'd be able to work rings around him with absolutely no training in investigation or police procedure."

Going back to the roommate thing, she asked, "So, you would act as my roommate, not a boyfriend?"

He hesitated before saying, "Correct. Playing a boyfriend would create another complete set of problems we don't need to get involved in at this time. You can explain it as a way of saving more money for school, which was one of the reasons Rachel was going to move in with you."

She understood his reasoning, but all she heard was how underneath it all, she was a problem. That led her to believe the quick kiss he gave her was a passing thing. Apparently, the kiss didn't mean as much to him as it did to her.

Not a problem. She could keep up the façade of disinterest. Her job made it easy to pretend, even when she felt otherwise. Wes had things all wrong. Dale wasn't interested in her and hadn't ever been. She was positive any interest in her as a girlfriend was gone when she became a major problem.

"Okay. Let me know when you're moving in," she agreed.

"Tomorrow morning. I'm going to be busy the rest of today, so I'll be here early in the morning." His beautiful gray-green eyes met hers. "Mariah, are you really okay?"

She dropped her eyes to the folded hands on her lap. The knuckles were white from gripping them together. She was unable to control the fear, loneliness, grief, anger and whatever else was lurking inside of her any longer. The tears she hadn't cried before came. Her world was crashing down around her, and she couldn't stop it.

Dale reached over, tugging on her hand. Without thinking, she stood and allowed him to pull her onto his lap. As she had with Wes, she curled into him before letting the crushing burden of the mixed emotions flood out of her with her tears. His arms made her feel safe and protected enough to cry.

When her sobs were replaced with sniffles, an overwhelming exhaustion settled over her. She succumbed to it, her head on his shoulder and her eyes closed. Dale's even breathing, and heartbeat were so soothing, she fell asleep in his arms. The sleep was deep and undisturbed by dreams.

It was close to ten when she awakened, still in Dale's arms. He ran a hand over her head, concern showing on his face. "Better?" he asked.

Unable to speak, she nodded, resting in his arms for a few more seconds before moving. When she stood, she couldn't look at him. "Sorry about the crying jag. You could have put me on the couch. I probably wouldn't have awakened."

The last time she had cried herself to sleep was when she found out her parents weren't coming back for her. Wes had held her while she slept that time. That night was the very first time Wes had said he loved her and how much he wanted her to be his little girl.

His wanting her had made up for some of the pain her parents had caused. That was until he told her to move out the day after her eighteenth birthday. She hadn't bargained or cried. He wasn't obligated to care for her once she became an adult. Wes had foregone the typical young man's carefree years to take care of her. The least she could do was move out and let him get on with his life.

Dale's touch made her jump. With gentle hands, he turned her to face him. "There's nothing to be sorry about. I didn't mind. If I hadn't wanted to hold you, I wouldn't have encouraged you to come to me. Truthfully, you made a dream come true."

"Really?" She had no idea what dream that would have been.

"Really." He put his arms around her, pulling her close to him. "You're the kind of woman most men only hold in their dreams. So yes, you made a dream come true. You've absolutely nothing to apologize for."

Mariah didn't want to move from his arms. The problem was that this wasn't the first time she had been called a dream girl. The bottom line to that declaration was how the man only saw the girl of his dreams. The problems arose when they discovered she wasn't a dream. She was real with all the faults and failings, along with the wants and needs, of a real person.

"In that case, thank you. I guess everything sort of came crashing down tonight. I promise I won't make a habit of it." Stepping back, she moved toward her bedroom. "I'll be right back."

It was more than a few minutes. She needed a shower to fully awaken. When she entered the kitchen, Dale smiled. "Love the towel on the hair look. Hope you don't mind, but I figured I'd fix you something to eat. I'm sure you haven't had supper."

Yes, she did mind, but would need to get over it seeing as how he was going to be moving in with her. "Thanks. I'm actually hungry."

"Good. Looks like you haven't been eating too well recently. You've lost weight from the last time I saw you."

She had slimmed down since her teenage years. She ate, but only when she got hungry. Plus, she ran or went to the gym almost daily. Her job kept her moving which meant she ate well while her weight stayed steady. The result was a loss of what she called baby fat. She was a fit hundred pounds, give or take a couple of pounds, and liked it.

"I eat like a horse but burn it all off. Besides, I like my weight where it's at. I can finally find clothes that fit." She wasn't sure if she liked the idea of him liking her heavier.

"You've always been thin, but if you lose much more, you'll be almost anorexic appearing. You look great and you're very muscular, making you burn more calories. All I'm saying is to make sure you aren't into negative calorie intake. I was for a while and the results weren't great."

She now knew his concerns. "Don't worry. I eat at least fourteen hundred calories a day. Usually more. I've no intention of becoming a skeleton. In fact, I don't worry about gaining weight and eat whatever I want within reason. But I normally keep it to healthy choices."

"Good. Grab a seat. This will be ready in a few minutes." He tended to a pot on the stove before asking, "When do you start your new job?"

"Officially Monday, but It will depend on what schedule they give me. I do know this week off is going to hurt financially. The good thing is that I'll be able to make it up once I get back to work."

Dale drained a pasta before adding it to the sauce he was keeping warm in a skillet. After mixing them, he took a bowl he had put on the counter, filled it with the pasta and added a slice of garlic bread before placing it before her. Her mouth watered at the aroma of the garlic and what appeared to be chicken Alfredo.

He dished up some for himself and joined her. As he had years ago, he put his hand on hers and said a simple grace. She had forgotten the simple ritual she had participated in while living with Wes.

She stuffed the memory of her time with Wes back into its box where it couldn't hurt her. Regardless of what he said earlier, she could tell he still didn't want her around. As for Dale, he would be gone as soon as she was out of danger. It wouldn't take him long to discover she wasn't what he expected. She wasn't the perfect dream girl.

Acting as if the grace was something she said daily, she picked up her fork and began to eat. The pasta tasted as good as it smelled. He was a good cook. She wouldn't complain about him being here if he cooked like this all the time. Most of her meals were as simple as she could make them. She had no reason to be fancy when she was the only one here to eat it.

His voice brought her back to the present. "One other thing. Please don't run without calling me to join you. If I can't make it, delay until I can get there. Wes told me about the men following you. I've a feeling they're waiting for the right time before making a move."

She nodded in understanding while not tacitly agreeing to his request. As if she would disturb him to go running with her at four AM. Chances are, he wouldn't be much help in the long run. She could outrun most men unless they were experienced runners, not joggers.

The rest of the meal was eaten in silence. When they were done, she did the cleanup as he watched her. A glance at him didn't give her a clue as to what he was thinking, not that his thoughts mattered. When she was finished, Dale asked, "You going to be okay for tonight?"

"Yes. I have enough work to do on my thesis to keep me busy. If you aren't here early tomorrow morning, I won't be back until close to five. My hours with the judge are from eight to four."

"I'll work around it. Please be careful, and don't let your guard down. You have my number, so call me if you have any concerns or need help."

His face was serious, but his eyes held what she had seen in them a long time ago. She sighed, realizing she would always be that dream girl to him, whatever that dream may have been.

Chapter Five

THE HOODED MAN STOOD before the statue on the alter, the light from the candles wavering as he caressed the green volcanic glass curved blade of the knife. The knife was old like the statue, from a time long past like their ritual.

He began to talk to the deity like it was inside the little stone replica of his god. "The blood is calling to us. Fifteen more days until the moon goes dark. Our power will increase with this one, but we need a virgin for the blood moon."

He smiled, caressing the blade with gentle fingers like it was a lover. "Only then will Xolotl be happy. I must make him happy or he will come with a death unlike any seen before. Dios de Los Muertos is too long to wait.

"The blood. It's all about the blood. Dark, red, salty, and warm. Blood. The life of us. Without it, we die. It gives us our power when we drink it. That is what I need. That is what Xolotl needs. Power. The power to escape this existence. Xolotl. I must remain one with him, for without him, it will all end."

His fingers closed around the handle. The tip of his tongue moved across the smile his lips wore. Anticipation filled him with a yearning he couldn't stop.

"Fifteen days. More blood. Sweet, warm blood to drink. The woman should be happy to serve Xolotl. Why are they so sad to join him?

"A virgin. We need to find the right virgin. One who won't be sad to join Xolotl. One who will find it an honor to serve him.

"Xolotl needs more blood. I need more. The Los Muertos ceremony. They don't know it yet, but they're all dead. We're all dead. We are all part of the walking dead. The sacrifice will be soon. I must wait."

He frowned, his thumb caressing the sharp edge of the knife.

"We need to find the virgin. Soon I will become one with you, Xolotl, just as you promised. Then they won't be able to find me. They won't see me, just like it has been for the past four thousand years."

Chapter Six

Wednesday, August 20, 2015

MARIAH WENT BACK TO work on her paper as soon as Dale left. It was one way to quit thinking about him, Wes, Rachel, and the mess her life had become. She didn't pay attention to the time since she didn't need to sleep. Besides, she had slept more today than she had in a long time. The phone rang, startling her, making her lose her train of thought.

Throwing down her pencil, she picked up the phone with a sigh. It was five AM. She didn't recognize the number.

"Hello," she answered wondering who would call anyone at this hour of the morning.

"Mariah, it's Danny. You okay? Zelda said you took the rest of the week off as vacation. Something about needing some time to pull yourself together." He sounded worried.

She smiled. He had cared enough to find out if she was okay. "I'm fine. I decided to take some time to grieve and what better time than now."

"You sure that's all? I know you and Rachel were close." He left it at that, not asking the obvious question about whether she was a lesbian and Rachel her lover as had been rumored at the club.

"I'm okay. I had a good cry and it seems to have helped. She was my best friend and I'm going to miss her a lot, but life goes on. So, how's the new job going? Still like it?" She needed to change the subject before she began to cry again. The tears were ready to fall at the slightest provocation.

"It's going great. I love it. The class of men are head and shoulders above anything the Golden Cat ever had. This is really a great place. We get a lot of business guys who come in for meals during the day, and several companies have booked a couple of meetings here. I know you'll like it a lot better."

Mariah could hear someone in the background talking to him when he paused. He chuckled.

"Mr. Becker asked if you wanted to start early. He can get your orientation out of the way in one evening. He handed me the schedule and has you down for Thursday, Friday, Saturday, and Sunday. If you want, you can come in for a few hours next Wednesday. It's usually slow and would be a great night to learn how things work around here."

He had to be hanging out at the club after work or he was working extra hours.

"I'll consider it. Let me get through the next couple of days and see how I feel."

"I understand. I miss you and can hardly wait for you to start here." Mariah heard the obvious longing in his voice. She knew how he felt about her, but had made sure he understood they would never be anything but friends. He accepted her parameters but still cared for her more than he should.

"I miss you too. Greg wasn't you when he walked me out to my truck. Let Mr. Becker know I'll call him on Monday about the orientation on Wednesday. Okay?"

"Yeah. You take care of yourself. I'll see you next week for sure."

"For sure. Bye." Mariah hung up. Danny was the only one to call her to make sure she wasn't totally falling apart today. She had earlier, but the worst was over. Now came the hard work of pushing the pain into the little hole she had for it, then keeping it there.

She closed her computer and decided to go for a run. She had no intention of calling Dale at this hour to run with her since it would be close to daylight by the time she dressed and drove to the river. With the daylight came a sense of safety, so she wasn't afraid of running alone.

The parking lot was empty when she arrived. The sun wasn't completely up yet but would be by the time she got back. At the halfway turn, Mariah stopped and drank a bottle of water before heading back. Two men popped out of the shadow of the bridge. They were moving at a run, not a jog. She sped up, hoping they couldn't keep up with her. Fear had her running faster, unsure if they had been waiting for her.

She was close to halfway back to her truck when she glanced back to see where the men were. They had fallen a good hundred yards back, but her heart rate increased. These men were runners. She kept her pace fast. When she reached her truck, the two men were out of sight. She was going up the ramp to the road before the men were close to the parking lot.

At the traffic signal, she had to stop for the red light. The men pulled up behind her. The car had to have been parked on the other side of the bridge out of sight. They turned the same direction as she did, keeping close to her.

Instead of going home, she pulled onto I-10, losing them in the heavy morning traffic. From there, she took a round-a-bout way home. No strange cars were in the lot. She entered her apartment without seeing anyone else.

Why were they chasing her? Then again, why didn't someone explain what was happening and why? From what had been said, this had something to do with the cartels, but what exactly? And which one or ones? Did she really uncover something in her research? If so, what?

All of this was so confusing. Was Rachel's death caused from her research or by something Rachel had discovered, and they believe she told her? So many questions and no answers.

Without thinking about what she was doing, she picked up her phone and called Wes. "Is everything all right, Mariah?" he answered, not saying hello. She could almost see his worried frown from the tone of his voice.

She hesitated before blurting out, "I'm okay. I need to know who's after me and why? I need the truth." Tears began to run over her cheeks. She was scared. Really, really scared, not sure if she was imagining things or they were real.

Her heart plummeted to her stomach. The silence meant he wasn't going to answer her. She flopped onto the couch, barely stopping herself from sending all the papers flying in frustration.

"Talk to Dale. I can't give you any more information. It'll have to come from him."

"Why?" She was crying, the fear sending prickling sensations all over her.

"It's his case. I'm only helping him. I can't give any information without clearing it with him."

She sniffled, swiping at the unwanted tears. "Then you got in trouble for talking with me the other day."

"No. I had the clearance to let you know how much trouble you're in, but that was the extent of it. Like I said, talk to him."

She plopped into the chair. "Right. He'll barely talk to me. Thanks anyway."

"Give him a chance. I know you're still attracted to him. He's at least talking to you."

"True, but I expect him to run away as soon as this is over. I hold no real hope for anything to develop even though he'll have as much of a chance as he did at the farm."

"I have to go. Talk to him if you want more information."

"Got it. Have a great day." Her voice was dripping with sarcasm. If she was lucky, he'd have as good a day as her. So much for learning what sort of mess she had gotten herself into without knowing how or why. Dale wasn't about to tell her a darn thing.

It was now six forty-five AM. She might as well get ready to go to the courthouse and finish the research for Judge Newcombe. She needed to be there by eight today. Not that the drive would take all that long, but there was a lack of parking spaces if you arrived later and they were picking juries. She didn't mind parking in the outer reaches of the parking lot, but on some days even those spaces were difficult to find.

She finished the last of her coffee while cleaning up the kitchen and putting the dishes in the dishwasher. A knock on the door had her throwing the dishrag into the sink and hurrying to the door. Hopefully whoever it was wouldn't hold her up for more than a few minutes. After checking the peephole, she opened the door to let Dale into the apartment. He had a box in his arms. The door to his Jeep was still open with several more boxes on the back seat.

"Need any help?" she asked, figuring she could at least make the offer.

"Nah, I don't have much. It looks like you're ready to take off for the day anyway."

"I am. Another five minutes and you would have missed me." Once he was past her, she followed him as far as the kitchen. She went to her bedroom to get her purse and bookbag. The shiny key to the apartment was on her bedside table. The key was the one she planned on giving to Rachel. Mariah picked it up, returning to the living room.

She stopped Dale on his way to get another box. "Here's a key for the place. I don't have a spare, so if you lose it, you'll have to get another one from the office or get me or Wes to let you in. Replacement keys costs fifty dollars."

"I'll take good care of it," he said putting it on his key ring. "I don't expect to be finished until around six or so this evening. Want me to pick up something for supper?"

"Not necessary. I laid out some hamburger to make a meatloaf. I've got to run. Remember to lock up when you leave." She didn't believe he needed the reminder, but you could never be sure about some people. Some who appeared responsible, weren't.

"Okay. Have a good day."

"You too." She gathered up the things she needed and headed to her vehicle. Mariah wasn't too sure about him essentially living with her. Maybe things would all work out in the end. She hadn't told him about Danny's call or the men who had followed her this morning. The last thing she needed was his scolding her for not calling him.

When Mariah arrived home, she noted that her living space hadn't been disturbed by his things. She put her books away and began to fix supper. She was hungry and needed to eat since lunch was long gone. It was going to be an oven meal where everything would cook with the meatloaf.

After setting the timer, she delved into the cartels and their organization. Engrossed in what she was doing, Mariah didn't hear the key in the lock or the door opening.

"Mmm, something smells good." Dale's voice brought her out of her reading. Her head popped up, startled to see him smiling at her.

"Oh, sorry. I didn't hear you come in. Supper should be ready shortly."

"Good. I'm starving. Lunch wasn't all that filling. Let me go and get cleaned up."

He was dressed like a bum and appeared to be dirty. Heaven only knew what he had been doing for the day. Returning to taking notes from the book she was reading; Mariah didn't attend to anything else around her until the oven timer sounded. Supper was done. All she needed to do was remove it from the oven and eat.

Mariah had the food on the table and the place settings ready by the time Dale came out of his room.

"Anything I can do to help?"

"Yes. Make sure there are no leftovers," she quipped, eliciting a chuckle from him.

"I'll see what I can do to help you out with that."

"Okay, grab a seat. What do you want to drink? I have iced tea, water, coffee or an orange soda."

"Water, please," he politely responded.

Mariah realized having him here was going to mean some changes. She wouldn't be able to run around in underwear or vacuum at two in the morning. With Rachel, there wouldn't have been much of a problem. But a man, well, that meant some minor changes. Her night shirts and PJs would be getting some use after all.

Dale again said grace, holding her hand as he had at the farm when eating with them. Wes had done that for as long as she could remember. Dale took healthy servings, giving her hope of having little food left. She took what she wanted and immediately started reading the book she had placed on the table. Reading while eating was her normal routine.

"Girl, you can take a break from studying to eat."

She pulled her eyes from the book. "Sorry. I'm not used to having someone around. I didn't mean to be rude."

He swallowed the bite of food he had in his mouth. "It isn't that you're rude, but you should pay attention to what you're putting into your mouth. Eating is one of the pleasures in life, and you need to stop long enough to enjoy it."

"Maybe for you. For me, it's one of those things I do to keep functioning like paying bills, doing the wash and going to work."

His studied her, his brows drawn together. "Life is to be enjoyed and experienced. It sounds like you're only existing, not caring what does or doesn't happen. You need to live your life and not let it pass you by until it's over."

While eating she mulled over what he said. He was right. She wasn't truly living. What he was advocating was too painful for her. Better to exist and let the time slip by until she could do something worthwhile. Existing was easy and kept her from falling apart when everything went down the tubes like now.

"You live your life like you want, and I'll live mine the way I want," she said without looking at him, hoping he would drop the subject. The last thing she needed was a lecture from someone who hadn't seen her in over eight years. That was after doing everything she could to let him know she wanted to get to know him better. Besides, he didn't know a damn thing about her life, or what it was like to be her.

Dale apparently knew to keep his mouth shut. Mariah concentrated on eating, not going back to her reading, but that didn't mean she wanted to talk and have him criticize her and her life. The quicker she finished eating the better. Then she could go back to her research and ignore him. His staying here wasn't going to change her routines.

When he put his hand on hers, the touch brought her head up. "You're right Mariah. You can live your life the way you want, but you need to understand that, like you. I found taking a risk difficult at best. To live, you have to risk being hurt. If you avoid the potential pain, humiliation and rejection that might or might not happen, you'll end up with nothing but the loneliness of empty days and nights. That dream you had will never come true, leaving nothing worthwhile to remember. I had to learn that the hard way."

He was right, up to a point. He didn't understand her life. Loving Wes had been a risk which hadn't paid off. She had attempted to get Dale's attention but failed. Her life had been uprooted when Wes told her to leave. Since then, the only thing she had to make her existence count was school and the possibility of doing some good once she became a lawyer.

Every time she tried to make friends at school, she had been rejected. Over and over and over again, the pattern never changed. So, he was right. She wasn't living her life, only existing in a world that had been forced upon her. Loneliness was something she had been required to deal with since that was all she had left with no one wanting her around.

Rachel had been her only real friend, and now she was gone. No, he didn't understand how she had risked time and time again and rarely been rewarded. What she had now was all that was left for her. No matter how you look at it, life is difficult when no one acknowledges your existence.

She played with the food she no longer wanted. "I understand what you're saying. What you don't know is how many times I put myself out there only to be rejected. Existing isn't so bad when you have a goal in sight. I do have a plan for what I want to do with my life."

"I'm not talking about goals and plans. I'm talking about living your life to the fullest."

She noticed the concern in his voice. "Don't worry about me. I'll manage just fine with the way things are. Sometimes circumstances force a person into a place they don't want to be." She didn't say anymore when he shook his head. She was right, he didn't understand. He hadn't walked that mile in her shoes.

"How did you end up in the DEA? I thought you wanted to stay on the farm."

Fork in hand, he now began to rearrange the food on his plate. "My brother's death from an overdose sort of pushed me there. He got hooked on heroin. It was cheap when he started using. No one knew until he was so far gone that we couldn't help him. Being an idealist, I thought I could make a difference. In reality, for every dealer I stop, there's another waiting to take his place. I refuse to give up though, hoping I'm saving a life or two by making it harder for them to operate."

He stopped, playing with his food before putting his fork down and facing her.

"You happened to get mixed up in a big operation without knowing it. There's a new drug being smuggled into the states that's extremely powerful. A quarter of an ounce will bring them millions. They can cut it to make one or two pounds or more. It sells for $1500 a quarter ounce and is snorted or injected. The problem is, if you take too much, it'll kill you because we don't have an antidote for it."

Mariah mentally sifted through her research. She didn't recall any specific information about the new drug on the market other than it was expensive and was being smuggled in over the Mexican border.

"I don't understand. I know minimal about the actual drugs and less about the purported new one which has only been mentioned in passing. I do know about the smuggling, how they commonly do it, the cartel setup and infighting, along with the corruption of the justice system. All of that is easily found with a simple internet search. Much of it is documented in the newspapers, so I have no idea of why someone thinks I know something that isn't common knowledge."

"Rachel."

His one-word answer had her staring at him.

"What do you mean?" she asked, even though she was afraid of his answer.

"She discovered something, and they think she told you. It's the reason she was murdered. We would love to know what she found and who she uncovered. For now, you're our only link. They're watching you and hoping to get you out of the picture."

"So, I'm not imagining being followed or chased in my truck."

"No, it's real. And not in your imagination. I'm aware you went running without me this morning, and two men followed you. Please don't run again without me. My running with you can be part of my cover as to why you're letting me rent the room. I like to run, and yes, I'll be able to keep up with you."

He was serious. She was in danger due to something Rachel knew and hadn't shared with her. If only she had shared it, she might still be alive today. Maybe she should follow his edict and let him run with her. What harm could his running with her for a while create?

"Okay. I'll call you unless I go at a time when people will be around. No more before dawn runs alone."

She wasn't happy. This would curtail her time to think and relax. The good thing was how it wouldn't be permanent, and hopefully, this case would go away reasonably soon. Until then, she could live having him run with her.

Dale offered to do the cleanup since she had cooked. Mariah nodded and went back to work on her paper, unaware of when he finished or went to bed. She wasn't going to change her habits because he was here other than doing no noisy things during the middle of the night or running around in underthings.

It was three AM before she went to rest. Resting was something she had learned to do, even when she didn't sleep. The two or three hours were spent in an imaginary perfect world where she had friends and someone who loved her. In the fantasy world, she got what she needed from the imaginary people, making life bearable. Once a day, she would rest and escape the reality of her existence.

Chapter Seven

MARIAH GOT UP AT five and fixed the coffee. She made extra, guessing Dale would want some too. She needed to go grocery shopping over the weekend. What groceries she had gotten earlier were based on cooking for one.

"Good morning," Dale said, startling her. "Going for a run this morning?"

"Yes. I don't have to be at the courthouse until ten, so I'll have time for my normal run and still be able to make it there on time."

"Why don't you go and do what you need to do, and I'll whip up something for us to eat."

"Great, thank you. I need to get dressed and organize my things for the day."

His ran his gaze from her head to her toes, a crooked grin on his face. "I can see the getting dressed bit. I don't believe El Paso is ready for you to be running in that get-up."

Heat flushed her face. She had forgotten she was dressed in a baby doll outfit. While covering more of her than her work outfit, it revealed more than he had ever seen of her. Unable to respond to his insinuations, she ran out of the kitchen to change. A housecoat from here on out was a must if he was going to be around.

Not until she caught her reflection in the mirror, did she understand what he saw. The red on her face deepened, imagining what he was thinking about her. A housecoat was a definite, along with some other changes while he was here. The desk in her room would finally be used for schoolwork instead of the living room sofa and coffee table.

Dressed in her running clothes, she joined Dale for breakfast. He gave her a once over scrutiny again.

He shook his head. "If I saw you running, I would run behind you and love every minute of it. It's amazing what clothes hide where you're concerned. I knew you had a good figure, but damn, it's no wonder they want you to dance."

Her face was heating again. He had finally noticed her, but it wasn't in the way she had dreamed of over the years. "Well, they can keep on wanting. I'll never be one of the dancers unless I can keep on all my clothes. I'll leave the stripping to the exhibitionists."

Dale studied her before asking, "Why no boyfriend?" You're this fantastic-looking woman most men would love to date."

"Then why didn't you ask me out?"

This time he turned red. "I didn't think you'd go out with me."

With an unladylike snort, she glared at him. "There you have it. No one will ask me out because they're afraid I'll turn them down. The result is how I've had exactly four dates in the last ten years. And you know what's funny? Three took me out then never called or asked me out again. Only one asked me for a second date. I've even asked men to go places with me, figuring they were scared, but that didn't work either. I've given up on dating and finding someone who wants to go out more than once.

His gaze had her turning away as she blinked back the welling tears from sharing the truth about her life with him. Like she told him last night, she had tried to live life. Instead, life dictated where she belonged, and that wasn't with friends and family since she had neither.

She took her plate and threw away what was left of her breakfast before rinsing the debris off and putting it in the dishwasher. He had finished eating and placed his plate with hers. She started to her bedroom, but his hand on her arm stopped her.

"Mariah, I get it. Wes did his best to get me to go out with you. Being young and terrified of this girl who was my idea of perfection, I couldn't screw up the courage to ask her out. When this is all over, I hope you'll give me the chance I didn't take back then."

A tear escaped and rolled along the side of her nose. He still thought of her as perfect, which she wasn't. Far from it. For many years her dream had been to go out with him. Now that he was proposing dating her, she was aware he was another of the one-date-and-disappear types. Oh well, one date would be better than no date.

Unable to comment on his offer, she pulled away and strode toward the living room. "Let's go for a run. I need the exercise today."

He followed her to the truck after putting on a warmup jacket and grabbing two bottles of water. He hadn't offered to drive his vehicle. Somehow, he seemed to understand this was her routine and she wanted to drive.

The sun was peeking over the horizon when she pulled into the empty parking lot. After they got out, she locked the doors before stuffing the keys into her pocket and taking the bottle of water he held out to her. She watched him scan the area.

At the point along the path where she normally turned, the two men who had followed her the last time came toward them. A fleeting glance to Dale showed he had seen them when they made the turn and started back to the truck. The men stayed a good distance back, so she didn't speed up this time. Dale remained beside her, not slowing her down, so she kept to her normal pace until they arrived at the truck.

The two men were still a good hundred yards back when Mariah pulled out. Having Dale with her had made them back off for now. Maybe having him run with her wouldn't be so bad since he had kept up with her without huffing and puffing.

Back at the apartment they both showered and dressed for the day. She was wearing leggings and a large shirt dress since she would be in the law library doing research for the day. Dale was in jeans and an old ratty t-shirt and sneakers which had seen better days.

"Were those the two who were behind you the other day?" he asked.

"Yes. They were even in the same clothes."

"Please don't go running alone. They know your routine and are waiting for orders about when to take you."

Laughing, she said, "They need to catch me first. They couldn't keep up with me the last time. I was out of the parking lot before they even got close."

Dale tilted his head back and stared at the ceiling, letting out a noisy breath.

"They'll chase you into two more in front of you. Please. Humor me and let me go running with you. I'm usually up before five, so I don't mind, and it would make them think twice about their plans."

"Okay," she said, not sure if she would use him or not.

For now, she really didn't want him or anyone else with her. Running was her time to let her mind go blank and simply enjoy the activity.

Since it was only eight, she had time to finish reading what she had started earlier.

Dale's voice interrupted her. "You up to doing some research concerning this case?"

"Sure. What do you need?" Contributing something to finding Rachel's killer would feel good.

"What I need is a search for all the murders using a specific method. Find ones of women who have an abdominal cut going from the xiphoid process to the pubis. They may or may not have open bowels. The abdominal cut is what I'm interested in for now. The newspapers for here and Ciudad Juárez should have most of them. We can't search police records because I don't want to raise any alarms yet."

"I can do it after I put in my internship hours today. I get out at noon and will be free for the rest of the day."

"Great. Get what you can. I know over the past three years the papers have reported other deaths similar to Rachel's. The pattern may go further back than that. Get the dates of each death, when found, and by whom if you can."

"Okay," Mariah said as she wrote the information he needed on a piece of scrap paper. She could use a few hours doing something different.

"Anything else?"

"No. I should be back around five or six this evening."

It was nice of him to tell her approximately what time he would be back.

"I should be home about then. I'll leave it up to you as to what you want for supper. I normally make Thursday my order-in day. By this time of the week, I'm over cooking."

Dale laughed. "No problem. I'll pick up something on my way home. See you this evening."

He took off, making sure the door was locked on his way out. He had good habits if nothing else.

Mariah finally quit on the research she was doing for Dale upon noticing it was close to five. She had found more articles than expected fitting the criteria Dale had given her. Female deaths with abdominal knife wounds had brought up hundreds of stories. She narrowed the search parameters until she found the ones killed in the same manner as Rachel. How she had died was something no one had bothered to tell her.

What she found was close to sixty murders over the past five years. Each was close to a month apart, occurring on both sides of the border. Before the last five years, two or three occurred each year going back at least thirty years, if not more. She quit at thirty years. After four hours, she had as much as she was going to get for this session. She gathered her things and left the basement of the library, waving to Alicia who thought she was doing research for school.

Mariah needed some answers and she wasn't going to back off asking Dale some hard questions. What she had found pointed to either a serial killer or a group performing a grisly ritual of some kind. Either way, a lot of dead girls were all murdered in the same fashion. How in the world could the police or border agents not see the pattern? Not even the news hungry journalist had noticed because most of the women were addicts.

It was after five when she got home. Dale wasn't back yet. After dropping her things on the coffee table, she decided to lie down. For some reason she was sleepy. If she didn't get at least an hour of sleep, she wouldn't be able to function tomorrow. In less than five minutes, she was out cold. When she woke, it was seven-thirty in the evening.

A note on the kitchen table read, "*Food is in the oven. Had to go out again. EAT! See you tomorrow, Dale.*"

Okay. He wasn't coming back tonight. Hopefully he was going to have an enjoyable time. The oven held a still-warm pizza with the toppings she liked on it. With two slices on her plate, she went to her room and began organizing her research. She went back for a third slice at about two AM. Dale still wasn't back.

Close to four, she heard his key in the lock. She didn't leave her room, not wanting to talk to him. A tear dropped onto her arm as she imagined him being with a woman until this hour.

The thought shouldn't hurt, but it did. Everyone had a normal life but her. She was a twenty-six-year-old virgin, not because she wanted to be, but because no one wanted her around them for more than one date, two at the most, regardless of how she looked.

Chapter Eight

AT FIVE AM, MARIAH decided to make coffee and something to eat. Out of habit, she started to fix an omelet. When she turned to the refrigerator, Dale was standing there studying her.

"Morning. Want an omelet?" she asked. Making enough for two wasn't any harder than for one.

"Yes, thank you. My night was long, and I'll admit to being hungry."

"Want toast or a bagel with it?"

"Bagel. Mind if I get a cup of that coffee?"

"Help yourself." The extreme politeness of their exchange grated on her nerves.

He was sitting at the table staring at the wall when she set his food in front of him before going back to get hers. She warmed his coffee before sitting to eat. With the dark circles under his eyes and his eyelids drooping, he looked as if he hadn't slept. Hopefully he didn't plan to work today. He wouldn't be able to stay awake if he did.

"Did you find anything in the newspapers yesterday?" He took a bite of his bagel, chewing as if it was hard work.

"Yes. I found there's been close to one murder a month for the past five years with Rachel being the last one on record. But what's surprising is how these specific murders go back at least thirty years." Mariah let that sink in as she took a sip of her coffee. "What was interesting was how there were only two or three a year prior to the last five years. That makes me think it's some sort of ritual, like a sacrifice. My question is why are they sacrificing women? That supposedly stopped with the Spanish invasion and the decimation of the Inca, Aztec and Mayan cities and peoples."

Dale swallowed his bite of bagel. "I'll need to see those notes. We need to figure out if the murders have a pattern to them. No one seems to have connected them all." He cut a piece off his omelet before saying, "I'm surprised one of the reporters didn't pick up on it. Thanks for doing the research for me. I've been trying to fit it in for the past three weeks."

"I get it. Seems like things pile up at times until you don't have a free moment to get done what you need to do."

The meal was finished in silence. He loaded the dishwasher while she retrieved her notes from the bedroom. She handed them to him, hoping he could read her scribbles. He pulled up calendars for the past five years and began to mark the dates. After a year, he stopped, chewing on his bottom lip, staring at the screen with a creased brow. Mariah moved behind him to see what he was looking at on the screen. Her eyes widened and her hand squeezed his shoulder.

She blurted out, "They're all on the new moon except for the equinox and solstices. That can't be a coincidence."

"It isn't. Your sacrifice idea may be correct. The ancient Inca and Mayans didn't sacrifice on the full moon. Let's see what the others show.

He opened a calendar for six years ago and marked the murders from that time. They were on the solstices, equinoxes and a solar eclipse. Dale sat back and kissed her hand.

"Great job there, Sherlock. It's a ritual that has been going on for over thirty years that someone changed five years ago."

"Okay, but how does that fit in with Rachel, drugs, and the money in her account?"

Dale turned back to the computer and scrubbed his hands over his face. "If I'm correct, a person or persons involved in the ritual is tied to the Sinaloa Cartel. This fits with the way the new drug is being smuggled into the States. Ten to fifteen small bags would get them close to a million dollars and would make the murders worthwhile."

Mariah frowned. "But they could use the regular ways of smuggling easier and with less risk. I don't understand why they would be committing murders once a month, upping the chances of getting caught."

Dale laid his hand on the one she had on his shoulder. "What they are doing isn't murder in their eyes. It's a sacrifice to their god or gods. I'm sure we'll discover this is a religious rite where they do the actual killing. The smuggling is someone's add-on to the ritual."

He hit *Print* so what he had done would be in a hard copy. She guessed he had a printer set up in his room. When the printing was complete, he powered off his computer.

Dale rotated on his chair to her. He held her hand. "Please don't go out alone. Whoever is doing this sees you as a danger to them. I have to get to work, but I'll be back later this evening."

"Okay, I have my last internship hours for the summer today and won't be back until after four."

Before he could get up, someone pounded on her door. "Jamison's back," she said, rolling her eyes and sighing. Dale grabbed his things and disappeared into his room.

Waiting for the second knock, she opened the door and leaned against the doorjamb. "What do you want now?" she snapped, a scowl on her face.

"I need to speak to you my dear. We have another problem." He was smiling, which meant this wasn't going to be good for her.

Stepping back, she let him and the young officer into the apartment. She hadn't bothered to clean up her papers from the living room, so they automatically strolled into the dining room and took seats without waiting for an invitation.

"Make yourselves at home." Sarcasm dripped from each word.

Jamison placed a folder on the table, waiting until she was seated. "We need an explanation for the $25,000 deposit made to your account." He sat back and folded his arms across his big belly, grinning like a Cheshire cat.

"I have no explanation and you know it. I haven't made a deposit in four days. My paycheck won't hit the bank until this afternoon, so you tell me about this deposit."

He pushed a photo from the folder across the table. She wanted to laugh. The man still didn't have it right.

With a snap of her wrist, she flung the paper at him. "You really need to get a life. First of all, I was in class at the time that deposit was made, so it isn't me in that picture. I have no idea who the man is, and there's no way I'd go all the way across town to that particular branch when they have one up the street from here. You might want to find out who these people are and ask them why the money is being put into my account."

The smile on Jamison's face faded as she talked. He picked up the photo and looked at the time. "You don't have any classes at that time, and I know that for a fact because we pulled your schedule."

Ah ha. The pieces ae beginning to fall into place.

"That may be, but I do have an airtight alibi. You might want to check with Judge Newcombe for that particular date and time. He has a record of me helping him find specific cases he needed to review." She let him digest that before asking, "Now is there anything else you wish to discuss? If not, I need to get ready to leave. I'd like to be on time for my last day with Judge Newcombe."

Jamison glared at her, his jaw muscles working overtime as he ground his teeth. "I'll get you. You can't continue to manufacture alibis. You better hope Judge Newcombe confirms you were there. If he doesn't, I'll be back for you."

The two men didn't wait for her to show them out. Jamison slammed the door, showing the anger at her foiling his attempt to frame her again. Dale stood in the doorway of his room. His arms were crossed over his chest, eyes on her.

"He really wants you off the streets. I guess someone higher up is pushing a few buttons to make him to keep trying to frame you. That's what, $65,000 they've put into your account so far?"

"Yes. I've put it into my savings until someone decides they want their money back. No one can get to the money without me. I set it up so the bank has to ask for a specific ID to withdraw the money from either account. They can't use my ATM card for anything other than deposits." The self-satisfied smile dared him to find holes in what she had done.

Dale stalked to the table and leaned over with his hands on the table so close she could smell the coffee on his breath. "Mariah, this isn't a game they're playing with you. Are you sure they don't know which ID they need?"

"I'm sure. I had it set up when someone attempted to take cash from my account shortly after I moved here. The request for the ID comes up on the screen when someone wants to withdraw money from my account. I also get notices when a withdrawal on my account is attempted, even me, so I would know if they did have the appropriate ID."

Dale gritted his teeth and stood up. He let out a snort. "Again, this isn't a game. These people will kill to get what they want. For now, they're attempting to get you out of circulation. If that doesn't succeed, I'm sure they'll come up with something nastier than a few days in jail on a trumped-up charge."

Mariah stood and took three steps toward her room before pivoting back to him.

"I'm not going to put my life on hold for you or anyone else. I have classes and a new job to go to starting next week. Besides, they have nothing to connect me to Rachel outside of work other than one trip where I went with her to visit her family.

"We didn't visit each other, we didn't really socialize, go shopping or anything else like that. Our main connection was via texts, and I'm sure all of those have been reviewed by now. If they have, I know they haven't found a damn thing."

Dale checked his watch before grating out, "I've got to go."

He was angry, but she didn't care. That was his problem not hers. No way she was going to give up the few slices of enjoyment she had carved out for herself regardless of what anyone did. If he was so worried, then let him put his life on hold and follow her around like a bodyguard.

At this point in time, she was so over the drama from Jamison and Dale. As for Wes, he could stay where he was and leave her the hell alone. Neither Wes nor Dale had cared whether she was alive or dead for years, so why should they care now?

Chapter Nine

MARIAH FINALLY CRASHED AFTER two days of not sleeping. Her clock was reading seven in the morning when she finally woke up. Dale was at the table working on his laptop. They hadn't said more than a few words to each other since Jamison's last visit. If he was still upset with her, that was his problem, not hers.

She fixed herself a cup of coffee, trying to decide what to have for breakfast. Dale, without looking up from his computer said, "There are pancakes in the oven if you want them."

She pulled out the plate he had fixed for her. It was still hot, so he hadn't been up long.

"Thank you." Like him, she remained overly polite.

There wasn't a choice where to eat, so she grabbed a fork and joined him at the table, eating in total silence. When finished she said, "I'm going for a run. I don't have to be in class until ten today."

"Give me a sec and I'll join you." He didn't even look up from the computer at her.

Leaving him to get ready, she changed into her running clothes. It was sixty-two degrees this morning, so she snagged her light windbreaker. Down by the river the air would be cooler. She was ready to leave when her phone rang.

"Hello," she said, not recognizing the phone number.

"Mariah, it's Mr. Becker. I don't know what your schedule is like, but tonight would be a wonderful time to do your orientation. I realize it's short notice, but I have a girl who'll be able to work with you and help you learn our system.

"Your uniforms came in and we have a locker for you. I think I forgot to tell you, but on Thursdays we exchange your dirty uniforms for clean ones, so you don't have to worry about laundering them. Theresa will show you what to do with the soiled ones. I have you down for Thursday through Sunday to work from seven PM to four AM and I'd like you to be comfortable for work on Thursday. The pit is usually busy, and you'll be on your own for the shift."

Sifting through what she had planned for the evening, she decided tonight would be better than tomorrow. Thursday was her seminar. The seminar would take longer to prepare for than her Wednesday classes.

"What time do you want me there?" His answer would determine if she could get there on time.

"Would six be too early?"

"No. Six is fine."

"Great. Plan on being here for about four or five hours. You'll be paid for it. I'll see you at six then."

"Okay. See you then." She hung up, looking forward to getting back to work. Sitting at home was boring, and she needed the money for school.

Dale was waiting for her in the living room. She picked up her keys before saying, "I'm going to be late this evening. I'm doing my orientation at the Platinum Slipper until ten or eleven."

He only nodded before following her to the truck. She didn't mind the silent treatment. Overall, nothing he did or didn't do mattered since he would be gone in a few weeks at the most.

Mariah pulled into the parking lot of the club at five-thirty. She stashed her books on the floor, having come directly from her last class. After grabbing her purse, she strode toward the building with hidden rainbow lights around it. Not many cars were in the parking lot, so she should have a chance to learn what was expected of her without being swamped. She was halfway to the door when Danny, with a big grin on his face, hurried to her. He picked her up, hugging her to him before giving her a kiss on the cheek.

"It's great to see you, girl. I've missed you," The brilliant smile backed up his words.

"Put me down," she giggled, happy to see him too.

They both laughed as he swung her around like she was a small child before putting her back on her feet. He was the only bouncer she had gotten close to, mainly because he had said up front that he only wanted to be her friend. Over the past eight years, he had been the only one she could talk to, crying on his shoulder more than once.

She had also comforted him when he broke up with his girlfriends, then supported him when he found a new girl. He was the one who had pulled a drunk customer off her as she left work one morning. Ever since then, he had walked her to her car. If he saw her pull into the parking lot, he would escort her into the club. His moving to here had been one of the reasons she'd applied for the job. She wanted to be near him since he would protect her. Even though she never admitted it, she was afraid of working in the clubs.

Danny escorted her to the anteroom of the locker rooms. He introduced her to Theresa, who smiled and shook her head. "Danny, if I didn't know you had a girlfriend, I'd say you were sweet on Mariah," she commented, giving him a hug.

"Nope. She's like my kid sister. I can tease the hell out of her, but nobody else had better bother my imp."

Theresa turned to Mariah for verification. "He's the big brother I can always call on for help no matter what. We've been close ever since he saved me from this creep. The guy thought I was one of the strippers when I left work one morning shortly after I began working as a waitress."

"Well, here are your outfits. When you're finished with your shift, put them in the bag with your name on it. They'll come back clean. If you find any damage or need a new one, let me know. Let me show you to your locker."

The locker room was spacious with a nice lounge and lunchroom. Each locker had a key, so she didn't need to worry about buying a lock, and it was big enough to hold all her uniforms without crushing them. She still couldn't believe how nice this place was compared to the Golden Cat. Talk about taking a step up in the world.

Theresa went into teaching mode, giving Mariah her spiel on her portion of the orientation process. "You can order from the menu on the table for your meal. It's a perk Mr. Becker insisted on for those who work here. Free food. You get a forty-five-minute break for meals. If you order fifteen minutes before your break, your food will be ready when you get here unless the kitchen is overly busy;

"There are showers in the back if you want to use them. You'll find the waitresses are on this end while the dancers have their area on the other side closer to the stage. If you need anything, let me know."

Mariah smiled. "Thank you. I appreciate it. I like it better here already. I'll get a chance to sit down and eat rather than having to stand and grab a bite when I can."

"Honey, if you need anything, don't be afraid to come to me. I know there will be a few girls who'll give you a tough time because Mr. Becker is putting you in the pit. From talking to Danny, he knows you'll do a lot better job than the others who have been working in that section. Danny has sung your praises from the time he started here. He told me you're a real class act and I can see why he thinks that of you." Theresa smiled, giving her a pat on the shoulder

Mariah felt the heat rise to her face at all the praise. To hide her blush, she faced her locker to pull out a uniform to wear for the evening. "Danny knows me better than most. I don't play around with the customers, and I refuse their advances in a way that keeps them from getting pissed off. I may work in a strip joint, but that doesn't mean I have to leave my self-respect at home."

"Just be careful. Mr. Becker won't be happy if the men complain. If you have a problem with them, let me or him know before Danny gets wind of it. Okay?"

"Sure thing. I seldom have problems though. I've learned how to refuse so nicely they end up teasing me and letting it go."

With a nod, Theresa left Mariah to get dressed. Once she had the uniform on, she was glad she had requested a size ten top. Even with that, the outfit showed more than she liked of her ample bust line. She needed to find a way to get the push-up pads out since she didn't need them. After putting on the new heels she had gotten to match the other girl's shoes, she closed her locker, putting the key in the small patch pocket on the front of the skimpy shorts.

Stopping at the mirror on the way out, she readjusted the top to show less of her breasts. The outfit was more revealing than those at the Golden Cat, but it was a lot more refined. It wasn't flashy and covered her butt, which she liked. She would trade the boobs showing versus the butt any day of the week.

The first people she saw upon leaving the locker room were Mr. Becker and Danny. Danny stopped talking when he noticed her, his eyes widening. Mr. Becker turned to see what he was staring at and had much the same reaction. She looked down and scanned her outfit, unsure if she had missed something before leaving the locker room. Unable to find anything out of place, she tilted her head and gave them a shy smile.

Mr. Becker recovered before Danny. His assessing scan told her he saw something she hadn't seen in the mirror.

"I can't believe what I'm seeing. Are you sure I can't talk you into dancing? I'll pay you three thousand a night plus the tips you get for two ten-minute shows."

"Sorry, but I'll stick with waitressing. I like being dressed in public."

"I won't be able to put you anywhere but the pit. I know of at least ten men who'll request you to wait on them once they see you." He glanced back at Danny. "You told me she would surprise me, but shock would have been a better word. Never in my wildest dreams would I have imagined a gorgeous sprite to show up."

Danny chuckled, joining them. "Yeah, she dresses up real nice. You should see her in a fancy dress. She turns heads just by walking into a room."

Mariah knew her face had turned a dark red at Danny's remarks. Mr. Becker put two fingers under her chin and raised her head until she met his gaze.

"Girl, that blush told me more than anything Danny has said to me. You keep that innocence for as long as you can. I'm usually around, so if you have a problem, send Danny or Theresa for me. I'll make sure you're kept safe. Danny told me, and you confirmed it, that you don't service the customers. I respect that morality. Theresa will also help you out if someone is too persistent and won't pay attention to a nice 'no' from you."

"Thank you. I appreciate it. Madeline was always pressuring me to service the customers, not understanding it was against my upbringing."

Mr. Becker put his arm across her shoulder, tucking her in next to him, before starting to walk down the hall. "Child, I do understand. Just because you work in a place like this, doesn't mean you have to leave your upbringing at home. I don't believe you'll have any problems, but I figured I'd throw it out there just in case it does happen."

"I'll definitely let you know if I can't handle a situation. When I have any problems with anyone, it's usually someone who's inebriated. A bouncer usually walks them out without making a scene. Oh, by the way, you don't need to put me in the pit. I don't mind working the outer reaches of the place."

Mr. Becker laughed, making her wonder what she had said that was so funny.

"Wrong, dear. I do have to put you in the pit. I want the best and most pleasant girls there. From the way you've said no to dancing, I can't imagine you upsetting any of the VIPs who reserve the pit."

Mariah let it go. She had no reason to create a problem on her first night. Besides, she knew she would get excellent tips being down front. During her years of work, she had learned how to coddle the men without them getting the wrong idea about her. Her eyes scanned the club as they neared the bar. Several groups were already in the pit watching the dancers, who were a lot better than the girls at the Golden Cat. But like those at the Cat, they needed to learn to work the poles they were using.

The girl working the pit was flirting with one of the men. From her actions, she would do more than bring food and drinks to get her tip. Mariah turned to the bar and smiled at the bartender who winked at her. He was going to make her life easy. She knew him from the Golden Cat. Bob was good at what he did and would make sure she had everything she needed when it came to taking care of her customers.

The girl finished getting her orders and headed back to the bar. She smiled at Mr. Becker and gave him an invitation with her eyes, which he ignored before turning to Mariah.

"Colleen, this is Mariah. I need you to show her the ropes. She's starting her regular shift on Thursday. She'll need to be able to handle an area by herself since we'll be short for the evening shift."

"Not a problem, Mr. Becker," Colleen purred before glaring at her.

Mariah knew she was going to have a problem getting all she needed to know from Colleen with just the one look. The girl's dislike was twofold. First was the way she looked and there was nothing she could do to stop the jealousy. The other was the way Mr. Becker had ignored the not so subtle invitation Colleen had given him. Mariah couldn't figure out why Colleen had been hired as a waitress. She would have been much better as a dancer with her flirtatious and suggestive actions.

"I'll see you before you leave," Becker said before moving away with Danny, heading toward the front door of the club.

As soon as the men left, Colleen changed into the bitch she was. "Look, honey," she said, sneering down at Mariah. "Don't think you're something special around here."

Mariah kept her smile in place. "Sweetie, I've been working in a cesspool and know how to handle myself around girls like you. Give me the basics, and I'll leave you to work on that man as much as you want. I'm here to serve drinks and food. Nothing more."

Bob cut into their conversation. "You have an order for me, Colleen?"

"Yeah," she responded and threw a napkin at him while glaring at Mariah. "Just don't cut into my customers, or you'll regret it," she warned before turning away and leaning on the bar so her backside looked it's best.

The girl was a piece of work. Her only thought was how to get the big tips. She was willing to do anything, including servicing them if that was what it took. She had a lot to learn about the better class of men who paid to be in the pit.

Mariah had learned the difference between the class act guys and the slime balls in less than two days. She expected several of the richer men who had come into the Golden Cat to follow her here. They had only gone there because she was their favorite waitress. Regardless of what section she was working, they would find her and then sit in her section.

Bob set a tray of drinks down for Colleen. She picked it up and looked down her nose at Mariah. "Wait here for me. I'll be right back."

As soon as she left, Bob, who was leaning on the bar, said, "She'll do what she can to make tonight difficult for you. Give me your orders for drinks and food. I'll set it all up for you. When the men want to cash out, let me know, and I'll give you the bill. You know how to do the rest. That's all you need to know."

"Thanks, Bob. I appreciate it. I knew when I saw you here that you'd help me out."

"Sweetheart, I'll do anything I can to help you. You'll add class to this place like they won't believe. Becker's been trying to find someone like you for the pit since the place opened."

"You're so good for my ego," Mariah said with a big grin.

"Hey, I know you'll make my night a lot easier and busier. You can work rings around her, and she knows it. She's also green with envy at the way you fill out that outfit."

Mariah glanced down, twisting her mouth before responding, "I'd give anything to fill it out a little less. I'm going to have to make some adjustments to the tops to get them to fit right." She glanced at Colleen before adding, "I wonder if she would want the padding from this top. Heaven only knows if it would improve her bust line, though."

Bob laughed, leaving her to wait on a customer. She knew she could say whatever she wanted to him, and it wouldn't go any farther, just like his comments wouldn't go beyond her. He had been at the Golden Cat for the first two years she had worked there as a waitress. She also knew she had been one of the few who listened to him, making life easier for both of them.

Colleen returned and started her orientation. "Okay. The tables have numbers on them. You give the bartender the order by the table numbers. You don't have to worry about the prices. Same for the food. You give them the menu if they ask for it. If they want separate checks, the seats are numbered from right to left so you have the correct check going to the right person."

Bob cut in and stated, "It's the opposite, Mariah. The seats are from left to right with the left one being number one if they want separate checks."

His interruption earned a glare from Colleen. She clearly had given the wrong seat order on purpose.

"You can follow me for the next half hour. My break starts then. Hopefully, you'll be able to muddle through for the hour I'll be on break."

Mariah didn't comment, fully aware she'd be able to do more than muddle through. Following Colleen, she kept to the background, letting the other girl do her thing as she watched. Several of the men asked about her. Colleen told them to ignore her since she was a newbie on the floor.

Mariah let Colleen push her into the background until a new group of men entered the pit. Colleen went to the table, but they ignored her. The short man, who Mariah knew was the CEO of a large company, met her and gave her a hug and a kiss on the cheek.

"Girl, you're a sight for sore eyes. Greg said you had come over here and you know I had to follow."

"Calvin, it's always a pleasure to see you. Do you want a menu or just drinks tonight?" she asked, walking with her arm around his waist to where he was sitting.

"Menus, please. You know what I want. You boys want your usual?" he asked, turning to the three men who had come with him.

The other men nodded and greeted her with a kiss. Letting them get settled, she handed them the menus she had grabbed, before saying, "I'll be right back with those drinks. From what I understand, the food is decent here. It's my first night, so I can't recommend anything."

"Not to worry, beautiful." Calvin said before perusing the menu.

Mariah headed to the bar with Colleen following behind. When out of hearing range of the men, the other girl snapped, "How dare you take my customers!"

Pivoting to the irate woman, Mariah said, "Honey, I've waited on those four men for over four years. If you can tell me what they drink, I'll let you have them."

Colleen clamped her mouth shut, stalking off to the table where the man she was flirting with earlier was sitting. Mariah stood at the bar and waited for Bob to notice her. When he came over, she said, "I need a Crown Royal on the rocks, a Jack Daniels Black label on the rocks, one screwdriver with the best vodka you have and a Manhattan."

"Coming right up for table three," Bob responded with a smile, nicely reminding her she needed to give him the table number. Mariah knew Calvin was paying the tab unless one of the others lost a bet with him.

Colleen came up beside Mariah, anger radiating from her. "Where's Bob? I have an order," she nastily demanded.

"He'll be right here. He's fixing the drinks for Calvin and his minions," Mariah sweetly replied, not letting the nastiness get to her.

Bob set the tray of drinks on the counter for her before taking Colleen's order, which she had again written on a napkin. Mariah took the tray, holding it at shoulder height while navigating the tables. Once each drink was placed before the correct man, she asked, "You all going to try the food?"

Calvin smiled up at her. "Of course. The food's got to be better here. I'll take the chicken cordon bleu. Boys, what are you having?"

The other three gave her their orders. She wrote them down because the one needed very specific changes to his meal due to multiple allergies. They handed her their menus before she asked, "Anything else you need?"

The man she knew as Bill stated with a big grin, "You to go out with me."

Laughing, Mariah told him, "Now you know better, Bill. I don't date my customers because I don't want to lose them." The men chuckled.

Bob was busy, so she waited, needing to explain the one order to be sure the kitchen got it right. When he saw her, he came and picked up the napkin and read it.

"I guess that one has a few food allergies."

"He does. Please make sure the chef is aware. These men are big spenders and they're a favorite group of mine from the Cat."

Bob leaned over and kissed her cheek. "Baby doll, anything for you."

Colleen arrived and glared at Bob. "You shouldn't play favorites here. It'll get you in trouble."

He crossed his arms, glowering while holding back the fiery temper that matched his red hair.

"Colleen, if you were half as pleasant as Mariah, you'd get the same type of service. We happen to be old friends and worked in the same place for several years. You might want to take a few lessons from her. It would improve your income if nothing else." He stalked away to turn in her order, ignoring the napkin Colleen had thrown on the bar.

"I'm going on break. Those drinks are for table ten," she said with a snarl before leaving, her heels hitting so hard she left black marks on the floor.

Okay, so she was on her own. Not a problem. Mariah had seen what table the drinks were meant for, so she wouldn't have any difficulty figuring out who got what. Bob came and picked up the napkin before glancing around for Colleen.

"She went on break. I'll take them out, even though she neglected to say who got what."

Bob shook his head before mixing the drinks and giving her the tray. She went to the new group of men and merrily inquired who got which drink. They each claimed their drinks with a smile while they teased her. Mariah didn't mind. They were a pleasant group who were just having fun. She inquired if they wanted menus, which they did. Colleen wouldn't have mentioned they could order food since she wasn't into doing any more work than required.

Colleen didn't return for almost two hours. Mariah had given Bob the tips from the tables Colleen had waited on prior to going on break. Mariah kept the tips she had gotten from those she had serviced, which, in her mind, was only fair if she did the work.

Mariah hadn't taken long to remember the table numbers for Bob and the seats if they wanted separate checks. Calvin had left her a hundred and promised to be back more frequently. He said the food was good, the place was great for relaxing, plus the dancers weren't half bad.

The smallest tip she had gotten was twenty–five dollars from a man who had come in by himself, drank two gin and tonics, then left. She enjoyed the better class of clients along with the bigger tips. If this night was slow, she could hardly wait for a busy one. She was going to be leaving with close to three hundred in tips for the evening.

Colleen's first words when she returned were, 'Where's my tips?"

"Bob has them. I'll finish tables eight and nine before I leave. Table five just got here and Bob is fixing their drinks now. They'll probably order a meal because they wanted menus."

When Bob put the tray down, Colleen grabbed it, going to table five. Mariah grinned at Bob. "I'm glad she came back. Those guys are right up her alley. They're tom cats looking for a female in heat." Bob chuckled before going to fill another order at the bar.

She made a final run on her two tables who were ready to leave. The men handed her the tip instead of leaving it on the table after a glance at Colleen. That told her more than anything how dishonest her instructor was. They also asked when she was working again. She expected to see them at some time during the weekend. The two tables had made up a large party of twelve men. Having a few regulars who tipped well would be nice.

Colleen was waiting for her at the bar. "Give me my tips, she commanded.

"Bob has your tips," Mariah repeated.

"Not the ones you just got, he doesn't," Colleen said, her lip curled in a sneer.

Mariah crossed her arms, glaring at the brash girl. "Look, I gave Bob the tips from the tables you started. The ones I did are mine. I'm not giving you what I earned."

"Those are my tips. You're orienting and don't get to keep tips."

"I do if I did all the work on those tables." Mariah didn't back down from the bigger girl.

"You give me my tips." Colleen stood over Mariah with balled fists.

Not rising to the threat, Mariah didn't move other than to tilt her head back to face the taller irate waitress. "I'll not give you what I earned."

Colleen reached out to grab Mariah. Before she could touch her, Mariah grabbed her wrist and twisted it until a gasp of pain escaped Colleen's gaping mouth. "Don't you ever attempt to bully me," Mariah warned.

Mr. Becker appeared at that moment beside them.

"What's the problem here?"

"She won't give me my tips," Colleen whined.

Becker turned to Mariah with raised eyebrows.

"I gave her the tips she earned and gave her a table I started. The tips I have, I got from tables I waited on, not her, and are rightfully mine."

Bob came over, dropping the money Mariah had given him for Colleen. "These are the tips from your tables, Colleen."

She grabbed the money and counted it. "I want the rest of my money."

"I'm not giving you my tips," Mariah repeated. "I handled the floor for two hours and what I earn, I keep. I split the tip from the table where you got the orders. I don't expect the same integrity from you for the table I started."

Mr. Becker held up his hand, stopping Colleen's reply. He took the money Colleen had earned from her and began to count it. "Are you sure she was gone for two hours?"

"Positive. Ask Bob and the bouncer there at the end of the bar. I've been working on my own for the past two hours. She got upset because a group of men came in who I knew from the Golden Cat. They always wanted me to wait on them no matter where I was working in the club. I had no intention of taking over the floor, but she left and didn't return until a few minutes ago."

Mr. Becker glared at Colleen before going to talk to the bouncer, ignoring Bob. When he returned, he wasn't happy.

"Colleen, you'll be docked an hour's pay for the extra hour you took for your break. Mariah gets to keep what she earned."

He held out his hand for Mariah's tips after he returned Colleen's to her. He counted the bills. Then recounted it. "I can see why you didn't want to give her your tips. That's more than anyone has gotten for a full shift on a slow night." He returned the money to her.

"I get paid for good service with a smile. Nothing more. Calvin will be back with his three minions. He liked the food and for as long as I'm here, they'll continue to come back. The hundred-dollar bill is from him."

Becker turned to Colleen. "Looks like you need to learn a few more things to work the pit. The chef has been busy all evening fixing meals for the tables in the pit, which tells me you aren't pushing the food. Also, for the two hours Mariah worked, she earned more than you do for two days, and I know her looks didn't get her those tips. She gave damn good service. I was watching from the office as she worked the floor. Not only did almost every table order food, she also made sure they had exactly what they wanted and spent the time to make sure they were satisfied."

Colleen scowled, staring in hatred at Mariah. "Bitch!" she spat before grabbing the tray of drinks from the bar, barely avoiding spilling them while stomping to the table.

"You've made an enemy there," Becker observed, frowning as his eyes followed Colleen.

"She hated me the moment she saw me. She gave me the wrong information to make sure I'd make mistakes in ordering. Other than the table numbers and seating, this is what I've been doing for the past five years." Mariah looked up at Becker. "She'll leave me alone or suffer the consequences. I won't start anything, but I won't back down either."

"I noticed. Bob let me know there was a problem. I'll make sure you two aren't working the same days. If you do happen to be on at the same time, I'll make sure she's in a totally different area of the club. I may make her dream come true and see if she'll do better as a dancer since she leaves a lot to be desired working the floor."

Mariah glanced back to where Colleen was chatting up the table of young men. "Probably a promising idea, but I'd make sure she was clean and using protection. Heaven only knows where her cat has been."

Becker sniggered, attempting to not laugh outright at her comment. "Girl, you're going to be a lot of fun to have around. Go home. You'll be paid for the full four hours for just putting up with Colleen."

"Thanks. I would be relegated to standing around like a statue if I stayed now that she knows she would have to split her tips if I did the work."

"Hey, fair's fair. I get it after seeing those tips you got. No wonder the owner of the Golden Cat did his best to convince me to not hire you."

Mariah stared at him, "You're kidding, right?"

"No, I'm not. They want you back. It seems a lot of their nicer clientele are going to be coming here." He was gleefully grinning at the thought of gaining more of the richer clientele.

Mariah gave a slight shrug, letting out a short sigh. "I was expecting Calvin. Al and his group will most likely show up. A couple of others might come also, but they're iffy because they like a couple of the strippers over there."

His fingers under her chin lifted her head so she was looking him in the eye. "You know that's not the full truth. I have a feeling there will be a mass exodus of those who can't do without their elfin waitress. You're damn good and I can't blame them. I'll see you Thursday at seven."

"Okay," she said before scurrying back to the locker room. She was almost afraid of what would happen when several other favorite regulars discovered where she was working. If the scum stayed away, she wouldn't mind. If ones like Calvin followed her, her tips would remain good.

Danny met her at the door as she was leaving. He put his arm around her as they walked to her truck. "Girl, when are you going to get a decent vehicle?"

"What's wrong with Whitey? He's been good to me and has a few more good years left in him. The dings and scratches are the sign of a good life." She loved the truck Wes had sold to her when she was sixteen.

"Well, Whitey could use some bodywork." When she opened the door, he lifted her and set her on the seat. "Watch your back. Colleen has several friends who work here. They may try to create problems for you."

Bending over, she kissed his cheek. "Warning not needed but appreciated. They can try, but they won't get away with it.

"But Colleen is a nasty adversary."

"And we won't be working together again. I've a feeling if she creates too much of a problem, she'll become history. I got the feeling that Mr. Becker doesn't want problems like what she created this evening."

Chuckling, Danny nodded in agreement. Mariah turned and put on her seatbelt. Danny moved close to her. His hand on her arm had her turning to him.

"Look, kid, Bob and I have your back. Go buy something nice with that money. Maybe a paint job for Whitey here. He could use a facelift."

With a giggle, she shook her head. "Not happening. So long as he runs well, I'm not going to worry about the minor things. He'll have to fall apart before I get rid of him." She could see the questions on Danny's face. "I bought this truck from the man who raised me. It has a great engine in a body which belies what it can do. Besides, I love the old thing and don't know if I'll be able to part with it even if it stops running."

"I get it. See you Thursday."

"Yep. Take care of yourself," she said with an impish grin. He gave her a merry laugh and closed the door when she started the engine. With a wave, she backed out and pulled off, looking forward to Thursday. The pit was going to be fun to work. The area was nicely laid out, enabling the waitresses to move around without blocking the view of the stage. Having a bartender who was efficient and a chef who made the food look as good as it tasted, according to her customers, was also a benefit.

When she got home, Dale looked up from his computer and smiled. "There's food in the oven for you. You might want to heat it up though. I turned the oven off over an hour ago."

He had made a casserole. Having food ready for her when she got home would be easy to get used to. Plus, Dale was an excellent cook. She popped a serving into the microwave. When it went off, she joined him at the table to eat.

"How was your orientation?" he asked, pausing in whatever he was doing on the computer.

She gave him a rundown of her evening and how Mr. Becker had handled the situation with Colleen. When she added what Danny had told her, Dale folded his arms and leaned on the table.

"You need to listen to Danny. I've a feeling there'll be more than a few very jealous girls with you being put where you get the bigger tips."

Mariah pulled out the tips she had made during the two hours and put it on the table. "I get it, but I made more in two hours than most of them get for a full shift on a busy night. Tonight was a slow night, supposedly, so that tells me they aren't working the tables correctly."

Dale counted the money she had fanned out on the table. "You have to be damn good to get that type of money for a couple of hours."

She swallowed the food she had in her mouth. "I'm exceptionally good and know it. I don't get money for playing around with the men. I give them great service with a smile and a light chatter. I also refuse their advances nicely with a smile.

"At the Cat on a busy night, I left with more than what most of the dancers made. I also had regular customers who would sit where I was working rather than have someone else wait on them. They liked that they seldom had to wait on refills and the food was served hot."

"I understand. I hate having to wait for someone to refill a drink and I despise cold food if it's supposed to be hot."

He returned to what he had been doing, allowing her to finish her meal. She cleaned up the kitchen and turned on the dishwasher which was full. After putting a lid on the casserole, she put it in the fridge. When she closed the door and turned, she found herself in Dale's arms. He held her for a few seconds before stepping back.

His face was serious. "Be really careful at this new place. Some people aren't who they seem to be."

"What are you getting at?" she asked, unsure what he meant. A stab of concern punctured her happiness at being in a better job.

"Exactly what I said," he responded before returning to his computer.

She washed the few things she never put in the dishwasher. When she completed wiping down the counter, she turned to find Dale behind her. This time he pulled her close to him. His head lowered until his lips met hers. The kiss started out gentle but ended up passionate, awakening a need she didn't know she had as their tongues danced with each other.

He raised his head but didn't let her go. "I've wanted to do that since I first met you."

Stunned at his admission, she leaned back and asked, "Then why didn't you?"

"I was afraid," he admitted with a wry smile before planting another kiss on her lips.

Stepping away from her, he picked up his computer and went to his room. Her thoughts were scattered by the emotions he had evoked within her. Why did he wait until now? Was he playing with her, or was he serious and wanting to move forward from being just friends?

She didn't have any answers. Other than his saying he wanted to talk to her once this mess was cleared up, she had no idea of what he wanted from her. Mariah let out a sigh, guessing he'd avoid the talk and walk away, leaving her to deal with what he had started. Such was life for her.

Chapter Ten

AT FIVE AM, MARIAH put the coffee on to brew. She needed to run this morning but was hesitant to wake Dale. While she was waiting for the coffee, he entered the kitchen and leaned against the counter.

"You want to run this morning?" he asked, startling her.

"Yes," she answered, not sure if he planned to repeat what he had done last night.

When he didn't move, she decided to try to forget the kiss he had given her, putting it down to a onetime thing. He took the coffee she handed him when it was done with a simple, "Thank you. I'll be ready in ten minutes."

Okay. He had a timetable to meet like she did this morning. they were on their way to Sunland Park in the then minutes he had given. Again, he was able to keep up with her during the run. He hadn't spoken to her since she gave him the coffee. Nothing like being shut out of what he was thinking.

The silence continued after returning home from their run. She was out the door by seven-thirty. but barely made her first class. Between school and work she had a full day. The earliest she would get home today was five, and she had to be at work by seven.

Her day didn't go smoothly, delaying her getting home until five-thirty. The savory scent of cooking food assailed her as she entered the apartment. Dale was dishing up the meal. He already had the table set for two. She put her books in her room and joined him for a meal of baked salmon, wild rice, and asparagus, along with fresh-baked bread, and a peach cobbler for dessert. If she kept eating like this, she would gain back the weight she had lost over the past eight years.

"How was your day?" Dale asked, filling his plate.

"Not bad. I have a ton of work to do before Tuesday though." She wasn't sure if he cared or was just making small talk.

"I'll be working most of the weekend, so I won't be here to disturb you. You're working the whole weekend, correct?"

"Yes. From tonight through Sunday night. I like the four days together as it gives me Monday through Wednesday off to study."

Dale chuckled. "With the way you sleep, you don't need tons of time off. I need at least five hours of sleep every twenty-four to function."

With a sadness she couldn't hide, Mariah admitted, "I guess being an insomniac has its perks. If I sleep more than three hours, I'm usually so groggy I can't function for at least an hour after I wake up."

Dale stared at his plate, playing with his food. He finally said, "If you could remember the names and faces of the people you meet at the club, it would be a tremendous help to us. We know several of the Sinaloa hang out there, but we need to know who."

"No problem. I'm fairly good with names and faces. I'll write them down for you and leave the list on the table if you aren't here," she offered, not sure what he was looking for with his request.

"Thanks. I appreciate it. It'll save us from having to have someone hang out there." He glanced at the clock. "If I were you, I wouldn't wait too long to leave. Traffic tends to be heavy from five to after six-thirty in the evenings on the interstate."

She finished her meal before taking a shower and washing her hair. Dale was cleaning up the kitchen when she re-entered the living area.

"Be careful," Dale cautioned as he watched her leave.

Mariah held back a sigh. The kiss was looking more like a onetime thing than a prelude to a relationship.

Night had fallen by the time Mariah pulled into the parking lot. She chose a parking spot at the back, leaving the spaces close to the building for customers. She was halfway across the lot when Danny met her with a big grin.

"It's about time you got here. I was worried you would be late with the heavy traffic," he commented after kissing her cheek

"I left early just in case it was heavier than expected. Overall, it wasn't too bad getting here."

She didn't miss how he kept scanning the parking lot and the club during their walk to the locker room. Bob had waved to her as they passed the bar. With him here, she knew it would be a good night. He would help her if needed. When there was no sign of Colleen, she relaxed, determined to have a good night.

She put on a uniform, removing the push up pads in the top. It fit a lot better without the padding. Slipping into her work shoes, she closed her locker and stuffed the key into the top of her uniform knowing it wouldn't move with the tight fit. She didn't trust the minuscule pocket on the shorts. The designer really needed to put decent pockets on the darn shorts so a girl could put a key and a couple of other small items in them if needed.

When she left the locker room, Mr. Becker was in the anteroom talking to Theresa. He glanced back at her then did a double take before shaking his head.

"Mariah, you sure you don't want to dance? That gorgeous figure and innocent look would get you more money than waiting tables."

"Thanks, but no thanks. My self-respect means more than the money," she repeated with a grin. "Besides, I'd rather wait tables. The men don't expect as much of us as they do the dancers.

He studied her before saying, "And you were raised to not disrobe in public. I do understand, but damn, you'd be great out there even if you didn't totally strip."

"Not happening," she merrily informed him.

He accepted her answer with a smile before walking with her to the bar. "You're in the pit. It'll be your station when you're working. Yvonne will let you know what is still pending as soon as she comes back to turn in her orders."

"Okay. I'll wait here for her. Thank you," she told him.

He left before Bob came over.

"Kid, I'm glad you're here. I'm sure we'll have fewer complaints with you out there. Yvonne is good, but she is too slow when it gets busy. I believe Becker and a few others will see your value after tonight."

"Thanks for the vote of confidence. I'll try to remember the table numbers and seating for you." She grinned at him knowing he would gently remind her if she forgot.

Yvonne came and stood beside her. She gave Bob her current order before turning to Mariah. "I take it you're my relief."

"Yes, I'm Mariah. It'll be my first full shift here," she informed the perky redhead.

"Great. Let me give you a rundown of what I have going." She went over all the tables and what each had pending.

When she was finished, Mariah said, "I'll leave your tips with Bob or Mr. Becker for all the ones you started."

Yvonne's eyes rounded as she stared at Mariah. "You're going to leave tips for me?"

"Of course. If you did all the work, you deserve the tips. Let me get these drinks out so those men don't think we've forgotten them," Mariah said with a grin.

She overheard Bob telling Yvonne, "She's a class act. You'll get all the tips from all but that one where she's taking the drinks to right now. That one she'll split fifty–fifty with you."

Mariah followed her normal routine and checked on each group in the pit before returning to the bar to give Bob two orders, remembering to state which tables. From what she could tell, she was going to have a busy evening. She was able to get several orders for meals and appetizers for the tables Yvonne had started. Hopefully it would add to the tips Yvonne would receive. She liked the girl.

A little before eight PM a group of well–dressed men came in and took table seven, which was toward the back and off to the far-left side of the pit. Mariah noticed Becker was watching them as the men chose their seats. From his intense gaze, she surmised she had some VIPs to handle. That guess was confirmed when Becker went to greet the men.

Assessing the newcomers, she worked her way toward them. One was tall and could pass for a Spanish Pierce Brosnan with his black hair, olive skin, dark eyes, and a beautiful smile with perfect white teeth. He was watching her as she made her way to their table.

Mr. Becker smiled when she stopped before the men. "This is Mariah. She'll be waiting on you this evening. I believe you'll enjoy your visit. If you need anything, let me know." He sauntered off, leaving her with the group.

"What would you all like to drink?" she asked, noting the handsome man still hadn't taken his eyes off her.

Without consulting the others, he said, "Mojitos for everyone."

When no one objected to his order, she asked, "Would you like menus this evening? The chef has a fish special that looks fantastic."

The man studied her before saying, "Menus, please."

"I'll be right back with your drinks and menus," she informed them before checking on a table on her way back to the bar.

When she gave the orders to Bob, he nodded before saying, "Take good care of those men. They're big spenders and tippers."

Flashing him a grin, she chided, "And since when haven't I taken care of a customer? You know me. They're all VIPs."

With a chuckle he went off to prepare the mojitos while she dropped off menus for the men then checked on several of the other tables. When she returned to the bar, Bob had the drinks ready for the two tables. She dropped off the drinks to the first table before heading to the VIP group.

She set the mojitos in front of the men before asking, "What would you like to eat?"

Two ordered the fish special. The next man grinned and stated, "I'll take you."

Without missing a beat, she said, "Sorry, but your only options are from the menu and I don't believe I'm one of the choices this evening."

"Oh, so when will you be on the menu?" he asked with a big grin.

She smiled and said, "Never."

The men laughed, but she could see he wasn't exactly happy. The handsome man said, "Julio, drop it. She isn't on the menu, so what do you want to eat."

Julio opted for the fish special as did the man who appeared to be the leader of the group. Before she left, she asked, "Is there anything else you need while I'm here?"

The handsome man answered her question. "Nothing for now. Thank you."

She left, feeling the eyes of the group following her as she made her rounds. When she returned to the bar with the orders from the tables, Bob glanced behind her before stating, "You have made a total conquest there. He hasn't taken his eyes off you since they came in this evening."

She looked up at the mirror that allowed her to see the pit. He was correct. The handsome man was watching her and not the girls on the stage. Dismissing the observation with a wave of her hand, she went to wait on two new groups. When she returned to the bar, the food for the VIP table had arrived. Taking the tray, she expertly wended her way through the tables until she reached table seven. Setting the tray on the area provided, she served the men as if they were at a fine restaurant.

One of the men said, "You really should be on the menu. You are so delectable."

Smiling sweetly as she put his food before him. "You would be quite disappointed. I tend to be slightly sour."

The next man asked, "Really?" He proceeded to try and pull her onto his lap.

Mariah twisted away from him, standing out of his reach, her hands on her hips, glaring at him. "The waitress isn't a toy. Please don't try to play with her while she is working." She served the man who hadn't quit watching her, his smile still in place with the incident over. She now knew to stay out of the one man's reach.

He smiled up at her, but his eyes were serious. Without looking away from her, he ordered, "Guys, leave her alone. Like she said, she's not a toy."

Julio grumbled something in Spanish. The man glared at him. "You have a choice. Leave her alone or leave."

No one attempted to grab her again, but they kept making innuendos which she turned into a joke. By the time the men left, Julio had shown he had a great sense of humor. If they were going to be regulars, she could count on the leader to keep them in line.

Sunday, August 30, 2015

Mariah was glad the weekend was almost over. Work had been remarkably busy, and she needed a break. The tall man had returned to the club every night. A couple of men were with him each night. He would watch her, instead of the dancers. She had no idea why.

The tall man had ordered the same drink every time he came in, so when she saw him, along with the two men who were with him yesterday, she knew what to bring them to drink along with the menus for a meal.

One of the men said, "Damn, I could get used to this. I haven't been any place where the waitress remembered what I drank, even after going there for a month."

"It's okay, sweetie," she said with a smile. "I'll remember what you drink. Usually after the third visit, if you keep to the same thing, I don't forget. Now if you go and change on me, you'll have to wait the next time you come in for me to find out what you want."

"No changes. I like the great service," he said, toasting her with his glass before taking a sip of the drink.

As before, they seemed to enjoy sitting and talking. She kept them supplied with drinks without being a nuisance. Once they understood she wouldn't allow them to maul her, she enjoyed the teasing and chatting as she checked on them.

Close to midnight, the tall man came over to where she was talking to Theresa and Bob. He waited until she turned to him before saying, "My name is Phillip Ortiz. Would you consider going out with me?"

With a smile she shook her head. "I'm sorry, but I have a rule about not going out with customers. It generally leads to problems if things go sour."

Bob cut into her conversation. "Mariah, you need to make an exception here. He's only asking you out and with what I know about him, he'll be a total gentleman where you're concerned."

Phillip added, "I still can't believe you are real. I only want to take you out to dinner."

Danny arrived as Phillip was speaking. He added his thoughts to what Bob said. "Go, Mariah. You'll have fun. If he doesn't behave, let me know."

Mariah turned to Theresa who grinned. "I agree. Go and have fun. Danny has warned him to behave."

She looked at Phillip, not sure if she was doing the right thing. "Okay. It's unanimous. Dinner it is."

A big smile lit his face. "Frank told me you don't work Sunday through Wednesday, so how about Tuesday evening about seven?"

"That'll work. Tuesday is my early day off from school." Mariah still wasn't sure she wasn't making a mistake.

"Want to meet me or have me pick you up?" Phillip asked. This was a first for her. Most men wanted to pick her up at her place.

Remembering Dale, she said, "Let's meet at the Sunland Park Mall. I'll park in the area between Macy's and Sears. I drive an old beat up truck, so you probably won't miss it."

"Let me have your phone number just in case," he requested.

"915–555–0102," she recited. He didn't write it down, so she hoped he would remember it.

"Thank you," he politely said before returning to his group.

Bob winked at her before returning to work. Danny leaned over and kissed her cheek before leaving her. Meanwhile she went back to work, unable to rid herself of the distinct sense she may have made a mistake.

At a few minutes before one AM, she took her break. The plate of food she had ordered was on the table with her name on it. She was eating when Theresa took the seat beside her.

"Mariah, whatever you do, don't cross Phillip. He's a really nice guy but can be really mean when he gets angry."

She stared at her food before asking, "Then why did you encourage me to go out with him."

"I believe you'll be good for him and him for you. Just don't get involved in his business dealings. I'll keep an eye on you and him, and you can let me know about any problems."

"So, you don't believe I made a mistake by agreeing to go out with him?"

"No, honey. You didn't. Enjoy yourself."

Theresa left to take care of a problem with a uniform while Mariah finished her break. She returned to work, noticing Phillip was still hanging out with the same three men. Near three AM he left, stopping her to say he would see her on Tuesday at seven. He handed her a business card with his cell phone number written on it.

She left work at four but wasn't ready to go home. Without thinking, she went for a run. At the point where she normally turned back, she noticed the two men following her again. They didn't follow her back to her truck this time. It was a tossup as to whether it was her imagination or not.

When she got home, Dale was pacing the floor. He ran his gaze over her shorts and running shoes before shaking his head.

"I can see you don't believe in safety. Breakfast is in the oven." He jerked his backpack from the chair and left.

She was surprised he hadn't slammed the door. Real nice. She arrives home, and he's gone in less than one minute, unable to get away from her fast enough. The last thing she needed was a hassle from Dale because she didn't do what he wanted. Maybe a date with Phillip wouldn't be so bad after all. At least she would have a pleasant meal with decent conversation and no drama.

Chapter Eleven

THE SMOKE OF THE candles drifted to the ceiling, the flames casting light upon the ancient stone statue. The big round eyes of the statue appeared to be dark holes in the dim light. A puff of air put the flames into writhing movements on their wicks. A robed figure stood before the shrine, eyes glittering with reflected candlelight.

"Xolotl, oh powerful one, soon we will be one. We have found what you require to make the jaguar sleep. This is one who is pure. Untouched by a man. So seldom are ones found like her. Imagine, a virgin for you. We will perform the special ceremony at the time of the equinox. No, maybe the solstice. Ah, I forgot about the time where the moon will hide. That would be perfect." He smiled, staring at the small statue. "I'm sure you will tell me at the next sacrifice which time it will be.

"She is at an age to understand what she must do. She will come to you with her eyes open. They tell me she is incredibly special. Because of that, she is being kept safe by your worshipers. I know once she meets you, she'll be happy with what must happen.

"The hawk was hunting, and he found her. He promises to bring her to us when we are ready. Xolotl, you must tell me which time will give you the most power. Until then, we will keep her fate a secret to prevent those who want to stop us from keeping her with them. We must make sure she remains worthy for when the jaguar eats the moon.

"We will bring another to you this time. She is but a poor substitute for the shining one. We can almost taste the bright one's blood. It will be sweet, untainted, giving us the power to continue for many years.

Her innocence is unheard of today and will give you what you have not had in over three centuries. Many years will pass before we find another like her. After her, we need to rest. I must keep those around her from finding the Hawk and you. Soon she will be ours. Soon, Xolotl. Soon.

Chapter Twelve

WITH CARE, MARIAH ASSEMBLED an outfit to wear to school for her presentation. The circular dark teal skirt, white blouse, and vest that matched the skirt was complemented by a pair of knee-high black boots. A delicate gold chain held a small pendant in the shape of a basket with gemstone flowers in blue, red and yellow set off with green leaves. Matching earrings completed the outfit. Not bothering with makeup, she smoothed her hair until it formed a glossy cap on her head. Ready, she grabbed her purse and keys not wanting to be late.

Mariah hadn't bothered to tell Dale where she was going for the evening. He only knew she wasn't going to be home. Not that it mattered if he knew where she was or not. Dale would say one thing, but then his actions didn't match his words. Time for her to get off the merry-go-round and move on and forget about him. Danny was right. It was time for her to find someone to go out with and have some fun. Someone who wasn't afraid to show they liked her and enjoyed being with her was all she wanted.

Her school day ended later than expected, so she went directly to the mall to wait for Phillip. After only a few minutes of being parked, a silver Hummer pulled in beside her. Phillip stepped out of the back, coming to her truck. He opened the door and waited for her to gather her purse and keys before lifting her down like she was a small child. At the Hummer, he lifted her onto the back seat, then made sure she was comfortable before instructing the driver to continue to the restaurant.

When they turned onto the main road, he handed her a glass of a light rosé wine from the small stocked bar.

"I wasn't sure what you liked, and Danny couldn't help me, so I hope that is acceptable." As he had at the club, he remained polite.

She took a sip of the wine. It was fruity and not too sweet. "It's quite good. Thank you."

He studied her for a few seconds, taking a sip of the expensive Bowmore 25 Scotch he drank at the club when he wasn't drinking mojitos. "I'm guessing you'd like to know more about me."

She gazed at her wine before admitting, "As long as you aren't married, I'm not worried about the other stuff this evening."

When she glanced at him, he was staring at her like she had grown a second head.

"Look, I don't date much, so for me, having a pleasant evening and enjoying someone's company is more important than a recitation of the personal information everyone else seems to find so important."

Mariah, took another sip of the wine before continuing. "My guess is you have a job or inherited a bundle to be able to afford the club and this type of vehicle. Like me, you didn't materialize out of nowhere, so I'm sure you have some sort of family. You have a decent education from the way you speak. So, what else do I need to know?"

Phillip chuckled, grinning. He took another sip of his drink. "Mariah, you are unique among women. By now, most would have questioned me about my income, family, where I went to school, where I work and so forth. The last thing they usually ask is if I'm married, which I'm not." He shifted on the seat to face her. "I'll give you a quick rundown. That way you won't have to ask later. I own a security company, and it pays quite well. I have a house up on the mountain overlooking El Paso. As to family, I'm one of six children. I was born in Mexico but came here legally as a child with my parents. I attended the University of Texas and have a degree in business."

Mariah raised her brows before saying, "So I was correct in everything I had surmised about you."

"What you didn't ask was if I had a girlfriend."

"So, do you?"

"No. I haven't found anyone who was more interested in me than my money. I inherited a goodly amount from my grandparents. Because of that, I can't go out to what most would call the better places without women doing what they can to get a date with me. The last woman I dated, claimed I had gotten her pregnant in an attempt to force me into marrying her. She lost her case when she refused the paternity test, but I knew it wasn't mine."

Out of curiosity, Mariah asked, "And how did you know that?"

"One of the things my father taught me was safe sex and how to prevent unwanted pregnancies. He understood what I would be up against when I started dating. I still thank him for his instructions."

Without thinking, Mariah blurted out, "So you're sort of like me. You don't go out because others don't see the person under the exterior stuff."

Phillip laid a gentle hand on her arm. "I do understand. I had guessed it before Danny told me that you don't date much. He said all the men see is the beauty and friendliness and never bother to consider what's underneath. I want to get to know the elf behind the face and body of a goddess. Like me, I'm sure she's quite lonely and needs a friend, not a lover."

Mariah blinked back the tears. He did appear to understand. If he would only remain the friend that she needed.

"I would love to have one friend who enjoys hanging out and doing fun things together."

Phillip took the glass from her nerveless fingers before gathering her into his arms.

"Let me be that friend, because heaven knows, I need one, too."

A tear escaped but she didn't notice. Phillip wiped it away. "I wasn't wrong about you needing a friend. Let's see how this evening goes. Then you can decide if you want to go out with me again. Okay?"

A nod of her head answered him. If she had attempted to speak, she would become a sobbing mess. Maybe she could have one friend. For her, his being a male didn't matter. She needed someone who cared about her and wanted to do fun things together.

Eight years of living here, and the only friends she had made were Rachel and Danny. But neither one was the kind of friend she could go out dancing with, see a movie with, goof off at the arcade with, or just hang with and have fun playing games. They were work friends.

He kissed her forehead before turning her loose to finish her wine while he told her about his family. She would need to share her particulars over the meal. Maybe she could gloss over most of her life.

They arrived at a quaint little Italian restaurant. It was one most would pass by without noticing. She was thrilled it wasn't one of the fancy places most of the wealthy frequented.

Like he had with her truck, he lifted her down from the Hummer as if she were a small child. In a way, she was a child compared to his height, and at a hundred pounds, she wasn't much heavier than most ten- or eleven-year-old children.

Phillip kept a hand at her waist as he escorted her into the restaurant. They were immediately taken to a secluded corner with a table set for two. The curved booth allowed them to sit close enough to talk without others overhearing their conversation. After she scooted into the space behind the table, Mariah glanced around the interior. The dining room was rustic and made to look like an old Italian building. The atmosphere was homey, down to the embroidered linens on the table.

A short older man with an apron tied around his expansive middle came to their table before they had a chance to open the menus. He smiled and began to talk in what Mariah assumed was Italian. Phillip answered him. He then glanced at her before saying something more to the man, who answered him and waited.

Phillip turned to her. "He wants to cook something special for us. He said a lady of so much beauty deserves the best he can make, but he won't tell me what he plans to prepare. What do you think?"

"I'm game if you are. You know this place, so I trust him if you do."

Chuckling, Phillip relayed their acceptance of the man's offer. Beaming, the man rattled off more words before heading back to the kitchen. Phillip took her menu and put it with his at the edge of the table.

"I've a feeling we're in for a wonderful treat. He's an excellent cook, making all the food to order. I hope you weren't in a hurry to get home."

"No hurry. I don't have a lot of homework, so the next couple of days will be easy for me."

"This is the second time you've mentioned school. What are you studying?"

"Criminal Justice at the University of Texas here in El Paso. I'm hoping to get one of the spots for law school in Dallas next year." The wide eyes and open-mouthed stare showed she had surprised him. "Hey being a cocktail waitress doesn't mean you don't have a brain. Besides, it was the only job I could find where I would earn enough to save money for school. I have enough for three years of law school right now. I hope to have the rest for housing and books before next fall."

He recovered from her unexpected revelation. "I'm sure you'll get enough working at the club. I know you get terrific tips from some of the men, and you deserve it. I've watched, and you give great service without compromising those morals of yours. Also, I'm aware that if it wasn't for Bob and Danny, you wouldn't have accepted my offer for a date."

She leaned back against the cushion of the curved bench, his words bringing back her normal results of dating. There was no reason to believe he would be any different than the couple of others she had dated.

"No, I probably wouldn't have. I know the typical kind of men who go to the clubs. They're into sex and don't care about the girl other than if she's willing to do what they want. Many are married and are cheating on their wives. Working at a club isn't conducive to meeting decent men who will respect you."

He took a sip of the wine the waitress had brought them. "I don't date girls like those at the club. They are only going out with you for what they can get. On top of all that, heaven only knows what you'd pick up from them. You're more of what I look for in a woman. The surface beauty is a plus."

When she met his eyes. She didn't know if he meant it or was a very accomplished liar. Time would tell which he was, so for now, she would accept his words at face value. He wasn't like most of the men who frequented the strip clubs.

Phillip seemed to be reading her mind. "I don't normally go to strip joints, but I provide the security there. The night we met; I came in to see if there was anything else needed. When I saw you, I had to come back again to make sure you weren't a figment of my imagination. You weren't." He hesitated then asked, "So why isn't your family helping you through school?"

Now it was her turn to pause. She took a sip of the wine to decide how much to tell him.

She stared at her wine glass. "I don't have any real family. I was raised by a cousin who told me to leave when I turned eighteen. I was no longer his responsibility. He also made it clear he wasn't going to help me, even in the form of a loan. I ended up here in El Paso, where I took a job at the

Golden Cat because they paid more than any place else and promised I could move to waitress when I turned twenty-one. They had a party for me on my twenty first birthday and trained me for waitressing the next night.

"I saved what I could and started school when I had enough to pay the tuition and books for one semester. I tightened my belt and put most of my money away and I now have enough for law school."

"What about your parents? You didn't mention them."

The question was one she had hoped he wouldn't ask. "I don't remember much about them. I know they had two other children. They dropped me off at my cousin's place one day, left, and never came back. He never explained why they left me there. All he told me was that he had agreed to care for me until I was old enough to be on my own."

"So, he did his duty, then threw you out," Phillip paraphrased.

"You could say that. It took me a while to realize he had given up his life to care for me. He's only ten years older than I am."

With brows drawn together, Phillip probed, "Why would someone that young take on the task of raising you?"

She shrugged. "You'd have to ask him. He never told me why."

Mariah glanced around the restaurant. Her breath caught when she noticed a woman who looked like Rachel from the side. A hope bloomed until the woman turned. She wasn't

Rachel. A tear escaped as she lowered her gaze to her wine. When would the pain of losing her end?"

"Are you okay?" Phillip asked. His voice was soft and caring, and his hand warm on her arm.

Nodding she used her napkin to dry the tears. "A woman over there reminded me of a friend who died recently. I still miss her."

"Tell me about her."

Mariah hesitated. His eyes held pain as if he understood hers.

"Her name was Rachel. She worked at the Golden Cat with me. She was a stripper. While she worked there, she started using drugs but had managed to get clean. We became good friends after she stopped using.

"She was supposed to move in with me and start school in the fall. The police seem to think she was using again and agreed to smuggle drugs from Mexico to here, but I don't believe that's true. She enjoyed being clean and was looking forward to getting out of the club and into a respectable job. Besides, she didn't need money, so why would she smuggle drugs?"

"I can't answer that for you since I didn't know her. There must be an explanation but that is something the police will need to figure out."

"Well, they aren't even going to try to figure it out. They want to believe she was smuggling drugs and are trying to tie me into whatever they think she was doing." Mariah was frowning and her voice held anger before realizing what she had told him.

She had said too much. Her eyes went to his. He was frowning.

He held her hand, an unexpected concern showing in the set of his features. "I can't see you ever being involved in something like that. They must be trying extremely hard to keep you from finding out what really happened to her."

"They are, but it'll eventually come out. Things just aren't fitting together, but I'm letting the authorities handle it."

"Good. Don't get involved. It could jeopardize your planned career."

"I know. They're trying to frame me. but I haven't a clue as to why. If it weren't for that, I would have let it go when they told me she was dead." Her fingers moved her silverware around, not willing to meet his intent look. She hadn't meant to tell him about what was happening to her. Now that she had told him, there was no taking back the words.

Phillip turned her head with gentle fingers on her chin until she was facing him. "Let it play out while staying out of what they are doing. If you don't, they'll make life a living hell for you. Please don't get involved any more than you are."

He seemed to be begging her to leave things alone. She could see fear in his eyes along with concern on his face. He actually cared about what happened to her.

"I'll leave it alone if they leave me alone. I've got too much at stake right now to get arrested for something I didn't do." She paused and gave him an apologetic smile. "Excuse me a minute. I need to use the lady's room."

He smiled as she stood. She could feel him watching her as she walked away.

Their entrées arrived just as Mariah rejoined him. The dish of veal and pasta was truly special, made in a way Mariah had never had before. She savored each flavorful mouthful. When they had their fill of the main course, cappuccino was served with a warm, sweet pastry. She felt like she had gained ten pounds by the time the meal was finished.

The conversation had remained neutral and pleasant as they compared their various interests. Phillip was extremely knowledgeable about the history of the area while she knew a lot about current events. They both liked sports which was a good thing. When it came time to leave, Phillip called for the car and escorted her out the door after paying for the meal and leaving a large tip on the table.

Once they were in the Hummer, Mariah said, "I'm sorry about being a downer earlier. Thinking the woman was Rachel hit me hard there for a few seconds."

"Take time to grieve," he advised. "Something like that doesn't go away in a few days."

They were silent until they pulled beside her truck in the parking lot of the mall. He looked out the window then back to her. "I'd like to go out with you again, if you would be willing."

She let out a gentle breath. "Let me think about it. Will you be at the club over the weekend?"

"Yes. It'll be the only way I'll get to see you," he admitted with a grin.

"I'll let you know when I see you the next time."

"I can wait until then. I do understand."

He lifted her down from the Hummer. She unlocked her truck and opened the door before stepping up on the running board. Turning back to him, she started to speak but was cut off when he took her in his arms and slowly lowered his head to kiss her. It was so tender and gentle, her mind quit working. Her wide eyes stared up at him.

"I probably shouldn't have done that, but I couldn't help myself," he admitted with a wry grin before lifting her onto the seat. "Go home and get some sleep. I'll see you Thursday." He shut the door to the truck and waited until she started the engine before going back to the Hummer. He watched as she left.

Mariah was home in ten minutes. Dale was at the table drinking a cup of coffee. His eyes followed her as she let the keys clatter into the bowl and slipped off her heels.

"How was your date?" he asked, his tone neutral.

She gave a slight shrug. "Okay. He took me to this Italian restaurant, and we talked."

When Dale didn't respond, she went to her room, to prevent him from seeing the tears. No way he was interested in her if he couldn't even show some concern about her going on a date with another man. Dale's reaction made the decision to go out again with Phillip very easy. At least she had someone who would take her out and enjoy being with her.

Phillip had been a pleasant dining partner and a total gentleman, even with his kiss. He wouldn't be pawing at her like most other men did on a date. Yes, he would get a second date, then as many others as he wanted for now. She was tired of being alone. She needed a friend. Dale didn't appear to want to be a friend in any shape or form.

After undressing she lay on the bed, letting the tears come as she grieved for Rachel and the loss of Dale. She had hoped he would fulfill her dreams about them. She now knew that dream wasn't going to come true.

Phillip was only temporary, and she knew it. He would tire of her soon when she didn't sleep with him. No matter what she did, everyone seemed destined to leave her without fulfilling any of her dreams.

Chapter Thirteen

THE CANDLES LIT THE picture of the one chosen for the time when the world would go dark. The woman was smiling with an innocent, childlike look in her eyes. Her hair was glossy and framed her face. The eyes were wide with wonder and followed him as he placed the picture below the old stone statue.

Rachel had sent her to them. She was perfect and would join Xolotl with that innocent smile. The blood moon and her blood would mix. The jaguar would drink her blood, and the moon would come back clean. Her blood would cleanse him of the evil and give him the power to stop the darkness creeping over them.

Yes, he needed to be cleansed. The rest were dirty like those they had used. All of them were making him dirty. Her heart. He could keep her heart. It was a pure heart. An innocent woman's heart. It would keep them clean, returning the ritual to its beginnings.

He turned his eyes up to the statue. "Xolotl, speak to me. Tell me what to do. Do I keep her heart or only drink her blood like you have instructed us to do? How do I get clean so

I can join you? I want to join you. Death is coming. Yes, it is coming. Soon. Very soon. The moon will hide, and the next one will honor you. Then the innocent one. She is the one who will give you life."

Chapter Fourteen

YESTERDAY MORNING DALE HAD run with her before she left for school, but he had barely said two words to her. This morning he handed her a cup of coffee and set food in front of her before leaving without a word. Okay, he was only a roommate. He was paying half the rent and utilities. Not a problem. It meant she could save more money for school and living expenses. Maybe she could finish the three years of law school with only working a few hours a week. She was almost there.

By this time next year, she hoped to be in Dallas starting her JD degree. After graduation, no one would find her. The plan was to move out of Texas to a completely new area. Nothing was keeping her here. When she left, she had no intention of telling Wes where she was going. That way, he didn't have to feel responsible for her.

If she moved somewhere else, she might be able to find someone who wanted her for who she was and not her looks. What she had now was no life. Wes and Dale didn't want her around, and Phillip would soon tire of her once he discovered she was a real woman with real feelings, thoughts, and needs. For now, she was his fantasy. From years of experience, Mariah knew fantasies didn't last.

When she arrived at work, she discovered Danny was off. Glancing around, she didn't know any of the bouncers, and it made her nervous. A tap on her left shoulder had her turning, then tilting her head back to see the smiling face of a giant man she hadn't met before.

"You have to be Mariah. I'm Quinn. Danny told me to look out for you tonight. I missed you pulling in. Let me know when you're ready to leave and I'll walk you out," the giant rattled off, grinning like a cat who had caught a mouse.

"Thanks Quinn. I wondered if Danny would arrange for someone to watch out for me." She couldn't stop staring at the handsome giant in awe. Few bouncers were as gorgeous as him.

A merry laugh rang out, drawing attention to them. "Honey, we almost had a free-for-all to see who was going to take his place tonight. Danny said I wouldn't scare you like the rest would."

She grinned up at him. "You don't scare me at all. I'll let you know when I'm ready to leave. I appreciate you stepping in for Danny. At least I know I'll have one other person making sure I'm okay."

"You bet. Signal me if you need help. You don't need to be hassled."

He moved away as quickly and silently as he had arrived, leaving her grinning. Danny knew she was partial to gentle giants. On her way to get changed, she noticed a different bartender mixing drinks. Her night could turn into a nightmare with all the changes in personnel.

When she left the locker room, Mr. Becker was talking to Theresa. She wasn't sure if he was there by chance or plan. He ran his eyes up and down her before shaking his head.

"Darling, you really should be dancing," he reiterated with a grin.

"Not happening and you know it," she responded with a laugh. "But I could teach those girls a thing or two about pole dancing. Only Sara has a clue what to do on a pole. The rest need to step it up to get the men's attention.

Theresa and Becker both stared at her, mouths agape. Becker recovered first.

"You know how to pole dance?" he squeaked, his voice an octave or more above normal.

Mariah laughed. They were clueless. Many women knew how to use a pole for exercise. The difference was that the exercise classes didn't have the sexy moves.

"Using a pole is taught at my gym as an exercise class. I took the class because it required a lot of upper body strength. I also like gymnastics. So yes, I know how to use a pole effectively. I'd be happy to teach them a few things, but I won't do it in front of a crowd, and I'll keep my clothes on, thank you."

Becker grinned. "Okay. Two-thirty during the break while the curtains are closed. I'll arrange for relief for you. I have to see this!"

"You're on," she said with a wink before walking away to go to work.

Phillip came in an hour into her shift with a man who appeared to be of Spanish descent. The man was around five-ten with dark-brown eyes, black hair, and dark skin. Even though he was thin, she got the impression he was physically fit. Since he was also a good-looking man, the two of them had heads turning when they walked into the pit and took their seats. Phillip and the new man both watched her as she made her way to their table. When she arrived, Phillip took her hand and pulled her over to him, tugging her down to kiss her cheek.

"I had to make sure you were still real," he whispered to her, causing heat to rise to her face. "Let me introduce you to Santiago. He's one of my friends. You'll frequently see us together."

"Nice to meet you, Santiago. Now, what may I get you two to drink?" she asked, returning to work mode.

"My usual," Phillip said before turning to Santiago. "He likes good tequila. Your bartender will know which one."

Santiago was still watching her as if he was trying to figure out something about her.

"Okay. Do you want menus?"

"Gracias, señorita," Santiago said. "I can see why my amigo can't stop talking about the woman–child he met. You are unbelievably beautiful, yet so unspoiled." Her face began to heat again at his compliment. "I would never expect someone working here to turn such a pretty shade of red. Phillippe, you have a rare treasure."

Phillip winked at her. "I know. I have no intention of letting her go anytime soon, if ever."

She rolled her eyes and said, "Men!" before leaving to the sounds of their laughter.

Mr. Becker was waiting for her at the bar. "You take good care of those two. They're special men around here."

She gave Carl, the bartender, her order before picking up two menus. "I treat all customers as VIPs. They're no different than the others except Phillip, like Calvin, gets to kiss my cheek. That's reserved for customers I know and trust."

She took the drinks to Phillip and Santiago, not paying attention to the smile on Becker's face. After checking on her other tables, she returned to get table seven's food order. Phillip took her hand and held her in place beside him.

"Santiago has suggested a double date for next Tuesday. You want to go?" He was clearly trying not to push her into anything.

"Sure. Why not?" she agreed with a smile.

"Pick you up at seven at the same place?" he asked, seeming to understand that she wasn't ready for him to know where she lived.

"Sounds good. Tuesday, September eighth, at seven," she repeated back as Phillip beamed at her and Santiago nodded with a big smile. Going out with Phillip might not be so bad after all. She might end up with a few more people she could hang out with until moving to Dallas.

At two–thirty, one of the girls relieved her. She went to her locker and put on the straps for her top. Mr. Becker met her with a smile before leading her to the stage, which was now curtained off. Mariah turned to him.

"You had better make sure those curtains stay closed or I'll quit right on the spot," she warned.

He nodded with pursed lips. Her guess had been correct. He had planned to open the curtains if she was any good. Her hand pulled on the pole close to her. It was solid and would take what she was going to do.

Keeping her voice soft, she had the girls move closer to her. "Poles are here to use. They aren't props. Instead, they are part of the action."

She swung around the pole as the girls watched.

"By not trying to be sexy, you'll end up being sexier on a pole. If you had been watching your boss, you would have seen how he was watching me, and I was doing nothing but twirling around the pole while having fun."

She hooked her leg around the pole and leaned out and twirled around again. The girls glanced at the men who were part of the stage crew. All of them were staring at Mariah, who was smiling at their intense interest in what she was doing.

"Ok, ladies. Let me show you a simple routine you can pick up at any exercise class that uses a pole."

Going from twirling with her leg around the pole, she leaned out, allowing her body to swing her around, her foot remaining at the base of the pole, her hand on the pole at shoulder height. She pulled herself back in and again hooked a knee around the pole before lifting her other foot from the floor. From there, she went into what most would think were feats of strength. They weren't.

"Ladies, the twirling is keeping me up on the pole, not strength. Try it. It's really quite easy and you'll find that adding a few things like this will improve your routine."

Two of the girls mimicked what she was doing and managed to stay up on the pole before letting the other girls try. The dancers were having fun with the new moves, which was what the show had lacked. The fun factor. Dropping to the ground, Mariah turned so she could see them.

"I'm now going to show you what you can do with a pole if you practice. I'd advise going to the gym where I exercise. They have pole classes all the time. I love the class. It's good exercise and helps me keep in shape.

She took hold of the pole and swung around, then went into a routine where she was upside down, sideways, and hanging sinuously from the pole, using it in a way none of the girls had ever seen it used.

When she dropped to the floor, she said, "That's how a pole should be used. If you have music, it all comes out as a sexy and sensual routine, but in reality, it's nothing more than exercise that will keep you working for years. It will add strength, and helps with abdominal, leg, chest, and arm musculature. No one needs to know you're having fun exercising for them.

"That is the other key. You need to enjoy it. If you don't, it'll become routine, and the men will quit paying attention. The fun you had when I first started to work here isn't there. The men know it and aren't paying attention to you. If you want them to attend to what you're doing and get those tips, you need to step it up a notch."

The girls went to the poles to attempt to replicate some of the simpler moves Mariah had done. When two of them began to play around together, they did a high five. They now had a way to make it fun again.

Mariah stopped before Mr. Becker. "No! Don't even ask!" She picked up a pad and pen from a table and wrote the name of her gym. "Here's where they offer the classes. You should encourage them to go or even pay for the classes. Not only will they have fun, but it'll also improve the shows here."

He cupped her chin. "Child, sure I can't get you to perform just once. Fully clothed. No stripping."

"No," she repeated shaking her head. "It isn't something I do in public. It's part of my exercise routine."

Walking away, she went to the lounge to complete her break. There was a plate of food for her, but she wasn't hungry. She shouldn't have let them know she knew how to use a pole. Then again, if it helped the men focus on the dancers and not her, her job would be a lot easier. No way should she be getting more attention than the girls on stage.

The rest of her night was uneventful. Phillip and Santiago had left while she was on break. Few customers were around at this hour, so she was glad to see her relief. Quinn smiled as he walked her to her truck.

"Let me know anytime you need a guard. Real ladies aren't common in this business, and I'll do what I can to make sure you're protected. I don't need Danny or Mr. Ortiz to tell me to keep an eye on you."

She stood on the running board of her truck to lean over and kiss his cheek. "Thanks Quinn. I appreciate it. I feel safer when someone is willing to watch out for me."

He beamed at her. "Got to protect the one lady I've met here. You be careful now. See you tonight."

She left him standing in the lot, watching her leave. She felt he was doing this more for himself than Danny. Underneath that big hulking persona was a man who saw what few others noticed. He knew she wasn't like the rest of the girls who worked there. She was different simply because she cared about herself

Chapter Fifteen

MARIAH PULLED OUT OF the Slipper's parking lot at close to five AM. She was restless and needed to exercise. No way would she call Dale to run with her, regardless of what he'd said.

The area by the river was dark with no moon to add light when she parked her truck. No other cars were in the lot. After putting on her running shoes and a light jacket, she took off along the paved path. When it ended, she continued onto the dirt road. The sounds of her feet hitting the hardened dirt were barely heard in the darkness.

About halfway to the midpoint of her run, she heard someone behind her. A glance back didn't reveal anyone close enough to see, but someone was there. She could hear feet hitting the ground and heavy breathing. Whoever it was, wasn't used to running.

Stepping up her pace, she looked for a place to hide. A couple of shadows off to her right told her where she was. Quickly, she turned and moved to the deepest part of the shadows next to the bushes that caused them, thankful for the hard dirt not showing footprints and her dark clothes. This time, she lay on the ground, watching as the men moved past her. They stopped a short distance beyond where she was hidden.

"Damn. We lost her," one of the men rasped. His voice was like the one she had heard after the thumps leading to what she now knew was a murder.

"Boss ain't goin' ta like this," the other man said, gasping for breath.

The raspy voice huffed, then said, "Let's go meet Joe as planned. Let him deal with it."

She could hear their footfalls as they ran away from her in the direction she had been going. Who was Joe and the Boss? And why were these men following her? Not until their footfalls faded into the distance, did she get up and jog back to her truck, unwilling to run into the men by going farther.

Her truck was still the only vehicle in the lot. She was pulling out as a car came down the ramp. The headlights of her truck raked over the car as she made the turn for the ramp. Three people were in the dark sedan.

At the first light, the car pulled up behind her. Double checking her locks, she hit the gas as soon as the light turned green. The car stayed behind her until she turned into the back entrance to the apartment complex. It kept going straight. She still wondered why the man named Joe and the two men were after her.

A light in the apartment window indicated Dale was up when she pulled into her parking space. When she entered the apartment, he stopped working to glare at her, his arms crossed over his chest.

"You were supposed to call me before going running. That was the deal."

Ignoring his attitude, she simply said, "I didn't go far. I needed some alone time and running is usually my time to be alone and think."

Without waiting for him to speak, she went to her room and shut the door. After showering, she lay on the bed, staring at the wall, letting the tears come as they wanted. She didn't attempt to stop the roller coaster ride of emotions concerning Dale. In the end, she relaxed, slipping into a daydream.

After nearly two hours, she rolled out of bed. The time spent crying and relaxing had left her rested, but now she was hungry. When she opened the door, Dale was still working at the table. He stopped to study her as if she were an insect he wanted to squash.

"You didn't mention the men who followed you this morning during your run. Or the car that followed you here. Want to explain what you were thinking?" His tone was flat, mouth grim, but with no visible anger.

"No explanation. Two men followed me while I ran, and I overheard them say they were supposed to meet someone named Joe. They were barely able to run a hundred yards without fighting for breath, so they had to know they couldn't catch me." She moved to the coffee pot and poured herself a cup, adding cream this time.

Dale moved to where she was standing and turned her to face him. She could see the controlled anger on his face. Meeting his gaze, she mutinously glared back at him.

"Mariah, you're a target. I don't know why yet, but you are. You need to be more careful. I don't want to lose you."

"Humph," she sounded and turned back to stir her coffee. "As if I'm all that important in the scheme of things."

Dale's fingers bit into her shoulder when he pulled her around to face him this time. "I care a lot about you. I can't show it right now due to what's happening, but I do care. A whole lot! Even if you aren't, I'm scared about what they'll do if they catch you. I don't know yet if these men are connected to those who killed Rachel, so please, don't go running without me. I'm sure they have a plan. You may have foiled them today, but the next time...." He let it hang there, searching her face, blinking back...tears?

What she had assumed was anger wasn't. It was fear. She lowered her head, not wanting him to see the confusion. He cared about her. Then again, that didn't mean he would be staying once this case was finished.

"Okay. No more runs by myself. I'm going out with Phillip again on Tuesday. I have no idea of how late I'll be," she said, head down to avoid looking at him.

"Not a problem. At least I know you'll be safe with him. I have to run."

He shut off his computer, grabbed it and left. Mariah frowned focusing on the front door. How did he know she would be safe with Phillip?

Dale was so confusing. He kept saying he cared, then ran out the door. He showed no outward sign of not wanting her to go out with Phillip. Mariah had to admit that her life was a disaster right now because of the men connected to her—all three of them.

As if on cue, her cellphone rang. The caller ID said *Wesley.* She picked it up with a grimace. "Hello, Wes. What's up?" She knew without a doubt there had to be a reason for his call.

"Just checking in on you. How's the new job going?".

"Great. I'll have enough for most of my living expenses if I keep getting tips like I have been. The Slipper is definitely a step up from the Golden Cat. Plus, I don't have to be afraid of a gunfight breaking out over one of the girls," she said, not sure what he was really wanting with his question.

"So, who are you dating from the club?"

Ah ha. She now understood the agenda. A second later, a spike of fear zinged through her. How had he discovered she was dating someone from the club? She answered her own question. Dale, who else?

"His name is Phillip Ortiz. He's been a perfect gentleman with me. We've only gone out one time and he took me to this wonderful Italian restaurant. We're going out next Tuesday on a double date."

Wes remained quiet when she finished. His silence created pain. He was disappointed with her again.

She decided to tell him the rest of it. "Look, Wes, Dale isn't about to ask me out. I'm twenty-six and have only been on five dates. What am I supposed to do? Sit and wait until I'm old and gray for him to man up? I'll not beg him to pay attention to me."

She sucked in a breath and let it out, blinking rapidly at the pain she couldn't stop as another sliver of her heart broke off.

"For now, Dale's my roommate. Other than cooking and conversation about the case, he hasn't said but three or four sentences that have been personal in nature. If he wants me, then he had better start showing it. Until then, I'm going to enjoy being with someone who seems to know I exist and need a friend."

Wes kept silent for another heartbeat before saying, "Mariah, if the pattern you and Dale found with your research is correct, the next body will show up sometime after September thirteenth. I don't want that body to be yours."

"Why would it be me?" What did he know but wasn't telling her?

"You're a target simply because you were friends with Rachel. Stick close to Dale regardless of what's going on between you two." He had just issued a rare command, not a request.

With a sadness she couldn't hide, she said, "He doesn't want me all that close."

Wes snorted. "You couldn't be more wrong, girl. Talk to him if he won't talk to you. Tell him what you need from him. Dating someone else won't get the response you are wanting."

"I'm not attempting to make him jealous, if that's what you're thinking."

"If you are, it won't work. He'll come to you when he won't be putting both of you in jeopardy with his undercover work. Have patience."

He hung up without saying goodbye. She tamped down the urge to throw her phone, just to see, feel and hear it break into pieces like she was inside. All this confusion wasn't what she needed. Besides, what did he know about her today? He hadn't bothered to talk to her for three long years.

As much as she would prefer being with Dale, she longed for someone who would take her away from what she was dealing with on a day-to-day basis. Phillip was doing that. Too bad no one liked it. Like she had told Wes, she was tired of sitting around and waiting.

Phillip wanted to take her places and show her off, if nothing else. He was also introducing her to new people, who also seemed to like her, not just her looks. Wes and Dale needed to accept it. If it wasn't for them, she wouldn't be in this situation to begin with. It hadn't been her choice to come here. She had been forced into moving and El Paso had been the closest city.

The ringing of her phone made her jump. She didn't recognize the number. "Hello. How may I help you?" came out automatically.

"It's Detective Jamison. You're off the hook for those deposits. Your alibis check out, but you aren't off the hook with me. I'll see you behind bars before this is all over. I know you're working with the smugglers. I'll get the proof, then you'll go down."

He didn't give her a chance to answer before hanging up, leaving his threats ringing in her ears. Why her? All he had to do was to run a background check on her to know she wouldn't be involved in drug smuggling or other illegal activities. Slowly she gathered her things for class, changing from hunted prey to student. For the next nine hours, she was going to concentrate on her future. That is, her future if she got through this mess in one piece.

Dale was at the apartment when she arrived home from school. She could smell the food he had fixed, but she wasn't hungry. What she wanted was to hide until she needed to leave for work. Going through her normal routine, she dropped the keys into the bowl, setting it to ringing, stepped out of her shoes and started to her room. A gentle hand on her arm stopped her.

"I'm worried about you. When was the last time you actually slept? You can't keep burning the candle at both ends, and you know that." She didn't miss the concern in his voice. Instead of focusing on him, she stared at the door to her room.

"Don't worry about me sleeping. I'm an insomniac. If I get two or three hours a couple of times a week, I'm fine. I can go up to three days without sleep with no ill effects. I do take time to rest. It helps if I can't sleep." She remained still, waiting for him to remove his hand.

"Did Wes call you today?" he asked.

"Yes." She waited for him to ask what they spoke about.

"I heard Jamison also backed away from the charges he was hoping to file when your alibi checked out."

She wondered where he got all his information. "Yes, he let me know, then threatened to get me before it was all over, so I guess I'll have to see what he does next to try and frame me."

Dale stepped in front of her, tilting her head up, enabling him to see her face. "I'm aware he's trying to frame you, but he was told to back off. Other than Phillip, who else have you met at the club who wasn't a regular at the Cat?"

She rattled off a list of names that included Santiago. He wrote them down as she gave them to him. "Why do you want the names from the Slipper? I'd have thought you'd have been more concerned with the Cat's clientele."

Dale's face was serious when he looked at her. "Not all things are as they seem. You have a deadlier clientele at the Platinum Slipper than you ever did at the Golden Cat."

"What?" she blurted out, staring at him.

"The place is filled with those tied to the Sinaloa Cartel. It is being used for money laundering, smuggling, selling, and who knows what else. Make sure you are aware of what is going on around you without being obvious. Also, use Quinn, not Danny, if you get into trouble. He's deep undercover and he'll protect you where Danny might not."

"Phillip?" she questioned.

"Don't worry about him. Let me do the worrying. You go and enjoy yourself while with him. I won't be far away. I'm not about to let anything happen to you." His voice was as tender as the hand that cupped her cheek.

"Why?" She needed to hear his answer.

"My reasons aren't all that important. Your safety is."

His answer took away what little hope she had that he really cared for her. Wes had to be the one who was having him watch her after learning about the type of place where she was working. She started to move away. His hand stopped her again.

"I have an appointment to see Father Rivers in the morning. Want to come with me?" He paused, waiting for her answer.

"Sure. I'd like to meet him and find out more about Rachel's treatment."

"Great. I'll see you in the morning. I'll be out for most of the night. Remember, go to Quinn if you get into big trouble. Not Danny."

"Got it," she said following him with her eyes as he left, locking the door.

She ate a lonely supper of chicken Alfredo. If nothing else, Dale was a great cook. The orders to go to Quinn let her know the club wasn't as safe as she'd thought when she started working there. Nicer clientele but still not a suitable place to work

Chapter Sixteen

MARIAH ARRIVED HOME AT four AM after a busy night. Not being tired, she decided to work on her paper, hoping to find a piece she was missing in the section she was reviewing. She was pulling up various articles from her previous research when a loud knock sounded on the door. Jamison. No one else would be pounding on her door at this time of the morning.

A peek through the security hole proved her correct. Jamison and the minion who had been with him the last time were standing on her doorstep. Sighing, she unlocked and opened the door.

"This had better be important because I'm in the middle of working on a paper," she said, not bothering to hide her annoyance.

"I need to speak to you," he said with a slight smile.

Moving back, she indicated with her hand they could enter. She had no reason to refuse Jamison entry. Whatever they were going to accuse her of doing, they were wrong. The two men again glanced at the papers on the sofa and coffee table before going to the dining room and taking seats. She picked up her coffee cup before joining them. She didn't offer them the normal hospitality.

Jamison barely waited for her to sit before demanding, "Tell me about this deposit."

He slid a sheet of paper across the table that listed a deposit, the time and another $20,000. With the paper in her hand, she had to question why he was pressing so hard to frame her.

"I've no idea where this deposit came from. Again, it wasn't me. I was in front of a class giving a presentation to approximately one hundred classmates." She faced him and dared him to prove her wrong.

"I want to know why these deposits are showing up in your account and who you are paying to make them." Like her, he didn't bother to hide his frustration.

"I've no idea why someone would pretend to be me and put money in my account. You're the detective, go and detect." At this point, she didn't care if he was angry with her.

Jamison stared at the sheet she had pushed back to him. "Where are you working?" he asked, keeping his eyes on the paper.

"At the Platinum Slipper," she told him. His head came up, eyes wide. "I'm not a dancer. I'm a waitress on the floor."

A second later his eyes narrowed. "Who are your friends there?"

She had no idea what he was after. "I don't have anyone I would call a friend. I have those I work with and my few regular customers."

"Who are you dating from there?"

He had seen her momentary reaction. "It's none of your business who I may or may not be dating."

He leaned forward with an evil grin. "You might as well tell me. I'll find out before the day is done even if you don't."

Of course he would. Then he would create problems for her in the bargain. "Phillip Ortiz," she said.

Jamison now had his turn to show surprise. He stared at her before drawing his brows down, then said, "I'll be in touch. You had better have told me the truth. We're watching you since we know there's something going on where you are concerned. People don't have large amounts of money deposited into their accounts unless there's a reason."

He glared and let out a huff before stomping to the door. She followed to close and lock it again. A small opening in the curtain gave her a view of the car the two men entered. They appeared to be having some sort of disagreement. Jamison wasn't happy and that most likely wasn't a good thing.

Dale's voice behind her caused her to pivot from the window to him. "He won't give up. I hope you know that."

"I know. You'd think he would have attempted something different this time."

She moved back to her spot on the couch where she had been working. Frustrated, she backed out of the websites and apps she had been using and shut her computer down. When she glanced up, Dale was staring at her, his face grim.

"Unless your boyfriend stops him, he'll keep trying." Dale's voice was flat. His face showed no emotion.

Her eyes speared him with the anger his words had sent spiraling through her. "I don't have a boyfriend. Phillip is only a friend. Besides, what does he have to do with all of this?"

She wasn't sure she really wanted an answer.

With troubled eyes, Dale ran a hand through his hair and shook his head. "Forget I said that." He let out a noisy breath. "We'll be leaving at eight to see Father Rivers," he said before going back to his room.

With a clenched jaw, she followed him with her eyes. What the hell was that all about? Was he jealous, or did he mean something different? Did he know something about Phillip she should know, or was he merely guessing? After sitting in thought for a few minutes, she picked up her laptop and went to her room to get ready to meet with Father Rivers.

She also needed something to eat. Since Dale was in a snit, she might as well fix breakfast. Talk about quick one-eighties—he was a pro at it.

By the time she'd finished dressing and entered the kitchen, Dale was already fixing breakfast. After a quick glance in her direction, he ignored her while finishing the meal. She returned the favor. She fixed the coffee then set the table before sitting down. That was the least she could do, seeing as how he was cooking a decent meal rather than the bowl of cereal she normally ate.

He put a ham and cheese omelet on her plate along with toast before serving himself. After he said grace, he pushed his food around his plate instead of eating.

Without moving his gaze from his plate, he said, "I'm sorry about my comment earlier. I guess I'm not handling things the way I should and showed some jealousy there. You need friends, be they male or female. Meanwhile I need to remain only a friend until this is over."

Okay. He apologized for the spurt of jealousy, but— was he really out of line with his comment, or was there something she didn't know? Either way, she had to get along with him while he was living in the apartment.

"Thank you. I appreciate your understanding." She didn't add to her statement, not wanting to deal with the fallout created by anything else she might say.

Dale began to eat, but he was acting as if he wasn't hungry. With his attitude, spending the day in his company promised to make the hours together uncomfortable. Hopefully all of this would be over soon, and he would soon be out of her life. She didn't need to be hurt like she had been before leaving the farm.

With their silent meal finished, Mariah did the cleanup. When the time arrived to leave, she noted they were taking his car. He held the door until she got in, then went to the driver's side. Once behind the wheel, he put the key in the ignition but didn't start the engine.

"Mariah, I really do care a lot for you. Because I'm working this case, I have no choice but to keep things on an impersonal basis. I'm aware that I have no right to ask you to wait, but I'm so afraid of losing you to someone else after all this time." He ran a shaking hand through his hair. "I don't know what to do to show you how much I care without getting into trouble with my boss."

Now she understood. He was under orders to keep things professional between them. He had just explained the Jekyll–Hyde thing he kept doing. Now what?

"I get it. Phillip's only a friend. I made that clear when I agreed to go out with him. I only need a friend and someone to go out with and have fun with. But...," she hesitated, then faced him, "What happens in my apartment, stays in my apartment. You don't have to be so uncaring when we're alone like you do in public. I won't tolerate your kisses one minute and a cold shoulder the next. I need you to pick one way and stick with it so I don't feel like I'm being jerked around every time I see you."

"Got it," he said, then started the engine, and pulled out.

He had better have gotten it. She wasn't tolerating his about-faces any longer. The emotional rollercoaster had to end. It remained to be seen which option he picked.

They arrived at the treatment center by nine. Dale escorted her into the door marked reception, waiting until the woman behind the desk finished a phone call.

"Good morning. May I help you?" the woman questioned in a pleasant professional manner, but her smile didn't match her voice. The smile appeared to have been painted on and she couldn't take it off.

"Yes. I have an appointment to see Father Rivers at nine."

"And you are?" she asked, looking at an appointment book on the desk.

"Dale Warner."

"Yes. He'll be a few minutes late. He's with a client. Please have a seat, and he'll be with you as soon as possible." The receptionist motioned to the hard chairs along the wall, then proceeded to ignore them.

They sat in silence as the woman typed and fielded phone calls. It was close to twenty minutes before a priest in a cassock strode down the hall. His broad, flat face revealed he was of Mexican heritage. He wasn't tall, of average build, but his erect posture conveyed authority.

The aura of energy around him belied the age showing on his face. The brown eyes were alert, but coupled with the serene smile, he appeared to be a man at peace with himself and his life. His stride was long and even, leaving the impression he was floating over the floor in the cassock.

Without speaking to the receptionist, he came directly to where they were sitting.

"Mr. Warner, I'm so sorry to keep you waiting. I had a minor crisis to attend to and couldn't leave," His voice was melodic, soothing, and almost mesmerizing with its deep tones.

"I understand. Your work comes first." Dale shook the priest's hand. "This is Mariah, a friend of mine, and she was a close friend to the person we came to talk to you about."

"Come with me to my office where we can talk in private."

They followed him down the hall to a comfortable room with a desk and a conversation area. Two of the walls were lined with book-filled shelves. A colorful material covered the overstuffed cushions on the rustic wood furniture, contrasting with the dull carpet and white walls. A round center table set on a colorful woven rug that matched the colors in the cushions. Several books lay on the table surrounding a dried flower arrangement.

Dale directed Mariah to the sofa before taking a seat beside her. The priest took the chair opposite them.

"Now, how may I help you?" He had his elbows on the arms of the chair and his hands folded over his abdomen.

Mariah glanced at Dale. He took a breath, let it out, then spoke. "What are you able to tell us about Rachel Hartley? I know she was here for inpatient treatment and continued to follow up once she was released and went back to work."

"As you know, any specifics about her treatment are confidential. I can tell you she was one who didn't have a relapse making her a splendid example for the others here. She worked the program and stuck to it. In the five years she came here, she was always open and honest about her problem and her ongoing fight against the urge to use again. Her work environment wasn't conducive to staying clean, but she managed to overcome that hurdle and was doing very well."

He paused, staring at the table, and letting out a sigh before continuing to speak. "I can't picture her using again, but the police seem to think she was, along with helping the smugglers. I can't imagine her relapsing unless something happened that I was unaware of within the last two weeks she was alive."

Dale had been watching the priest as he talked. To Mariah, Rivers had gone from serene to sad then somewhat confused. Dale didn't show what he was thinking.

"Did she keep her appointment on the twelfth?"

Rivers shook his head. His forehead creased between his eyes, his face changing to troubled, his thumb rubbing his finger. He was almost like a chameleon.

"No. It was so unlike her to miss an appointment. She said she had something important to discuss with me when she scheduled the meeting, but then never showed up. I tried calling her, but all I got was a message that said her phone wasn't in service and to try again later."

"I take it she never called to cancel or explain why she couldn't be here," Dale stated for clarification.

"If she called, I never got the message. If she had contacted me, I would have gone and gotten her no matter where she was, and she knew it. I do the same for all of those who have completed rehabilitation and have a relapse."

He sat forward, moving a book on the table before speaking again, his voice changing back to sad. "She was a special lady who had experienced a hard life with a family who gave her everything but what she needed. The last time I saw her, she was happy. She told me she was moving in with her best friend and starting school."

When he raised his head, tears where running over his face. "It's so hard to lose someone like Rachel. I don't believe we'll ever know the truth about what happened to her."

Mariah swallowed hard, blinking back tears. "It was me she was going to move in with after I encouraged her to go back to school so she could get a respectable job."

Father Rivers smiled. "You meant the world to her. She talked about you often but never gave your name. You gave her hope for a better life than what she was living. She described you as this happy little fairy who flitted around, spreading joy and happiness to everyone who encountered her. Along with all of that, she said you showed her how to live a decent moral life while working in an environment which wasn't favorable to that type of lifestyle."

With a slight shrug, Mariah explained her philosophy. "It's a job, not a lifestyle. There was no way I was going to lower myself to what many of the girls are doing in those places. All I told her was that what she did as a job wasn't who she was and not to confuse the two."

Dale and Father Rivers stared at her as if she had said something unusual. Rivers commented, "Child, you're wise beyond your years. Many people will never see that one fact. You can keep your moral standards while working jobs which don't appear to allow you to uphold them."

Mariah glanced at Dale before saying, "I work as a cocktail waitress. It doesn't mean I have to date the customers or allow them to demean me or do things I find morally wrong. Rachel liked what she did because it gave her the money to live well, but she didn't date the customers or work the back rooms like many of them do. She told me one time that what she did was less objectionable than some antics she had seen on TV from entertainers who were fully dressed."

"Rachel also spoke to me about her reasons for keeping her moral standards and how she kept herself from being like the others. She said you were the best example of how to work in a job that didn't fit your morality," Father Rivers said.

Dale smiled. "Mariah had a good family who taught her well."

The heat rushed to her face at Dale's words. He was correct. Wes had already shown he would disown her if she was doing something against what she had been taught. The way

Dale said the simple statement showed he was like Wes with the same expectations.

"Would you like to see the facility?" Father Rivers asked.

"I'd love to," Dale said with a glance at her. "I've heard a lot of good about this place. From what I understand, you have an exceptionally high success rate. From everything I've read, and from what some of your past clients have said, this is an excellent rehab."

"We do our best. The biggest problem is the lack of beds for those needing inpatient treatment. We can't push people out who aren't ready. Crowding the facility with more than we can handle would only make us like many other treatment centers. Our waiting list is long, but we do the best we can." Father Rivers led them down a hall which connected to another building as he talked.

He took close to an hour to show them the facility and explain the different treatment modalities. The place was extensive, and as he said, it was full. The patients were all busy doing crafts, housekeeping, cooking, or other activities, but they also appeared to be happy with what they were doing. Father Rivers believed idle hands were open to the devil's work, so he made sure everyone did something they enjoyed while in recovery.

When he had completed the tour, they returned to his office. "I've been praying for Rachel's soul. Let me know if I can do anything more for you without breaching confidentiality," he offered.

Dale shook River's hand. "Thank you for your time, Father. I'll be in touch if there's anything else we need."

The ride home was silent. He seemed to be as deep in thought as she was. When they arrived back at the apartment, Mariah headed toward her room. She wasn't sure what Dale's plans were, but until he made it clear what he wanted from her, she was going to avoid him. His hand on her arm, stopped her.

"We do need to talk," he stated.

"About what?"

"You and me among other things."

She turned and flopped down on the couch, arms crossed and feet on the coffee table. "Okay. Talk."

Dale sat in the chair, leaning forward with his elbows on his knees and his hands clasped in front of him. He took a deep breath and let it out. "What is your relationship with Phillip?"

"Friend. I told you that this morning. He's taking me out to places where I can have some fun. We talk a little, but that's it. He's been a total gentleman with me. He says he has to make sure I'm real each time he sees me." She stopped and watched Dale who hadn't looked at her.

Dale stared at the wall while saying, "I care a lot about you. I know I'm not handling you going out with him very well."

Mariah rolled her eyes and sighed. "You aren't handling anything concerning me really well."

He lowered his head before admitting, "I really want to be more than a roommate, but I'm not sure how to keep things so they stay in the apartment. If anything about our relationship goes beyond here, we both could be put at risk. I don't want to expose you to more danger than you are already in."

She wanted to throw something at him but instead snapped, "If you care for me, then you had better start showing it on a regular basis. I'm not going to wait the rest of my life for someone who won't let me know how they feel. As it is, I've tried for eight years to get over you. I'll not wait another eight years for you to make up your mind as to what you want to do."

Mariah stood and stalked out of the room. He now had to decide if he wanted her. If he really cared about her, then he had better start consistently showing her how he felt. Until then, she was going to go out with Phillip and enjoy the attention he gave her.

She needed something better than the hit-or-miss courting Dale was doing. The bottom line to the whole situation was that she was tired of waiting. There was no way she was going to beg him for attention. He was a man and there was no better time than now for him to act like one.

Chapter Seventeen

PHILLIP WAS ALREADY AT the club when Mariah arrived for work. He was watching the girls on stage for a change, along with Santiago and two other men. The girls had improved their skills in using the pole. Well, at least they were acting like they were having fun while using the poles more than they had been. When she arrived at Phillip's table, he smiled at her.

"Good to see you Mariah. Santiago was pointing out the improvement in the girl's dancing. They must have taken a lesson or two with the pole." The two men returned to watching the girls.

Mariah watched for a few seconds. The dancers had a long way to go to even be considered decent. Without thinking she said, "They really need to take some classes to be good. At least they are having fun tonight."

With a crooked grin, Phillip turned to her. "And how do you know what it takes to be good on a pole?"

The heat rushed to her face when she realized what she said and his take on her words. Nothing like opening her mouth and inserting a foot. "They give classes in pole dancing at several gyms. It's great exercise but does take some practice," she informed him without saying she had taken the classes.

The attention of both Phillip and Santiago flipped completely to her. Phillip tilted his head, a smile playing across his lips. "If I'm not mistaken, you have taken one or two of those classes," he said, daring her to deny it.

"One or two. Like I said, it's great exercise." Okay. The men had the truth. She knew how to use a pole.

Santiago chuckled before saying, "I'd love to see you do a routine on one of those poles."

Her sharp glare had both men laughing at her. "I don't strip!" she snapped, indignant at Santiago's insinuation.

Phillip drew her fiery gaze to his when he took her hand. "I would never dream of asking you to strip, but I'd like to see that routine. I would love to see what a pole is really supposed to be used for other than to hang onto while barely moving."

"You're welcome to join me at the gym this Wednesday evening. That's when I take the class," she said, hoping they would now drop the issue.

Becker came to see what was holding her up at the table, not sure if there was a problem. Phillip grinned but didn't turn loose of her hand. "I would love to see her use that pole. She just admitted she takes classes at the gym to learn how to do it right."

"I'd pay her two thousand cash to do one exhibition. I've seen her routine and you wouldn't believe what can be done with one pole and someone who knows how to use it," Becker grinned at her. She glared at him, ready to run and hide.

The last thing she wanted Phillip and Santiago to know was that he had seen one of her routines. Two thousand was the pay for a week for most of the dancers, plus their tips. Becker wanted her on stage, not serving drinks.

"Not happening. I'm a waitress, not a dancer," she informed them, her face still hot from all the attention.

One of the men said, "I'll add another two thousand if you do one exhibition, totally clothed."

Santiago and the other man also agreed to give her two thousand for one routine. Phillip saying, "I'll double it all for one exhibition," had her staring at him. That would be a total of $16,000 for a simple routine on a pole.

Phillip tugged her closer to him. "Please Mariah. One time only. For me. You can change into sweats for all I care. I just want to see what you can do with a pole and some music."

She glanced down at her outfit. She could do it in what she had on if she added the straps that came with the top. She lifted her eyes to Phillip. He mouthed the word *"please"* to her.

Knowing it was wrong, she said, "Okay. Fully dressed. One time only." She turned to Becker. "Don't ever ask me again. If you do, I'll quit."

Becker rubbed his hands together, a big smile on his face. "Boys, you are in for a real treat." He inclined his head toward Mariah. "Next show since this one's almost completed." He left to make sure everything was ready for her.

She took the orders for the table, needing to focus on the customers until time for the next show. She had a half hour to wait. What had she gotten herself into? When she delivered the drinks to Phillip's table, he pulled her down to talk so the others couldn't hear.

"This is the only time I'll allow you to do this, darling. You better make sure you stay covered."

Her eyes widened at his words. He didn't want her to strip. Apparently, he had a standard for the women he dated and it didn't include removing their clothes in public.

Becker met her at the bar, motioning her to him. "You have five minutes. Go pick out your music and whatever else you need to do to get ready."

She nodded and left him to go to her locker. She attached the straps to the top, hoping she wouldn't fall out of it while upside down. The shoes she could remove before going on stage since she needed her bare feet or soft shoes for what she was going to be doing.

Backstage, she chose the music she wanted to use. Quinn, who was the backstage guard for the evening, studied her before commenting, "I wouldn't have ever expected you to dance on stage."

She bent her head to hide her fear and shame. "I'm not dancing. I'm giving a pole exercise exhibition fully dressed. It's a onetime only thing." She glanced at him before adding,

"It'll be nothing more than a gym routine I do twice a week. I'm not even going to attempt to make it sexy because it's exercise for me."

He continued to stare at her. "Okay. I'll be here if you need me." He looked away before saying, "I guess the guys offering to pay big money helps make it worth doing. I let Danny know you weren't stripping. He was having a meltdown over his little elf dancing."

She took her shoes off and let out a big breath. "I can imagine. This is as close as I'll ever get to dancing. Like I said, one time only."

"I guess Phillip had something to do with you agreeing to this." His eyes sought hers.

She met his direct stare before glancing at Becker, who was talking to the girls who were scheduled for this show. "Yes, he did. He told me to make sure I stayed covered."

Quinn smiled before bending over and startling her with a kiss on the cheek. "I guessed as much. Like Danny, he doesn't want to share his elf. I agree with them, too."

She flashed him a smile, less ashamed of what she was about to do before heading to the center pole to wait for the curtain to go up. Two of the girls were going to be on the other poles, but she knew they wouldn't be getting much attention this show.

The curtain rose, and the music started. Without looking at the audience, she twirled around the pole until the song's introduction was over. Listening to the music, she did the routine she had perfected at the gym. It was very athletic but followed the music. On the stage, she didn't hear the gasps and appreciative murmurs from what she was doing. The routine took a full thirty minutes to complete. When the last bars of the music sounded, she twisted and dropped from the pole and swung around it. She curtsied before the curtain was dropped.

Becker rushed to her, picked her up and hugged her. "That was fantastic. Absolutely fantastic." He walked her off the stage, then stopped. "Look, I'll pay you six Gs a week for one show on Friday and two on Saturday. You can keep your clothes on."

She hung onto the chair as she put on her shoes before answering him. Even though he was offering a lot of money, she couldn't accept the offer. If she did, that would change her from waitress to pole dancer. "Thanks for the offer but this was a onetime thing. I told you that before I said I'd do it. Register a couple of the girls in the class who really want to do what I did. You'll get what you want with less money and more shows."

He moved so he was blocking her exit. "They wouldn't be the same. You have this innocent, mystic quality that captured every man the minute the curtain went up."

She understood what he was saying. "That would only last for a few weeks. After that, they would want to see more and more of me. Not happening."

A smile crossed his face. "My guess is Phillip is behind the onetime only thing."

With a raised brow she said, "He wanted to see the routine only. I wasn't about to strip, and he knew it."

Mariah turned and went toward the locker room, only to run into Phillip entering the darkened hallway. He bent over and gave her a passionate kiss. Fear coursed through her, now worried he would want more than she was willing to give.

"Sweetheart, that was beyond believable! It was worth every penny we offered to pay you." He handed her a wad of cash with a big smile. "You'll have to collect from Becker, but this is from our table plus a few tips from those around us. Your friend Calvin added a really big tip before telling me I was one very lucky man."

The cash was more than she had ever held in her life. Phillip had handed her over $25,000. Tears welled at the realization of what she had done, even if it was one time only. She had joined the dancers.

Her head hung as she blinked back the tears. "Thank you. This will almost pay the tuition for a year at law school." A tear escaped, dropping onto her hand. "I shouldn't have done it."

She attempted to push past him, but his arms came around her. Tears of shame coursed down her face. He held her for a few seconds before picking her up and moving to a more secluded area, holding her on his lap as she cried.

"Don't cry, mi querida amor. I do understand. I see how your self-respect means more than the money we offered." His arms tightened around her.

"I shouldn't have done it. Even the one time." She began to cry again, hating herself for agreeing to the exhibition.

"Querida, I understand. I really do. I won't ask you to do anything like this again. Ever."

Her eyes met his. He was serious. He would never request her to pole dance again in public. Somehow, he understood what it had cost her to do the one show. He kissed her forehead and held her tighter to him.

"Please forgive me for pushing you into doing the routine, even though it was one time only. Deep down, I knew better. I'm so sorry. How can I make it up to you?" his voice hitched as if he were ready to cry as well.

Unable to look at him, she nestled further into his embrace. "I had a choice. You didn't push me. It was a challenge and I took it, not thinking like I should have. Not until Becker offered me a ton of money for three shows a week fully clothed did it enter what I had done."

Soft fingers under her chin tilted her head so she was looking up at him. "You didn't do a darn thing wrong. An exhibition of gymnastic pole dancing isn't the same as stripping, even if done in a strip joint. You have nothing to be ashamed of. Nothing at all. In fact, what you did was amazing in how you took it from the sleaziness, which is normally associated with pole dancing, to something that was beautiful, innocent and extremely athletic."

Her eyelids covered her eyes as she played with a button on his shirt. "I still feel like I did something wrong. I shouldn't have done it."

"Look, mi amor, you have nothing to be ashamed of in that routine. Not one thing was suggestive or sexualized in the whole exhibition. I now know where you get all those muscles you have." He ended with a chuckle.

She met his gaze. He was proud of her, along with something else she couldn't understand. "Okay. I guess I can live with the innuendos and increased proposals for the next couple of weeks."

"If they don't back off, let me know. I won't let anyone hassle my elf."

Her eyes widened at his words. His elf? Was she really his? He smiled as if reading her thoughts.

"You're my girl and my elf. Regardless of what I think or want, it's up to you where we go in our relationship. I won't push you for more than you're willing to give, now or in the future.

"I'll only be a phone call away if you need anything. Day or night. You didn't lose my respect with what you did out there. If anything, your reaction showed your real character. Tell me if I ever ask you to do something against your moral code. I don't want to ever see you cry again because of me."

Her arm went around his neck. She pulled him down and kissed him. A smile lit his face before he set her back on her feet.

"You'd better get back to work, and I'd better rejoin my friends before rumors start."

He was right. The others would assume they had gone to a private room. If that made the rounds, she would have more problems than she wanted to deal with now or ever.

Without asking her, Phillip undid the straps from the back of her top. With a wink, he gave her a quick kiss on her cheek and left. She was back on the floor a few minutes later. Bob, who was tending bar, came and handed her a wad of cash. He wasn't smiling.

"That's from the men in the pit. I'm sure the other girls kept what the others told them to give to you." He started to leave, but she put her hand on his arm.

"Bob, what you saw was a onetime mistake. I'll not do it again. Ever." She sighed and turned away from him, the shame making her want to cry again.

"Ahem," Bob sounded, clearing his throat. "I'll accept that, but don't you ever disappoint me again, Mariah. You aren't one of the sleazy show girls. You're classy and don't need to show off to get tips."

"I know. I let a challenge push me into doing something I shouldn't have ever done. Trust me. This isn't something I'll ever do again." She met his gaze, her eyes pleading for his understanding.

He nodded. "Okay. I believe you. I also saw you weren't trying to get attention or make things sexy in your routine. You are one of the few girls with morals and I'd like to see you keep them."

Okay. She had disappointed him, herself and several others. Never again.

Danny met Mariah at the end of her shift when she was ready to leave. They were outside before he said, "Great show you did. You're damn good. The girls really need to learn how to do that."

Mariah took his hand in hers as they walked. "That was a gym routine. They can learn it if they want. I use it to keep in shape a couple of times a week."

Danny stopped, holding her in place as he scanned the parking lot. She glanced at him, then noticed the flat tire on the front of her truck.

"Damn it! That was a brand-new tire," she cried when she saw the slice. Danny handed her a note from under her wiper blade. Opening it, she held it in numb fingers.

"What does it say?"

She handed him the note. It read: *Back off or you will follow Rachel."* Danny scanned the lot again, moving closer to her.

"Mariah, whatever you are doing, leave it alone. Let the police handle it. This is a warning and one you need to heed," he said in a quiet voice as if someone could hear them.

"I haven't been doing a darn thing," she informed him before catching her bottom lip in her teeth. "Danny, I'm scared. I haven't done anything, and I keep getting threatened by the police and now this"

Danny held her for a few seconds before asking, "Do you have a spare?"

"No. I dropped it off to have a new tire put on. I had a sliced tire the other day at school. I put new tires on all the way around, believing the tire had blown out. I'll call the tow service come and tow it." She pulled out her phone and spent the next ten minutes giving information. She would have an hour to wait before they could get there.

"I'll send Quinn out to stay with you. I don't get off for another two hours and he's off now. Lock yourself in the truck until Quinn gets here," he ordered before hurrying back to the club.

A few minutes later, Quinn strode across the lot, not smiling. She opened her door to talk to him.

"Call Dale and let him know you have a flat without a spare so he doesn't go all bonkers," Quinn commanded.

With reluctance, she called and left a message on his phone. Quinn noticed the note in her hand. He took it from her and read it.

"You're in big trouble Mariah. Stick close to Dale and Phillip. They'll protect you." Her head popped up at his words. Dale *and* Phillip? A chuckle escaped him at her stare. "Yes, both for much the same reason. I'm keeping an eye on you here." He sobered. "I know you trust Danny, but I don't. Be careful where he's concerned. Phillip won't let anything happen to you for now. I'll let you know if that changes."

What in the hell did he mean? Not trust Danny? And Phillip wouldn't let anything happen to her *for now*? So much for safety.

Who could she trust? Wes? In a pinch, maybe, but unless she were in big trouble, he wouldn't help her. Dale? Sure, he would come to her aid, then throw her away like yesterday's garbage when it was all over. Phillip seemed to be suspect, according to Quinn, but then again, why should she trust Quinn? From what she could see, she had no one safe to turn to if this all went down the drain. She was on her own—only, she had no idea of what was happening or why.

Quinn didn't try to make conversation while they waited. His presence was comforting, but she didn't trust him. She had no idea who he was really working for. As the minutes dragged on, she leaned against the seat, unable to decide what to do next.

The tow truck showed up over an hour later. The driver refused to let her go with him. He was taking her truck to the tow lot. It would be delivered to the tire place in the morning since no one was there to receive it tonight. This meant another hundred added to the tow fees for a cab home, then to the tire place in the morning. It also met missing school in the morning or getting a rental for the day.

Quinn stopped her protest with a hand on her arm. "I'll take you home. You don't need to be hanging out at the tow lot and a taxi would cost a fortune from here."

"Okay. Let's go," she said as the tow truck left, pulling her truck behind it. Not until Quinn turned into the apartment complex did she remember that she hadn't given him her address. "How did you know where I live?"

"Dale," he responded with a smile. "I work with him on occasion, and he told me he had moved in to watch over you. He always knows where I'm living like I always know where he's at.

"Oh," she responded, remembering that Quinn was working undercover. "Thanks for the ride."

She was ready to close the door, when Quinn said, "You be careful. These are only warnings. I'd hate to have anything bad happen to you on my watch. Let Dale handle the investigation and you stay out of it."

She closed the door without answering him. He waited until she was in the apartment before leaving. The bowl rang as her keys hit it. The light over the stove was on, showing a paper on the table. It was a note from Dale.

"I got your message. Had to go out and don't know when I'll be back. Use Quinn if you feel threatened. Go to

Phillip if you need someone to stay with in an emergency. I know he'll protect you. Dale"

She threw the note back on the table. Okay. It looked like he was wanting to get rid of her. Either that, or he was admitting he couldn't protect her like Phillip could. With Dale telling her to go to Phillip, she could only wonder about what ties Phillip had that made it so he could protect her better than Dale.

Chapter Eighteen

THE MAN IN THE mask stood before the statue, his hand caressing the old knife. He took a deep breath and closed his eyes. The smell of burning wax took him back to when he was a child, witnessing the special ceremony. Unlike the other priest, he had fulfilled his promises to Xolotl. He was the God of Death and death he had given him.

Two more days until the darkness came again. She was ready for Xolotl. She was the last before the special one who shone. That one would help them celebrate the moon going into hiding.

"Xolotl, help us keep her close. It's her blood you want. She is the virgin you require. We only need to keep her innocent. Her blood will be sweet with the power of the innocent. It will be like when you asked for the first one. This one will be your bride. A gift for you."

He ran his hand over the picture he held, a loving smile on his lips. "So much to do in so little time. She will be ready. For you Xolotl. She is for you."

Chapter Nineteen

Tuesday, September 8, 2015

MARIAH TOOK ONE LAST look in the mirror to verify she was ready for her date with Phillip. With a sigh, she worried her bottom lip. Dale had barely been here Sunday. He had taken her to the tire place Monday afternoon, leaving her to wait for them to put a new tire on her truck. She figured he was avoiding her. She hadn't talked to him since he admitted he cared for her after talking to Father Rivers.

Sadness filled her, resigning herself to Dale ignoring her until the case was completed. It wasn't what she wanted, but it did make sense. Would he step up when this was all done? Or would he continue to shy away? She knew what she wanted, but did he want the same thing?

She met Phillip in the same general area of the lot where he had picked her up for their last date. Phillip understood that where she lived was off limits to everyone. Santiago greeted her with a kiss on her cheek and a big smile.

"Mariah, let me introduce you to my girlfriend, Deanna."

Deanna assessed her with deep brown exotic eyes set in a perfectly oval face. Her mouth was wide with full lips topped by a narrow aristocratic Spanish nose. Long black hair fell in thick waves to the middle of her back. Mariah pushed back at the spike of jealousy for the exotic beauty.

Deanna and Santiago kept the conversation going until they pulled into a bowling alley. Mariah turned to Phillip with an eyebrow raised in question.

"I will admit—I like bowling, and I don't care what others think."

Santiago chuckled. "Señorita, he has liked bowling ever since he was a boy. He could have done anything he wanted, but he would go bowling every weekend. He saw bowling as a challenge for him to knock all the pins down. I go with him just to see if he will have a perfect game." Santiago lightly punched Phillip on the arm before he exited the Hummer and helped Deanna out.

Phillip followed after Deanna, then lifted Mariah from the high vehicle. Even though she wanted to tell him she could get in and out without help, she knew it would hurt his feelings. His smile, and the look in his eyes let her know he enjoyed touching her for those few seconds. She was his fairy or elf, and he wanted to treat her as such.

Phillip wasn't just a good bowler; he was an excellent bowler. Santiago wasn't a slouch either. She and Deanna weren't horrible, but they weren't in the same league and the men. The men scored over two hundred for all three games.

Meanwhile, Deanna kept her score in the hundred and thirties, Mariah had an average of one hundred and fifty-eight. Before changing jobs, she had bowled with the league at the Golden Cat, it being one of the few group things she participated in since moving to El Paso.

"Hey, you didn't have a bad score." Phillip's soothing voice caressed her. His hand brushed her hair back from her face.

Mariah raised her head. "It wasn't my best score. I'm going to miss the league this year. I bowled on the team from the Golden Cat."

"Check with the bowling alley you like to use and see if they have any teams that need an extra player. I'd offer you a spot on my team, but our night is Thursday and you work."

She knew he would have made room for her on his team if she wasn't working.

"Ready to go dancing?" he asked.

"Only if it's someplace we girls won't look out of place in what we have on," Deanna said, giving Santiago a sharp glare of displeasure.

"Country goes with jeans," Phillip said, giving Deanna a hug.

"Yeah," she said, sending another glare at Santiago. "Come on, Mariah. Let's go freshen up."

While moving through the bowling alley, the beautiful girl groused, "They do this to me all the time. We're going bowling, so I dress for bowling. Then they decide to go somewhere else. I hate it when they do that!"

Mariah giggled. "It's a man thing. They don't see that we'll look out of place in some of the clubs in old ratty jeans and tees."

"I guess so." Deanna's face lit with a smile. "At least this time I'm not alone in looking odd. I guess tennis shoes will work for country dances."

"They will for you. For me, I'll look like a dwarf next to Phillip in tennis shoes." Mariah tilted her head up to grin at Deanna who was at least a head taller than her. She turned to the mirror to check her makeup.

Deanna leaned against the counter. "I would give anything to be shorter. At five-seven, I guess I'm average, but you are so darn cute. I'm totally jealous."

Mariah met Deanna's eyes in the mirror. "Cute is okay, but it only goes so far. At five-one, I'm like a miniature next to most men. On top of that, I have to watch my weight, or I begin to look like the Michelin man." She lowered her eyes to her hands. "Deanna, I want to say how great it is being out with another woman who's so nice and not green with envy over my looks."

"I can't say I'm not envious of your looks, but I know I attract attention with my appearance, too. Besides, you're so good for Phillip. I haven't seen him so happy and relaxed in ages."

Mariah, without thinking, said, "I hope we can be friends with or without the men. I miss having my best friend around. I haven't had another woman to talk with since she's been gone."

"Oh. What happened to her? Did she move?"

The questions let Marian know she didn't think before speaking. If They were going to be friends, she might as well be truthful.

"No. She was murdered."

A pause ensued. Deanna asked, "What was her name?"

"Rachel. Rachel Hartley."

Tears formed in the beautiful girl's eyes. Deanna slowly turned to her. She put a hand on Mariah's arm.

"You knew Rachel?"

"Yes, we worked together." Mariah blinked back tears.

A gentle hand on her shoulder had Mariah looking into Deanna's exotic eyes. "I understand. She came to visit me on the eleventh and stayed overnight. Her excitement at starting school had her almost bouncing with joy. She told me she had a lunch date on the twelfth.

"The police came and talked to me two days later. They said she'd been doing drugs, but I don't believe them. Why would she use when she was going back to school and was so excited to be moving in with a close friend who she loved dearly."

"Like you, I don't believe she was using either."

Deanna sighed, "Rachel and I had been friends since grade school. I saw the worst and the best of her life. She was so put together when I last saw her. Happiness radiated off her as she talked about her plans."

"I was that best friend." Mariah wiped away a tear.

"Oh, my God," Deanna exclaimed, her eyes wide. A smile lit Deanna's face when she leaned over to hug her. "I'm so glad to meet you. You did so much for her after she got clean. I was the one who encouraged her to go to Father Rivers and get into treatment. Santiago said it was the best rehab center in the area. I wish I knew what really happened to her."

"Me, too. I know they have it all wrong, but proving it is another whole story." Mariah took a deep breath before saying, "We'd better get back to the men before they send in a search party for us."

With a musical giggle, Deanna agreed. "You're so right. Let's go."

The men didn't comment on their time away from them. They ended up going to several clubs before deciding to quit for the night. On the way back to her truck, Mariah became quiet as she thought over what she and Deanna had discussed.

"You okay, Mariah?" Phillip asked.

"I'm okay. I was just thinking about Rachel." She didn't notice the look between Phillip and Santiago as she smiled at Deanna. "I found out Deanna and Santiago knew her and helped her to get clean. I still can't see her relapsing when everything was going right for her."

"Celebration maybe?" Phillip said.

With a shake of her head, Mariah said, "It doesn't fit. We were going to celebrate by going for a two-day spa treatment. It was her idea. She said it would make us both feel like different people."

A tear escaped and ran over her cheek. Phillip's gentle thumb wiped it away before tilting her head up. "Honey, you need to take the time to grieve for her. You may never know the truth about what happened, so you need to come to terms with that, also."

"You're right. I've been taking time to grieve, but trivial things keep bringing back memories. The pain of losing her is still fresh. I'm sure that with time, it won't hurt so much."

"Things will get better," he promised before kissing her forehead and pulling her closer to him, not turning her loose until the Hummer stopped beside her truck.

"Next Tuesday?" he asked.

Giggling, she answered, "Sure. I guess I'm your Tuesday girl."

"My only girl," he corrected.

"Really?" she said, not believing him. "I can't see you going out with only one girl."

Santiago chuckled then said, "You're his only girl. I'm surprised he's taken you out twice, let alone asked for a third date." He grinned at Phillip, but he had an undertone to his voice that made her turn back to Phillip, who had reddened beneath his swarthy skin.

"Like I said, I don't date much because most women aren't interested in the real me." He met her gaze with pain and hope showing in eyes that were normally neutral.

"I understand. I don't date much since most men aren't interested in what's under the exterior. You're the first man I've agreed to go out with for a third time," she admitted.

With a nod, he got out and lifted her down. After she unlocked her truck, he opened the door, then lifted her onto the seat. They gazed into each other's eyes. He leaned in and gave her a tender kiss.

"I'm interested in you. Please give me time to get to know the lovely lady under the otherworldly exterior."

Her heart skipped a beat. He was afraid she wouldn't continue to go out with him. Her hand touched his face and tracked his jaw. "You'll have time to get to know me as I hope to have the time to get to know you." Like him, she was afraid.

"All the time you need," he murmured before brushing his lips across hers again.

She swiveled so she was facing the windshield. Phillip closed the door. He waited for her to start the truck and pull out. Mariah did what she could do to keep from crying on the way home. He was doing everything right, but he wasn't Dale.

At home, her keys rang as they hit the bowl after she locked the door. She curled into the corner of the couch, laying her head on her hands. She attempted to figure out what she had missed in her conversation with Deanna. Whatever it was, it was important. Then there was what Phillip had insinuated about his feelings for her as they parted. She had little experience with men, and absolutely none with men like him.

Deep in thought, she didn't see or hear Dale until he leaned over and kissed her cheek. She peered up at him, her eyes troubled. He sat beside her and pulled her onto his lap and held her, cuddling her into him. The tears welled up, spilled over, and rolled off her chin. She missed Rachel. The safety of Dale's arms made her comfortable enough to show her emotions.

When she was down to sniffles, Dale held her close to him and asked, "You okay now?"

"I think so." She wiped away the last of the tears, not wanting to move from his embrace.

"Want to discuss what brought this on?"

She curled closer to him before telling him about her conversation with Deanna. She then gave Phillip's take on it on the way back to her truck. He tensed when she talked about Phillip, but he didn't walk away from her as she feared he would. Instead he handed her a tissue before running a hand over her hair.

He gave her a few more minutes before asking, "Did Deanna know who Rachel was meeting?"

That was what she had missed! "She didn't say, and I didn't think to ask."

"I understand," he said, not condemning her for not getting all the information.

He laid his head on hers, his arms pulling her closer to him. He didn't talk, yet he appeared to know that she had needed someone who cared enough to let her cry and miss her friend. She closed her eyes and listened to his heart and soft breaths.

The next thing she remembered was waking up in bed alone. Her crying then falling asleep in his arms was becoming a habit. She closed her eyes again, emptying her thoughts while relaxing, letting her body regenerate for a while longer. For the first time in an exceedingly long time, she was comfortable lying down and didn't want to leave her bed.

Chapter Twenty

MARIAH WAS ALREADY UP and working on her paper when Dale joined her at five AM. He sat quietly until she finished typing before speaking.

"You want to go for a run this morning? I need the exercise and time to think," he said,

Apparently, he also used running time to sort out issues in his life. If he didn't insist on talking, she could handle him running with her a couple of days a week.

"Sure. Let me go and change."

He was waiting for her when she left the bedroom. From the keys in his hand, they were taking his vehicle today. He parked where she normally did. When they made the turn for the trip back to the car, she recognized the two men following them. Dale gave a slight nod that he had also seen the two men. This time the black sedan didn't follow them back to the apartment.

She showered and changed for class. Before she left, Dale said, "Be careful. I'll see you this evening."

His stare said it all. She felt like the chastised child and him the parent. He was right, she did need to be more careful. The men had been in the open and could be recognized which was a warning in and of itself.

"Okay. I need to get some groceries, so I'll be about an hour later getting home."

He acknowledged her information with a nod. She had something to look forward to for this evening. He would be there, but which Dale would show up?

Her last class was canceled for the day due to the professor having an emergency. Their assignment had been left on the board. This meant she could take some extra time at the grocery store, getting everything she needed without having to rush.

She was putting the last of her groceries in the truck when two men in suits moved in her direction. She pushed the cart away and climbed in the truck, locking the doors. The men stepped up their pace toward her.

Adrenaline pulsed through her veins. Her heart sped up until it was like a pianist playing 'The Flight of the Bumble Bee.' When the engine came to life, she threw the truck into gear. The tires squealed when she punched the gas backing out of the parking spot. She shifted into first gear. One of the men tried to open her door. Giving the truck more gas, she saw him fall. The second man stopped to help him up.

With a quick check for traffic, she pulled out onto the street before checking her mirrors to see if anyone was following her. After making several turns to ensure she wasn't being followed, she headed home. Two blocks from the apartment complex, she passed a police car parked at the curb.

She had barely gotten past them when the car pulled out behind her, lights flashing. Her speedometer showed she was speeding. A ticket she could handle. But the two men who had been after her, she wasn't so sure she could handle them.

A half a block later, she found a safe place to pull over. The parking lot of a strip mall was the best she could do to avoid having them following her into the apartment complex. By the time the officer got to her door, she had her license, registration and insurance card in her hand and her window down. She waited for him to speak.

"Get out of the truck," he ordered.

She unlocked the door and slid down from the seat before reaching back for her purse.

"Don't move," the officer commanded.

Freezing, she slowly turned her head to find a gun pointed at her. "I was only getting my purse," she informed him.

"Back away from the vehicle," he demanded.

Doing as ordered, she moved away from her truck, keeping her hands visible. The last thing she needed was them shooting at her. Two more police cars pulled into the parking lot, blocking her truck in and stopping anyone but the police from getting close. They opened their doors, guns drawn. She froze where she was and put her hands on her head to show she was no threat.

A female officer frisked her thoroughly before saying, "You can put your hands down."

"What is the problem?" Mariah asked, watching as the officers started searching her truck.

The officer who had stopped her asked, "Where were you going in such a hurry?"

"Home. I was at the grocery store and two men accosted me, but I got away. I didn't realize I was speeding until you turned on your lights."

"Humph," he sounded, watching the others who were tearing her truck apart.

One came over to him with a baggie in his hand. Her eyes rounded as she watched them grin at each other. She now knew what was happening, and she had no way of stopping them.

The officer turned to her. "Appears to me that you have a slight problem here. Possession with intent to sell on top of speeding and eluding a police officer...." He let it hang with a smile.

She kept her mouth shut. Nothing she said would change things. Anything she said or did would be held against her. The officer put the evidence in another baggie before coming over to her. He took a hand and put the cuff around her wrist and tightened it.

Mariah felt her world falling apart while he recited her rights and cuffed her other wrist. She glanced up to see Jamison with a crocodile grin on his face. He had finally framed her. This time she had no alibi.

After booking her at the jail, they gave her back her phone to contact whoever she needed for help. She tried Dale first. No answer, so she left him a message, saying, "I wanted to let you know Jamison picked me up on charges of holding with intent to sell. I don't know when I'll be home."

She then sent him a text. Wes was the same. No answer. She didn't bother to leave a message. She typed "Thanks for not answering." After pushing send, she turned off the phone and handed it back to the officer.

Less than an hour later, she was taken to a courtroom for arraignment. With the evidence the officers gave, her bail was set at $50,000. Neither Dale, nor Wes, had that type of money. Before she was taken back to her cell, she asked, "May I call my employer to find someone to cover me?

They handed her cell phone to her. She called Becker at the number he had used to notify her about her orientation. He answered on the second ring.

"Mariah, what can I do for you?" he asked.

"I'm in jail. They say I had drugs in my truck with the intent to sell them. I don't have the money for bail, so I don't know when I'll be back at work," she said in a rush, swiping at the tears running down her cheek.

"What? You've got to be joking! Jail?" She heard the disbelief in his voice.

"I'm not joking. I wanted you to know. Like I said, I don't have the $50,000 bail, so I'll have to sit here until my court date. I don't know when that will be."

She didn't bother with the tears that were now dripping onto the floor. With nothing else she could do, she said, "I've got to go. They're indicating my time is up."

Becker quickly said, "Don't you worry. I'll let Phillip know. He'll get you out."

He hung up before she could get out that she would rather sit here. She turned off her phone and handed it back to the officer. Considering she wouldn't be able to answer a call, there was no sense in letting the battery go dead. Besides, if the phone was out of service, hopefully Wes or Dale would know she was in trouble.

The officer at the desk took her phone before she was put in a cell by herself. She sat on the cot with her arms wrapped around her midsection. The severity of her situation led to a sense of helplessness, hopelessness and fear. She couldn't expect Phillip to pay $50,000, or even $5,000 to a bondsman, to get her out of jail. No one she knew had that type of money lying around. At least Dale would know where she was if he ever got her text. The hope that he would have read her message and answered it was dashed when she had no messages. If she didn't answer after reading her text, he should know she was still in jail.

A female officer came to her cell after what seemed like an eternity of sitting and shivering in the dreary cell. "Lansing, let's go," the officer ordered and opened the cell door.

Not sure what was happening, Mariah exited the cell and walked before the officer to the end of the row of cells. The door opened and she went through it. After being let through the next set of doors, they walked down a short hall. When the door at the end of the hall opened, she saw Phillip standing there watching her come through.

"Let's get your things and get you out of here," he said when she neared him.

He remained close to her while she signed the required paperwork. They handed her purse to her, then her cellphone. She checked to see if her keys were in her purse. They weren't. That meant she couldn't go home. They had apparently left them with the truck.

"What about my truck?" she questioned, not having much hope of being able to get it tonight.

"Being held for evidence," the officer on the desk said, handing her the papers that said she was free to go and had to show up for court so Phillip could get his money back.

They were pointed to the exit. Phillip pulled out his phone and hit a button. A few seconds later, the Hummer stopped at the curb. He opened the door and lifted her onto the seat. She scooted over so he could get in. She sat with her head down and her hands folded on her lap.

"Where do you need to go?" he asked, studying her. "Don't you dare say work. Don't even think of going in tonight!"

"I'm not sure. Give me a minute to see if my roommate is at home."

Mariah turned on her phone and checked it. No calls or texts. She sent a text to Dale. *"Are you at home?"* While giving him a chance to answer the message, she sent a message to Wes letting him know she was out of jail on bail.

When Dale didn't answer the text, she sighed. "I guess a motel. The police have my keys and I can't get into my apartment until tomorrow."

"Not happening. I'll not leave you at some motel for the night." He faced the driver in the mirror. "Diego, home."

She couldn't look at him. "I can't stay with you."

"I won't leave you at a motel. Unless you have another option, you're coming home with me for the night. I have a big place with locks on the doors. You'll be safe. Now tell me what happened."

"Jamison found a way to frame me. Two men came at me in the grocery store parking lot. I got away but then got pulled over for speeding. Instead of giving me a ticket, the officer had me get out of the truck at gunpoint. They searched it and found a bag of dope that they said I was going to sell."

A heaviness settled in her stomach. All her plans, gone. All her hard work, gone. All her hopes, gone. All her dreams, gone.

"It was planted, but I can't prove it. I guess my chance of ever becoming a lawyer just fell off a cliff and crashed on the rocks. I'll end up in prison with a record because I have no way of fighting them."

She turned her head away to keep Phillip from seeing the tears. This meant starting all over someplace else with a new job, a new major, and a new career choice. Maybe she could earn enough at the Slipper before moving so she could just go to school. The realization that school would be useless entered her consciousness. Decent jobs would be closed to her with a felony drug charge and prison time. She was now stuck working in clubs or low-paying jobs for the rest of her life.

Phillip tugged her into his embrace. "It'll all work out. I know a decent lawyer who'll get the charges dropped. You'll still get to be that great lawyer you want to be."

Unable to face him she mumbled, "I can't afford a decent lawyer. I'll have to use what I have to pay you back for getting me out of jail. My guess is they'll figure out a way to make you lose the bail money."

"No, they won't, I won't be out a dime once you go to court, so don't sweat it. I'll make sure of the court date and time, so you don't need to worry about being there. I'm just glad Becker called me." He lifted her head until she was facing him before asking, "Why didn't you call your family?"

Her eyelids lowered. More tears welled and over flowed. "I did, but no one answered. I even sent a text and got no response. I guess they decided to let me extricate myself."

She wasn't about to tell him who her family was, or about Dale. With Dale not answering her last text, she figured he didn't really care what happened to her.

Phillip lifted her phone from her hand and went to her contacts. He added his name and phone numbers.

"Don't worry. I'll always answer. You now have someone to call."

He put her phone back in her hands.

Unable to take her gaze from her phone, she said, "Thank you."

Tears dripped from her face. He kissed her forehead before holding her close.

"I won't let anything happen to you, so relax."

The tears wouldn't stop. A man she barely knew had come to her rescue. Meanwhile, those who professed to love her, hadn't even bothered to attempt to contact her to find out what trouble she was in, or if she needed them. She rechecked her phone. No calls. No texts. Wes she could understand not answering her messages. At four AM, over ten hours had passed, and Dale still hadn't bothered to get in touch with her, even with the text asking if he was at home. Maybe he felt she was safer in jail. The least he could have done was to let her know that so she would get it when she got out.

The Hummer stopped in a circular drive. Phillip lifted her out of the vehicle. He walked her to the door of a large house in what she knew was a high-end subdivision. From what she could see, his business had to be profitable. The entry confirmed that he was either seriously in debt or had money to burn. It had marble floors, antique tables and an expensive vase, even if it was only an imitation. The mirrors had gilt frames and the picture was an original or a fantastic copy.

He guided her into the den. Once she was seated, he poured a drink for her, then one for himself. "Drink it. You need something after what you've gone through."

She took a sip of the expensive whiskey he drank. It went down smoothly. By the time she finished what he had poured for her, she knew she was drunk. Being sloshed was better than what she had been feeling.

"What about your truck?" Phillip asked.

Mariah ran her hand over her leg. The more she considered things, the more money she saw flying out of her bank account.

"They're holding it for evidence. I need to get my keys from them along with my groceries. I'm sure all the meat and refrigerated stuff will be spoiled. I guess I'll have to rent a car until I can get it back. That is if I can ever get it back."

What was she going to do? She had been honest in how she couldn't afford any lawyer he would recommend. Most of what she had saved would be used to get a car and hire a lawyer. Then she owed him for the bail money. He might need that money before they set a trial date. So much for school. All her time and money wasted.

When she finished this semester, she would graduate. But now, she could forget about trying to get out of the club. While working there, she would save as much as she could, then find something else to do to make ends meet. Maybe a waitress in some restaurant somewhere.

With nothing else to be done, Mariah saw her dreams shattering into tiny pieces. The criminal justice degree would never be used. No one would want a felon working for them.

Phillip sat next to her, pulling her out of the morose thoughts. "You don't need to rent a car. I have one you can use until you get your truck back. As to the lawyer, I'll pay him. He owes me, so he'll only charge me a tenth of what he normally would to defend you."

"I can't let you spend that much on me. I can afford to rent a car for a while. If the case looks like it'll drag on for a long time, I'll get a cheap junker until I get Whitey back." This is if they didn't invoke the right to sell it because she committed a felony.

He chuckled at the name for her truck. "I have a car you can use. It mostly sits here unless one of my staff wants to use it. No one will miss it, least of all me." He stopped her objection with a finger on her lips. "I won't accept a refusal. If you want to pay me back for something, then make it the bail money. It was my emergency fund."

She studied him before saying, "I can have that back to you in a couple of days. I need to get it from where I have it stashed."

"Deal. So, what can I do to make it easier for you to get home?" he asked.

"I need to get my house keys and the groceries from the impound lot. Once I have my keys, I can get into my apartment. I really don't want the manager to let me in because I lost my spare key."

The excuse was a partial truth. She had *lost* her spare key to Dale.

"Okay. Let me show you to a bedroom. You need to lie down and rest. I'll get you up at six. The police impound lot opens at seven. Hopefully I can have you home by eight and you can make your class."

At the bedroom door on the second floor, she turned to him.

"Thank you," she said, unable to think of anything else appropriate. The drink he had given her muddled her brain.

Phillip ran a hand over her hair. She looked up at him, unsure of how she felt about this man who had bailed her out of jail. He bent over and kissed her.

The kiss showed how he felt about her. Mariah wished more than anything that she could see him as more than a friend. A tear tracked down her cheek. He lightly wiped it away with his thumb.

"I'm sorry. I shouldn't have kissed you that way. Don't worry. I won't push for more than you want to give. All I ask is for you to let me feel what I do while I can. Like any fairy or elf, I know you'll disappear, and all I'll have left are the memories of my time with you."

She didn't stop the tears that followed the first one. "I would give anything to care for you in that way. You'll always be special to me." She couldn't help but see Phillip's true feelings. His face showed a love she had always dreamed of having, not even trying to hide it.

He turned her to face the room. "Go to bed. I'll wake you in time to eat and freshen up. You can find a nightgown in the closet if you want to use one. I'm sure my sister wouldn't mind."

Phillip left, closing the door behind him. Standing where he had left her, she closed her eyes, letting the tears run in rivulets over her face. If only she could love him like he deserved to be loved. She wouldn't short-change him or herself. They both deserved more.

She took a shower before putting on a nightgown from the closet and curling up on the bed to rest. No matter what she did, her life seemed to always end up in a tangled mess. Phillip loved her but she only loved him as a friend. Dale said he loved her, but she wasn't sure if that was true because of his actions. Wes, well, she had no idea how he felt about her. He had been her father figure for ten years, then coldly pushed her out and away from him, not bothering to contact her for years. He had even believed others that she was stripping without asking her about it.

Maybe the best idea after all was leaving and starting over someplace else. When the legal matters were resolved, that was something to consider. That is, if it was ever over. If she went to jail, she would be moving away and restarting her life where no one knew her. She would have no reason to stay here. No one would want her near them after she served time, even if it was for something she didn't do.

The knock on the door pulled her from the daydream she had conjured up to relax. "Yes?" she answered.

"Time to get up and get moving. "I'll meet you downstairs," Phillip said through the closed door.

She had to give him credit. He didn't push her for more than she was willing to give. The man would be hard to let go, even if she didn't love him like he did her.

She put on her clothes from the day before. They would have to do until she could get home and change. Going down the stairs, Phillip met her with a smile. He stopped her when she was on the third step from the bottom.

"I'm going to be very bad," he warned before pulling her close to him.

This time, his kiss was deep, and passionate. She couldn't stop herself from responding. She didn't want it to end, but knew if they continued, she wouldn't be leaving with everything intact, including her heart.

She hid her face in his shoulder, attempting to make sense of what had just happened. Why had her body responded so strongly to him? She didn't love him yet wanted him physically. This was a conundrum she never had to face before now.

"Mariah, I won't say I'm sorry about that kiss, because I'm not. I wanted to see if my elf had the fire I could see in her eyes. She does. It's up to you what to do with that fire."

"I can't," she said, plucking at his shirt before gathering the courage to let him know why, hoping he would understand. "This situation is like stripping. That's all part of the self-respect I was taught. You don't have sex until you're married, and you marry the one you love."

He scanned her face. She wasn't sure what he was looking for so intently.

"You're still a virgin!" The shock showed on his face when he realized what she said.

Mariah moved out of his embrace to sit on the steps, her arms around her knees. "It isn't a disease. It's a choice. I don't believe I'd still be one if I'd met you six years ago and you kissed me like that."

He joined her on the step. "I now understand. I wondered when I kissed you the first time and you reacted the way you did, like you didn't really know what was happening."

He stared at the wall and sighed. "You were raised with the highest moral standards. That, and I'm sure the lack of dates helped. If the man you're waiting on doesn't keep you, I'll take what you have to give and not complain."

Keeping her head down, she repeated what she had said last night. "I wish I loved you like you do me. I'll keep your offer in mind. If he walks away again, I may take you up on the offer. I know I'd never find another who would love me like you do."

He kissed her forehead. "Come. Breakfast is ready, and you need to eat." Phillip stood and helped her up. He displayed a calmness she wanted. Inside another slice of her heart fell, letting drops of pain spill from it.

Breakfast ended up being a lot of fun. Phillip started teasing her until she was giggling in merriment. When they were finished, he took two sets of keys from the cabinet by the kitchen door before leading her into a huge garage. Five cars were parked in it, but no Hummer.

"Okay, you can choose between the Lexus or the Mustang. Personally, I believe you'd like the Mustang better. It has a six-speed on the floor and enough horsepower to go from zero to sixty in less than forty seconds. The Lexus is comfortable, but more sedate. It's an automatic, gets great gas mileage and is dependable."

She eyed the two cars. He was right. She loved the Mustang. It would be fun to drive.

"The Mustang it is," he said without her saying which one she wanted, a knowing smile forming on his lips. He took out his cellphone and called one of his minions. "Bert, I need you to deliver the Mustang to..." he waited. She gave him the address. He repeated it to Bert before hanging up the phone. "It's insured for anyone to drive it. All I ask is for you to try to keep it in one piece. It's my play car when I want to be a teenager and street race."

She could see him doing just that. He was still a kid at heart when it came to cars. The Lexus was the only luxury sedan in the garage. There was a Jeep, the Mustang, a Camaro, a Corvette and what appeared to be a Ferrari. He liked fast muscle cars.

The garage door opened and one of the men she had seen at the club ambled to where they stood. He held out a hand for the keys. Phillip dropped them into the open hand. "I'll pick you up at her apartment, so wait for me. We need to take a detour to the impound lot first."

Bert nodded before going to the Mustang. "Boss, you take extra good care of her. I know of at least three people who'll come after you if anything happens to her."

Phillip chuckled. "I won't let anyone get to her. I have a vested interest myself."

Mariah had no idea what he meant, so she let it pass.

They were at the impound lot in less than thirty minutes. The man at the desk watched as she took the truck key off her key ring. She handed him the key and kept the rest of her keys. He stood outside and watched as she took the groceries from the back of the truck. No one had bothered to check what was in the bags. She lifted the bag of meat and walked to the trash and dropped it into the can. Fifty dollars wasted. She also trashed the melted ice cream, a half-gallon of milk, and ten containers of yogurt. The rest of the groceries quickly disappeared into the trunk of the Lexus.

She also took all her personal items from the cab of the truck. The man kept watch but didn't stop her or comment on what she was taking with her. The last thing she removed was a cooler bag. She put it in the trunk with everything else.

"That's it," she told Phillip.

He closed the trunk and escorted her to the passenger side, opening the door for her. She slid in and had her seatbelt on by the time he got into the car. When they pulled out onto the main road, she let her breath out with a whoosh.

"Okay, what was that all about?" he asked.

She caught her bottom lip in her teeth before saying, "I know this was all a setup because they didn't search my truck. If they had, they would have found the loaded gun in that cooler I put in the trunk. It's registered to me. I do have a concealed carry permit, but I normally open carry. I can't conceal anything of a decent caliber with more than two bullets unless I put the gun in my purse."

"What caliber is this one?"

"It's a forty-five. I bought it when I started to work at the Golden Cat. It lives in my truck and is normally where I can get to it without being seen. I still can't believe they didn't find it."

He glanced over at her before saying, "They didn't find it because they weren't looking for a gun. They were more interested in getting the drugs into the truck then finding them. I believe you just gave your lawyer a way of proving you were set up."

"I hope so. I don't need a record, especially where drugs are concerned."

He reached over and patted her leg. "You won't have a record. I want you to complete law school. You'll make a good lawyer."

"So I've been told by others," she said with a chuckle.

He pulled into the apartment complex, going directly to her building. Bert was there with the Mustang. Dale's car wasn't there, so he wasn't at home.

"Okay. You have my number. Call me if you run into any problems. Understand?" he instructed, his voice stern.

"I understand. Hopefully I won't have to use it to get me out of a jam again."

He leaned over and kissed her. "I don't mind. I'll see you tonight."

When she got out of the car, Bret handed her the keys to the Mustang. "Take good care of her. She's special," he said with a grin before helping Phillip bring in what groceries were left, along with the items she had taken from the truck.

She could see the men assessing her place. She still had papers all over the living room for her thesis. At least the kitchen was clean, and the dining room table didn't have a note on it. Apparently, Dale hadn't been home since he left yesterday morning.

Bert left Phillip with her, going out and taking the seat she had vacated in the Lexus. Phillip lifted her and sat her on the kitchen counter. He took a deep breath and let it out.

"Mariah, I'm worried about you and how you're being targeted. Please, if you get scared, call me, or just show up at the house. Someone will let you in if I'm not there. If I thought I could convince you to stay there for a while, I'd do so, but I know you won't."

She put a hand on his face. "Phillip, I can't stay with you. We'd both end up regretting it if I did. If I get scared, I'll come. But for now, most of what has been done to me is more of an annoyance than anything."

With a nod, he pursed his lips, staring above her head. "I'm going to have a couple of the guys check on you. I've got to know you're okay."

She smiled before saying, "Just don't mistake my roommate for a bad guy. I let him rent the extra room because he runs with me in the mornings. I've had a couple of guys following me, so he volunteered to be a bodyguard when I run to keep them away. Other than that, I don't see him much because he seems to work all the time."

He accepted her explanation of Dale. "I'll let them know. Stay close to home. If you want, I'll give you a bodyguard who can be on call for when you go places."

"Thanks, but I'll pass for now," she told him with a grin.

"It's an open-ended offer. Let me know if you change your mind."

He gave her a quick kiss before lifting her from the counter and striding to the door. He stopped, his hand on the knob. "Mariah, please check in with me a couple of times during the day and in the evenings when you are home, okay?"

"I can do that," she said with a smile. She would find the time to call him. At least he was worried about her, unlike Dale who still hadn't answered her text.

She watched as he pulled out before closing the door and locking it. Today, she was going to skip classes and work on her paper. She needed a day of losing herself in another world.

The time on her computer showed almost two PM when Dale opened the door and walked into the living room. She glanced at him, nodded and went back to what she was doing. He locked the door, then stood looking down at her.

"Where's your truck?" he asked.

Without looking up, she said, "The impound lot."

"What?" His voice sharp, his forehead a map of creases. He stared at her.

Mariah stopped what she was doing and glared at him. "If you'd read your texts, you'd know what happened." Sarcasm and condemnation fell from her words, landing between them.

"What texts?" he asked, frowning.

She picked up her phone and showed him what she had sent. It was the last one at the bottom of the ongoing text between them.

He checked his phone, lowering himself to the chair, staring at the text before running his hand through his hair.

"How did you get out of jail?"

"I'm out, so why does it matter to you how I got out? I called you first and sent you the text. I called Wes. Neither one of you responded. My last call was to Becker to let him know that I didn't know when I'd return to work. You figure out how I got out."

She closed her laptop and threw it on the papers littering the couch before taking a step toward her bedroom. Dale reached out and grabbed her wrist, stopping her.

"I honestly didn't see that text. My phone has been in silent mode since I left here yesterday. I was where I couldn't have it going off. I'm sorry."

"I understand."

"Do you want me to take you to get a rental until you get your truck back?'

"No. I have a car to use. The only cost is that I need to let the owner know I'm all right a couple of times a day. I also owe him the bail money. It was probably for the best that neither one of you answered. You couldn't have bailed me out and he could."

"You're talking about Phillip, right?"

With a sadness that swelled from deep inside of her, she nodded. "Becker called him. Somehow he figured out I didn't have Phillip's number with me."

She kept her face impassive, unwilling to let him know how he had hurt her by not responding. She hadn't expected Wes to call her when she didn't leave a message, but Dale, she had left a message and texted him more than once.

"I'm really sorry. What a nightmare for you. If I had gotten the messages, I would have dropped everything and done what I could to get you out."

"I didn't expect you to drop everything. A simple call back that you got the message was all I wanted. I needed to know you were there for me. As it was, Phillip had me out by one in the morning. He took me to his place until I could get the keys to the apartment. With you not responding when I asked if you were home, I figured it was worthless to call you to let me into the place."

Dale dropped his hand from her wrist. She didn't wait for what he would come up with to excuse his lack of response. When she closed the door to her room, she didn't slam it as she wanted. Instead, the door closed with barely a sound.

With the click of the latch, she closed the door to the chapter of her life where Dale and Wes were concerned. Neither one of them cared enough to find out why she had called. She wasn't important enough in their lives to pick up the phone even though they kept saying she was in danger. Now she had no one to rely on other than Phillip. Even he might become iffy if things got much worse.

Curling onto her side, she closed her eyes, going into the dream world where someone loved her, and she loved them back. The man no longer had a face, returning to the nameless, faceless person who was a total fantasy. An ethereal being who disappeared in the light of the day.

Chapter Twenty-One

Friday, September 11, 2015 Xolotl

THE DRUMS ARE CALLING. It is always the same. The sound becomes a part of me, echoing inside of me, pulling me into the ceremony. The drums and the blood. These are the things which haven't changed in the many years of my leading my people. No one understands the need for me to be here. If only we were many like we once were. This is a poor representation of the past, but Xolotl protects us like he has from the time the outsiders came and took away our lands and our religion. We will survive.

The long robe he wore swayed to the rhythm of the drums and chanting singers on his walk to the alter. The scent of the burning wax of the candles swirled around him as it always did. His grandmother had been right. He had been destined to lead the worshipers in their praise of Xolotl and saving the moon from the jaguar.

His sonorous voice joined the others in their praise of Xolotl. He began preparing the ancient green knife and the special cloth for the sacrifice, blessing them so Xolotl would be honored. He had done this so often it was now without conscious thought. He held the photograph of the current sacrifice to the flames. When it was consumed by the flames other than the corner he held, he put it on the metal plate to become ash, the symbol of her passing.

The photograph of the next sacrifice was placed face down to the left of the statue. He remembered the smile in the picture. She would be the worthiest sacrifice in memory.

When he closed his eyes, the sounds of the drum moved to inside of him, giving him the peace and courage to do what he must for Xolotl. The changing rhythm took his spirit to the underworld where Xolotl waited for him. A rush of sensations sent a shiver rippling through him as he and Xolotl became one, the ecstasy swelling him until he was no longer contained in the vessel the others saw. Xolotl was here, pleased with what he was doing.

The rhythm of the drums changed. He waited until the chant was said the required seven times before turning to watch the sacrificial offering being led to the alter. He was no longer the earthly being the others saw.

This woman wasn't worthy, needing drugs so she wouldn't object to what was required of her. This would be an easy one, but Xolotl wasn't happy. She wasn't clean, let alone a virgin, but she would appease the jaguar for now.

He smiled behind his mask. Soon. Soon he would have his virgin. When he finished that ceremony, he would become Xolotl, no longer melding with him only for the ceremonies.

Xolotl will live again through him, the high priest of the remaining Nahua.

Chapter Twenty-Two

SAMUEL MARTINEZ SAW THE cloud of flies in the bushes. There was only a slight smell, but he was certain something dead was the cause. Whatever it was had to have an open wound for so many flies.

In his twenty years with the border patrol he had seen it all. The small children who had perished on the way north. The coyotes who guided them, not caring if the illegals had food or water in the harsh, hot land. On top of all of that were the murders. Way too many over the past five years. He thought he had seen everything, but after finding four women brutally murdered, all in the same way over the past year, he wasn't so sure.

His partner, Hector, sat in the passenger seat, not moving. "Sam, you thinking what I'm thinking?"

With a grimace, Sam said, "Probably. It's about the right time and place. I wish they would find somewhere else to drop the bodies. I'm fucking tired of finding their garbage."

Hector's jaw muscles jumped from gritting his teeth, steeling himself for what he would see. "How many does this make for you?"

"It'll be my fifth this year. Let's go and see if I'm right." Sam reluctantly opened the driver's side door to the SUV and stepped out to the buzzing of the flies and the smell of death.

The noise became louder as they neared the bush. The men scanned the area for footprints or any other evidence they might find. Sam pulled the bush back and saw the body. Another woman, her abdomen slashed down the middle and the intestines sliced open. Why in the hell couldn't they find a better way to smuggle their drugs? Even if it was an addict, they didn't deserve a death like this.

Sam moved so he could see the woman's face, staring at a countenance he knew well. She was out of her misery. No longer suffering from the addiction she had embraced for over ten years. Slowly releasing the breath that he had been holding, Sam backed out of the bush. He pulled out a radio, making the call to notify their boss.

Hector glanced at the woman before turning away in haste. This was his first mutilated corpse. Rushing away from the body, he began emptying his stomach of his lunch and probably breakfast. Sam understood. He had done the same on the first two he had found. His boss, Wesley Lansing answered the phone.

"Sam, what's the problem."

"We have another body. Same as the other four, only this one I know."

"Who is it?"

"Maria Lopez. She used anything she could score. Worked as a mule for whoever would pay her in drugs." Sam turned away from Hector before saying, "Wes, whoever is doing this has to be demented. You can't mutilate women like this and be sane."

"We're working on a profile of the person. So far, we think the person is connected to a cult that still worships the old gods and believes in sacrifices. Our best guess is that someone in the cult is tied in with one of the cartels. From the autopsies, they are using the bodies to smuggle drugs if the intestines are cut open. They sacrifice the person, then someone retrieves the drug packets after the body is dumped on this side of the border."

Sam could hear Wes tapping his pen on his desk, a habit his boss had when thinking. "You going to let Dale know, or do you want me to call him? He'll want to check the scene before the others get here and destroy the evidence."

"I'll call him. Stay there. I'll let you know when he'll arrive," Wes ordered before hanging up.

Sam sighed. This was going to be an exceedingly long shift. "Hector, you better get it together. We're here until the DEA gets here."

"Dammit Sam. You could have warned me what she would look like," Hector said, drawing in a deep breath and swallowing hard.

"As if it would have done any good. You'll get used to it after finding a few more. This one isn't too bad. At least it's fresh. Wait until you find one three or four days old. Those are the ones you'll hate. The smell alone is enough to make you empty your stomach of the past three days of food."

Hector turned back to the bush, gagging again. Sam grinned. Yeah, the kid had a lot to learn about this job and some of the horrors he would find on patrol. Sam returned to the SUV to get comfortable until Dale showed up to see the fresh scene without someone trampling all over the evidence.

Dale and Mariah were finishing breakfast when his cellphone rang. He glanced at Mariah, listening to Wes telling him what Sam had found.

"Thanks. Let him know I'll be there within the hour. Tell him to make sure no one goes near that scene until I get there. I'd like to examine one without it being totally contaminated."

"No problem. You going to bring Mariah so she can see what they're doing to the girls?" Wes asked.

"Why?"

"I take it you haven't explained who Ortiz is yet. Don't keep her in the dark too long. She needs to know about him and Santiago."

"Not yet," he said, avoiding looking at Mariah. "I'll see what the plans are for the day and go from there." Wes would guess Mariah was listening from his answers.

"Boy, you better not mess it up this time. She's been waiting for you for a long time. Her going out with Phillip is because she's desperate for someone to notice her along with wanting to have some fun. You're the one she'd rather be with, so get a move on, and let her know in no uncertain terms you love her and want her."

"Soon," he said before hanging up. Wes was right. He did need to make sure she knew he wanted her, and only her, but until this case was finished, he couldn't put her at more risk than she was already.

He studied his phone before speaking, keeping his voice neutral. "They found another body. Same pattern. Want to go with me to investigate this one? Before you answer, the body will be in bad shape. The last two were quite gruesome."

She didn't answer for a few seconds. "Sure, if you don't think I'll be in the way. I'd like to see what you do at a crime scene."

He hoped her wanting to go was for professional experience. If this was personal, he wasn't sure her coming with him was such a good thing.

"Be ready in five. I told them I'd be there in an hour."

Dale went to his room. He needed his gun, crime scene kit and ID. What he had on would work since the clothes were old and could be trashed if they got contaminated.

Mariah was ready when he reentered the dining room. She had cleaned up the dishes and changed into jeans, a t-shirt, and tennis shoes. Her hair looked like a glossy cap on her head, the light making it shimmer. He wanted to know how she managed to make it stay in place and shine like a halo around her head. She was so beautiful with a natural coloring around her eyes and on her cheeks. She didn't need to wear makeup to make her skin glow. The lips he wanted to kiss were always a rosy color.

He pulled his thoughts back to the murder, pushing away the yearning to kiss Mariah until she melted into him. Now wasn't the time. Later. When this was all over.

When they arrived at the crime scene, Mariah noted that Wes was there with the two border patrol agents. Anger spiked, making her tense. It was an anger she hadn't expected.

"Did you know he was going to be here?" she asked, ready to stay in the car and forget she ever agreed to come with him.

Dale frowned, glancing at Wes then back to her. "Of course. He's their supervisor and is required to be here. Wes was the one who notified me of the body."

She didn't say anything more, wishing Dale had warned her that Wes was going to be at the scene. Then again, Wes was her problem, not Dale's. She waited at the Jeep while Dale talked to Wes and the other men, wondering what she could find out about the murders while she was here. After a few minutes, being careful not to cross into the area the men were guarding, she walked around the perimeter, looking for anything out of place. She didn't want to disrupt the men's conversation.

No one paid attention to her as she made a circle around the bush containing the buzzing flies. On her second circuit, a glint of white caught her attention. The small clear plastic bag contained a white material. She took the tweezers from the grooming kit in her purse and picked up the small packet, putting it in a tissue from the pack Phillip had given her on the way to his house.

A few seconds later, she found a second packet near a footprint. Leaving the packet there, she headed back to Dale and Wes who were still talking.

Her hand on Dale's arm made him stop in midsentence. He turned his head to look at her.

"Need something, Mariah?"

"I think you might want to see what I found over there." She pointed to the area where she'd been walking.

"Can it wait a few minutes?" Wes's voice showed his displeasure at her interrupting them.

She took Dale's hand and placed the tissue on it before carefully opening it, not touching the packet it contained.

Her eyes were on Dale when she spoke, ignoring Wes. "There's another like it over there near a footprint. I didn't touch that one. I used tweezers to pick this one up. I can show you exactly where it was."

Her eyes slid to Wes's glowering face before she pivoted to walked away. Dale didn't need to get in trouble with Wes because of her. A gentle hand holding her wrist stopped her. She waited to see what the person wanted, not sure if it was Dale or Wes.

Wes's soft drawl commanded, "Show us where you found this and where the other one is."

Without looking back, she took them to the footprint, staying on the path she had taken earlier. When she stopped, Wes held her in place as she pointed to the location where she found the other packet.

"Well, can we say someone screwed up?" Wes said, not releasing her.

Dale took a step closer to the footprint, scanning the area closely. He squatted and studied something she couldn't see. The expression on his face was grim.

"Looks like two people and they were in a big hurry. I wonder if someone intruded on their little dissection party?" Dale said before standing.

"Let me get the troops looking for a second body. If they were discovered before getting all the drugs, they may have killed the intruder, then took off, not waiting to see if he had buddies around." Wes strode back to where the cars were parked.

"Good find," Dale said, smiling down at her. "We most likely would have missed this. I knew I had a reason I wanted you to come with me."

She mirrored his smile before saying, "If you're looking for a second body, try over there under that tree. I see a concentration of flies over there."

Dale scanned the area where she was pointing. Turning back to her, he asked, "Sure you haven't had training in crime scene investigation?"

"I haven't, but what I have done is to study crime scene descriptions and how the investigators worked to prevent destroying evidence for a couple of my classes. I hope my picking up that one packet doesn't create a problem for you."

Dale chuckled. "Honey, you did more to preserve the evidence than many experienced crime scene workers. I'll need a team here to get a cast of that print and pictures. I'll let Wes know to start over at that tree for the second body."

Dale joined her, keeping to where he had stepped. When he got to her, he put his arm across her shoulders, before walking back the way they had come. "You are about to see what these people are doing to the women. What you read in the newspapers is nothing like seeing the real thing. This is the way we found Rachel's body."

He didn't turn her loose, guiding her to where Sam was watching Wes photograph the body for his records. Mariah stopped, staring at the woman's corpse. She was naked except for a gauzy robe. Her face was a bluish color, but the rest of her skin was the color of tallow wax. The eyes were open and staring at the sky. Meanwhile, her mouth looked like she was screaming. Moving down the body, Mariah noted the gaping wound to the abdomen. Someone had pulled out the entrails which were sliced open starting with the stomach. From what she could see, the abdominal cut appeared almost surgical in nature with the clean sharp edges, but the bowels were a mess.

"I can see why they didn't include photos of the bodies in the paper. With that clean abdominal slice, I would think medical or a ritual of some sort. Since there isn't any blood, she wasn't killed here." She turned to him, frowning. "Were all the rest drained of blood before being deposited where you found them?"

"Yes. All of them. It was one of the connecting features for me. No blood. According to the coroner's reports, they all had a puncture wound to the heart. Putting it all together, them being killed in some sort of ritual makes sense." Dale had kept his arm across her shoulders. He now pulled her close to him.

She leaned into him before asking, "What do you think is in those packets I found?"

"My best guess is the new stuff they're running. Even without those two, they'll have gotten over five million from the body. Those little baggies are worth close to, if not more, than a half a million once they are cut and repackaged for sale."

"Where are they selling it? I've only heard rumors about a new drug on the market." She tilted her head to view his face.

"You wouldn't have heard about it yet. It's still with the users who are big spenders. It's extremely expensive due to the limited amount they can get. From what we can tell, they've only sold a fraction of what they've gotten from the women. Our guess is they're stockpiling it until they see how well it sells or if any major problems arise with the drug, like a high death rate. If that's the case, they won't continue to sell it except to a select group of dealers."

"Humph," Mariah sounded. "They need to find some other way to earn money."

"Oh, they have other ways of making money, but drugs are the biggest and easiest money maker for them. As long as people want drugs, they'll sell them."

"People are so stupid. You can stay high on life which makes using drugs unnecessary," she said, more to herself than Dale.

Dale didn't comment about her observation. Instead, he told her, "Go on back to the car. I need to speak to Sam before I leave."

Dale waited until she was on her way to the car before going to Sam. Like Wes, he had worked with the older man since he had joined the DEA.

"Sam, you have anything for me besides what I see here?"

Sam turned and walked away from the other men who had shown up. When they were at a spot where they couldn't be overheard, he kept his voice low, giving Dale what information he had.

"I spoke to Javier of Juárez a couple of days ago. He was over here trying to drum up some business. He mentioned he had heard that the Sinaloa Cartel is using a religious cult to get their new stuff across the border. He also said quite a few women have disappeared over the last couple of years and all were found dead. He heard about a connection to the cult and the murders."

Dale stood for a few seconds, digesting the information. "Any way of substantiating any of what he said or heard?"

Sam stared off at the men who were working the crime scene. "Not unless you believe him when he said there has been one murder a month for over three years that he knows about. All women. All with an abdominal wound and opened bowels. All the women can be connected to the Sinaloa in some way. He also mentioned the last one, a woman named Rachel, was used because she had discovered the connection."

Their eyes met. One more piece in the puzzle now fit. That would explain her diary entry just prior to her death. She must have discovered who the leader was or what they were doing. "Makes me wonder if she discovered the path of the drugs from the makers to the dealers."

Sam shook his head. "I don't think so. I believe she stumbled upon who. That's what Javier thinks too. She had to go. What more fitting way could they have come up with than using the method she had discovered."

"And what she found has put Mariah in the mix since they were good friends," Dale added.

Things were beginning to come together. The problem was finding out who, then getting the proof to arrest them. Dale sighed. Mariah didn't know she had gone from bad to worse when she changed jobs. At the Golden Cat, the bad guys were obvious. At the Platinum Slipper, they weren't seen, but they were there, and were much more dangerous.

"Thanks Sam. I appreciate it."

Sam put a hand on Dale's arm before he could walk away. "Dale, you better keep a good eye on her. The word is she's the next one on the list. According to what Javier said, she will be the main attraction at the upcoming blood moon ritual."

This time Sam didn't stop him as he walked away. Dale needed to find out about this blood moon and when it was to happen. His resources were stretched to the max and Wes couldn't help him. He was also without enough people for this case.

Dale questioned if Ortiz was part of the cult. He knew the man and was even friends with him, but if he was, Mariah was in major danger. If he wasn't, did he know about the cult and could he keep Mariah safe? Way too many *ifs* floated around. He was beginning to think he needed to go and talk to Javier himself.

He found Mariah leaning against the Jeep. He had locked it and she couldn't get in to sit down.

"Sorry," he apologized, hitting the unlock button on the keychain.

"Not a problem." She opened the door and slid into the seat. Before Dale started the car, she said, "I've seen little bags of white powder changing hands at the club. I thought it was cocaine, but now I wonder if it's the new stuff."

The spike of fear whizzed through him at her words causing him to stiffen. "Is anyone aware of you seeing the exchanges?"

"I don't think so. I act like I haven't noticed a thing and do my job. The last thing I need is for someone to target me for seeing them make a deal."

"Keep acting like you don't see a thing." He paused. "I'm going to drop you off at the apartment. I need to go and see someone this afternoon. I shouldn't be gone too long."

She nodded, then said, "Okay. I have some typing to do. I won't be going any place until time to go to work."

After leaving her at the apartment, Dale headed back to the crime scene. He picked up his cell phone and punched in a number. Wes answered on the second ring.

"Need something, Dale?" Wes asked, not bothering with the normal hello.

"Wanted to know if you'd like to go and have a chat with Javier Gutiérrez of Juárez with me."

Wes chuckled. "Does Shell have gas? Meet me at the substation. I have to drop this stuff off first."

"Sure thing. Mariah's at home. Hopefully she'll stay there until I get back." He knew Wes was worried about her.

"You do have someone watching the place, right?"

"Not today. I'm stretched so thin you can see the gaps."

The pause told Dale more than words could say. "You had better hope nothing happens to her. She means more to me than you could ever imagine."

Dale didn't say what he was thinking. "I'm doing my best. She's not exactly cooperative at times."

He could hear Wes talking to someone before he came back to the phone. "I have to go. See you in an hour."

Wes was waiting when he arrived at the substation. They headed to the meeting point with Javier. Being one of the Juárez Cartel, he was willing to rat out the Sinaloa in hopes of getting ahead when they were shut down. The Sinaloa was the biggest and baddest, attempting to put all the others out of business or pull them into their cartel. Javier said more than once he preferred the competition. It helped to keep prices reasonable and made it so the cartels had to be inventive to get a share of the business.

The shack where Javier met them had nothing around it. Dale knew if Javier was caught meeting with them, he was a dead man. He had agreed to the meet because he didn't like what was happening with the murders and new drug. Those deaths gave all the cartels a worse reputation than they already had. It also made it harder to recruit people to work for them.

Dale parked so his vehicle couldn't be seen. They went inside. Javier sent a man outside to guard the place with an order to let him know if anyone showed up unexpectedly.

"Señor, you said you wanted information on the Sinaloa," Javier said, waving a hand for them to join him at the small scarred wooden table in the kitchen.

"Yes. Sam said you had learned the Sinaloa was responsible for the women we have been finding with their stomachs cut open." Dale kept to his policy of being honest with the man who was helping them.

"Sí. They are using the bodies to move their new stuff. We have been hearing about the women showing up all over with the same way of dying. So, we wait and watch. Santiago, Ortiz's man, has been seen with all the women except the last one. One, maybe two days before they show up dead." Javier stopped, studying his hands. His face was grim.

"So, Santiago is in charge of moving the new stuff."

"Sí, señor. He gets protection from Ortiz. Santiago picks up the goods, is seen with the girl, and then the girl, with the goods inside is dropped in a remote location when they are finished with her. The dogs are sent to get the delivery after the body is dropped. They get the stuff from the body and deliver it to the man at the second lab who cuts the stuff."

Javier stopped again, drumming his fingers on the table. The habit was a sign that he was upset. He raised his head and studied Dale.

"This new drug. It is like Krokodile, only it kills fast. It is bad. They are making a million on less than an ounce, but it isn't like coke. One snort too many or a fraction of an ounce more than you should shoot up and you're dead. No one can do anything to help you. We don't want this stuff on the street."

"Where's the lab?" Wes asked.

They were pushing Javier beyond what they usually asked of him.

"Not sure," he answered with another glance at Dale.

"Then get sure. We want this stuff off the street as much as you do." Dale was irritated at Javier holding back information after giving them what he had so far.

Javier shrugged, obviously relenting. "In a basement two places to the right of Maria's Cantina. It has a lot of guards and alarms. You'll never get to them. They will destroy the lab and start a new one someplace else."

"Who's making the stuff?" Wes asked.

Dale nodded. It was worth a try to get a name.

Javier chuckled. "Señor, about time you asked. A man named Parker Fulton. He is training two others, but they aren't ready. If you mix it wrong, you will blow yourself up. It requires very exact measurements and a precise way of cooking. They use these HAZMAT suits and masks. One guy tried to make a batch and ended up killing himself. If you can get Fulton, you will stop them cold."

Dale grinned at Wes. Wes nodded. They knew who Fulton was and where to find him. Time to shut the new drug down.

Chapter Twenty–Three

IT IS DONE. OUR virgin has been selected. She will be easy to find. We only hope the one who is watching her won't ruin her before the moon turns to blood. She needs to remain innocent or we will need to start over.

"You will be happy Xolotl. It will be the last like you requested. She will come to you on the blood moon, rejoicing in what she must do for you. We will find another for the next blood moon, but it is so difficult to find one who is pure.

"Blood. It is all about the blood. It gives life and power. It is the color of fire. Our face must be red this time to signify the fire of the blood. Yes. Heat. Fire.

"You will be pleased Xolotl. We can join and defeat death with this ceremony. It's all I've ever wanted. To join you. Please, let me join you. The blood will sing like her name. Mariah. It sings like we will when she gives up her blood for you. This time we will become one with the power she will give us."

Chapter Twenty-Four

MARIAH RELUCTANTLY PREPARED FOR work. She didn't want to face Phillip tonight. She needed another couple of days to pay him back the money he used to bail her out of jail. She couldn't pinpoint when her life began to break apart, but she did know that the downward spiral had moved into warp speed after Rachel's death.

Dale hadn't been around except for early in the morning since she returned home. They ran together Sunday, Tuesday, and this morning. Other than their runs together, he was gone. Doing what, she didn't know, but it kept him out most nights.

It was probably for the best. He paid half of the rent and she had a roommate who didn't annoy her. What more could she ask for?

Before she could get the door opened to the Mustang, Danny was walking to her. She waited for him, avoiding for a few more seconds going into the club. Her door opened. Danny leaned on it watching her. He wasn't smiling but she couldn't tell what he was thinking.

"Is everything okay, Mariah?"

She nodded and turned to get out of the car. "Yeah. My life sucks right now, but it's as good as it's going to get for now."

"Where's that pretty smile? I can't remember ever seeing you without it." He helped her to stand.

"I'll have it in place by the time I get dressed," she said, the heaviness inside of her holding her in place.

"Hey, girl, you're out of jail. That's a good thing."

Mariah knew he was trying to coax a smile from her.

"I guess it's a good thing, but it came with a price. Jail wasn't all that bad and I probably should have stayed there and saved the money."

Danny put his arm around her as they strolled toward the club. "So how much was the bail?"

"Fifty thousand. Phillip got me out, but now I owe him. I have it, but I need to transfer it from where I keep my extra funds. This will mean another six months of working to earn that money back." She rubbed her eyes to keep the tears that had formed in place. No one needed to know how much all of this was affecting her.

Danny stopped, frowning down at her. "You're kidding, right? Fifty thou?"

"I'm not kidding. I wish I was." The heaviness increased with the mention of the amount she owed Phillip. "What sucks is that I had the money, but not where I could access it. When I called Mr. Becker, he called Phillip who paid the bail without asking me. In a way, I wish he hadn't paid it. I may end up needing that money for a decent lawyer."

They continued to the club, moving slowly. Danny gave her a quick hug. "You be careful. Someone out there doesn't like you for some reason."

"I got that message right after Rachel died. I'd better get a move on it. I have ten minutes to get to the floor."

Danny walked her to the anteroom for the lockers before removing his arm from her shoulders. She gave him a fleeting smile before going to change. Avoiding Phillip would be impossible. She needed to find a way to see him in private to tell him when he would get his money back. It would take her until next week for it to be in her account.

What she wanted to avoid was creating a problem for him or her. This was the first time she had ever owed anyone money other than a couple of dollars for a meal when she first came to El Paso. The idea of being in debt to anybody didn't sit well with her.

Phillip arrived later than normal. Mariah had begun to think he wasn't going to show up. He took his normal table, gave her a smile and a wink, then waited for her to get to him. He ordered his usual mojito. She provided her normal service, but without her typical cheeriness. No matter how she looked at the situation, tonight was going to be difficult. She was uncomfortable with Phillip and Becker learning about her arrest and time in jail.

She had to wait on the drinks since the bartender was new and he was slower than the regular guys. She jumped when a hand touched her shoulder. Turning slightly, she met Phillip's worried face. He took her arm and pulled her into the hall, putting them out of sight of all but a couple of the customers at the bar.

"Are you okay?" He had a crease between his brows, and a gentle hand on her shoulder.

She bit her lower lip, gazing at the carpeting while blinking rapidly. "Not really, but I need to work."

His hand stroked her arm. "No, you don't need to work. You need to take the rest of the weekend off and take care of yourself."

Sighing, she shook her head before reaching for the check she had folded and put in her top. She handed it to him. "Here's a check for your money. Please wait until Wednesday to deposit it to ensure the transfer is completed."

Phillip looked at the check then back to her. "You don't need to pay me back all at once. You can make it in a couple of payments."

"I had it saved. I couldn't access it from jail. Who knows, I may need your help again with the way things are going." She still couldn't face him. He had helped her, but now she would need to work as much as she could to replace the money.

His arms pulled her into a hug. "Angel, you can call me for help anytime. Anytime at all."

"Thanks," she mumbled. "I better get back to work. I'll be okay in a bit."

"I hope so. I like my effervescent little elf." He kissed her cheek and walked her back to the bar.

The rest of the night went by in a blur. She knew Phillip was concerned by the way he kept watching her. No matter what she did, she would need a few more days for things to get back to normal for her.

Friday, September 18, 2015

Mariah decided to go for a run. She needed the exercise to get rid of the emotions which were drowning her. Not until she was at the end of the paved section of the trail, did she remember that she hadn't called Dale.

When two men stepped from the shadows of the bushes alongside the path, Mariah turned and began to run away from them. One man caught her arm, pulling her off balance and into him. He was big and had her restrained, including her feet in a matter of seconds.

She couldn't see them in the dim light from the streetlights on road above. A gag was forced into her mouth, her arms and legs were tied, before a cloth bag was put over her head. The man who had been holding her, picked her up and carried her to a waiting vehicle. She was placed horizontally on a bench seat. A man lifted her head and sat, holding her head on his lap, a hand on her arm. During it all, neither man had spoken. All she heard was heavy breathing and a couple of grunts from them.

Fighting them wasn't an option. She was securely bound and couldn't scream with the gag. She took deep breaths through her nose, hoping to keep what she had in her stomach in her stomach. There was a good reason why the cloth in her mouth was called a gag. Her eyes watered as her throat constricted. After swallowing several times, she hoped the cloth would be removed soon.

A good twenty minutes later the car stopped. She was dragged off the seat and carried into a building and unceremoniously dumped on a sticky, gritty floor. The door closed and the lock clicked into place. She was alone with her stomach rebelling at the cloth in her mouth. If she couldn't control the urge to vomit, she would drown on the stomach contents.

She moved her hands, but whatever they had used to tie them together had no give in it. Her legs were the same way. She had only one option. That was to wait and see what they had in store for her. She prayed she could last until the gag was removed.

Dale got up at four AM. He made the coffee and was waiting for Mariah to get home before starting breakfast. When six came and went, he picked up the phone and called Wes.

"Something wrong?" Wes answered.

"Yeah. Mariah hasn't shown up. I'm going to where she normally parks to run and see if the car is there." Dale was unable to hide the worry and fear he was feeling.

After a pregnant pause Wes spoke. "She was picked up at about four-fifteen by two men. The team lost them on the east end of El Paso. The two men were known Sinaloa members."

Dale frowned. "Why in the hell didn't the team stop them from taking her?"

"They were too far away."

"What in the hell was she thinking? She knew she was supposed to call me before going to run. She promised." Dale's voice was sharp with fear along with anger at her not listening to him.

"She probably didn't remember until too late. In case you haven't noticed, she's been overwhelmed with everything after being arrested," Wes said in her defense.

Dale sat at the table, chewing on the corner of his lower lip. "That's a vast area to search and they may have taken her to Juárez. Let me call Juan and see if he can give us some help."

"Can't hurt," Wes agreed. "I'll admit I'm at a loss as to what to do right now." His voice hitched when he said, "She's all I have in the way of family and I don't want to lose her this way."

"I understand. I don't want to find her like the other girls." Dale tamped down the fear which was flooding him. "Let me call Juan and get things moving."

When they hung up, Dale called Juan, their Mexican counterpart. He explained what had happened.

Juan said, "Let me shake a tree or two and see what fruit falls to the ground."

For now, Dale had to wait until Juan called him back. There was nothing more he could do without more information.

Juan went to work. After a few phone calls, he had the names of the two men who had taken Mariah and confirmed they were Sinaloa. Time to go and see one of the big players in the cartel. Santiago Herrera wouldn't give him much of a problem with this request, or so he hoped. The names of the two men were the only link he had by noon. Time was something they didn't have a lot of if they wanted to get Mariah back alive.

Juan pulled into Santiago's driveway and parked. The guards had let him through, aware that he would come back with more men and legal papers if they didn't. The door opened without him knocking.

"He is on the patio. Right this way," the man at the door stated politely.

Santiago motioned for Deanna, his girlfriend, to leave as Juan hesitated in the doorway, awaiting an invitation to join him.

"Come and sit, amigo. What do you need?" Santiago said as soon as Deanna was inside.

"First, I'm not your amigo, but I do need to ask a few questions." Juan kept his voice calm and polite.

Santiago nodded and indicated for him to sit with a wave of his hand. Choosing a chair where he could see the man's face, Juan put his hands on the table, ensuring the guards and Santiago knew he wasn't here to create a problem.

"A woman was taken this morning by two of the Sinaloa. She needs to be returned." Juan watched his adversary closely.

Santiago fingered his fork on the table, lips pursed. He lowered his eyelids and tilted his head before asking, "And what makes you think I know anything about this missing woman?"

Juan tsked, shaking his head, his eyes never leaving the face of the man opposite him. "Santiago, you know everything that happens in the Sinaloa. These two men have had her since early this morning. Much trouble will come to you if she isn't home soon. We have not had any problems until now. It is bad enough the police have been harassing her, now this. This isn't good."

"I'll see what I can do. I'm not sure who took this woman, but if I find out, I'll see if she can be returned safely." He raised his head and faced Juan, his face composed, but eyes wary. "I can't promise anything at this point. First I'll need to find out why she was taken and who ordered it."

Juan gave a slight nod of his head. "I understand. If anything happens to her, be aware it will not go well for your people. As it is, many things are being investigated, one of which is a string of murders of numerous women. The pattern is of concern to multiple agencies in the States. I'd not like to see you go to prison for murder," Juan warned.

"Gracias. I'll look into it and get back to you in a couple of hours. I have your number."

Juan knew he was dismissed. Rising from the table, he nodded. The house guard escorted him to the door. Once in the car, he called and informed Dale that he would hopefully have some information in a few hours.

Mariah knew hours had passed since she had been dumped on the floor. She needed to use the bathroom. Closing her eyes, she attempted to concentrate on relaxing and not retching. Nothing was working well as her bodily needs increased by the minute.

The click of the lock had her stiffening. Fresh air swirled in as the door was opened. The sound of shoes let her know someone had entered the room.

A hand brushed her lower leg before the restraint on her ankles was removed. Someone picked her up and stood her on her feet with only a grunt. The hand tugged on her right arm. Her legs felt heavy, but she made them work, stumbling along behind the person.

Another hand took her left arm and guided her through a door. She was turned and backed against something cold. Her shorts and underwear were pulled down before the person put their hands on her shoulders, indicating for her to sit. It was a commode and none too soon. Her bladder felt like it was going to burst.

When she was done, the person wiped her like she was a child. A tug on her arm indicated she was to stand. They pulled up her clothes. She was then guided out of the bathroom and into another room before being turned, and again, pressure on her shoulders indicated she was to sit. Maybe now she would find out why she was here and what they wanted.

As the seconds ticked by, the uncertainty began to push her fear into terror.

A hand touched the back of her neck.

She jumped.

A man's voice said, "Sit still. I'm going to remove the gag. If you scream, you're dead. Understood?'

She nodded understanding.

With the gag removed, she took a deep breath and let it out, hoping the nausea would go away. She swallowed a couple of times, then attempted to calm herself. The advantage was all theirs. She couldn't do anything with her head covered and her arms tied behind her.

The hair on her body stood up with the sound of a chair being moved closer to her. A spike of fear whipped through her then settled in her chest, making it hard to breathe. Mariah moved away from the soft voice near her. The voice terrified her with its extreme calmness and lack of emotion.

"Tell me what you know about Rachel's death," the voice ordered.

After several tries, she was able to speak. She related what she knew, not mentioning what Rachel's diary had said or her suspicions. Yes, she was lying by omission, but the man wouldn't know that unless he knew about the diary.

"What do you know about other women being murdered?" The voice sent a shiver along her spine with his question.

Okay. He seemed aware that she knew something about the other women. Again, she told him the truth about checking to see if any other murders were like Rachel's. She admitted to finding a pattern of women being killed near the new moon each month.

"What do you want to do?" the voice questioned.

"I want to go home and get back to work. I missed several classes today, so I'll need to get my assignments."

"Tell me about Wesley Lansing and his relationship to you?"

The question was unexpected. He must know they were related or knew each other somehow.

"He's my cousin but was a surrogate father to me. He raised me from the time I was eight. He works for the Border Patrol, but that's about all I know. He didn't talk about his job when I lived with him and we haven't talked much since he threw me out at age eighteen."

Hopefully he had enough information about Wes to satisfy him.

"What about Dale Warner?"

This person knew a lot about her and the people in her life. "He's an acquaintance from my teenage years when he worked on Wes's farm." She was keeping to the truth—just not the complete truth.

"Explain the large deposits made into your account and why you were arrested."

Sighing, she slogged through her problems with Jamison and why she was arrested. She stressed how she had been framed for something she didn't do. So far, she hadn't outright lied to the scary voice.

"Who bailed you out of jail?"

This question surprised her as much as the ones about Wes and Dale. This was something she had expected them to know. This must be a fact finding question and answer session to see how much she knew and if it matched what they knew.

"Phillip Ortiz. My boss, Mr. Becker notified him, and he paid my bail. I paid him back. Before you ask, I had the money saved for school, but I couldn't access it from jail or my phone. That means I'll need to work longer before going back to school.

She didn't miss the pause before the man asked, "Ortiz? What is your relationship with him?"

"We're friends. I've gone out with him a few times. That's all."

"Hmm. I don't know too many friends who would put up that kind of money to bail someone out of jail."

"You would have to ask him why he bailed me out. I didn't ask him to do it. He did it on his own without consulting me, not that I minded."

The silence lengthened as her nerves tightened and stretched to the point where she wanted to scream. The voice made her jump.

"Thank you," the man said before standing and walking away.

The interrogation was finished. She didn't know what they wanted, but she had given them verifiable information. She hadn't lied. The man hadn't asked if she suspected anyone for the murders or anything else along that line.

Someone moved next to her. She could smell food. A hand lifted the edge of the cover over her head and pushed a spoon against her lips. Opening her mouth, she took the food off the spoon. It was a TV dinner, but she didn't care. Right now, food was just that, food. She was hungry and ate until no more was offered to her. A straw was pushed next to her mouth. She drank the warm water.

When the person finished feeding her, she was pulled to her feet and taken back to the room without furniture and pushed to the floor. Her legs were restrained again. She curled up and closed her eyes, going into one of her daydreams to try to get some rest. It was their call as to what happened next.

Chapter Twenty-Five

THE SOUND OF THE door opening sent a shock zipping around from chest to stomach and back again bringing Mariah to full alert. She had been daydreaming to keep her mind off what was happening. The sound sent her crashing back into reality and the uncertainty of her situation. Holding her breath, she waited. The noise of two different shoes meant there was more than one person entering the room.

Gentle hands lifted her until she was standing. A man picked her up and put her over his shoulder like she was a sack of grain. Her arms felt like they were being wrenched out of their sockets, but she didn't complain, hoping that whatever they were planning would be over soon. Confusion set in when she was carefully laid on the seat of a vehicle. Whoever had been carrying her, adjusted her so he would be able to sit on the seat and hold her in a reclining position.

Again, they drove for at least a half hour before turning onto a bumpy incline.

The car stopped.

The doors opened.

She was removed from the seat and placed on damp grass. The restraints on her arms and legs were removed. The soft voice from earlier spoke.

"Do not remove the head covering until you can no longer hear the car. This isn't over, so be careful in what you do."

The soft warning sent a zing of real fear bouncing around in her stomach, bringing back the nausea. She couldn't ignore the voice's threat. The voice, devoid of emotion, had woven through it a deadly intent.

Doing as instructed, she waited until she could no longer hear the car. Her purse and her phone were beside her along with the keys to Phillip's Mustang. It was still parked where she had left it. She had multiple missed calls from Dale, Wes and Phillip. They must be aware she was missing. Maybe they did care a little after all.

She pulled up Wes's number, hit autodial, and waited for him to answer.

"Mariah, where are you?" he asked without a greeting.

"I'm here by the car. I'll fill you in on the details when I get home. I wanted to let you know I was okay. All I want right now is to come home, take a shower and get something to eat."

"I'm here with Dale. We'll see you in a few minutes then."

"Right. In a few."

She sighed as she stared at the screen on her phone. It did appear he was worried enough about her to be in El Paso. He never came here unless it was important.

When she checked the time on her phone. It was three AM. He was worried since he hadn't been asleep. Maybe she still meant something to him after all.

When she arrived, Wes opened the apartment door before she had even gotten out of the car. Tentatively, she approached him, her eyes searching his stern face. He reached out, pulling her to him, holding her as he had when she was younger. The hug was what she needed. The fear finally began to recede, leaving tears of relief behind.

He guided her into the apartment, keeping his arm around her.

"Are you all right, girl?" he questioned, keeping her close to him.

With a sniffle, she told him, "Yes. I was scared, but they didn't hurt me."

Dale lifted her arm, studying the thin line left behind by whatever they had used to restrain her. "Looks like they wanted to make sure you didn't run away."

She glanced up at Wes, who was watching her. Time to explain what happened. Taking a shaky breath, she moved out of his arms to sit in her favorite spot on the couch.

Unable to look at them after breaking her promise to Dale, she recounted what happened. When done, she wanted to get up, but remained seated, ready for the two men to tell her how stupid she had been. She expected them to inform her that she wasn't going to be allowed to go anywhere without a bodyguard.

"You were lucky this time. I hope you know that. This could have turned out a lot differently than it did," Dale said, his face a mask.

She was unable to read his face. He had to be in work mode, covering his feelings with the work mask. Her eyes went to Wes, who watched her like he had when she misbehaved as a child. Okay, she had disregarded the safety instructions they requested that she follow. What happened was her own fault.

"I know," she said, her eyes on the fingers twisting in her lap. "I won't be doing it again. As I said before, I was upset and didn't even remember until I was quite a distance from the car."

"Girl, I know you're going to be going to school away from here and this mess. If you need help, let me know," Wes said.

Staring at him with wide eyes, she blurted out, "Really?" She hoped he meant it.

"Really. I want you out of this area where you'll be away from all of this and hopefully into a safer environment."

How odd for him to be worried about her now. He hadn't been concerned when she was forced to take the job in the club to survive. A little bit of help back then would have kept her in a safer environment instead of having to learn about the worst side of El Paso. She kept her mouth shut and her face composed. If she commented on his statement, she would be condemning him for throwing her to the wolves at eighteen.

"I'm going to go and take a shower," she said.

When they didn't object, she left them to discuss her and her ordeal. Neither one of them understood what they had done to her eight years ago. For them to be so worried about her now didn't make much sense. She was glad to have them here, but she didn't need them like she had when she was eighteen. She had learned from the school of hard knocks how to survive in a world that didn't make life easy.

A few minutes after she completed her shower, a knock on the bedroom door startled her.

"Mariah, you're needed out here," Wes said.

She wondered what was going on now. Slipping into shorts and a tank top, she walked out to see Jamison grinning at her. A different uniformed officer was at his side. Flicking a glance at Dale, then Wes, she returned her gaze to the detective who was doing his best to make sure her life was as miserable as he could make it.

"You will need to come with me," Jamison said, his grin widening.

"For what?" she questioned.

"Well, this new deposit was found in your account, and then more drugs were found in your backpack."

Her hand went out, palm up. "I want to see the warrant you needed to search my personal belongings and to access my bank account. You need a new one for each access and I expect to see them all," she demanded.

The grin slipped from Jamison's face. He blinked at her like an owl in daylight. Stammering, he said, "I—I don't have them with me."

She turned to the officer with him. "Go and retrieve those warrants and return here. Detective Jamison will wait for you."

Silence filled the room. The two officers exchanged a telling look. If she were a betting person, she would bet they only had the very first warrant.

"When was the last deposit made?" she asked.

"Yesterday."

"Well it wasn't me since I was lying on a dirty floor in a room with a hood over my head. My hands and feet were tied so I couldn't move. As to what you say you found in my backpack, unless you can produce a warrant, you performed an illegal search and seizure. Anything you might have found will not be able to be used as evidence." She stood with her arms folded, daring him to argue with her.

She waited for him to answer. When he didn't, she said, "The next time you accuse me of dealing, holding or anything else about drugs, you had better have a legal warrant in your hands. Now please leave my apartment and leave me the fuck alone."

Jamison, with his minion following, couldn't get out fast enough. She glared at Wes and Dale before returning to her room, slamming the door hard enough that the wall rattled. The least they could have done was to help her with Jamison considering they were both in law enforcement.

Dale's phone rang with the slam of Mariah's door. He answered the call, glaring at Wes who was holding back his laughter.

"Hello," Dale said.

"Dale, it's Juan. Javier wants to meet with you and Mariah. He specified that she had to be there after telling me she had been returned to her car."

"Did he say what he wanted?" Dale asked, watching Wes, who had gotten a cup of coffee and was merrily staring into it.

"No, señor. He said for you to be there in two hours."

Dale had no idea of what Javier wanted with Mariah, but he guessed it was important. "Okay, tell me where."

Juan gave directions to a place barely on the US side of the border outside of El Paso. He would have to hurry if he was to get there in the time allotted. After hanging up, he turned to Wes. Dale shook his head, not sure what the man was finding so funny.

"That was Juan, Javier wants to meet with Mariah and me in two hours," Dale said.

"No problem. Let me light a fire under her," Wes said before chuckling.

Dale reached out and took Wes's arm, stopping him. "What's so funny?"

Wes grinned, glancing at the door to Mariah's bedroom. "She still has that temper. If Jamison pisses her off anymore, he'll find himself behind bars. She's not one you want angry at you and that slammed door told me she was beyond furious."

Dale released him so he could let Mariah know what was happening. He changed clothes, put on his weapon, and a Kevlar vest. Javier hadn't made any move to harm him, but he never knew with these guys.

Mariah had taken a quick shower and was sitting at her desk, fuming when a knock sounded on her door. She knew who it was without even opening it.

"Come in, Wes," she said loud enough for him to hear.

"Is it safe?" he joked after opening the door, but not entering the room.

"Depends on what you want," she retorted, pivoting toward him on the chair, a scowl on her face.

"Well, it seems that Javier, one of our informants, wants to talk to you and Dale. He set a time limit on getting to the meeting. My guess is he is being watched and has made a detour for this meet."

"Do you know why he wants to talk to me?"

"No, and neither does Dale."

"All right. Give me a couple of minutes to put on decent shoes," she said, turning back to her computer to shut it down. She had dressed in jeans and a t-shirt and was as ready as she was going to get after putting on her tennis shoes.

Dale escorted her to his Jeep. He didn't talk during the drive to the meeting place. Mariah wasn't sure if she should be glad or pissed with him giving her the silent treatment.

They arrived before Javier. The little house was located on a side road in a poor section of the county. Dale's Jeep fit right in with the surrounding area since it was old with dents and chipped paint. What it did have was a motor that said *power* in the way it ran.

They were expected. When they neared the house, the door opened, and they were ushered in after the man did a quick scan of the street.

Javier sauntered in less than five minutes later. Pulling out a chair at the table where they were seated, he turned it around and straddled it, his eyes never leaving her face.

"You're Ortiz's girl." Javier's eyes narrowed.

"Not really," Mariah said. "He's only a friend I go out with to have some fun. I'm nobody's girl at this time."

"That's not what I hear. In fact, I was told he's so gone over you, that he bucked the hierarchy to protect you." Javier's voice was calm.

Mariah glared at Dale, then studied Javier before saying, "If Phillip is involved in any of this, I'll turn on him so quick his head will be spinning for a week."

An eyebrow rose at her words before he flashed her a smile and nodded. He turned to Dale, dismissing her now that he knew her true feelings. "The place you are looking for is under the pharmacy on the southeast side of Juárez. The entrance is through the back of the office. Fulton will be there tomorrow about five to finish this last batch and start a new one. This time, there will be only three guards.

"They are making a half kilo every couple of weeks. So far, they have carried out three bodies in the last two months. This drug is extremely dangerous to make. One mistake, and kleech," He drew his finger across his throat like a knife slicing the throat. "It is a bad drug. I like money but not if it is going to kill like this one does."

"What else can you tell me about the place?" Dale asked.

Javier shrugged. "Sinaloa stronghold. Benito and Humberto run that territory. The place is always well guarded with six men, but not this time. Seems there is something important going on where they have pulled the men from there.

"Oh, before I forget, Santiago is doing the transporting. You might want to ask him about all those women who have been murdered over the past five years. He may know more than he's said so far."

Dale frowned, studying the man who was putting his life on the line to talk to him.

"Why are you telling me all this?"

Javier pulled on his lower lip. He glanced at the man who was standing at the door. The man inclined his head.

"Because they won't share in anything. We were willing to make a deal and stick to what we do best, but they want it all. I want to see them lose that big money maker. Now that I know how dangerous it really is, I'm glad they cut us out."

"I understand. I'll let the appropriate people know. They will take out the lab." Dale hesitated then asked, "Do you know anything else about the murders of all the women?"

Javier wasn't the one who answered. The man at the door began to speak. "Sí señor. Old Mayan cult that has been around since the Mayans disappeared. From what I was told, a new leader took over about ten or fifteen years ago. He calls himself Xolotl and controls the new drug. He was the one who introduced it to the Sinaloa. From what I've been told, they are using it in the ritual. They sacrifice the girl and use her body to transport the drug across the border. Been doing it once a month for maybe four or five years. He said the ritual is done to keep Xolotl and the jaguar happy."

Dale asked," Do you know where?"

"No, señor," the man said before turning away.

Javier added, "They do not talk much about their gods. He was lucky to learn that much. This has been going on for hundreds of years. They were able to hide what they were doing since they would make a human sacrifice only a couple of times a year. These guys are giving us all a bad name with what they are doing."

"We're trying to shut them down, but we have to find them first," Dale said.

Javier glanced at her before saying, "Danny was seen with Rachel on the afternoon of the day she disappeared. You might want to ask him where he dropped her off."

"You're talking about the bouncer at the Platinum Slipper?" Dale asked.

"Sí. He has been seen with several of the girls who later showed up dead. He was with them the day before they were found." Javier studied his hands, mouth in a grim line.

"Anything else you can tell me?" Dale asked.

"Nothing other than asking Humberto where he was during all those times. He disappears right after each girl. You now have everything I know. Good luck catching them. I would bet Benito and Humberto are in the thick of it. Or Santiago. They all like blood." He turned to her. "You be careful, señorita. Ortiz can't stop this Xolotl if he wants to live. You are in great danger."

A chill went down her spine before making her shake in a shiver. He had just informed her in a roundabout way that Danny, Santiago, and Phillip were all involved in these murders. No wonder Theresa, Quinn, and Dale told her not to trust any of them. She turned her gaze to Dale. He didn't flinch or turn away. What had she gotten herself into by believing Danny was her friend and dating Phillip?

Chapter Twenty-Six

*Saturday, September 19. 2015,
Afternoon*

WHEN THEY RETURNED TO the apartment, Mariah decided she needed to call Becker and talk to him if she wanted to keep her job. She hesitated, attempting to figure out how to tell him what happened without creating too much concern.

She picked up the phone and placed the call. Mr. Becker answered on the third ring.

"Becker here. How may I help you?" He sounded distracted.

"Hi. It's Mariah."

"Mariah. Are you all right? When you didn't show up or call, everyone panicked, including me." She had his full attention.

"I'm all right. I ran into a major problem and was unable to let anyone know what happened." She waited for the expected questions.

"What happened? I know you, and for you to not call whatever occurred had to be something extraordinary."

She let a couple of responses flit through her brain before opting for honesty. Her eyes went to Dale, who was listening to her as she talked to Becker.

"Well, I was kidnapped while I was running yesterday morning. They asked me some questions, then let me go. I've no idea of what they wanted, but they apparently decided I wasn't any threat to them for now."

The silence stretched for an extended period when she finished speaking. His voice changed to concern when he asked, "Look, if you need tonight off, I'll understand. I can find coverage. Just call Phillip. He is beside himself with worry."

She let out the breath she had been holding, wondering if the worry was for himself or her. "I'll be in tonight. I'll call him and let him know I'm all right."

"Okay. I'll see you at seven. Thank you for calling and letting me know what happened."

She paused before saying, "Please don't spread around what actually happened. Leave it as a personal emergency."

He chuckled. "You got it. See you tonight."

She hung up, waiting for Dale to comment. When he didn't, she put off calling Phillip by calling Danny instead.

"Mariah, are you all right? What happened?" Danny sounded worried. "You never miss work.

"I'm fine. Just a minor problem that is over now. I'll be at work this evening."

"You sure you're all right?" he asked, his voice still holding concern.

"I'm totally fine. I wanted to let you know so you didn't go nuts when you saw me this evening."

"Yeah, well, I was wondering what happened to you. It's the first time you've missed work without advance notice."

"I know, but everything is fine, so quit worrying," she told him.

"I will, now that I've heard from you. I'll see you tonight then. Bye."

Dale, with a raised brow questioned, "Was he really concerned or playing along?"

She chewed on her lower lip, going back over what Danny had said before answering, "He wasn't that concerned, but he put up a good front. Something didn't sound right, but I can't place what it was."

"Call Phillip," Dale instructed. "Speaking to him might show you what you missed with Danny."

Phillip answered on the first ring. "Mariah! Where are you? Is everything okay? Please tell me you're not hurt?" Phillip blurted out. She could almost see his face and the real concern and caring it would show. That was what was missing with Danny.

"I'm not hurt. I was taken and held for the night. They asked me some questions, then let me go this morning. Other than being uncomfortable, it wasn't bad," she informed him, making light of her fear.

"Are you taking the night off or working?"

"I'll be at work. You'll get to see that I'm okay then." She knew he would want to see for himself that she hadn't been hurt.

"I would feel better if you had a bodyguard. I don't want anything to happen to you."

She was tempted to take him up on the offer. "That's not necessary. I'll be fine. Look, I'll see you tonight. We can discuss it on my break." He would have to come up with a compelling reason for her to agree to someone following her around all the time.

"Look, I'll be there to pick you up in twenty minutes. You don't need to be alone." His voice made her feel like he really did care about her. He was going to do what it took to see she was safe.

"You don't need to do that. I'm fine here," she said, a warm fuzzy feeling pushing away that last of her fear.

"No. I insist. Bring what you need for work and I'll take you there and bring you home. I really want you close to me."

Okay, he was going to be the macho male now. "Fine. Let me get my things together. I'll see you in twenty minutes."

After hanging up, she understood the difference between Danny and Phillip. Danny didn't really care about her. Dale was right. She couldn't trust him, but Philip was a totally different story. He was genuinely concerned about her no matter what his role was in the recent events.

She jumped when Dale put a hand on her shoulder. Raising her gaze to his, she wondered what he was thinking. His face was composed, but she felt that slight shake in his hand that showed he wasn't as calm as he appeared. He sat on the arm of the couch, keeping his hand on her.

"Look, I know Phillip really cares for you, but please, be careful with him," Dale warned, not really telling her why he was cautioning her.

She crossed her legs Indian style on the couch before she answered. "I'm watching my step with him, but..." She stopped not sure how to continue.

Dale finished the sentence for her. "You care about him, but not like he cares for you. I've seen how he looks at you. You are special to him, just like you are to me.

He smiled when she turned to him, shocked. "Yes, I've been keeping a close watch on you since you seem to be a key to what is happening. I've seen the difference in him when he is with you. I'll not interfere. It's up to you to decide who you want."

Anger swept through her. The idiot still didn't understand that he was the one she wanted. Phillip was a stop gap friend to keep her from being lonely. How could she get Dale to see how much she wanted him? Only him. This was a question she needed to be able to figure out and answer soon.

"He's coming to get me. He wants to keep me close to him and will take me to work and bring me home in the morning."

Dale gave her a hug. "I understand. I get it from his point of view. For now, your being with him will be the safest place to be. He has enough men to protect you. I'll admit I don't, and you need that right now."

She stared at him, not sure what he was saying. "So, you think I should use him to stay safe?"

"Yes. I don't have the resources he does, and I know he won't let anything happen to you. So, yes, use his resources and help for now. You can straighten it out later."

She searched his face before lowering her head having seen what she didn't expect. The fear she saw confirmed his real concern for her safety. Using Phillip was an option and one he was advocating until things settled down.

"Okay, let me go and get ready," she said before hurrying away to gather her things for the rest of the day and night. She knew Phillip planned on taking her to his place until time for her to go to work.

She packed what she needed and was ready for Phillip when he arrived. Dale had disappeared while she was packing. Before she could pick up her backpack, Phillip embraced her, running his hand over her head, then tilting her head up so he could see her face.

"Darling, I was panicking when you called. Let's get you someplace that's safer than here."

The man with him picked up her backpack while Phillip guided her to the Hummer. He lifted her up, placing her on the back seat. She scooted over, giving him room to sit beside her. The driver pulled out of the parking space without Phillip speaking. He knew where they were going.

Phillip kept close to her side, an arm around her. He let out a big breath before speaking. "I've never been so scared for someone in my whole life than I was last night when you didn't come to work." He put a finger under her chin, raising her head so she was facing him. "It makes me realize how much you mean to me."

Tears welled and threatened to spill over. "Please, Phillip. Don't get attached to me."

"I already am," he admitted with a wry smile, using his thumb to wipe away a tear that had escaped.

He held her close, his hand intermittently running over her head. When they arrived at his place, he lifted her down from the Hummer. With an arm around her, they walked into his home. She went to the divan. This time he sat beside her instead of going to the chair.

"What happened, Mariah?"

Curling into him, she went over the events from the time she decided to run to returning home. When she finished, she mumbled, "Rachel seems to be connected to all of this somehow. I don't know how or why, but I do know it has something to do with drugs. I'm being set up." She peered up at him. "I'm scared."

He pulled her onto his lap like she was a small child. Relaxing in his arms, a few tears ran over her cheeks. Calling what she had felt over the past twenty-four hours scared was an understatement. Totally terrified would be a better description. Then his admission of how he was attached to her didn't help matters. What was she to do now?

"You'll be okay. I know the cartels are fighting and somehow Rachel, and now you, have been caught up in what is happening. I understand Rachel was your friend, but let the police handle her death. Your becoming involved will put you at more risk of getting hurt."

His words were a repeat of what he had said before. The difference was that this time he said it with feeling and some fear. Like Dale, he was afraid for her.

"Would you consider moving in with me until this is all over?" he asked before tugging her closer to him, pressing her head into his shoulder.

She wiped away some tears before saying, "I can't. I have school plus work. Besides, I don't sleep much which would drive you nuts. I wander around in the middle of the night, keeping myself busy."

"Think about it. You would have all the freedom you want other than going out by yourself. I would have a guard be with you when you aren't here. It would only be temporary."

He was almost begging. He had to be extremely scared to offer her sanctuary in his home.

"I can't," she said without explanation.

He didn't push the issue. Changing the subject, they continued talking. Soon she was laughing and joking around with him. When the time came to get ready for work, he showed her to a room that had been decorated for a woman. Before he left her, he said, "This is your room anytime you want to come here. No strings attached. No expectations."

Reaching up, she pulled him down and kissed his cheek. "I appreciate it more than I can tell you. I'll consider staying here if anything else happens."

He held her in place, giving her a kiss filled with passion before leaving her to get ready for work. The love she saw in his expression had her crying, but the water running over her face hid the tears.

She knew he would do whatever it took to keep her safe, only she didn't love him. The easy way would be to stay here and let him care for her, but she couldn't do it. Her heart was with Dale, who she had loved since she was a teenager even though he hadn't said more than a few words to her until now. Each time he touched her, the connection between them had strengthened.

Phillip made sure she was to work on time. Becker and Theresa both expressed concern for her safety. Danny stayed back, which she assumed was due to Phillip being with her. Quinn was in the background, watching. He gave her a slight nod before moving away.

During her shift, she noticed Quinn kept a close eye on her. Phillip was continuously monitoring where she was and what she was doing. As tempted as she was to take him up on his offer, she couldn't justify doing so.

The fear of what would happen if she did was almost as strong as the fear of being kidnapped again. The kiss had shown how easy it would be to succumb to him. She would end up breaking the promise she had made to herself as a teen. The promise to not sleep with a man prior to marrying.

At the end of her shift, Phillip walked her to the Hummer. Once she was inside, he asked, "My place or yours?"

Blinking back tears, she told him, "Mine."

They were almost at her apartment when he handed her a tissue, aware she had been silently crying.

"It will all work out, sweetheart," he murmured. "I understand."

She looked up at him, searching his face before asking, "Do you really?"

He gave her a quick kiss on the lips. "I do. Please stay close to home. I'll call you later."

He waited until she was inside before leaving. She had a feeling he really did understand why she wasn't staying with him. Sighing, she dropped her keys into the bowl and headed to her room. As she passed through the kitchen, she saw a note on the table.

"I don't know when I'll be back. I'll contact you as soon as I can. If you need help, call Wes or Phillip. Love, Dale."

She dropped it back on the table. So much for protection from him. She went to her bedroom to work on her assignments. Today was going to be a long day.

Chapter Twenty-Seven

Sunday, September 20, 2019,
Morning

MARIAH WAS TYPING WHEN a phone rang. It rang again. She opened the door to see Dale at the table, his cellphone to his ear. He turned to her, a frown on his face.

"Thank you, Juan. I appreciate you letting me know. We're close to being able to bust the lab with your help." He listened again before saying, "I'll let you know. Thanks again."

He hung up and stared at his phone before taking a deep breath, blinking rapidly. She moved into the room and stood behind a chair, her hands on the back of it.

"What did Juan want?"

Dale raised his gaze to hers. "He called to let me know that Javier paid with his life for what he gave us. He was found this morning along with the man he had been with at the meeting. Both were executed with a bullet to the back of the head."

She pulled out the chair and sat before saying, "So someone who was with him when he met with us ratted on him."

"Yes. I believe I know which one it was. Juan knew when he asked for the meeting that he was a dead man."

She concentrated on tracing a pattern on the table. "How is Danny involved?"

When Dale didn't answer right away, she glanced up at him. He was playing with his phone on the table. "I'm not exactly sure what his role is in all of this, but he does have major ties to the Sinaloa." He looked at her, his expression grim. "Santiago's real deep into all of it. He's a major player."

Mariah took a few seconds to process the meaning behind the words. "Deanna isn't involved, but she loves him, and I believe he loves her."

Dale met her gaze. "What about you and Phillip?"

Pausing, she knew why he was asking, but how did she really feel about Phillip? She cared about him. He was the first man who showed how much he liked her. Yes, her looks drew him to her, but he had seen beyond that and loved the real person beneath the exterior. If she were totally honest with herself, she loved him, but not in the way she loved Dale.

"I care deeply for him." She stared at her hands, hoping Dale would understand what she was telling him. "He's easy to be around and I know he loves me, not my looks. Staying with him would be so easy, but it would be unfair to him."

She sniffed and swiped at the ever-present tears.

"I would never love him like he deserves to be loved. He's this wonderful, caring man who will do whatever it takes to make me happy." She gave up and let the tears run unchecked over her face. "He'll always be special to me if for no other reason than how much he loves me."

Dale's hands covered hers. Mariah raised her head to face him. "It's okay. Too bad he's on the wrong side. He's one of the big players in the Sinaloa cartel. He's the reason your kidnappers let you go. No one wants him angry with them since he makes a very nasty adversary."

Not sure she wanted to know, Mariah asked, "What exactly is his position with them?"

"Enforcer and protection," Dale responded without hesitation.

That explained his being at the club all the time, and why he said that he was in the security business. He had a secret side he wasn't willing to share with her. He was two different people depending on whether he was working or just being himself.

Musing aloud, she murmured, "I wonder how he got involved with the Sinaloa and into the security business for them."

"Through his older brother. Phillip has this icy temper. When he gets angry with someone, he's very cold and calculating in how he gets even with them. His brother had Phillip protect him as he ran drugs for the Sinaloa. His brother was caught skimming and was killed by another enforcer. That man was later found dead, murdered in a way that had made him suffer before he died.

"No one was able to prove it was Phillip, but the Sinaloa leaders all knew it was him. From that point on, Phillip did his job with them, but he kept his private life separate from what he saw as a job and nothing more. As he told Quinn not too long ago, what he does isn't who he is. He knows he won't get out alive, but he has men surrounding him who are loyal to him, not the cartel. He did that so he could survive as long as possible in a world where most are dead by age fifty."

"I wonder what he would have done if his brother hadn't gotten him involved with the cartel," she said, learning more about the man who was so kind and loving to her.

Dale was silent for a few seconds before he said, "He wanted to be a detective and own his own agency. He really does run a legitimate security business and is good at it, making enough off it to live like he does without what he gets from the cartel." Dale squeezed one of her hands. "If he gets caught by the cartel helping us, they'll kill him."

Staring at him, she let what he had said percolate through her brain until it made sense. "He's helping you?" she asked, needing verification of what he had imparted.

"Yes. That's how I know how he feels about you, It's also why I said to use him if you couldn't get to me or Wes for help. We're working on extracting him from the Sinaloa, but it's going to take some time to do it and keep him alive."

She now understood. Dale liked Phillip and was doing his best to help him. The kind man deserved to live the life he wanted, not the one thrust upon him by his brother. He may have done some nasty things, but that wasn't him. That was another persona he developed to keep from being killed. She now had the explanation why he had his bodyguards living in his compound. They were the only ones he trusted to keep him safe.

Her head spun with the new information. She admitted, "He seems to be there for me when no one else is."

Dale gave her hand another squeeze. "I know. I'm working undercover a lot and didn't take that phone with me, so I didn't know you needed help."

"Wes didn't respond either, so you weren't the only one. He's all I've got in the way of family. I didn't call Phillip. Mr. Becker did, but he had to have started working on my release right away."

She met Dale's gaze with hers.

"So that you know, I paid him back. It'll mean working an extra six months or so to recoup that money. It was part of what I had saved for my tuition and living expenses for law school." She paused, then admitted in defeat, "Then again, becoming a lawyer might end up only a dream that won't come true if I can't get out of this mess."

"Wes and I wouldn't have been much help to you even if we had gotten your messages right away. Neither one of us have that kind of money," Dale admitted.

"I had the money, but I couldn't get to it while in jail. Wes has the money but he's not responsible for me and neither are you. I can take care of myself but need to get past all of this to get back on track."

"Mariah, everyone needs someone sometime, be it a relative, sibling, friend, or even an acquaintance." He gripped her hand tighter. "I hated that I wasn't there for you when you needed me."

She pulled her hands from his, folding them in her lap, withdrawing into herself. She put up a wall around her inner self, not willing to trust him. "That may be true, but for me, it's like everyone disappears when I really need them. I've found I'm better off not counting on anyone to be there. I appreciated that Phillip got me out, but I would have preferred staying in jail and saving that money for a decent lawyer. As it is, I know Wes won't help me. He was glad to get rid of me and get his life back."

Dale quickly said, "You're wrong. Wes loves you and says you're his child. He would have only left you there to keep you safe. If it's proven you were framed, you'll get your money back."

"Yeah, when pigs fly," she said before scooting back from the table.

She returned to her room and closed the door, not giving him a chance to refute her beliefs. Lying on her bed, she mulled over their conversation. Phillip was temporary. That fact was brought home by what Dale had revealed.

Dale was wrong about Wes, though. He hadn't seen Wes's face when he told her to leave. She had. His face was cold, hard, and unyielding. This wasn't the first time he hadn't responded to her when she needed him. The one time he answered, he told her to deal with it on her own.

Then Dale, like Phillip, was temporary. The chances of his sticking around were slim. Regardless of what he said, his actions showed he wouldn't be staying.

She had no one else now. Rachel had been the only close friend she'd had since moving to El Paso. Being alone sucked at times, but it prevented being torn apart like now with Phillip and Dale. She wiped away the wetness on her cheeks, putting more mortar in the bricks of the wall she had erected around her heart. Now was the time to reinforce the barricade for when this was finished, and everyone left. The only person she could count on was herself, regardless of what Dale had said.

Chapter Twenty-Eight

Sunday, September 20, 2015, Evening

AFTER ACCEPTING THAT NO one in her life was there for the long term, Mariah returned to her normal self. She needed to plan on working in the club to earn the money she might need for a decent lawyer and recoup the fifty thousand she had given to Phillip. While doing all of that, she also needed to come up with an alternative plan for her life. Hopefully things would work out, but if they didn't, she needed a backup plan.

When she left her room a couple of hours later, Dale was gone again. After fixing lunch, she went back to her homework, continuing to study until time to go to work. Stuffing all her problems into a little compartment, she put a smile on her face. Tonight she would have fun socializing with the men and few women who came into the club.

Danny was beside the car before she could gather her things together. He must have been watching for her. She smiled when he opened the door. Even if she couldn't trust him from what she had learned over the past few days, it was nice how he took care of her while at work.

"Hey girl, I don't need another scare like the other day." His face was serious.

"Me neither," she said him before turning to get out of the car.

His big hands pulled her to her feet. He took her keys from the ignition and handed them to her before locking the door and closing it.

"You really need to go someplace safe," he admonished, his arm about her shoulders as they walked to the side door of the club.

"I'm in as safe a place as I can get right now. I'll have to stop running for a while and go to the gym instead." She didn't tell him about Phillip's offer.

"You could go and stay with Phillip. He would keep you safe." Danny hadn't looked at her as he voiced the suggestion.

Okay. The two men must have talked at some point in time, or Danny was attempting to make her safe from himself. He needed to hear the truth about why she wasn't staying with Phillip.

"Danny, he's only a friend for me, but for him, I'm his perfect woman. I can't stay there and let him get more attached to me. Besides, I refuse to have someone following me everywhere I go. I'll be all right at home. I'll have to curtail some of my normal activities, but I can handle that for a while."

"You need to go stay with him. Trust me on this one, Mariah. He can protect you when no one else can. You're in danger, and I don't want anything to happen to my favorite elf."

She stopped and faced him. "What do you know about what is happening?"

He stared over the top of her head, his face grim. She didn't think he was going to answer when he softly said, "This isn't about me. It's about you, and regardless of what else happens, I want you to be safe." He lowered his eyes to hers. Tears shone in them. "Please. Go and stay with Phillip. That's the only way you'll be safe."

There was no mistaking the fear she saw in his expression. She had seen something similar when Dale had encouraged her to use Phillip. She didn't think either one of them meant for her to live with him.

"I'll think about it. Right now, I need to get to work and then school tomorrow." She turned and started to the door again.

Danny stopped her, "Please. I'm begging you. Go and stay with Phillip and accept his protection."

A lead weight settled in her stomach at his statement, the worry on his face, and the fear in his voice. Maybe it wouldn't be such a bad idea after all. She really needed to talk to Dale before making that type of decision. All she needed to do was to catch him at the apartment.

"I'll see. Right now, I'm going to get through tonight. I'll worry about everything else after work." Even though this wasn't what he wanted to hear, it was the best she could do for now.

He was quiet for the rest of the walk to the locker room. She really wanted to know why he was so worried that he felt she needed Phillip's protection. Did he know why she had been kidnapped? Or was it something else?

Mr. Becker and Theresa were in the anteroom when she left the locker room. He motioned her over with his hand. Reluctantly, she joined them.

"I should have insisted you take the night off," he said, studying her face.

With a shake of her head, she said, "No. I need to work to keep myself sane. I'd rather be here than at home thinking and worrying."

"I understand," Theresa agreed. "What are you going to do now?"

The two of them watched her and waited for a response. She was aware that flippancy wouldn't work. The truth wouldn't be easy to forget.

"I really don't know. If I knew what they were after, then I could plan for what to do. Why I'm a target is a mystery to me and has been from the start. I guess taking things day by day is all I can do."

Theresa leaned on the high table between them. "Take Phillip up on his offer to protect you." She was totally serious.

Mr. Becker nodded in agreement. Why was everyone pushing her to go to Phillip? What sort of power did he have that would protect her from whoever was after her?

"I'm considering it," she said, unsure what else to say.

"Do more than consider it," Mr. Becker said. "We all want to keep our little sprite with us."

With a sense of things closing in around her, she repeated, "I'm considering it. I have this thing about staying with a man I don't know very well, especially when he is attached to me and I'm not attached to him."

A gentle hand on her shoulder had her facing Becker. "He understands and will be a perfect gentleman. He's the only one who can protect you right now. Go and stay with him," he advised, his eyes boring into hers.

"I'll think about it." She glanced at the clock. "Time for me to get to the floor. Thanks for the concern."

Theresa surprised her by saying, "Quit thinking about it and do it, Mariah."

Okay. That made four people pushing her to stay with Phillip. What she wouldn't give for Wes to put his arms around her and talk with her about what to do. That wasn't going to happen. Those days were long gone.

She hurried away, blinking back the tears unexpectedly forming at the thought of the loss of her only family. He wasn't dead but might as well be with the three-year estrangement. She stuffed the pain back into its little box, dismissing the things she couldn't change while waiting for the girl she was to relieve to report off to her. She scanned the tables in the pit, her eyes coming to rest on Phillip, who smiled when he saw her looking at him. He winked and tilted his head before returning to his conversation with the men who were with him.

A girl she hadn't met but had seen before greeted her. "Hi, I'm Molly. I take it you're my relief?"

"Yes. I'm Mariah," she said with a big smile for the pleasant girl.

Molly gave a quick rundown of the customers and their orders before saying, "You're a hard act to lead into. Several of the men have been asking if you were coming in tonight, including that handsome guy at table seven. Calvin said to tell you he would be here tonight since he missed you last night. He also said you had better have a good reason for not being here," she merrily said.

Mariah laughed. "I'm sure. He's an old friend and followed me here. I take it you covered my shift last night."

Molly nodded. "Yes. You must be a great waitress. Since I began to work here, I never got so many tips. Bob told me what you do, and it even worked today."

"Thanks for covering for me. Something came up that I couldn't control. If you want, ask Mr. Becker if you can stay over for an hour or so and work with me to see how I do it," she offered, not aware the man in question had come up behind her.

His voice had her turning to him. "I don't mind. In fact, I think Molly would benefit from working with you for a few hours."

Without thinking, Mariah gave him a quick hug. "Thank you. She's one of the ones who's willing to learn, or Bob wouldn't have given her hints."

Becker bent over and kissed her cheek. "I know. I'll see you later."

Mariah and Molly watched him walk away. Molly turned to Mariah, her eyes round. "How in the world did you ever thaw out the ice man? He's never touched, let alone kissed, any of the girls since the place opened."

"I didn't do a thing. Maybe he likes elves," Mariah joked with a grin.

Mariah took the tray for the order Molly had given to Bob before saying, "Give me a chance to introduce myself to the tables first, then we'll work the room together."

She delivered the drinks and took a food order from the men there. Going to each occupied table, she joked around after ensuring they didn't need anything, leaving table seven for the last. When she approached the men, Phillip captured her hand and held her next to him, studying her closely.

"Looks like you're doing okay," he said, his eyes not leaving hers.

"For now," she replied to his unasked question.

He squeezed her hand. "My offer is open ended. I'm only a call away."

"I know," she said shifting under the stares of the other men. "Anything you gentlemen need?" she asked, needing to turn the conversation away from her.

One of the men chuckled. "Honey, that question could get you in a lot of trouble."

With a hand on her hip, she told him, "I'm not on the menu, so you'll need to look elsewhere for that need."

Santiago pointed to the man using both hands and merrily laughed. "Gotchya."

"She'll never be on the menu," Phillip informed the men. "We're set for now. Go back to work. I'll talk to you on your break."

With a nod, she left the group, wondering what he wanted to talk to her about. He normally didn't disturb her breaks.

Molly followed her, listening to how she talked to the men and watching what she was doing. When they were waiting for orders at the bar, Mariah instructed her in how to improve her service with the admonition to develop her own style of interaction. She stressed how she didn't need to service the men to get generous tips.

By the time she was ready for a break, she had given Molly part of the pit to work, keeping an eye on what the pert girl did. She gave her feedback on how to give the best service. When the time came for her to break, she reported to Molly and headed to the break room.

Phillip appeared in the hallway. "I had your meal delivered to a conference room. I hope you don't mind. I need to talk to you in private."

"No problem as long as you don't mind me scarfing down my meal."

She studied him for a few seconds. The smile on his face didn't reach his eyes as he scanned the room behind her before leading her down the hall. A frisson of concern ran up and down her spine when she noticed his tenseness. Another ton of rocks hit her stomach.

When the door to the room closed, Phillip gathered her into an embrace before giving her a kiss. It was tender and full of the feelings he didn't show. Sadness slipped into her at being unable to return what he felt for her.

"I had to make sure you were still real," he joked, his eyes showing it wasn't the truth.

"I'm real and you know it," she chided.

He didn't release her. "Mariah, I'm worried about you."

She leaned back and studied his face. He was no longer smiling.

"Please let me provide some protection for you," he requested, his hand cupping her head as he held her gaze.

"I can't let you take responsibility for me." She lowered her eyelids so he didn't see the emotions she knew she couldn't hide. Letting him take control would be so easy, but she couldn't do it. Not yet.

"You are the sweetest woman I've ever met. So innocent, yet sexy and beautiful, all wrapped up in this cute elfin exterior." He kissed her again, then released her. "I better let you eat," he said before pulling out the chair where her food was waiting.

Once she was seated, he took the chair next to her, watching as she began to eat.

"I'm going out of town tomorrow for a few days," He put a hand on her arm. "I would rest a lot easier if you were at my place while I'm gone. The guys would watch over you and make sure you're safe."

"Safe from what?" she asked, not expecting him to answer.

"From those who are after you."

"Do you know who they are?"

He looked away from her, his face a mask. "I have a reasonable idea as to who is behind this, and if I'm correct," he paused, then met her gaze before continuing, "they won't give up." His handsome face was grim. "Let me provide the protection you need until this blows over."

She didn't miss the worry in his voice or the fear in his eyes. What should she do? Would they come back for her again? Somewhere, somehow, her life had spiraled downward until she was in the whirlpool going into drowning mode and had no idea of what to do next, where to turn or who to trust.

"Let me think on it. As I said before, I may still take you up on your offer."

He changed the subject to where he wanted to take her on Tuesday, saying he would be back in two days at the most. Before she had finished eating, he had her laughing with his stories, but the smile on his face still didn't reach the soft brown eyes that seldom left her face. What she saw and felt told her she would have to remind him of her not wanting a romantic relationship with him. No matter how she said it, she would hurt him. That hurt would mean losing a person she would love to keep as a friend.

When she finished eating, Mariah returned to work. Molly thanked her before leaving, happy with what she had learned while going home with more tips than she normally got in two or three days. Mariah had no illusions where Molly was concerned. They would have a good working relationship, but they would never be friends.

Stuffing the emotions Phillip had brought to the forefront deep inside, she returned to work. The banter and work kept her problems at bay. Things were going well until Santiago stopped her in the hall as she was taking a quick break.

"You sure you're all right?" he asked, his face reflecting the concern in his voice.

"I'm fine," she said, avoiding meeting his scrutiny. "It was a hiccup in my messed-up life."

His hand on her shoulder made her raise her head to face him.

"You do need to take Phillip up on the protection he's offering, even if you don't stay at his place," he advised. "He's worried about all that has happened. You need to let him take care of you for a week or so."

She caught her lower lip in her teeth, turning her head so she was staring at the picture just beyond his head. "I'm not sure I should saddle him with my problems."

Phillip's voice and his hand on her other shoulder had her turning to him. "I'll happily take on your problems any time."

Santiago grinned. "See. He doesn't mind. Before I forget it, Deanna said for you to call her. She likes you and loved hanging with you the other night." He handed her Deanna's phone number, written on his business card.

Mariah kept her eyes on Phillip. "We'll do it again soon. I enjoyed myself. I'll call her tomorrow after school."

Phillip bent over and gave her a quick kiss. "We'll repeat it when I get back." He stood staring down at her for a few seconds. "Call me if you decide to use my place so I can let my men know to expect you."

She nodded, then watched the two men head out the door. She needed to decide within the next few hours what she was going to do. The more she thought about it, the more she was tempted to take Phillip up on his protection offer.

The rest of her shift passed in a blur. She must have covered her distraction well. She had received more than her normal tips even though the night was slow. When she went to change, her mind was in a fog, keeping her from seeing things clearly along with slowing her movements. The problem wasn't that she was tired. She just felt out of touch with the things around her.

Her plan was to go straight home, but as she was leaving, Theresa stopped her. "Let's go and get some breakfast. I'd really like to get to know you better," the woman who always seemed to be close by requested.

"Sure," Mariah said, not really wanting to go home, afraid Dale would still be there, yet wanting to see him.

She followed Theresa to a diner that was open twenty-four hours a day. They took a booth away from most of the other customers. After they had ordered their meals, Theresa gave the reason for the invitation.

"I know you were told to trust Quinn and me." She stopped and took a sip of her coffee. "You have become involved in this through Rachel. Danny has pulled you further into it without you knowing what he and the others are doing and planning."

"So I've been told," Mariah said, wondering where the pretty brunette was going with this conversation.

"What have you learned about the club and those who frequent it?" Theresa asked.

Not sure where Theresa fit in all of this, Mariah decided to keep her answer general. "Something was said about drug trafficking and how several at the club were involved. I was also told to go to you or Quinn if I needed help."

"You're in way over your head in this. Danny isn't the only one involved. Phillip, Santiago, and Becker are working for the Sinaloa. They don't know who is threatening you, which is why Phillip is offering the protection of his men."

Mariah frowned, the fear popping out of its box, making it difficult to think. "How do you know all of this?"

Leaning forward on the table, arms crossed, Theresa imparted. "I'm undercover. So is Quinn. Dale instructed me to let you in on some of what is happening. Becker oversees getting and distributing the drugs on this side of the border. Phillip is enforcement and Santiago transports. Danny is involved up to his eyeballs and does what he's told, including getting you to come to work at the club so they could keep tabs on you."

Their meal came, giving Mariah time to digest what Theresa had told her. She had believed she was going from a bad place to a better one. Instead she had gone from bad to worse. She ate for a few seconds in silence before asking the question no one would answer.

"Why me? I have nothing to do with them or drugs."

"Rachel is the tie. They know you two were close and aren't sure if she talked to you. They've been watching you. They saw you with Dale when he talked to Javier. You're making some higher-ups extremely nervous because you're getting too close, so they're stepping up the heat."

"Close to what?" she asked, not sure she wanted to know.

Theresa chewed the bite of toast she had in her mouth and swallowed before answering, taking her time.

"Their operation," she responded. "We know Rachel's body was used to hide the drugs along with the rest of the girls who've been found murdered in the same fashion. Someone who goes by the name of Xolotl is the one in control. Currently, no one knows who this person is or where he is. We have a couple of suspects, including Santiago who seems to know most of the players. Most of what we have is pointing toward him."

Mariah shook her head. "He isn't the head guy. He may know who is or be in contact with him frequently, but I don't believe he's in charge. Someone is telling him what to do. I know he's concerned about my safety due to how much Phillip cares for me. For now, he'll protect me, but I'm not sure that would continue to hold true if things begin to get really nasty."

Theresa sighed, lowering her head. "Phillip is in love with you, but if it comes down to you or him, he'll throw you out there to protect himself. He's done it before."

Her words confirmed much of what Mariah had surmised from what little she had learned from Dale and Wes, yet they both had pushed her to use Phillip. Why? What did they know that she didn't?

"I'm not sure he would this time," Mariah said, watching Theresa's reaction.

"What makes you think that?"

Mariah took a few seconds to gather her emotions and thoughts together. "Phillip won't allow anything to happen to me because he's in love with me, and Santiago knows it. That's why he also told me to go to Phillip for protection last night. Because of Phillip's love for me, they're going against their boss." She lowered her head. "He'll do whatever it takes to keep me safe." Tears welled when she gave Theresa the rest of the truth. "Even though he knows I don't love him, he would marry me if I'd agree to it."

Theresa squeezed her hand. "You haven't seen the other side of him. I hope you never get to see it, but I have. In his job, he's ruthless, cold, and calculating. He's exceptionally good at what he does for the Sinaloa." She sat back before saying, "It's like he's two people. At work, he's this ruthless man who can kill without batting an eye. Meanwhile with you, he's this tender loving person."

Blinking back the tears, Mariah didn't comment about her take on Phillip. Instead she asked, "What about Danny? I sort of feel like he's my biggest problem."

Theresa smiled. "He is, but let Dale take care of him. He's working on neutralizing him and a couple of others you aren't aware of who have been dogging you. Again, use Phillip and his love for you to stay safe. If Santiago is telling you to go to him, you might want to do so. Right now, your safety is extremely important to more people than just Dale and Phillip."

Staring at the woman, Mariah felt the weight of all her problems descend on her like an imploded building. Theresa had added more issues for her to consider. Santiago was also trying to protect her even though he was highly involved in the organization attempting to neutralize her. None were aware she didn't know what Rachel had discovered. Phillip was this complex person who could kill without emotion. then come to her with all the love and caring a woman could ever want. With all the information, she had no idea of what to do or even who to trust. She could use Wes's level head right now, but she wasn't positive she could trust him any more than the rest of the people around her.

Chapter Twenty-Nine

Monday, September 21, 2015

MARIAH RETURNED HOME, PUSHING back the urge to go running to get her thoughts together. Things were way too complicated. She let herself into the apartment, the ring of the metal keys dropping into the glass bowl echoed in the silent room.

She stiffened when Dale's soft voice said, "You're late. I was worried something had happened to you."

"I went to breakfast with Theresa." Facing the mantel, she began to rearrange the knick-knacks, unwilling to let him see her face.

An intense sadness settled over her, leaving her short of breath with the pain radiating throughout her chest. She wanted him to love her like Phillip did, but it wasn't going to happen. He was watching over her because that was his job.

With a sigh, she curled into her normal spot on the couch, feeling a tiredness beyond her normal. All she wanted was for this to be over so she could get on with her life.

Dale frowned, watching her. "I'm worried about you. I've never seen you so down."

She refused to look at him. "I'm all right. It's nothing I won't get over."

He took the chair next to her, a gentle hand on hers. "Talk to me."

Slipping her hand from his, she curled tighter into the corner. "There's nothing to talk about. These issues I need to deal with on my own."

"What issues?"

Not caring what he thought, she rattled off all the things she was dealing with. ."Jamison trying to frame me. Phillip. You. Wes. Work. The pending charges against me. Them holding my truck hostage. School, and all the other stuff which has popped up since Rachel was murdered."

He didn't seem to hear any of it except one thing. "What issues with me?"

Her shoulders lifted in a shrug. "The issues are all in my head, so don't get concerned about it. I'm just waiting for this to all blow over and for my life to get back to normal?"

"Normal?" Dale asked as if he didn't know what she meant.

"Yeah. You know. Like it was. No one around so I can concentrate on school, work, and the peace and quiet I had before this all happened. Essentially getting back to my normal routine."

She glanced at him but quickly looked away. Routine. It would ease the pain that would come when he left.

"Is that what you want?" His question had her pulling further into herself.

"It doesn't matter what I want. I need to get back to what my life was and will be again. All of this is only temporary, and when all is said and done, my life will return to what it was with only a few minor changes."

The defeat added to the tiredness pulled her down further into the corner. Over the years she had learned to accept what she couldn't change.

"I'm not one of the temporary problems now that I've found you."

"All you had to do was ask Wes. He knew where I was. I had no one else to use as a contact when I rented the apartment or when I got a job."

Mariah didn't want him to learn about the loneliness that was part of her life since leaving the only real home she had ever known.

Dale stared at his hands. "He wouldn't tell me, saying you didn't need to be disturbed. I had my chance at the farm and blew it."

Twisting her mouth to the side, her voice was laced with disgust. "Yeah. Sounds like him. He told me to forget the past and move on to the future. The next sentence was that I needed to move out and I had two weeks to decide where to go, find a job, get packed, and leave. He did offer to help me get a place. That was the end of my life as I knew it. Other than a couple of trips back for a visit and the calls for the first few years, I've had little contact with him since I left."

Dale leaned forward, placing his elbows on his knees, hands clasped together. "Wes adores you and has missed you a lot since you left. He felt you needed to develop your own life without depending on him. The reason was that he wasn't sure he would be there for you with his job. That was why he wanted you to be self-sufficient."

"Well, that I am. I'm not dependent on anyone." Her voice remained flat and emotionless. "I learned early on just how temporary people are in life."

Not knowing how much he knew about her and Wes, she left it at that. The lesson of how temporary families could be was learned at the age of eight when her parents left without telling her. Then ten years later, Wes, without emotion, told her to leave. Then there were the so-called friends. Other than Rachel, every one of them had simply disappeared after a fleeting bit of time in her life. With Rachel gone, she didn't have one person she could trust, and yes, that included Wes, Dale, and Phillip.

She flicked a glance at Dale. A crease had formed between his eyes as he studied her. "What do you mean?"

Okay. He didn't know the story. While keeping all emotion out of her voice, she told him about her past.

"My parents took off with my brother and sister and left me behind. I was eight. Wes is my cousin, not my father. I don't know why he kept me, but I guess after ten years he felt he had been saddled with me long enough.

"I was expecting him to turn me out at some point, but not in the way he did it." She started to stop but continued after a few seconds. "He gave me two weeks, but I was gone in two days. I had no reason to stay. I had some money I had saved for school, thinking he would let me stay until I had completed my education. I took that and used it for my apartment. I had the job at the club by the end of the first month."

"Why did your parent's leave you?"

She stared at her hands, swallowing the sharp pain she still felt when remembering being told they were gone.

"I've no idea unless it was because of my insomnia. Ever since I was a baby, I've only slept a few hours every couple of days. I guess they couldn't deal with it.

"Wes never seemed to mind since he took care of me a lot before they left. He appeared to like me being there until he started losing girlfriends on account of me.

"Let's face it. He didn't need me hanging around and let me know it. He wanted a life without having me in the way."

Dale was silent for so long that she thought the conversation was over.

"I didn't know you weren't his child."

"I sort of figured that you didn't. Only those who had access to my file at the school knew. It's part of the reason he told me to leave. He had done his duty and wanted me out of his life."

She wasn't sure if that was correct or not, but it was the lasting impression she had gotten from the way he told her to get out.

"Did you ever hear from your parents?" Dale asked,

"Yes, if you call a card from Alaska a few months after they left 'hearing from them.' The enclosed note told me not to contact them and to ask Wes to explain why. I asked, but he only said the reason wasn't important. That was the last time I heard from them and the last time I ever asked Wes about them."

The pain of her family leaving had been magnified when Wes hadn't explained why they had left her there. Then again, she knew she was different and never felt like she was a part of her family. They clothed and fed her, but that was the extent of the actual care she had received from them. Her parents played with her siblings, took them places and did special things with them. She was left at home. They were aware she could fend for herself by age five. Because of that, she hadn't been included in the trips, parties, or even playtime.

That was life for her, and she had accepted not being included, so she had no real reason to be upset when they left her behind. Like now. She had no reason to get all bent out of shape about being left to figure out on her own how to get out of the mess she was in.

"Ask him again. He may tell you now," Dale advised.

Moriah pulled further into herself, not wanting to discuss her past life. "The reasons don't matter any longer. I'll stay in contact with him because he's the only family I have. Other than that, I'm on my own. He made it clear he doesn't want me around."

Dale frowned. "So, rather than learning the truth, you suck it up, pretending the reasons don't bother you."

She let the spike of anger his words had sent through her abate before speaking. "Not really. I learned by age five to not expect anything from anyone and to rely on myself. I learned to accept my life simply because I wasn't like everyone else. Like I said before, people come, and people go. I learned to deal with it as part of my life."

By the way he was staring at her, he didn't believe her. That was fine. No one, including Wes, understood how she had accepted her lot in life.

"Talk to him, Mariah. He has what you need to know. For your information, I've no intention of disappearing. I may have made major mistakes the first time around, but I won't this time."

"Right. And pigs can fly. I'm not that teenager you knew. I've grown up, and the fact that nothing is forever has been reinforced repeatedly over the years," she explained. That was her truth. One that had been reinforced multiple times over the years.

Dale smiled before moving to beside her on the couch. He tugged her close to him. The kiss he gave her was tender yet passionate. "I liked that teenager a lot, but I love the woman she's become. All I want is for you to give me a fair chance to show you how much I love you when this is finished."

Leaning into him, she simply said, "Okay."

As nice as the thought was, it wasn't likely to happen. She added a couple of more bricks to the wall around her heart, not wanting to be hurt when he found out she wasn't who he thought she was, just like all the rest the men she had dated.

He kissed her forehead before letting her go. "You need to get ready for school and I need to get to work. I'll see you this evening," he said, leaving her on the couch.

Her day ended up being uneventful. She returned to the apartment after class to find Dale cooking and talking on the phone. He smiled at her before returning to his conversation and dicing potatoes. She put her books away, took a shower and changed into comfortable clothes, having no intention of going anywhere until class in the morning.

Dale had just set the food on the table when she entered the kitchen.

"Grab a seat. I have some good news for you," he said, darting a glance at her.

She sat and waited while he said grace before helping herself to the food, not pressing him to give her the good news. When they were both eating, he told her what he had learned while on the phone.

"One problem solved. Jamison was arrested this morning along with four other officers. One of them rolled and told them how he was framing you and several others by falsifying evidence. All the charges against you have been dropped and the bail money will be refunded. You can also pick up your truck tomorrow once the paperwork is processed. You won't have to pay any charges for storage either."

Calmly putting her fork on the plate, she folded her hands in her lap before asking, "How did they catch him?"

Dale kept his head down. "A lawyer who was looking into a case involving Jamison said his client would sue the department for false arrest, harassment, and then ask for five million in damages due to the preponderance of evidence which showed they were being framed. The judge agreed and ordered Jamison and four other officer's arrests. All his cases, going back to when he was promoted to detective, will be examined."

As he was speaking, she stared at him. Unbelievable! No more Jamison knocking on her door before class.

"So, to keep the lawyer from suing them, they're giving back the money for the bail and my truck without having to pay for it," she verified.

"Yep. Oh, before I forget. The money they deposited in your account is yours to keep. The internal affairs at the police department believe the Sinaloa fronted the cash but can't prove it. So other than needing the bank statements to show when it was deposited along with the pictures in your file that proved he had something to do with it, it's yours to keep. The lawyer arranged that for you since he was investigating your case specifically.

Okay. She could breathe easy. The lawyer made sure there would be no felony drug possession with intent to sell on her background check. Now she had to find how much she owed to Phillip for his help. Phillip's car could be returned when he got back from his trip. Thinking aloud, she asked, "Why can't I get my truck back tonight?"

Dale picked up the phone and made a call. When he hung up, he said, "We can get it after seven, so you might want to put on some clothes."

Dale drove her to the impound lot. She waited patiently for the man behind the counter to finish on the phone. When he turned to her, she explained who she was and that she was there to get her truck. He slapped some paperwork on the counter before showing her where to sign. He gave her keys to another man to bring her truck to the front of the building.

After checking to verify nothing was missing, she signed the release papers and got behind the wheel. She felt good at having her own vehicle again. Yes, the Mustang had been fun to drive, but she loved her old truck.

Dale left while she finished inspecting the vehicle, so she expected him to be back at the apartment already. When she parked in her normal spot, she noticed Dale's Jeep with Wes's truck beside it. Why was he here? What had happened now?

She hopped out of the truck and locked it before staring at the door to the apartment. With a deep breath, she steeled herself for unwelcome news before forcing herself to open the door. Wes and Dale stood in the middle of the living room talking.

She dropped her keys into the bowl before going to Wes and giving him a hug. He didn't release her immediately like he had done since she had left home. She leaned back and looked up at him, studying his face. Something was wrong. The signs were all there in the way he was holding her and avoiding her direct gaze.

"Okay. Out with it. What's gone wrong now?" she demanded, moving out of his embrace.

Wes had her sit in the chair before saying, "Phillip was picked up today in Dallas. He called me and requested to have you come to see him. He also wants me and Dale to come with you."

Her eyes went from Wes to Dale, then back to Wes. The feeling they were hiding something strengthened. "Why?" she asked, not sure she wanted to know.

"He said it concerned Rachel, and you needed to hear it too. He's willing to turn state's evidence depending on you." Wes gritted his teeth before reluctantly adding, "Seems the man cares a lot about you."

"I know," she said, facing away from him. He could read her face like it spoke to him.

Wes sat on the arm of her chair. His hand was gentle on her shoulder. "Mariah, be honest with him. Don't lead him to think you'll be waiting for him if it isn't true."

"He already knows how I feel about him. When are we supposed to meet with him?"

"Tomorrow. Okay if I use your couch for the night?"

"If you want. Or you can have my bed, and I'll stay out here. I'm used to it," she offered, hoping he would take her bed.

"You can share my room. I can sleep on the futon," Dale said, leaving them alone to prepare the room in response to the slight nod Wes had given him.

When Dale left them alone, Wes lifted her head, staring into her eyes intently. She closed her eyes, trying to hide what she knew he was looking for in his study of her face.

"It's decision time, Mariah. I know Phillip and Dale both love you. You need to decide what to do where they're concerned."

She stood by the fireplace, her back to him, a hand on the mantel. A heaviness settled in her chest when another piece of her heart fell away, the pain consuming her.

"As I said, Phillip knows how I feel about him. He'll always be special, but he knows I don't love him. As to Dale, well…" She let her voice trail off before walking away, going to her room and closing the door.

She sat on her bed, with her back to the headboard before she folded and crossed her legs. No decision needed to be made. She loved Dale, only he would disappear, and she could do nothing about it. Phillip would never be forgotten. He was the first man who had shown her how much he loved her. If it weren't for his being on the wrong side of the law, she would have seriously considered settling for the love he would have freely given her.

Her head fell back against the headboard. She closed her eyes to clear her mind. The sadness couldn't be blocked. It was always there with her, but she could block the pain of loss. Another person she cared about would be leaving her. As she had told Dale earlier, this was her life, and she had learned to deal with it before the age of five.

Chapter Thirty

Tuesday, September 22, 2015

FOR ALMOST AN HOUR Mariah rested, leaning against the headboard. She had avoided letting her mind go back to Phillip and Dale. When she got up, she began the task of polishing her senior thesis. The research was done. Now was the time for fact checking and proofing the document for context errors. When she closed her computer, the clock read close to three and she needed a break.

Not wanting to turn on the light in the kitchen, she used the dim glow from her room to make tea. Her mind drifted back to what Wes had said earlier. She had been totally honest with Phillip, but not with herself. He was more than a friend. She loved him. It was the real reason she would have considered marrying him if he would have asked.

As to Dale, she wanted to believe he wouldn't disappear, only there wasn't much hope he would stay with her. He would never know how much she wanted to believe him. This was one of those times she would negate the words he kept repeating. He needed to prove to her he meant what he said. Until then, she would go on as she had for the past eight years.

Mariah consciously decided she wouldn't ever let another person get so close to her. The pain of them disappearing hurt too much. Not caring if she would miss a lot of life, she knew her decision would keep someone else from ripping out pieces of her heart to take with them.

A slight noise had her raising her head to see Wes watching her, his face hidden in the shadows. Lowering her eyelids, she watched the tea swirl in her cup, not wanting to talk. She glanced at him again, a sadness she hadn't felt in a long time engulfing her. He pulled out a chair and sat beside her. To avoid speaking, she took a sip of her tea then set the cup on the table, staring at it, hoping to avoid whatever he wanted to say.

Gentle fingers turned her head until she faced him. "Talk to me Mariah. I can't help you unless you do."

Turning away from him, the first words out of her mouth were, "Why didn't my parents want me? I need the truth, not an admonishment to forget about it."

He turned and leaned on the table, letting out a heavy sigh. She waited. He remained silent. Mariah pushed her cup away and started to get up when his voice stopped her. It was filled with sadness and pain.

"Your mother's first love wasn't the man you called your father. She married him after the one she loved left her for another woman. She never gave up hope that her first love would come back for her. That man is your biological father.

"Your mother had an affair with him when he returned to town, and you were the result of that affair. She didn't admit she was pregnant until it was too late for an abortion. She quickly had your brother and sister to appease her husband."

Wes lifted his head. His mouth twitched. She waited for the rest of the story.

"Because you were so different from the others, neither one of them really wanted you around. You were a good kid, but they had no idea how to deal with the unique issues you presented by being awake all the time. Then they ran into some financial issues which created more tension in the marriage."

He slid a glance to her then went back to staring at his hands. From his actions, this was hard for him. Waiting patiently, she wondered what was so difficult about telling her how her mother didn't want her.

He began speaking again. "You were a constant reminder of the man your mother had loved enough to bear and keep his child. Eventually she had to decide on abandoning you or her husband abandoning her. By this time, your mother knew your father would never marry her, even if she were free. He didn't want you either. He was having too much fun playing the field, and a child would cramp his style."

He turned his head and sent a smile filled with sadness in her direction.

"I'd been babysitting you from the time you were born. I loved this little girl with the beautiful eyes who would ask the darnedest questions, then wait for the answers.

"I was so scared they would drop you off someplace and walk away, blaming you for their problems. I offered to take you as long as they gave me enough money to feed and clothe you. That's one decision I've never regretted."

After the past eight years, she didn't believe the last sentence. At least now, she had the *why.* The man she had thought of as her father, really wasn't. Her mother was a real trip, cheating on her husband with a man who didn't give two hoots about her or his child. She had been nothing but a reminder of a big mistake.

"Are they still together?" she asked.

"Yes. Things smoothed out once they moved from here and you were no longer around. According to what they've written, they're quite happy," he said, not shying away from saying he had remained in contact with them.

She ran her fingers over her cup before saying, "That means my mother didn't want me once she found out my real father was a total jerk."

"Right," he confirmed.

"Why did you volunteer to take me?"

"The decision was easy. As I said, I started taking care of you when you were a baby. My parents helped, but I liked the little baby doll who moved and didn't sleep. You were with me more than you were at home. By the time I was sixteen, I saw where it was headed, and I couldn't let them destroy the adorable little girl I had come to love as my own.

"When they said they were moving away, I asked if I could keep you with me. They were more than happy to leave you behind. So happy that they left without even telling you they were going."

He shifted his chair to face her. "I loved my little girl so much I adopted her as soon as I got a decent job and had saved the money. It's the reason you have my last name. You're my daughter even though I didn't father you. They signed the papers and returned them in less than a week. As soon as it was final, they quit paying support and no longer contacted me. Your brother has kept me in the loop about what has been happening with them over the years."

"Why didn't you tell me when I asked before?" She was more curious than angry.

Wes shrugged, "I guess I was thinking your mother would realize how special you were and come back for you, but she never did. By the time you were old enough to ask, I didn't think it really mattered anymore. You were my daughter, and I loved you. I couldn't imagine not having you around. I'll always think of you as my daughter, no matter what happens in the future." He glanced at her before adding, "Don't ask about your biological father. I don't know who he is. That's something you'd have to ask your mother, only she won't talk to you. For her, you don't exist."

Mariah studied him in the dim light. She asked a question she had wondered about over the years. "Why would a ten-year-old boy volunteer to take care of a baby then keep her as a teenager?"

Again, Wes took his time in answering. "Part of it was the fascination of this little creature who didn't seem to ever sleep. I guess I needed the love you so freely gave to me. As you grew and followed me around on the farm, I got so I didn't want you to leave. Being an only child isn't much fun and you gave me a companionship I wouldn't have had otherwise.

"My parents thought I was crazy when I kept you, but before they died, they understood why. The happy smile you always wore and the love you gave so freely showed them why I wanted you with me."

She studied her hands folded in her lap. "I didn't think you wanted me around when you told me to leave."

"Nothing could be further from the truth. I made you leave because the longer you were with me, the harder it was for me to let you go. Also, if you had stayed dependent on me, you wouldn't have grown into the lovely woman you are now. Every time I see you, I want to keep you with me, protecting you from ever being hurt. I knew the real world was cruel to people who are different, and I'd done everything I could to protect you from it until you were through with high school."

She asked, "Did I run off all the girls you dated?"

Wes chuckled. "No, I did. None of them were as special as the little girl I was raising. You set this high standard for women in my world, and none of them have measured up to you."

She punched his shoulder. "I'm not all that perfect, and you know it." After a pause, she responded to his admission of why he had her leave. "You're probably right. I wouldn't have grown until I left home. At least I know I have a wonderful dad I can go to if I need to when things get wonky.

"Yes, you do. Even if I appear to be cold, I'm there for you. I heard you when you called for help when you were in jail. I couldn't help you figure out what to do. I had orders to not get involved in your problems from my superior when he discovered you were my daughter."

Okay. He wasn't perfect, but he loved her enough to adopt her and raise her as his. She now understood what he had done and why. Due to his age and how close he was to her and Dale, she was aware he couldn't help her much with the Phillip and Dale issues. She needed to decide what to do with the two of them.

As if he were reading her thoughts, Wes asked, "So, what are you going to do about Phillip?"

"I guess I'll talk to him. I'll admit he's incredibly special to me, so I need to find out what he wants. Things will sort of hinge on what he says to me."

Wes hadn't taken his eyes off her as she spoke. He inclined his head. "I take it you could say you love him."

She nodded in agreement. "Yes, the part Phillip has shown me is that of a special man who would go to the ends of the earth for me if I only asked. I guess I need to see the other side of him to get the total picture, but what I saw, I liked more than a little."

Wes pulled her over onto his lap. "Honey, he wouldn't have ever let you see that part of him. He loves you more than you'll ever know. I'm wondering if he'll be man enough to be honest with you."

She burrowed into his embrace, needing the closeness he was giving her. "He'll be honest with me. He knows if he isn't, I'll walk away and never talk to him again."

Wes hugged her tightly, his cheek resting on the top of her head.

Dale joined them, fully dressed. "You two need to get ready if you want to get there at a reasonable hour. Dallas isn't all that close."

Wes set Mariah on her feet before standing and leaving the room. She started to her bedroom when Dale stopped her by saying, "I want you to know I'll be around no matter what you decide. There's no way I'll be able to walk away from you or let you walk away from me."

She nodded before saying, "I need to talk to Phillip. A lot hinges on what he tells me. After that, I'll decide what I need to do."

Dale gave her a hug. "I wouldn't have expected any less from you."

They arrived in Dallas in the late afternoon. Dale called the contact he had been given for the planned meeting with Phillip. He was told it was postponed until nine in the morning. One of the people who needed to be there was unavailable.

Mariah had packed her schoolbooks and computer, so she decided to use the time to study. She had gotten her assignments from her professors after saying she had a personal emergency. Wes and Dale talked softly as she read and took notes. She was so involved in what she was doing, she didn't notice when they became quiet.

She finally glanced up from her book, surveying them before asking, "What?"

Wes chuckled. "We were wondering if you wanted to go and get something to eat."

"Sure," she said, putting her book down. The two men were almost giggling. "Okay. What's so funny?"

"You," Dale said with a grin. "You were so involved in what you were doing that you never heard us ask if you were hungry."

Wes added, "You took a full ten minutes to realize we were quiet. Your power of concentration is something else."

She stood and stretched her back. "You get that way when you don't have anything to disturb you."

Her words hung there with no comment. She didn't mean her words as a scolding for them staying away, but from the way the two of them sobered, that was the way they took it. Dale and Wes were attentive for the rest of the evening. When the waitress believed the two of them were her boyfriends, Mariah teased them. On the way back to the motel, she wished it could always be like the last couple of hours. As nice of a dream as it was, the time with them today wasn't real life.

They were at the jail early in the morning to go through all the necessary paperwork and scanning to get in to see Phillip. The district attorney met them outside the room. He studied Mariah closely. "I've agreed to a private meeting between Mariah and Ortiz. He knows he only has a half hour maximum with her." His gaze hadn't left her as he spoke.

She glanced at Wes, looking for guidance. Becoming the father she loved, he told her, "Listen to him. He'll guide you about what you'll need to do."

A glance at the DA let her know he had misunderstood what Wes was telling her, but she knew what he meant. It was like her work with the horses on the farm. If she paid attention, they would tell her what to do. Phillip would, too.

She was admitted to a large room with a table and several chairs on both sides. The officer motioned for her to sit at the table on the side where she had entered the visitation room. He left her there, not saying if they could touch or not.

Phillip was let in through the door at the back of the large room. His handcuffs were removed before the officer left through the door where Phillip had entered. Phillip stood studying her. She got up and went around the table and into his arms when she noticed the tears rolling down his cheeks.

"I'm so sorry, Mariah. I didn't want you to ever find out what I did for a living. I had hoped I would be able to do like my father did with my mother and keep you from ever knowing about my other life."

She kept her arms around him but admitted, "I think I knew when I met Santiago." She leaned back and scanned his face. "For me, you'll never be that other person I've been told you are."

He cupped her cheek. "I fell in love with this lovely angel then almost destroyed her."

"How?" Mariah questioned, not understanding what he meant.

"I knew why they were setting you up. They didn't want you to clear Rachel's name because, if you did, you would expose them. I told them to back off, but Jamison wouldn't. That's the reason I paid your bail. I wanted to show them I wasn't going to allow them to hurt you in any way. By the way, I'll never cash that check you gave me, no matter what happens, so add that money back to your account."

"Why?"

"You didn't do one thing wrong. I told them to back off. When they didn't, I used their money to bail you out." He shrugged as if it didn't matter.

"The state is going to give you back the money. I got my truck back and they're letting me keep the money deposited to my account by Jamison since they can't prove where it came from originally." Like him, she shrugged. "The department did it as a way of keeping me from suing the hell out of them since it was a whole lot cheaper."

He shook his head, his lips turning up in a quick smile. "Consider the fees for the lawyer my way of saying I'm sorry."

Mariah saw no use in arguing with him. She took his hand and led him to the table and chairs. Once they were seated, she held his hand, not quite sure of where to go from there.

"What's next?" she asked, hoping he had an answer.

He squeezed her hand. "Now that I've seen you for the last time, I'll be going to prison for a very, very long time for what I've done, no matter what I do. Chances are, I won't live past a few months. Because you believed in me, I'm going to give them the information they want.

"What I needed to tell you is to forget about me. Find that perfect man for you and love him. I knew when I met you, I'd never be able to keep you. For a short time, I lived the dream of having my angel who cared about the person I really am." Pausing, he attempted to keep the tears from running down his cheeks. Sniffling, he told her. "I'm not that other person. That was a man forced to do things he hated. Any time I was him, I had to bury who I was deep inside. With you, I got to see how beautiful life could be with you in it."

He ran a shaking hand through her hair. "That afternoon when I held you as you slept is something I'll never forget. To have an innocent woman trust me to care for her, even if only for a few hours, touched me so deeply I'll always treasure the memory."

She moved to his lap, cuddling into him like she would have Wes. "What if I don't want to move on?"

He hugged her tightly. "You have to. After today, we won't see each other again. I know there is a man out there who'll love you like I do, and you'll love him back. Go and find him. Have that beautiful life you deserve."

She reached up and pulled him down, initiating a kiss neither of them would ever forget. When they parted, she said, "I won't ever forget the wonderful man who loved me for a short time."

"Good. I did something right," he said, holding her close to him.

"Yes, you did," she agreed, staying in his arms for a few more seconds before moving.

Unable to look back, she left him, passing Dale and Wes with the DA on their way in to talk to him. She sat huddled in a chair crying for the man who had to hide who he was in order to survive in a world that made a person choose between life and death daily. Few ever saw or understood that part of the cartels or gangs. On top of all of that, he was sacrificing himself by helping Dale and Wes to keep her safe.

Several hours later Wes and Dale joined her. The tears started again when she saw them. Wes squatted beside her and dried her tears with his thumbs.

"Well?" was all he asked.

She sniffed then blew her nose on a tissue from the small pack one of the officers had given her.

"He sent me away from him. He loves me enough to not destroy my life. His talking to you is because I never saw the bad side, only the good."

Dale took the chair beside her. He, like Wes, dried a tear with his thumb.

"He also saw how much he could hurt you if he continued to deny what he was doing with the cartel."

She refused to look at either of them when she said, "He told me to find the one who would love me and make my life complete. He knew it wasn't him as much as he wanted it to be."

Wes stood and held out a hand to her before saying, "Smart man."

From what Phillip had said to her, she was aware he wouldn't live long once the trial was completed. This had been their last goodbye. He was right. The time had come for her to move forward with her life.

Chapter Thirty-One

Wednesday, September 23, 2015
8:00AM

AFTER MARIAH WENT TO school, Wes, Dale, and Juan made their way to Santiago's compound to verify what Phillip had told them. Phillip had insisted Mariah not be told about what information he had given them. His work with the Sinaloa was the part he never wanted her to know about or see. Dale agreed to keep it from her over Wes's objections. Dale understood why Phillip had asked it of them. Wes didn't.

During the long interrogation, Phillip had given them details of the Sinaloa operation, including the names of the people who were involved and their roles within the organization. Some they knew about already, but many they didn't. Now they had enough proof to arrest many of those the DEA had been observing. The members taken off the street wouldn't shut down the Sinaloa. The goal, short term, was to slow the cartel's operations and stop the new drug.

They arrived at Santiago's estate shortly before eight in the morning. Wes took the lead, ringing the doorbell. The guards at the gate watched them closely but didn't stop them from entering the compound. Clearly, they didn't want problems with the authorities be it US or Mexican.

The door opened to reveal a marble-floored foyer, an antique table with a painted vase on its polished surface. The flowers in the vase were fresh, reflected in the mirror behind them. The man holding the door was heavily muscled, a partially concealed gun showing under his left arm.

"May I help you?" the man asked with extreme politeness, his voice not matching the examining glare.

Wes smiled. "I hope so. We need to speak to Santiago Herrera concerning some information we were recently given."

"And who may I say is calling?" the man asked, staying in the role of butler."

"Wesley Lansing of the US Border Patrol. Dale Warner of the DEA, and I'm sure you know Juan Lopez of the local police."

The man let them into the foyer. "If you would kindly wait here, I'll see if he's able to receive you at this time."

Less than two minutes later the man returned. "Right this way gentlemen." He guided them through the well-appointed rooms. The appearance was old money, not new, with the understated elegance of old and new things. Dale wondered who Santiago really was in his other life. Like Phillip, he had two separate lives.

The man led them to the patio where Santiago was finishing breakfast. There was an extra place setting. Another person had either left or been sent away.

"What may I do for you gentlemen?" Santiago waved a hand for them to take a seat, giving the maid time to remove the dirty dishes.

Once they were seated, Wes, in his soft drawl asked, "Rachel Hartley. What do you know about her?"

Santiago took a sip of his coffee before setting the delicate cup on the saucer with a clink. He pursed his lips with lowered eyelids, remaining quiet so long Dale wasn't sure he was going to answer. He finally looked up at Wes, who had asked for the information.

"She was a stripper at the Golden Cat Gentlemen's Club. She and my girlfriend, Deanna, were good friends." He stopped and waited for the next question.

"What do you know about her death?" Wes asked.

Dale watched the man who was about Wes's age.

"Her death wasn't pleasant from what I've been told. I was also informed she had a relapse and was using a lot of different drugs over a brief period of time."

Dale jumped in with, "How brief?"

Giving a shrug, Santiago stated, "Twenty-four hours more or less."

"How do you know that?" Wes asked.

"She was here the day before she died, and she wasn't using when she was here."

Wes's expression didn't change. Dale leaned on the table, head tilted, observing the man opposite him closely.

"Tell us about her visit here," Dale requested.

Santiago shifted in his chair, moving back from the table. He crossed his legs, then motioned for the guard to leave. He faced them, an unexpected sadness showing on his face.

"She came to visit with Deanna. They normally got together every week or so to talk and have fun together. They knew each other from when they were children, having gone to school together. Deanna watched her go from a bubbly girl to a user who would do almost anything for a fix.

"Rachel started using about ten years ago to deaden the pain of being rejected by her family, then the loss of a man she had loved deeply. She, with the help of Deanna, decided to get clean. Rachel went to Father Rivers' clinic which is the best in El Paso. She stayed there until she felt she could go back to work and not return to using."

He stopped, staring at a point on the wall behind them, blinking rapidly. He released a breath before continuing. "She remained clean for over five years. When she got here, she was so happy. She informed us that she was moving in with a girl named Mariah. They had become good friends over the time they worked together. She talked about going to school and how Mariah was this lovely tiny elfin girl who always had a smile for everyone.

"Rachel and Deanna went shopping for a present for her. Deanna invited Rachel to lunch, but she said she would take a raincheck as Danny, one of the bouncers for the club, was picking her up for lunch. She left here before noon. The next thing I heard about her was a couple of days later. That was when I learned Rachel was dead."

He stopped, eyes down, and shoulders slumped. Dale studied him, dismissing the notion that Santiago was acting.

"You liked Rachel." Dale hoped his observation would encourage the man to add to what he already told them.

"Yes. When sober, she was a lady. I enjoyed having her around. Away from the club, you wouldn't ever be able to tell she worked as a stripper. I keep looking for her to show up so she and Deanna can take off for a fun day in town.

"Do you know where she was planning to meet Danny?" Wes asked.

"No. She never mentioned where, just that she was meeting him."

Dale glanced at Wes before asking, "Do you know anything about an old cult where Xolotl is the main god?"

The slight tensing of his muscles was the only show of surprise Santiago betrayed.

"I've heard of a group of people who still worship in the old Incan and Mayan ways. They never strayed from their religion, worshipping in secret to keep it alive. Other than that, I know nothing about them."

"So, you can't tell us anything about Xolotl," Dale said.

"No. What does that have to do with Rachel?"

Dale glanced at Wes, gauging how much to reveal of what they suspected. "We have a reason to believe they are involved in several murders, including Rachel's."

Santiago didn't react other than to glance at the doorway where one of his guards hovered.

"I've heard rumors of them, but that is all," he said, his direct look letting Dale know he wouldn't answer any more questions on that subject.

Wes's finger played a tattoo on the arm of his chair before he roused himself. "I guess we need to have a talk with Danny," he said before turning to Santiago. "I'd like to thank you for your time."

"Anytime," Santiago returned, a slight crease on his forehead. He sent another quick glance at the doorway.

He shook hands with Dale, palming a piece of paper into his hand before shaking hands with Wes. Dale nodded, keeping the paper hidden as they headed to the door. Santiago had someone he couldn't trust as a guard. Whether the problem was old or new, was a tossup. Either way, he had given them what they needed to know for now.

They were away from the compound and had made sure they weren't being followed before relaxing slightly. Dale opened the folded paper Santiago slipped him. He read it, then reread it.

"What did he give you?" Wes asked, flicking a glance at Dale.

"A warning about Mariah."

"Well, are you going to tell me what it says, or do I have to stop the car to read it?".

Dale reread the note before sharing its contents.

"Keep Mariah under guard. She is the next one Xolotl wants. The date is September 27th, the blood moon eclipse. I promised Phillip to protect her, but someone is watching me now that he has been arrested. Use his men if you need to. They will help you."

"Do you believe him that Ortiz's men will help us?" Wes asked.

"Yes. They're loyal to him, not the organization," Dale replied. "They're still at his house, waiting for me to let them know what to do on his orders. I believe it's time to use them. Santiago knows she's the next target."

Wes drove for a couple of blocks before saying, "He doesn't know who this Xolotl is, but he knows who does. Let's go and talk to Danny and see what information he has for us."

"I was thinking the same thing since he was the last person to see Rachel before she was murdered."

Wes headed to the address they had for Danny. Dale kept watch to see if anyone was tailing them. When no one was following them, he became worried. The Sinaloa had to know they would visit Danny after talking to Santiago.

Also, why was Santiago warning him about Mariah? The answer jumped up and slapped him. Rachel was his girlfriend's long-term friend. Deanna had gone out of her way to help Rachel, only to see her best friend murdered. Santiago was helping them because of Phillip and Deanna, the two people who were closest to him. The pieces fit, making sense to Dale.

11:00 AM

They left Juan at police headquarters in Juárez. Wes parked on the street in front of Danny's apartment building. For someone who got a good paycheck, he lived in an area that left a lot to be desired. Wes scanned the street and surrounding buildings.

"Let's hope we have wheels on the car when we come back out." Wes focused on a group of men on the corner who were watching them.

Dale got out and motioned to one of the men standing on the corner. A man of indeterminate age ambled to where Dale was standing. "Mario, if anything happens to this car, I'll pull that warrant and make sure you're serving time by next week. Understand?"

The small man grinned, showing nothing but nubs where his teeth should have been. "Sí, señor. Pretty car will still be pretty when you come back."

Dale glared at him. "And it will need to run like it does now. Pretty doesn't get it if it doesn't run."

Mario giggled. "It will run, señor."

Wes joined Dale as he strode to the door of the building. "You trust him to watch the car?" Wes glanced back at Mario, who had rejoined the other men.

"He'll watch it. If he doesn't, he'll be serving hard time, and he knows it, along with the rest of the men with him." Dale opened the door and let Wes go in first.

The smell of cooking food, urine, and garbage assaulted Dale's nostrils. They made their way up the stairs to apartment 204. Wes knocked on the door twice only to have it swing open. Exchanging a glance, they pulled their weapons and entered.

Working together with Dale clearing a room then Wes, they cleared the kitchen, half bath and living room and balcony. The bathroom was empty. Wes nudged the door to the bedroom open. Danny's body was on the floor in a pool of congealed blood. Dale checked the rest of the room while Wes felt for a pulse. The body was cold. He had been dead for hours.

They holstered their guns before searching the room for clues, putting on gloves so they wouldn't leave fingerprints. Wes handed him two papers. They contained instructions for how to lure Mariah into a trap.

"Santiago was right. They want her." Dale held the printouts confirming what the note had said.

Dale moved the mouse for the laptop. The screen lit up, showing emails. The original email was on the screen. Going to saved mail, he opened another from Xolotl. It was instructions for Rachel. As he opened more of them, he found Danny had been the one to deliver the last five women who had been murdered. Hitting *print* for those he had seen, he closed them as soon as he had the hard copy.

"Now if we could only trace these to find out who Xolotl is," Dale said.

"Not happening and you know it. It'll all be erased before anyone else gets to it," Wes said with disgust.

Dale noticed a second laptop. He smiled at Wes. "Not so quick. I do believe I need to have the computer he borrowed from me returned,"

Wes quirked an eyebrow. "That isn't quite within the law."

"I know. But we need leads, and this'll be the best chance we'll have. I can justify it by citing the corruption within the local police department. You can verify that I sealed it and didn't let it out of my possession until we got back to the office and it was logged into the evidence room." Dale dared Wes to negate what he was doing.

They gathered the papers Dale had printed, the computer and a cell phone they had found before leaving the apartment, pulling the door almost closed like it had been when they arrived. Dale had the computer, along with the papers, in a bag so it couldn't be seen. Mario nodded to him as they got into the car and pulled off. Dale knew the men wouldn't give the police any information about them having been there.

Dale pulled out a throw away phone and called 911, reporting a murder. When done, he had Wes pull over so he could put the phone in the trash after removing the SIM card. Returning to the car, he removed the gloves and put them in his pocket to dispose of later.

"You'd have made a good criminal," Wes commented, giving the young man a sidelong glance as he drove.

Dale scanned the mirrors, then concentrated on the scene before him. "Probably, but I like being on the right side of the law. I'm not fond of cages."

Wes's jaw muscle tensed from gritting his teeth. He drove for several blocks before asking, "You ever confront them?"

Dale didn't answer for a few seconds. "Yeah. They wanted me to come for a family outing. I went but it didn't go quite the way they wanted when Dad joked about putting me back in the cage because I said something he didn't like. I don't believe they'll ask me to attend any more family functions."

"About time."

Dale added with a chuckle. "I felt damn good telling him how he needed to watch what he said, or I'd put him in the cage and take the key with me to see just how much he liked it. You would have loved his face. My mother was the one who got angry. I cut her off and told her I could arrange an adjoining cage for her."

"What did your brother say?"

"Not a damn thing. He knew better. I told them they were no longer my family, just the people who raised me, treating me worse than they did the dogs. I let them know I had found my real family after leaving them. On my way out, I wished them a happy life. If they bother me again, I'll sue them for cruel and inhumane treatment."

"Who's your new family?"

Dale hesitated then said, "You and hopefully Mariah. You were more of a father to me than he ever was."

Wes pulled into the parking spot at Dale's office building before speaking again. "You had better not let her slip away. You'll never find another like her," he warned before opening the door and exiting the car.

Dale followed suit, retrieving the computer and papers they had taken. "I'm going to marry her. She needn't think I'm going to let her disappear on me."

Wes clapped him on the shoulder before he opened the door. Dale hoped Mariah wouldn't reject him. He wanted this case done. Until then, he had to hide how much he loved her.

5:00PM

Mariah was looking for mistakes in her paper when her cellphone rang. The noise pulled her from the world of the cartels and their organization. Rereading the last sentence again, she picked up the phone and pressed answer without looking at the caller ID.

"Hello."

"Mariah, it's Zelda."

Mariah put the paper down and leaned back in the chair. "Oh, hi. What's up?" she asked not sure what crisis had prompted Zelda to call her.

"Have you heard from Danny today?"

Mariah could hear the worry in Zelda's voice.

"No. I only see him at work. He's only called me a couple of times over the years I've known him. I won't see him until tomorrow night. Why?"

Zelda said something to someone before saying, "Well, he promised to call me last night and he didn't. I've tried calling him all day, but his phone goes right to voice mail."

Fear skittered through Mariah. Memories of trying to call Rachel before she was found murdered came rushing back. Stuffing the fear into a little corner, Mariah attempted to conjure a reason he wouldn't call or answer the phone.

"Maybe he's shacked up with a girl," Mariah said. "He's done that before and didn't return calls or answer the phone."

Zelda took a few seconds before saying, "Maybe that's it, but he usually calls me when he promises he will, even if he's with another girl. Let me know if he contacts you, okay?"

"Sure thing," Mariah agreed before Zelda hung up.

"Men," she muttered before returning to her paper. She wasn't Danny's keeper.

7:00 PM

The sound of the key in the lock let Mariah know that Wes and Dale were back. She saved her work and closed her laptop. Wes sat in the chair while Dale perched on the arm of the couch.

Immediately, she knew something had happened. The question was what.

Dale asked, "How well did you know Danny?"

She frowned, her eyes going to Wes, then back to Dale. "I know him from work. He watched out for me after a customer tried to rape me in the parking lot. I know he dated Zelda and several of the other dancers at the Cat. He brought me home one time when I had to have my truck towed after it wouldn't start. He wouldn't leave me until I was safely inside."

She didn't ask why he had asked the question. Wes shifted in his chair. He and Dale exchanged a glance before turning back to her.

"We went to see him today and found him dead in his apartment. It was an execution. He'd been dead for close to a day from what I could tell," Wes said, watching her. "We know who it wasn't. Do you have any idea of who would want him dead?"

"No. Almost everyone who knew him liked him, but then again, I only know what he was like at work."

"What can you tell me about Miguel and Rico?" Dale asked.

She wondered what they had to do with Danny besides working together. "They're bouncers at the Slipper. I've seen them talking to Becker and Phillip. Other than that, I don't know anything about them."

"Okay. Finished with the questions," Dale said before leaning over and giving her a quick kiss.

She stared up at him, then glanced at Wes, who was smiling. Maybe Dale wouldn't disappear right away after all. The two men went to Dale's room. She reopened her laptop, unwilling to mull over Danny's death and the questions Dale had asked. Even though she had been fond of him for a long time, he had destroyed their friendship when Jamison was framing her and he passed it off as nothing to worry about.

11:00PM

Mariah's cellphone rang. She picked it up and recognized the number. "Hello, Deanna. Everything all right?" At this hour of the night, the chances of this being a social call was nil.

"Santiago wants to talk to you," she said. A male voice came on the line.

"I can't talk long, so just listen to me," Santiago ordered.

Mariah placed her feet on the floor, totally alert now.

"Xolotl. I don't know who he is, but he's in charge of the smuggling. I only handle the normal drugs, but he handles the new stuff. There's this cult he's part of. I don't know where or how they do the murders, but I do know they want you next. Have your men check with Humberto Garcia. He's very close to Xolotl and the cult, if not in it. Let them know I haven't had anything to do with those murders. I try to keep my mules alive so I can use them again."

The phone went dead. She raised puzzled eyes to Wes and Dale who had reentered the living room when her phone rang.

"It was Santiago. He said for you to check with a man named Humberto Garcia, who is supposedly close to Xolotl and possibly the cult. He also said he hasn't had a thing to do with those murders or the drugs they're running.

Wes turned to Dale. "I guess shaking the tree did some good after all."

Dale nodded in agreement. "I do believe a visit to one Humberto Garcia is on the agenda for early tomorrow."

Chapter Thirty-Two

MARIAH WAS PUTTING THE books she needed for the day in her backpack when her cellphone rang. A glance at the clock showed it was only eight in the morning. The number on the screen wasn't one she recognized, so she answered it thinking it was a call canceling a class.

"Hello."

"Mariah, it's Phillip."

Moving to her bed to sit, she tamped down the fear at what this call might be about. "It's good to hear your voice." The love for the man he could have been sent a pain she wasn't expecting through her chest.

"The same for me. Your voice is like a slice of heaven. I can picture the lovely woman who goes with the voice. I wish I was there to give you a hug and a kiss."

"I could use both right now," she said, If only things were different. She remembered how tender and respectful he had been with her. "Is everything okay?" she asked, wondering why he had phoned, aware he had limited time on calls.

"Things have been better, but I honestly can't complain. I don't get hassled by the others, so it isn't too bad."

She could hear the defeat in his voice. He was having a tough time being locked up.

"I do have a reason for calling. Your two men made it so I could talk to you without having to wait for the weekly call time."

Her forehead creased. What was he talking about? She quickly realized that Dale and Wes must have bargained for him to have a few privileges for helping them.

"They can be nice when they want to be. They do look out for me when in the area."

That was the problem. To many times Dale and Wes weren't around when she needed them.

He chuckled. "Mariah, those two will go to the ends of the universe for you, just like I would. I don't know what your relationship is to Wes, but he's one tough man if he believes someone's going to hurt you. Dale was easy to figure out. He loves you like I do."

"Really?" She had no clue as to how he come to those conclusions?

"Really. I guess I'd better let you know why I called. They didn't ask a few questions that I was expecting, so I'm going to give you the information since it involves your safety."

She leaned forward, listening intently to what he had to say. He was still worried about her even though he was looking at a lot of years in prison and possibly being executed while there.

"Danny was involved in the murders. He would pick up the girls chosen by Xolotl and drop them off at a specified address that was changed with each woman. He would then leave. Louis Martinez would set them up and get them ready for whatever they were going to do to them. From what I was told, you're the next one on their list. That's the reason I want you to be guarded. From what one of my friends told me, Danny is dead, so Xolotl has to come up with another way to get to you."

"I take it that Rachel met Danny because she trusted him. They thought I would be like Rachel, meeting him because I thought he was a friend." She hoped she was correct.

"Yes. With you refusing the guards, I put a couple on him instead. One of the big bosses ordered Danny's execution. Danny apparently discovered what they were doing. He was scared and was going to talk to save himself, only he wasn't too bright. He called Jamison, not aware he was working for the cartel. That call resulted in Jamison's arrest and Danny being executed."

"Where do we go from here?" she asked.

"I do know Rachel saw Father Rivers after she left Santiago and Deanna. Danny let that slip when I was talking to him right after Rachel died."

Mariah rubbed her forehead. Father Rivers had denied seeing her. Why? Phillip's voice pulled her back to the phone.

"Honey, I don't know what I'd do if anything happened to you. If Xolotl gets you, he'll kill you. Stay close to Wes or Dale.

Use my men. They'll watch over you and do their best to protect you."

"Thanks for telling me. I owe you." She would never be able to repay him for what he was doing for her.

"You don't owe me a thing. I owe you more than I'll ever be able to repay. Just call my cell. Alfonso has it and will set up the guards for you so only you will know they're there." She heard a voice in the background talking. "I have to go. I love you. Stay safe." He ended the call, not giving her time to say goodbye.

He had to be very afraid to have called her at this hour. She stared at her phone, then hit the quick dial for Phillip's cellphone, hoping she wasn't making a mistake using his men. His call pushed her from major concern to body numbing fear. If she was taken, there was nothing Wes or Dale could do to save her. She wasn't even sure Phillip's men could keep them from getting to her.

"Alfonso here," came the voice of the man who had been the driver of the Hummer.

"It's Mariah. Phillip told me to call you." She didn't know what else to say.

"I was wondering how long it would take you to contact me. You about ready to go to class?"

With that question, she knew he already had a decent idea of her schedule. "Yes. I was almost ready to leave when he called me."

"I have a man a block away. He'll watch over you. Phillip has one on campus who'll make sure no one gets to you while you're there. Use this number to let me know if someone makes you nervous or you need help."

They had been watching over her even without her permission. "How long have you all been following me?"

He laughed. "Honey, we've been doing our best to keep tabs on you ever since you agreed to go out with him. We all volunteered to do it when we saw what he loved about you after you were taken by his boss. Don't worry. We're also working with Dale on Phillip's orders since he trusts Dale and Wesley. Just let me know if you change your routine."

At least they wouldn't be hovering over her. That was a good thing. "Thanks, Alfonso. He didn't say it, but I got the feeling he is more afraid for me now that Danny's dead."

"It changes things. They will need to alter how they get to you. Don't be afraid to call me, even if it seems silly or stupid. Sometimes the trivial things are what gives us a clue about what they're planning. Be sure to let me know if you feel something is wrong, out of place, or simply different. It'll help us to keep you out of their clutches."

"Will do. Thanks again. I'd better get going or I'm going to be late for my class."

"Talk to you later," Alfonso said before breaking the connection.

She hoped he was telling the truth about working with Dale. If not, no one other than Phillip's men would know if something happened to her. She grabbed her backpack and purse from the sofa, then her keys from the bowl, locking the door automatically before heading to school. Her mind already on her first class.

She didn't notice the cars following her as she wended her way through traffic, or the men who followed her as she hurried to class. Like when running, she used the time to think and go over her day, noting only what she needed to accomplish. She had dismissed her conversation with Phillip and Alfonso when her thoughts jumped to her classes.

Mariah didn't return home to the empty apartment until after six PM. She had no idea when Dale and Wes left, not having seen them before leaving in the morning. There was no note, so she didn't know if, or when, to expect either of them to return.

She showered before putting on comfortable clothes and hurrying out the door to make it to work on time. Parking in her normal spot, she glanced around, looking for Danny before remembering he was dead. She was on her way into the building when Quinn joined her.

"Sorry. I didn't see you pull in," he said, shortening his stride to stay at her side.

"No problem. I don't worry so much about coming into work. I get concerned when time to leave because that's when the drunks are in the parking lot."

"Leaving you to walk in alone isn't okay," he said. "I promised Danny I would watch over you."

She gave him a quick glance before saying, "And Dale. I know you're working with him."

"Wrong. I don't work *with* him. I work *for* him. He's my boss."

Mariah stopped and stared up at the big man. "You're kidding, right?"

Quinn chuckled, his big hand turning her back to the entrance, walking a few steps before saying, "No. I'm not kidding. He's the head of this division. Dale took less than a year to become the boss. He's damn good at what he does out in the field. I'd give anything to be half as good."

Nice how she learned from one of his underlings that Dale was more than a field agent. Then again, she hadn't bothered to ask him about his job. Plus, he hadn't volunteered any information other than the agency he worked for during their infrequent conversations. Maybe now was the time for that talk where she got caught up with his life. He already knew about hers.

Quinn walked her to the anteroom for the lockers. "I'll catch you later," he said before disappearing.

Theresa wasn't in the small room. Everything appeared to have changed since last week. No one was where they normally were when she came to work.

She dressed and made the last-minute adjustments to her costume before leaving the locker room. Theresa and Mr. Becker were now in the anteroom. She picked up her order sheets before saying, "Good evening. Any changes I need to know about?"

Becker turned to her, his brows drawn together. "Have you heard from Danny?" he asked. "He hasn't shown up for work for two nights and I can't get through on his phone."

"No. I don't normally talk to him other than at work. I haven't heard from him since Monday morning." She remained factual in her answer.

He let out a big breath. "I wonder if he's all right."

"I don't know," she lied, aware he was dead but not willing to tell them what she knew. It hadn't been in the paper or on the news. "Zelda called me yesterday saying he hadn't called her as promised which is sort of strange. He usually follows through on what he says he'll do."

"I hope he calls me today, or I'll have to let him go. He's a good worker, but without knowing what's happening with him, I won't have a choice. I hope he isn't in any trouble."

"Me, too," Mariah said. "He's my guard dog."

Becker laughed. "You have plenty of others." He sobered before asking, "Have you heard from Phillip?"

She lowered her head, hiding the tears his question had caused. "Yes. He called me. He was arrested in Dallas. I'm worried about him. All this stuff seems to be happening all at once."

A hand rested on her shoulder. She wiped the tears from her face before raising her head. The kindness in his eyes, had her crying again. He took his handkerchief and dried the tears.

"I'm sure he'll be all right, along with Danny. Don't you worry about them," he told her with a glance at Theresa.

"I hope so. I don't have so many friends that I can lose two at once," she said, her voice laced with fear and sadness.

Theresa glanced at Mr. Becker then back to her. "I'm still here, so if you need to talk, let me know."

Mariah let a smile flit across her lips. "I guess I'd better get to work before Molly thinks I didn't show up," she said, leaving them to discuss her and Phillip. Tonight was going to be long without him here to brighten it with his smile.

As Molly was giving her report, she noticed Santiago entering the pit and taking his normal seat. He had two men she hadn't seen before with him. She hoped he wouldn't disappear now that Phillip wasn't around.

Chapter Thirty-Three

Friday, September 25, 2015,
Midnight Xolotl

SHE IS SAFE, XOLOTL. I got rid of the one who would defile her. You will love her beauty and innocence. A woman-child who is a virgin. She will give us both what we want. When the moon shows red and goes dark, she will be yours. Unlike all the others, she is pure. Wait until you see her, oh great one. You will keep her. With her you will have taken a big piece of the light's power."

The statue grinned in the candlelight as the flames danced in a light breeze. His hand touched the smiling face of the perfect unspoiled woman in the picture before returning to his talk with Xolotl.

"I'm tempted to defile her, but I'm your servant and you need her unspoiled. I can see her soul in her eyes. She is so trusting. I know you will love her. With her, I'll join you. We will love her as one. She will draw others to us because your power will multiply greatly with the blood she will shed for you.

"Wait until you touch her. You will feel it like I did. A power we have been lacking. It is there within her. She has the face of an angel, but it is her eyes. I can't forget them. They are the gray of a misty morning before the sun rises fully, with flecks of a clear blue sky. She has so much beauty within her. She shines like a rainbow as the sun comes through it, shimmering in the light."

"I'm saving her for you. As a man, I want her, but I'll get so much more when she comes to you unspoiled. We will share her blood.

"Think of it. The power of innocence! I can feel it when near her. I can only imagine what it will be like when I have that innocence within me."

"It won't be long now. Soon we will join and revel in the power she will give us with her blood. Soon. Very soon."

Chapter Thirty-Four

*Saturday, September 26, 2015,
Morning*

MARIAH ARRIVED HOME BEFORE five in the morning. The apartment was silent. Dale still wasn't here. She checked the door to ensure it was locked, then went to get some sleep. She hadn't slept in three days. The stress since Phillip's arrest had tired her to the point where she needed more than just resting.

After changing into a nightshirt, she curled into a ball on the bed, closed her eyes and drifted to sleep. Swift moving dreams of the events which had occurred over the past week filled her sleep. She was dreaming of Wes's hand on her shoulder when his voice pulled her from the dream.

When she opened her eyes, he was sitting on the edge of the bed. The dark circles under his eyes and stubble on his face showed he hadn't slept or shaved in over twenty-four hours. He was studying her intently as if to memorize her face. Whatever was happening had to be important for him to awaken her.

"You look like you need to sleep as much as I did," she said, sitting up to talk to him.

"I'll sleep later," he said. "Are you all right baby girl?" A gentle hand pushed a strand of hair off her face.

"I'm fine. I hadn't slept in three days and needed to crash for a couple of hours." She glanced at the clock. She had been asleep for more than four hours, but that was something he didn't need to know. He seemed to have enough problems to handle without adding hers to them.

"We need to talk to Father Rivers again. Dale asked me to find out if you wanted to go with him."

Why hadn't Dale come and ask her himself? She let it pass.

"Sure. Let me get ready."

"I'll let him know," he said before leaving as silently as he had come.

Her gaze remained on the door as she questioned what they had been doing that hadn't allowed Wes to shave or sleep. The dream he had awakened her from came back to her. She hoped it wasn't a precursor of things to come. He had been telling her goodbye. In her dream the separation was one where he wouldn't ever return.

She sat for a few more seconds before dressing. Fear of Wes's dying was something she had lived with ever since she had learned what he did outside of the farm. The chance of his dying was more real now that she knew more about the dangers of his job. If she lost him, she wouldn't have any family left. Even though they had been estranged, he was still her family and was there in the background. Until recently, he was that emergency person she knew would come if she was hurt or in major trouble. Without him, she would have no one at all, leaving her out there twirling in the wind by herself.

Life was fragile. So were the connections to those around her. What she needed was at least one person who would be there for her other than Wes. Rachel had been that person, but now she was dead. Danny had proven to be a false friend. Phillip would have been there for her, but he was now incarcerated due to the other life he led. Dale? He said he loved her, yet he might still disappear when this was all over. All the other people she knew were only acquaintances. They would become memories when she switched jobs or moved from El Paso.

She was an island with no connection to the land around her, the water of life slowly eroding her, showing how insignificant she was in the scheme of things. Like the island, her survival depended on her foundation. Wes had given her a good base, but she wasn't sure about all the surrounding things which she thought of holding her in place. Things like school, job, friends, and everything else that made life livable. Only time would tell if she could survive what was happening to her.

She dressed and brushed her hair. Studying herself in the mirror, she had no idea of what men saw in her. She had nothing unusual about her other than being short and having unusual gray eyes. Her figure was decent, but nothing others didn't have. Whatever they saw, she didn't see it in the mirror.

After unplugging her phone from the charger, she put it in her purse before joining Dale. He was waiting for her in the living room. Like Wes, his face was lined with exhaustion, but he had shaved.

"You look like you should get a couple of hours of sleep before going anywhere," she told him, pausing in the doorway.

He ran a hand over his face. "I'll sleep when we get back."

She moved to the door. He opened it and let her go out first. She glimpsed one of Phillip's men getting into a car. Alfonso had made good on his promise to make sure someone was always watching her.

Dale's hand guided her to the passenger side of his jeep. He opened the door before saying, "I'm glad you took Phillip up on his offer to have his men guard you."

She took her seat and waited for him to join her in the car. "How do you know I took him up on it?"

"Al called me and let me know and how many he had on you. He wanted to make sure we would have full coverage."

Staring at him for a few seconds, she asked, "So you've had someone following me?"

"Not until after you were kidnapped. I couldn't get enough agents until then. Phillip's had a couple keeping tabs on you since then as well. We decided to join forces when he found out I was staying here with you."

He had started the car and backed out of the parking space as he talked. His explanation had her head reeling. He and Phillip were working together, yet his agency had arrested him. Nothing was making sense!

"How well do you know Phillip?" she asked.

He stopped at a red light. Scrutinizing his mask-like face didn't give her any answers.

"Well enough for him to ask me about you after his man saw me going in and out of your place. We agreed not to fight over you. That's how I knew he loved you as much as I do and would do everything in his power to keep you safe."

"Which explains why you told me to go to him," she said, needing verification of what she thought was correct.

"Yes. He has more resources at his disposal than I do. He also has a group of men who are loyal to him, and only him. He made sure they knew to keep you safe." Dale kept his eyes on the road.

"So, he knew about you?"

"He didn't know about our relationship. I've never lied to him, so when he asked how I felt about you, I was honest. He could tell there was someone else you loved other than him. Unlike Wes, he told me that if I ever hurt you, he would make sure I felt the same pain you did. He'll carry through on that threat no matter what happens."

Dale briefly met her eyes. Nothing made sense. They both loved her, yet they were protective of her and her feelings. She cared for them both, but Dale was the one she wanted. Phillip was that dream man any girl would want, but Dale was her reality—the one she had loved for years.

She was sixteen when she discovered how much Dale meant to her. He thought she was asleep on the couch when he kissed her that one time. When he had moved away from her, she had opened her eyes and smiled at him. He stared at her until he finally said Wes wanted her down at the barn before disappearing. Until now, that was the only time he had ever kissed her. No way would she ever tell him she had been awake and remembered it all these years.

Was she wrong to have loved him like she had, waiting for him to come to her? Each kiss he had given her over the past few weeks had strengthened her feelings for him. Now, to find out that Phillip knew about him and hadn't attempted to break them apart; instead, he only threatened to hurt Dale if he hurt her, was unreal.

Pulling her thoughts together, she smiled, "Then I guess you had better make sure you don't hurt me."

He grinned. "True. I only needed to know who you wanted."

Her brows shot up at his statement. "I'm not some fickle female who falls in and out of love at every turn. As much as I care for Phillip, I've never lost my feelings for you."

"That's good, because I've never lost mine for you. I'm hoping we can manage to help Phillip get out of this mess by having him cooperate with all the different agencies. If he can, you'll have that best friend you need."

She frowned, turning to him. He was smiling.

"You can't be serious!" What Dale said was unbelievable.

Dale laughed after glancing at her. "I'm totally serious. He and I have been friends for years. I've known what he does right from the start, but we're still close friends. Both of us loving you is the universe's joke on us. He'll be there for you like me and Wes."

She couldn't imagine him allowing her to remain friends with Phillip, aware of how much he loved her.

Dale reached over and squeezed her hand. "I've no reason to be jealous of him. You're the one who will choose who you want. No matter what you decide, we both will accept your choice and support the other person. Like him, I'll be your best friend if you decide you want him and not me."

None of this made sense to her. But then again, what she knew about men would barely cover the bottom of a child's teacup. The rest of the drive to the rehabilitation center was done in silence, giving her time to mull over what Dale had told her.

They only had to wait for a few minutes for Father Rivers to join them this time.

"Mr. Warner, Miss Lansing. What a pleasure to see you again." His saintly smile was friendly and welcoming. "To what do I owe this pleasure?"

The kindly man began to stroll through the garden where they had been directed to meet him. "From what I've been told, you did see Rachel on the day she died," Dale said, observing the priest.

He sighed. "Yes, I saw her. She showed up here about one. I only had a few minutes to spend with her. I can't divulge what we discussed in those few minutes since it was confidential. She was with a man named Danny. I expected her to be here at two, which was the time for her appointment, but she left and didn't return. I was with her for less than five minutes."

Dale walked a few steps with the priest before saying, "Danny is dead. There seems to be some sort of tie to an ancient Nahua cult. Do you know anything about them?"

Father Rivers drew his brows down, concentrating on the walkway as they followed it through the flowers and plants. "I can't say that I do. I didn't study cults, preferring to learn about the church and how to get and keep those who want to be saved. I've not heard any mention of any cults in this area."

Dale stopped and held out his hand. Father Rivers shook it. "Thank you for your time. I wasn't sure if you would have heard anything in your work with the addicts or in a confession. If you hear anything about them, you have my card. Please call me. I'm attempting to tie up a few loose ends."

They left Father Rivers to finish his walk in the garden, returning to Dale's Jeep. Dale stopped and looked back at the buildings, his lips pursed, but didn't comment on the exchange with the priest.

He didn't talk on the way back to the apartment either. Mariah didn't attempt any conversation, having her own thoughts to ponder from their conversation this morning. What she needed was Phillip's confirmation of what Dale had said.

After they entered the apartment, Mariah commented, "That was a wasted trip since it was a dead end."

"Maybe," Dale answered as he stared at the wall, frowning.

Wes entered the room, looking less haggard than earlier. He had shaved and appeared to have slept a little. "You ready to go and find Humberto?" he asked.

Dale pulled himself from his thoughts. "Give me a couple of minutes. We do need to get to them before they run to their holes like the rats they are."

Mariah sat on the couch while Wes made coffee. She could hear them talking.

"This Xolotl has them all running scared," Dale said. "I don't know who he is, but whoever it is, he wields a lot of power."

"My bet is Antonio or someone close to him. I can see him using a cult or being in one. If you noticed, they were all staying away from him during the meeting," Wes responded.

"I'm not so sure about that. He's the head of a group there in Juárez, but I can't see him as the leader of a cult. Phillip was leaning toward Humberto. Again, I can't see him as Xolotl even though he keeps talking about the moon and how it will be eaten soon."

Mariah leaned against the doorframe before saying, "The jaguar will eat the moon when it's red. There's a blood moon eclipse on the twenty-seventh of this month and the new moon is on the twelfth of October. Phillip said I was next. They will make a move for me before one of those two dates. My guess is they will try to get me today for tomorrow night."

The men stared at her. She knew what they were thinking. No one could get to her. They were wrong. These people would find a way, just like they had found a way to kill Danny. Like they had Santiago running scared. Like they had Phillip arrested so he was out of the way.

Wes moved next to her. The worry lines on his forehead deepened as he stared into her eyes. "How do you know you are next?"

"Phillip. He called me yesterday morning and told me. He also said Danny was the one who took the girls to the drop off point. Louis Martinez took them from there and Danny would leave. Danny didn't know what was happening to them until Rachel was found dead. Phillip also mentioned that Rachel had seen Father Rivers on the twelfth of August.

Wes turned to Dale. "You have everything in place?"

"Yes. If we knew who Xolotl was, this would be so much easier."

"We do have a line on the other players. We need to make sure Mariah is watched extra closely for the next couple of weeks." Wes turned back to her. "One of the reasons Jamison was framing you is that they wanted you tied to the drug smuggling and the cartel. It would create a reason for your death to be dismissed like Rachel's."

Dale came to where she was standing. "Please stay here until we get back. That should be somewhere around five. Al and one of my men will be near."

She understood his concern. Having done her research, she knew the danger she was in until after tomorrow. By the clock, it was one-thirty now. She would only be alone for three and a half hours. "Okay," she said, agreeing easily but knowing so much could happen in three hours.

Both men kissed her before leaving. She wanted to tell them not to leave her alone, but they had a job to do. Even though she had guards, she didn't feel any safer. Everyone was underestimating the resourcefulness of the enemy. That was why they would get to her, even with the men on guard duty.

Going to the couch, she sat in her favorite spot. Crossing her legs, she breathed deeply, centering herself until she was meditating. This was the only way to prepare herself for what was to come. Until Phillip's call, she had expected to skate through this unscathed. But she now knew that wasn't going to happen. The bit about the jaguar and the moon told her differently. She was going to be used to appease the jaguar. It was a ritual thought to have been abandoned. Mariah was certain it had been kept alive by the Nahua, used by the Sinaloa and she was next.

Chapter Thirty-Five

*Saturday, September 26, 2015,
Afternoon*

A KNOCK ON THE door disturbed Mariah's concentration on her thesis. She checked the time on her computer. Who would be here at this time of day on the weekend? She checked the peephole. It was Zelda. Mariah cracked open the door, leaving off the security chain, wondering why Zelda was here instead of calling.

"Zelda. What can I do for you?"

Two men she hadn't seen pushed the door open. One grabbed her. She let out a squeal. He pulled her into the room. The one on the left gagged her before she could gather enough breath to scream.

Zelda entered with the men. Her satisfied smile as she watched them tie her arms and legs made Mariah more afraid than what the men were doing to her. When Zelda looked down at her as the men held her in place, Mariah's intestines contracted, sending pain up to her chest. She now understood that Zelda knew what had happened to Rachel because she was working with the cartel. It was all making more sense. She had known about Rachel's death when they had talked at the Golden Cat. She had probably helped set Rachel up for Danny.

"You were told to leave Rachel's death alone. You didn't. Because of you my Danny's dead. Now your turn has come Miss High and Mighty. You'll honor Xolotl by giving your life to him. A fitting end for a Miss Goody Two-shoes like you, I do believe."

Zelda opened the door for the men to carry her to the waiting van. They hid how she wasn't walking and was gagged, using their size and keeping her sandwiched between them. One of the men joined Mariah in the back while the other one drove. They didn't care if she recognized them. That and Zelda's words told her what her fate was to be. She was the next sacrifice. The one planned for the eclipse of the blood moon.

Zelda was the last person she expected to be involved in something like this. Sure, she used, but she didn't seem to consort with others who were using or selling. Mariah now guessed what Rachel had found out. Somehow, she had connected Zelda and Danny to the killings and the new drug.

Mariah made herself as comfortable as possible. She was prepared for what she expected to be a long drive. They would need to cross the border where no one would check the van. That meant at least an hour or more drive from El Paso.

The van stopped at a gas station where the driver filled the tank. The next stop was more than an hour later and involved the driver talking to someone. They joked around, then the van moved again. They were across the border. About an hour later, the van slowed. Mariah guessed they were in a town or city from the traffic and noises. Several turns later they left the town before the van turned onto a dirt road. Each turned took them onto worse roads until the van slowed and stopped. The driver turned off the engine.

The men pulled her from the van, carrying her through wooden gates set in an old stone wall enclosure. The gates closed behind them. They opened the door to a small wooden building to the right of the gates. She was carefully placed on a narrow wooden bed with a thin mattress then covered in clean sheets with the creases still in them.

The driver turned to the man who was waiting in the shadows. "Here she is, Louis. Xolotl wants her ready by tomorrow night."

Louis stepped into the light, staring down at her. Mariah recognized him as one of the men who had been with Phillip on several occasions.

"She'll be ready," he said before looping a rope across her middle and tightening it. He did the same at her neck and across her legs. He had done this more than once from the way he had everything prepared to tie her to the bed.

Going to the cabinet he took out a syringe and filled it from a bottle which was sitting on the table. Her eyes followed him as he returned to where she was tied. He bent over, cleaned her arm, then injected whatever the drug was into the muscle.

Louis watched in silence while the drug began to take effect. She felt like she was drunk. Soon her muscles felt like they had melted. She could barely keep her eyes opened. Louis hadn't taken his gaze off her. He removed the gag. She attempted to stay awake. Afraid of what would happen if she didn't.

"Feeling pretty good now?" Louis asked, lips turned up in a smile.

She let her eyes drift shut, not bothering to stop the tears. He loosened the ropes before untying her legs, then her hands. He leaned over and kissed her. Her eyelids felt like they had lead weights attached, but she forced them open to stare at him.

"Don't worry, little one. That's all I'll ever do. Can't have you falling asleep on me just yet." He sat her up before moving her to a chair with arms on it. He slipped a harness-type contraption over her. She wasn't sure if it was to keep her upright or from escaping.

He poured a clear liquid from a big dark glass bottle into a glass before coming back to her. "You need to drink this. It will help with what is to come," he said, no longer smiling.

She took the glass from him. It felt like it weighed pounds instead of ounces. Whatever the glass held, it tasted awful. She managed to swallow it, but it didn't stay down. He had a bucket ready as if he expected the reaction. He had her drink another glass of the vile liquid with the same result.

The next glass of liquid he gave her tasted better. She followed his instructions to drink it all. An hour or so later she told him she needed to use the restroom. He moved her to a portable commode before giving her more of the liquid, leaving her on the commode, with the harness hooked to where she couldn't undo it. Mariah was thankful he had left her there when the full effects of what he had given her took hold. Through the drug haze, she knew he was making sure her bowels were clean for the drugs they were going to make her swallow.

Hours later, when she was empty, he moved her back to the chair, refastening the harness to it before giving her another injection. He had her drink the first liquid he had given her, which again made her sick. When he was satisfied that she had nothing left inside her, he pulled out the reason for all the internal cleaning.

Handing her a thick liquid and a packet, Louis ordered, "Swallow it, Mariah."

From the feel of the little bag, she would be unable to bite through it before he could get it away from her. The covering was strong enough the withstand the acid in her stomach and would be hard to puncture or tear. She had no options. Putting the packet in her mouth, she took a drink of the liquid and swallowed. Louis repeated the process until she had twelve little packets inside of her.

After she swallowed the last one, Louis took the glass from her. Her fate was sealed. A calm sadness overtook her as she accepted what was to come, the drugs he had given her masking the fear. The tears which ran down her face were for the future she would never see. All her struggles had been for nothing.

Louis raised her bowed head. She met his eyes, without fear, the drunken feeling now gone. "I can see why Phillip fell for you. A man could drown in those beautiful gray eyes. They are like the mist in early morning with flecks of blue. They show this strong, yet innocent child, who's all woman. If I could, you're one I'd save from him."

"Please," was all she could say.

Louis shook his head. "Not happening, doll. He'd kill me and find you. Neither one of our deaths would be easy or painless. This is the way things are and for now, I'd like to keep on living."

She gave a slight shrug. "It's okay. I was a horrible mistake who was allowed to be born. If she would have aborted me, it would have saved everyone a lot of trouble."

Mariah closed her eyes, letting the last tendrils of the drug pull her into a resting state. Phillip had sacrificed himself for her, only to have her die like Rachel. She would never find out if Dale would stay with her. Wes was going to miss her, but not for long. She had been a shadow person her whole life, flickering briefly in and out of other people's lives. As soon as she was gone from sight, she was forgotten, an ethereal being from the edge of a fantasy.

Dale and Wes met Juan at the border. He came with them to pick-up Humberto. They found him at the pharmacy where the lab was located.

Juan said, "You need to come with us, amigo."

Humberto didn't object. The three men had counted on him going with them to prevent them from searching the pharmacy. What he didn't know was that as soon as they left, a group of DEA and Mexican police would close down the lab. They knew Fulton was there and getting him was the team's priority.

When they arrived with Humberto at the police station, he was taken to an interrogation room. Dale watched through the two-way mirror as Juan handcuffed the calm man to a chair that was bolted to the floor. A few minutes later, Dale and Wes entered the room. The two of them sat so one was on each side of the cuffed man.

Humberto bravely bragged, "I'll be out of here before you get home, gringos."

Dale tilted his head. He studied the man like a lion would a tasty free meal. "You sure about that?"

Humberto lost some of his bravado. "I'm sure." His gaze was flicking between the two men, uncertainty showing in his actions. Juan entered the room and sat on the edge of the table facing him.

Juan calmly said, "Humberto, you won't be leaving this jail until just before your trial. That will be after the extradition papers are processed for said trial in the United States. You see, there are charges for murder against you in the States and I already have the extradition approved.

Fear took the place of his earlier boasting. "They can't tie me to any murders," he said, eyes darting between the three men.

"Yes, I can," Wes informed him. "I have a trail that leads directly to you for at least four murders and we are working on the other fifty-six linked to Rachel Hartley's murder. She was an American citizen and her murder concerns us. We'll prosecute you in Texas for all of the related murders."

Dale sat back and crossed his legs, straightening the crease in his jeans. "I can keep you on this side of the border, but I need some help here. I need to know where to locate the Nahua."

"I can't help you," Humberto said, shrinking back in his chair, his eyes wide, like he was watching a horror show.

Juan glanced at Dale and Wes before saying, "Fine. You're looking at the death penalty in Texas and hanging here."

"Why?" Humberto asked, unsure who to concentrate on for the answer.

"Murder, amigo. Sixty murders at this point to be exact. By the time you get to trial, the count may have risen. We only have to tie you to one to make the rest stick," Juan said like this was something he did every day.

"I didn't murder anyone." Humberto's voice rose to a squeak.

"Then who did?" Juan asked, arms folded across his chest.

"Xolotl kills them. He sacrifices them," Humberto said with a swiftness that showed he wasn't going to take a murder rap for anyone.

"Who is Xolotl?" Juan asked, not changing his stance or expression.

"I don't know. I've never seen him without a mask. You might want to ask Louis Martinez. He talks to him all the time. I haven't killed any of those women."

"You know where the meeting grounds are. Tell me where to find him," Juan commanded.

Humberto began to cry. "They'll kill me."

Dale faced the very frightened man. "Not if you were far away from here and under my agency's protection."

"How far away?" Humberto asked, hope in his voice as he licked his lips.

"Far enough they won't find you until we get them," Wes said.

Dale added, "I can get you away from here, but I need to know who Xolotl is. I know I'll find him where the Nahua meet. Tell me where and I'll arrange for you to get out of here and make sure you aren't charged with anything more than an accessory to what Xolotl has been doing. We'll decrease your sentence for helping us."

"If you lie to us, the deal is off," Wes said. "You become a state witness and we'll hide you where they won't find you."

Humberto sniveled before asking, "How many years will I have to be in jail?"

"Five if you're telling the truth and had nothing to do with the murders. We'll charge you with the manufacturing of drugs with intent to sell. You have no record in the States, so you'll get a light sentence for helping us. Again, you lie to me and I'll make sure you never see freedom again," Dale warned.

"I'll take it," Humberto said, visibly shaking.

"Where will I find the meeting grounds?" Dale asked again.

"It's on the Sanchez rancheria southwest of Juárez. There is a walled enclosure there on the edge of the property. They will have guards along the top of the wall, along with two patrolling outside and inside the gates. Four men will be in the building on the left and Louis will have the girl in the one on the right of the main gate.

"The gate is closed with a wooden bar on the inside once Xolotl enters the grounds. If you are facing the gate on the outside, on the left wall is a hidden opening, also closed with a wooden bar." He took a deep breath, fear in his eyes, before saying, "There is a ceremony tonight for the eclipse. The girl should already be there. Louis has orders to kill her if the place is attacked."

Dale exchanged a glance with Wes. A spike of fear went through him. "If you are lying Humberto, I'll hang you out so all the wolves can have a piece of you. Understood?"

"Understood," he said before turning to Juan. "I'm dead if you put me in a cell."

"Not to worry. As soon as they let me know that what you told us is true, you will be spirited out of here to a safe place," Juan promised.

Dale hit the icon for Mariah. Her cellphone went to voice mail on the second ring. He hung up and called Alfonso.

"Al, check Mariah. Her cellphone is turned off." He hung up. "Let's go. If they have Mariah, we need to get to her before the ceremony."

Wes made several calls, setting in motion the teams who would be helping them. He glanced at his watch and frowned before lifting worried eyes to Dale.

Dale checked his phone. They were running out of time. The eclipse was due to start at nine PM Sunday evening with the moon fully covered at ten forty-seven PM. They had just over twenty-four hours to save Mariah

Chapter Thirty-Six

DALE AND WES HEADED back to El Paso while Juan and his men put the plan they had come up with into action. The closer they got to Mariah's apartment, the more apprehensive Dale got. He jumped at the ringing of his phone, making him glad Wes was driving.

"Talk to me Al," Dale commanded.

"She's not here. I'm questioning my men as to why they didn't know she was gone. I'll have answers by the time you get here," he said before hanging up.

"They have Mariah," Dale said, his voice not betraying the fear poking him like thousands of needle making him jittery. Different scenarios, none of them good, whizzed through his thoughts.

"If anything happens to her...," Wes let the statement hang in the air, not finishing the threat.

Dale knew Alfonso would question all the men, including his, about how Mariah was taken without anyone noticing. He would have answers, but no one would like them. He blamed himself for not taking her with him. Wes had talked him out of it, saying she was safer at home. He had been wrong and now time was critical if they were going to save her.

They arrived at the apartment less than thirty minutes after Alfonso called. He was waiting for them by the door, face grim.

"Dale, Wes. Come on in. I know how they got her without being seen. "He opened the door and waited for them to enter.

"What happened?" Wes asked, anger making his soft voice clipped and gravelly.

"The guards at the back were watching a young man who was going from door to door trying to open them. Meanwhile, out front, a salesman was giving the tenant on the end a problem. A girl went to Mariah's door. Before it opened, a big dog began barking at Benito and Vince. They concentrated on the dog. When they got rid of it, the girl who had been at the door was leaving, but she was alone."

"Which meant they thought Mariah was still in the apartment. Nice." Dale ran a hand through his hair and let out breath of frustration.

Taking Mariah had been so easy for them. They knew approximately how long they would need to get Mariah out of the apartment. At least two men and the woman had been involved along with the salesman and the pretend robber.

Dale scanned the living room and noticed Mariah's phone on the coffee table. He picked it up and smiled. He now knew why it had gone to voice mail. He shut off the recording, then hit *play*. They all listened as Zelda said her piece. Dale shut it off when he heard the door click shut.

"The filthy bitch," Vince spat.

"Who's Zelda?" Wes asked.

"One of the strippers at the Golden Cat. She was supposedly Rachel and Mariah's friend," Dale answered.

"With friends like that, who needs enemies?" Alfonso asked. "What now?"

"Okay. We know where they have her. We need a plan to get to her before the eclipse." Wes ran a hand through his short hair.

Dale placed a call to Juan. When he answered, Dale told him, "They have Mariah. She was set up by Zelda. We're going to need that backup we talked about yesterday."

"How many are we talking about?"

"I can get about twenty there in two hours. To make it airtight, we'll need maybe ten or twelve more. I'll bring Phillip's four men who are here if you're okay with that."

"Bring them. I'll meet you at the crossing to keep you from waiting in line."

Dale glanced at Wes. "Wes is coming back with me. The woman they have is his daughter."

"What time do I need to have everyone together?"

"The eclipse starts at nine PM. It is midnight now, Make it six AM. That will give us time to scope out the place, make final plans and get into position to see who all goes in and out and verify their defenses."

"You got it. I'll meet you at four AM at Paso del Norte Port. Our songbird is safe for now. He's been singing a pretty song ever since you left. He is doing everything he can to prove he had nothing to do with those murders," Juan said, a smile in his voice, before hanging up the phone.

Dale didn't have a chance to say he would be singing too if threatened with life in a Mexican prison or death by hanging. They all found a place to sleep until three when they left Mariah's apartment, using the Hummer since everyone could fit into it. Sometimes it paid to have rich friends.

Chapter Thirty-Seven

SHE IS MINE. THEY are preparing her now. I will become one with you tonight Xolotl. Our darkness will reign with the blood of the virgin. The power we will have!

"The green knife will sing with the power of her blood. Your voice will rise to the stars, rejoicing for what I have done. The power you had will return through her. Your loyal subjects will revel in the blood of the virgin."

With a cackle, he stared at the knife. "Thank you, Phillippe for saving her for me. Too bad you won't be able to enjoy what she will give me."

Gathering the knife, his robes, and the mask he would need for the ceremony, he prepared to leave his simple room. The small room was all he needed. He had riches most only dreamed about, but that was for Xolotl to use, not him. With this sacrifice, he would become Xolotl and rule as a god. Xolotl had promised him that when he told him about the perfect virgin he had found.

Today all his dreams would come true. All the years of waiting would be worth the result...bonding with Xolotl. With his bag in hand, he hurried to his car. The hours were passing, and he needed to talk to her. She needed to accept her fate, rejoicing in going to Xolotl. If only she would come to him, singing like the girls of old.

Chapter Thirty-Eight

DALE, WES AND JUAN met with Jorge Sanchez, the owner of the ranch where the Nahua held their rituals. He was a friend of Juan's and had quickly agreed to meet with them. When Dale asked him about the compound, Jorge informed them that the religious group had leased the compound for the last hundred years. They paid their lease on time and hadn't created any problems in the area.

Juan asked his old friend, "Do you have the plans for the ranch and the stockade. I know the Spanish had to send their plans to the governor with what they were planning to build."

Jorge took them to his den. He opened a container with the original plans. Unrolling the hand drawn maps of the ranch, he pulled out the one with the walled compound on it, using items on his desk to hold the map open.

Jorge explained, "My family built the stockade for protection during the Indian wars. The original buildings shown on the plans were burnt in a raid before Geronimo surrendered. The two guard shacks beside the main gate were built in the late

1800s but the rest were never rebuilt since the Indian wars were over."

The old plans showed the two entrances that Humberto had mentioned. The dimensions of the buildings, the windows, doors and other pertinent information on the old stockade were written on the plans. Wes, Alfonso and Dale studied the plans, pointing out possible entry points and things to cover in rescuing Mariah.

Jorge listened to them discussing how to get into the enclosure with the least amount of trouble before speaking. "Just what are these people doing? They've been here for several generations with no complaints from anyone."

Juan answered him, not hiding the truth. "They are the Nahua and are practicing human sacrifices as their forefathers did before the Spanish came to this area." Jorge blanched. "They have Wes's daughter, and we are attempting to save her. From what we've discovered, the group is using the bodies to transport drugs."

The horror which Jorge had shown turned into anger when what they had told him registered. He took a deep breath before saying, "There's one thing not on that map. I don't believe they know about it. A tunnel that has an opening in this area is hidden by a group of rocks." He pointed to the area on the map. "I found it when I was a child. The opening is here, behind this building. It isn't very big but would enable a couple of men to get into the compound unseen. I can take you to it if you want."

Having someone on the inside to let them into the compound through the side entrance would be a major help. "We would appreciate it. If we can get a couple of men in there, we might be able to get Mariah out alive," Wes said before Dale could. Their priority was to save Mariah. They would round up the group after she was safe.

From Rachel's murder and the drugs in her system, Dale guessed Mariah would be drugged, which meant she might not be able to move on her own. They would need to keep her safe until the people in the cult were under control. Since Humberto had told them where all the guards were stationed, directing the team to their posts wouldn't be difficult. Dale took three men and followed Jorge to the tunnel entrance. They wouldn't have found it without his help. Before he went into the tunnel, he contacted Wes.

"We're going in, so we'll be out of contact. I'll give two clicks to let you know when we're in position. We'll wait for you to create a distraction before entering the compound."

"Got it. Keep the faith. She'll be all right."

"I'm praying she is. I want to see those beautiful eyes looking at me again," Dale said, stuffing the fear of her death back inside.

"You shouldn't have let her get away in the first place." Wes's voice was gruff.

"True. I won't let her go this time."

"She almost did get away. Be glad Phillip sent her back to you or you'd be working really hard to get her."

"I'm still going to have to work hard for her. She cares for him more than she's shown you."

"Use the past to your advantage. She's been drawn to you since she was a teenager." Mariah had told Wes how much she liked Dale and had asked for his advice. It was one of the reasons he had encouraged Dale to ask her out.

"Planning on it as soon as Xolotl is in custody."

"Then get going," Wes told him. "I want him too."

6:00 PM

Mariah awakened from the drug induced sleep. Louis was watching her. She wondered how long he had been sitting there, doing nothing more than staring at her.

"It's a shame you're going to be sacrificed to a God only a few have ever heard about," Louis said. "Is it true you're a virgin?"

She tilted her head back until she was gazing at the ceiling. "It's true. Sad isn't it. I get to die before I know what all the hoopla over sex is about."

"True," he agreed. "You'll end up in a place of light and beauty while I end up in hell."

She faced him. "It's a hell of your own making. It's the way of a lot of mankind. They're offered heaven and they choose hell."

He sat staring at his hands, his shoulders slumped before shrugging. "Want to go back to la-la land. There's still three hours to wait."

"Not yet. Maybe later. I'd like to enjoy being alive for a while longer." She relaxed in the chair, hooking a small table with her toe to pull it over so she could rest her feet on it. Louis notice what she was doing. He scooted it over and put a pillow under her heels.

"You're the first I've been able to talk to. The rest chose the drugs," he told her when she was comfortable.

She studied him. He was a nice-looking man who had made a lot of wrong choices to end up here.

"That's because they didn't enjoy life. I do."

His face showed his confusion. "It seems to me that yours couldn't have been all that great with having to work at the clubs."

"Wrong. It was a choice I had in how I wanted to live. I wanted to go to school, so I needed a job which would pay well. The clubs pay well. I'm on my last semester at the university. I've saved enough to pay for law school, a place to live and for all the necessities without having to work more than three days a week."

Louis laughed. "Figures. I can see you with Phillip, keeping him out of jail."

She turned her face away from him, blinking rapidly to no avail. The tears seeped from her eyes creating rivulets on her cheeks.

"Why are you crying over him?" Louis asked, turning her head so he could see her face.

She sniffed and wiped the tears away. "He loved me enough to give me my freedom. I know he had an evil side to him, but with me, he was so gentle and loving."

"You love him, don't you?" Louis stared at her in disbelief.

"I do."

He smiled, shaking his head. "Yeah, he fell big time for you. I can see why. Santiago told me you were special. He had never seen Phillip act the way he did with you with any other woman he dated. It was totally out of character for him."

"That's where you are wrong. What I saw was the real him."

Louis was speechless. Mariah could see he didn't know the real Phillip. Santiago did. He understood why Phillip had hidden his other side from her. She was honest when she said she loved him. The problem was that he loved her more than she did him. If it wasn't for Dale, she could see herself with Phillip.

Chapter Thirty-Nine

AT FOUR IN THE evening, people began to arrive at the stockade. The gates were open for the men and women who got out of their cars and trucks, dressed in heavily embroidered robes and dresses. There was one child, a boy, who had been taken into the compound. Wes and Juan counted the people as they entered. There was twenty. Twelve men and eight women, not including the child. Six guards had been in the compound since they had taken up their positions. None of them had seen Louis or Mariah.

At seven-thirty, a car with Texas plates pulled into the parking area. The man who got out had a mask over his face. The mask and his robes glittered with gold and were a dark red in color. He spoke to the guards as he strode through the gates. When he was inside, the gates were closed. Xolotl was there and the ceremony was about to start.

A couple of clicks on Wes's radio notified him that Dale and his men were in position. He gave the signal for the rest of the men to move to their assigned spots. The three guards, who had been patrolling the outside of the stockade, had followed

Xolotl through the gates. When the drums started, all the men surrounding the compound were aware there was no turning back. If they did, an innocent woman would die.

Mariah could hear people talking. It had to be close to time for the ceremony. Louis picked up the syringe and raised an eyebrow. She hesitated then decided she wasn't that brave. With a nod of her head, he gave her another dose of the drug.

The hours spent with Louis showed he wasn't all bad. He had gotten into the cartel to feed his family when he was still a child. There hadn't been many options when their fields had been burned on a regular basis.

His family had been kept safe and were now in a place where they could live without fear. He was a realist. There was no way he'd ever be able to leave the cartel alive. It was a fact he had accepted years ago. His younger brother would need to keep the family going with the money he had put into an account for them.

In their conversation, she also discovered he had dreams of a different life. One where he could have a family of his own, and a large enough place to have a vineyard where he could make wine to sell. It was a dream. One which would never be fulfilled. She pitied the man who hadn't had a life without killing, drugs, hiding and fear.

The drums began a steady beat and she could hear chanting from the people who had arrived. When the door opened, she turned her head to see a man in a mask which covered his upper face. He was dressed in a long-embroidered robe. His smile was welcoming as he entered the room.

"I knew you were different," he said to her.

She sighed and leaned back in the chair, recognizing his distinctive voice.

He chuckled. "I see you weren't expecting me."

"No, I wasn't," Mariah admitted. "Why?"

The man who called himself Xolotl moved to the chair Louis had vacated, motioning for him to stay away so he could talk to her. "I am Nahua. My people have been keeping the old ways alive for centuries. This is a ritual which has been done for thousands of years. Xolotl is a very demanding God."

She stared at him, her parted lips and wide eyes showing her disbelief.

He gave a short bark of laughter. "Of course, there is the money. Things aren't cheap today and there wasn't a good reason not to combine things."

"Why Rachel?" She needed to understand why he had chosen her.

"She got too close to the truth, like you. Only you are incredibly unique. This ceremony won't be able to be topped in my lifetime. Everyone will benefit from your death. True adult virgins are extremely difficult to find. Especially ones who have experienced life to some degree. The Gods will love you and I'll have what I've been striving for all my life."

Mariah lowered her eyes then lifted them to him. "Will you have what you want, or is it all an illusion?" She let him ponder her question before saying, "I know when I die where I'll be. Do you know where you will go?"

"It matters not where I will go when I leave this life. For now, I'm keeping Xolotl and the jaguar happy."

She studied the masked man who was smiling. "It will matter when the end comes, whether you believe it will or not."

His deep laughter made her believe he wasn't totally sane. "No, it doesn't. I've been saved by the blood like the others here have been. Of course, you can't see it." He brushed a hand across her cheek. "Your blood will be extra sweet to us. It will hold a lot of power because of how special you are."

Without removing her gaze from him, her voice calm, she said, "Louis, the drug please. Make it a double."

Louis moved so he could see her face. She met his dark eyes. He nodded and moved to honor her request. After cleaning her arm, Louis gave her a chance to stop him. When she didn't, he injected the medication.

The masked man grinned. "It makes no difference if you are drugged. So long as you are still breathing, you will serve your purpose." He left with a swish of robes as the drums began a slow cadence.

Louis sighed. "You won't be conscious, so sweet dreams, angel."

She swiped at the unwanted tears. "Thank you. He'll pay with his soul. You need to get out. You and Santiago. There's a life away from all of this and you need to find it."

The drug was taking effect. She began to nod, not seeing the tears running down Louis's face, but she did hear him say, "I'll figure out a way, angel."

Wes and Juan listened to the drums as the sunset progressed. They had to wait until the sun set and the darkness settled over the area to enter the compound. It was now nine fifty PM. The total eclipse was at ten forty-five. No matter how you looked at it, they were cutting it close.

The men were in place. With a set of clicks, several men dressed in dark clothes climbed the walls. Dale and his men entered the grounds from the hidden tunnel. They moved into the shadow of the building to the left of the entrance. No one was guarding the gate. They were all at the ceremony or in the buildings.

Dale and his men moved further into the shadow as four men exited the hut beside them. He held back a gasp as he watched them carrying Mariah. A slight movement of her hand showed him she was still alive. Pulling his eyes from the group, he verified everyone was in place.

Two of the men entered the building they were hiding behind, as Dale and another man made their way to the one where Mariah had been. They silently entered to find Louis sitting on a chair holding a syringe in his hand. Dale grabbed it from him, not noticing it was empty. It had taken them close to fifteen minutes to make it into the building.

Louis lifted his tear stained face to Dale. "You have less than thirty minutes to save her."

"What happens next?" Dale asked, not sure if he would get an answer.

"They'll continue the chant until it becomes a frenzy, then it will stop. If you aren't there, she'll die with a knife to the heart." Louis put a hand on Dale's arm. "You need to stop him before he kills her."

Dale studied the crying man. "Why?"

"He's evil. She's an angel. You can't let him kill an angel."

The man with Dale stayed with Louis. One of the men opened the main gate, letting the rest of the team in while another opened the side gate. Like moving shadows, they spread out around the edges of the wooden stockade, using the dark shadows at the base of the walls to hide them. One of the men gagged and tied up the boy who was sitting along the wall, watching the ceremony.

By the time, everyone was in place, the drums had increased in speed. They had seconds to save Mariah. The priest had his back to the stone slab where Mariah had been placed. The man was praying as he held an object high, offering it to the stone statue above him. Giving the signal, Dale joined the men. They entered the dancers like moving shadows.

The commotion reached the priest, who turned, assessing the situation. His voice rang out. "You are too late." He raised the object in his hand above Mariah, who hadn't moved.

Dale pivoted when the man spoke, his gun in his hand. He fired, the flash from the muzzle showing the bullet had left the gun. He fired again. The reports echoed in the sudden silence. The priest moved back two steps but began to move forward again, grinning. The priest was wearing a bulletproof vest. Sprinting faster than he ever had, he dove over Mariah, knocking the priest to the ground.

The man stabbed at Dale with the odd curved knife he held in his hand. Dale felt a sharp pain in his left arm. Ignoring it, he grabbed the priest's wrist below the hand holding the knife. The priest cursed at him in Spanish and English fighting Dale with every ounce of strength he had.

Dale didn't see who grabbed the hand with the knife. The two of them got the man under control, and placed handcuffs on his wrists. The priest laughed, then began to babble in an unknown language. Juan picked up the knife from the ground and studied it. Dale knelt on the ground, attempting to catch his breath, a hand over the throbbing area on his left arm.

Wes was bending over Mariah. "We have a problem," Wes said, his voice overly calm while taking her pulse.

Louis ran to them, having broken away from the man who had been holding him. He checked her eyes and assessed her breathing. "I have the antidote in the room. Let me go get it," He begged, turning to Dale, the tears still flowing over his cheeks unchecked.

Wes said, "Go," not waiting for Dale to give permission.

Louis raced to the building. He was gone less than a minute before he came racing back to them, a syringe in his hand. He skidded to a stop, put a tourniquet on before tearing open an alcohol pad to clean the inside of her elbow. There was fear on his face as he injected the medication into her vein. He rubbed the spot after releasing the tourniquet, staring at Mariah.

"Please angel. Come back to us," he begged, waiting for the medication to do its job. He held her hand, continuing to cry. "Come on. You can't let them take you. Open those beautiful innocent eyes for me."

Mariah took in a deep breath, her head rolling to the side on the thin decorated pillow.

"Angel, come on. Wake up. It's all over," Louis said, placing a hand on her cheek before checking her eyes again.

A few seconds later, her eyes fluttered open. She smiled at Louis.

"That's my girl. Welcome back. The cavalry got here in the nick of time, just like in the movies." He patted her cheek before moving back from her.

Dale, who had managed to drag himself from the ground, rested a hip on the stone alter. "Good to see those beautiful eyes. I was beginning to believe we weren't going to make it in time. The things I go through for you," he joked.

Mariah smiled and squeezed his hand before attempting to sit up. Wes draped her with a decorated blanket one of his men thrust into his hand. All she had on was a gauzy gown, that she hadn't noticed, but everyone else had. It wasn't until she moved her legs over the side of the stone slab and the blanket came open, she noticed her state of undress. Her brain was still foggy. It took a few minutes to get rid of the cobwebs. Her eyes went to Louis, who was smiling as he watched her.

"Thank you," she said.

Louis moved to her side and kissed her cheek. "No thanks needed. My life looks pretty bad, but you'll be okay." He scanned the men who were gathered around her. "It appears there are a few more, other than Phillip, who love you."

Mariah flicked a glance at Wes and Dale. "You're right. There are a couple more." Her eyes met his. "But I owe you my life."

He gave what she called the Latino shrug. "Considering I was praying for a way of rescuing you, I believe you need to thank the one above, not me."

Wes studied Louis. "You could have let her die."

Louis clamped his lips together before saying. "No, I couldn't. I was ready to come out here and stop him. Your rescue team showed up right on time."

"Why would you want to save her?" Dale asked, his right arm around Mariah, holding her steady.

"Because she's special. She gave me the key to life without ever knowing it while we were waiting. I would have died to save her."

"You sure about that?" Wes asked.

Louis grinned. "Positive. Santiago saw it too. He called me before going into hiding. He said he couldn't let her die and had contacted a DEA agent to help save her. He also said he couldn't do what he was doing any longer. Neither can I. A druggie on their last legs is one thing, but angels—not happening."

Wes turned back to her, his arm helping Dale to support her. "Better?" he asked, scanning her eyes.

"I'm all right. That priest is insane. I hope you know that."

Dale's gaze went to where the man was sitting, babbling to voices no one else heard. His mask had been removed, revealing the one person, none of them had seriously suspected.

"Yes, he is. Too bad the voices are still talking to him. He's responsible for over sixty murders in the last five years.

Mariah leaned into Wes, needing his comfort. "I couldn't believe it when he began to talk to me. He didn't have a clue how you and Wes would come after me."

"Good for us. Bad for him," Wes responded, helping her to stand.

Her legs were unsteady, but she could stand if she held onto something.

"Who is he?" Louis asked, studying the man who was sitting in his own little world.

Mariah stared at the man with the lovely voice. "Father Rivers of the St. Vincent of LeonTreatment Center. It's were Rachel went to get sober. He did some wonderful work there."

"Well, damn. No wonder he knew who to tap for sacrifices," Louis exclaimed. "I don't believe anyone would have suspected him in a million years."

"Correct," Dale stated. "No one did until Rachel. He made a mistake and she caught it. His big mistake was in attempting to frame Mariah. He didn't know there were a lot of people who cared about her."

Juan came to them. "Do you want him, or do I keep him?"

Dale chuckled. "You can keep him in exchange for Louis, Santiago, and Humberto."

"Deal. We'll make sure he's never allowed to be free again," Juan promised, motioning for his men to take the priest away.

Louis stared at Dale, fear creeping into his eyes. "Why are you taking me?"

Dale smiled. "Because you deserve another chance. You screw up, and you'll pay big time, but for now, you get that chance you wanted to live a normal life."

Mariah attempted to take a step. She began to fall. Wes scooped her up in his arms, carrying her as he had multiple times as she was growing up. "Girl, you need to eat. You aren't much heavier now than you were at eight," he scolded.

She giggled. "I'm not much bigger than I was back then."

Wes chuckled. It was true. She wasn't much taller than she had been at eight years old. Relaxing in his arms, she didn't object to him carrying her. He placed her in the back of the Hummer, wiping away the tears which had started when she saw it.

"He'll be all right," Wes told her, aware of what had caused the tears.

Scooting her over, he joined her on the seat, holding her close to him as the stress of the night eased with the quiet tears she cried. Dale silently took the seat on the other side of her. His hand on her shoulder let her know he was there, but for now, she needed her father and the comfort and safety only he could provide.

Chapter Forty

SHE HADN'T BEEN GIVEN the choice to walk into her apartment. Wes carried her, letting Alfonso open the door for him. He set her on the couch and joined her, his arm across her shoulders, staying next to her. Alfonso took the chair, not willing to leave them alone until Dale finished his paperwork and joined them.

Wes rested his cheek on her head. "Girl, you're something else. All the men are singing this beautiful tune just for you."

She burrowed closer to him. "Not for me. For themselves. They saw the light at the end of the tunnel and want to get to it."

Wes asked. "What about Phillip?"

"He'll get there if allowed." She knew that wasn't what he was asking though. "He set me free. He said he knew he would ruin my life. He wouldn't have, but I took the freedom. For now, he needs to decide what he wants to do with his life. He's a gentle loving man when he's allowed to be himself."

"So, what do you plan on doing?"

Mariah moved her shoulders, getting more comfortable. "It's up to Dale. He's been keeping me at a distance during all of this. I promised him a chance. He now has the choice of taking it or not."

"You love him, don't you?"

She lay in his embrace, feeling as if all her bones had turned to mush. "Yes. Ever since he kissed me, thinking I was asleep. I opened my eyes and looked into these beautiful brown ones which told me how he felt about me."

Wes chuckled. "I figured as much. It surprised me he didn't come after you before now."

"He's scared of me, but I don't know why," she told him, not bothering to stuff the fear of being left alone back into its box.

"Beauty does that to a man, and it isn't just the external. It's also the internal. Your outer beauty gets their attention, but it's the internal which captures them, then scares them to death. Dale is terrified of not being worthy of the lovely woman you've become since leaving the farm. I had to see if I was right about you. I was."

She pulled away from him, staring at his face. "Huh?"

"You waited on him. Phillip was as close as you could get to someone like him. He was on the wrong side of the law, but you saw the man he really was, hidden inside. The same with Louis, Santiago, and Dale."

"Maybe," she said, returning to his embrace. "It remains to be seen if Dale mans-up or runs away from me again."

Wes and Alfonso laughed. Alfonso was the one who spoke. "He'll man-up. He knows if he doesn't, he'll lose you and he can't accept that possibility."

It was close to noon when Dale entered the room. He had dark circles under his eyes, lines on his face, and a dressing on his left arm. Alfonso stood motioning for him to take the chair. Nodding to him, Dale fell into the comfortable seat, leaning back and closing his eyes. He stretched his legs out under the coffee table.

"They're rounding them up on both sides of the border. Santiago showed up at my office asking for a deal and protection. The Sinaloa will fill their spots, but they have lost a lot of really good men over the past couple of months, along with the lab and the chemist." Dale hadn't opened his eyes as he spoke.

"What is this new stuff?" Mariah asked.

Alfonso answered. "It's a synthetic cocaine which is concentrated to the point where you can take an ounce and make three kilos from it. It lasts longer than coke, but the problem is, if you take too much, you die.

"The rash of overdoses is what alerted the authorities to it. Phillip and Santiago both attempted to get them to leave it alone. All the bosses could see were dollar signs with the ease it could be transported before cut."

"Without thinking, Mariah snapped, "Idiots! I don't know why anyone would ever use that stuff. It'll eventually kill you, no matter what drug it is."

Wes grinned when he said, "Not even if it was like the stuff Louis gave you?"

She elbowed him. "Especially if it was like that. It removes you from life. You can't live life if you aren't present in it. You know that since it's what you taught me."

Dale murmured, "But that's the whole purpose of taking drugs. If you don't like your life, you use drugs to escape it for as long as the drug lasts."

"Humph. Stupid if you ask me. If you don't like your life, then change it." She turned to Wes. "Okay. What do I do with the drugs they made me swallow when the packets come out?"

Dale popped up, hitting his leg on the coffee table. Wes turned to her. "What?" he asked.

"They made me swallow these little packages with a white powder in them. When they come out, what do you want me to do with them?"

"Do you have any laxatives in the house?" Wes asked.

"No."

"I'll go get some," Dale said, motioning for Afonso to come with him.

She watched them leave. "Why is he so afraid of me?"

"You'll have to ask him, not me. I told you what I believe it is." Wes pulled her back into his arms.

Dale was back in under twenty minutes. He handed Wes the bag. A few minutes later, there was a knock on the door. A woman entered when Alfonso opened it. She had a doctor's bag with her.

"Have you taken the laxatives yet?" she asked, setting her bag on the papers on the coffee table.

"Not yet."

"Okay, let me see what you have there," she requested, holding out her hand for the bag Dale had given Wes.

She examined the contents. "Come with me," she ordered, picking up her bag before leading the way to Mariah's bedroom.

The woman asked multiple questioned about the packages she had swallowed before giving her the laxatives. She also had her drink some fluid from a bottle she had in her bag. There was no reason to not trust the woman when she had introduced herself as Dr. Lilith Coleman.

It took a good share of the day and night for everything to work. Mariah safely passed all twelve of the little packets. As it stood now, if she never had to take another laxative in her lifetime, it would be too quick. It made her wonder how the girls could purge themselves voluntarily.

Dr. Coleman insisted on fixing her something to eat, not trusting the men to feed her. She insisted Mariah stay in the bedroom while she ate, then gave orders for her to rest. Mariah didn't complain, feeling too weak to get up and move, not sure if it was the purging, the drugs she had been given, or both. Curling on the bed, holding a pillow, she closed her eyes to rest, only to fall into a deep sleep.

A hand on her face brought Mariah awake. She stared into the brown eyes she loved. "Wes was worried when you didn't join us. I convinced him to let you rest for a while longer," Dale said as he inspected her face.

"I feel pretty normal now. I guess the drugs are finally out of my system. What I am is hungry. What I ate earlier didn't do much other than take the edge off,"

"Supper is ready. You can join us, or I'll bring you a tray."

"I'll join you. Give me a few minutes," she said.

He didn't move from where he was sitting. "Mariah?"

"Yes."

"I—uh. I—uh." He stopped, his hand playing with her hair.

"Spit it out, Dale. I don't bite."

He hung his head. "Right. I wanted to say I love you and have from the moment I saw you the first time with the sun all around you. I'm not sure what to do now."

She reached up and rapped him on the head with her knuckles. "Dodo brain. You stay with me and show me how you feel."

"You sure?" He asked, letting her take the lead.

"Of course, I'm sure. I find it strange how you're so sure of yourself when you aren't around me. I've seen you be brave, strong, and efficient on the farm and when you are working. Meanwhile, around me you turn into this quivering mass of jello. Hello! I've been waiting on you since I was sixteen. I'm not going to wait forever." She had shown him when she dated Phillip that she was tired of waiting.

He met her gaze. "I guess that means you won't throw me out."

"I won't throw you out. I might give you a knock upside the head to rattle those brains which go into hiding when you're around me."

"Umhmm," he sounded, before pulling her onto his lap. She wrapped her arms around him. He lowered his head and kissed her. He didn't stop with a quick kiss, keeping it going until a heaviness settled in her pelvis. She didn't want him to stop when he pulled away.

"I believe you got the message," she said, not moving from his embrace.

"I did. No more running away," he promised, holding her tightly, his heart racing.

"You better not," She warned. "I have a lot of friends who'll hunt you down and make you pay."

Dale laughed. He was aware of her friends, starting with Alfonso, Louis, Santiago and Phillip. She wasn't above using them if needed to keep him with her.

The End

Thank you for reading to the end. If you enjoyed this book, please leave a review. It will help other readers to find the book and enjoy it.

Historical Facts

Xolotl was the **Nahuatl** god of fire and lightning. He was also god of twins, monsters, misfortune, sickness, and deformities. **Xolotl** is the canine brother and twin of Quetzalcoatl, the pair being sons of the virgin Coatlicue. He is the dark personification of Venus, the evening star, and was associated with heavenly fire.

In the religion of the Aztec Empire, **Xolotl** was a god of fire, lightning, deformities and death. He was the dark twin of Quetzalcoatl, responsible for guiding the Sun through Mictlán, the Underworld.

The Aztec canine god **Xolotl** was responsible for accompanying the dead to Mictlan (the underworld), guarded the sun, and was the god of bad luck.

I used the Nahui who are descendants from the first world and still worshiped the old Gods. There is proof that human sacrifice was practiced but I took it a step further into a cult who used the sacrifices as a way to keep the jaguar from eating the moon (also in the legends of the Inca/Mayans). Please remember this is fiction and not based on any real happenings today or in the past or any actual beliefs of the Nahui. The idea actually came about when I was studying the cartels, the Mexican heritage and the old beliefs since the Day of the Dead caught my attention as a holiday...murder, cult and drugs. It all fit in this story.

About the Author

Picture curtesy of Henry Greer, taken in New Hampshire in 2015.

I'm one of those old people who refuse to sit in a rocking chair and slowly fade away or become one of the condo denizens. I enjoy keeping busy. I did retire from nursing and followed my plan to travel, seeing as much of the United States as I could until the money ran out. I used the trike and trailer in the picture above while camping whenever I could. It was a trip to remember where I saw all these beautiful places and met a lot of wonderful people.

Unlike most authors I didn't start writing as a child. I was too busy reading every book I could get my hands on. I didn't begin writing until 2014 when a friend was finishing her book. I mentioned that I had always wanted to write the stories that popped up in my brain like hopping bunnies. To me, they all sounded horrible and I never got past the first page or two. Her advice was, "Start that the beginning and write until you're done. Don't worry about what it sounds like, just complete it."

I did that and will be editing that 500,000-word saga for quite some time. Meanwhile, I'm working on other books which will be easier to fix.

Previous books

Abilene: No Place to Hide

The Jillian Factor

The Jillian Factor: The Prequel

Website: https://www.bamealer.com

Facebook: https://www.facbook.com/bamealer

Pinterest: https://www.pinterest.com/bobiem91